BITTER SWEET HEART

New York Times Bestselling Author **HELENA HUNTING**
writing as

H. HUNTING

From the outside looking in, I live a charmed life: hockey legend for a father, my own promising future in the league, a great family, awesome friends. It's not untrue, but it's not quite that simple either.

My dad's advice has always been to make hockey my number-one priority—at least until I make it to the pros. So, going into my senior year of college, I have a plan. I'll put in the effort required to pass my classes, play hockey like my life depends on it, and avoid relationships. All I have to do is stay focused on the end game, and I'll walk away with a degree and into a career in the NHL.

It should be easy.

But when a woman literally floats into my dock, just before summer ends and my senior year begins, I can't resist one last hookup. What harm could a one-night stand do? It's not like we even exchanged numbers.

Everything is fine until I run into her on campus.

It's a big school. I should be able to avoid her.

Except she happens to be in my class.

And she's not a student.

She's my professor.

BITTER SWEET HEART

ACKNOWLEDGMENTS

Husband and kidlet, you inspire me every day. Thank you for your love.

Deb, I adore you. Thank you for being the Pepper to my Salt.

Kimberly thank you for everything you do, even when it isn't easy.

Sarah, you're incredible and wonderful and I'm forever grateful for you.

Hustlers, you're my cheerleaders and my book family and I'm so grateful for each and every one of you.

My SS team, your eagle eyes are amazing and I appreciate your input and support.

Denise, thank you for sharing your hockey knowledge and insight with me. You're truly incredible and I'm honored to have your support.

Tijan, thank you for being such a great source of encouragement when I need it most.

Jessica, Christa, Julia, Amanda, thank you so much for working on this project with me and helping me make it sparkle.

To my entire Social Butterfly team, you're fabulous and I couldn't do it without you.

Sarah and Gel, thank you for being graphic gurus. Your incredible talent never ceases to amaze me.

Beavers, thank you for giving me a safe place to land, and for always being excited about what's next.

Deb, Tijan, Kat, Marnie, Krystin, Laurie, Angie, Angela; thank you for being such wonderful and inspiring women in my life. I'm lucky to have your friendship.

Readers, bloggers, bookstagrammers and booktokers, your passion for love stories is unparalleled, thank you for all that you do for the reading community.

*For the protectors who put the people they love ahead of
themselves, even when it hurts.*

BITTER SWEET HEART CAST

MAVERICK WATERS

Siblings
ROBBIE
LAVENDER (LITTLE LIES)
RIVER

Parents
ALEX & VIOLET WATERS
PUCKED SERIES:
PUCKED/FOREVER PUCKED

CLOVER SWEET

Siblings
BLAINE

Parents
DAWN & LENNON SWEET

SOPHIA

CLOVER'S BESTIE,
COUNSELLOR AT THE COLLEGE

GABRIEL LOCKWOOD
CLOVER'S EX

KODIAK BOWMAN

BEST FRIEND/TEAMMATE

Siblings
ASPEN
DAKOTA

Parents
ROOK & LAINEY BOWMAN
ALL IN SERIES: A LIE FOR A LIE

BJ BALLISTIC

(FRIEND/COUSIN) HOUSEMATE TO KODY & QUINN

Parents
RANDY & LILY BALLISTIC (HALF SISTER TO VIOLET)
MAV'S AUNT & UNCLE

LOGAN BUTTERSON

COUSIN TO MAVERICK. POLICE OFFICER

Siblings
LIAM & LANE
LAUGHLIN
LOVEY & LACEY

Parents
SUNNY AND MILLER
BUTTERSON
MAV'S AUNT AND UNCLE

QUINN ROMERO

TEAMMATE/HOUSEMATE TO KODY & BJ

Siblings
CELESTE
HEATHER

Parents
LANCE & POPPY ROMERO
PUCKED SERIES: PUCKED OFF

Floating on this Cloud

MAVERICK

I flip the lid open on the cooler. "Who needs another beer?"

My cousin BJ holds out his hand. "This guy right here."

I glance over at my best friend, Kody, who I've known my entire life. "What about you?"

"I'll have water, or a soda as long as it doesn't have caffeine." He doesn't look up from the textbook he's reading.

"Seriously, dude, take a break. That textbook isn't going anywhere, and we have limited lazy dock days left." I pass him a beer instead of his requested water or decaf soda. When he doesn't reach for it right away, I tack on, "It's light and only two percent. You'd need to drink an entire case to catch a buzz."

He's slow to drag his gaze away from whatever he's reading.

"I want to get a jumpstart on my bio-chem class. It was my lowest grade last year."

"Which was what, ninety-seven percent?" BJ snorts.

"Ninety-five point four."

The way he says it makes it sound like he almost failed, but he finally grabs the beer I'm still holding out.

"I don't understand why you get so bent out of shape about your grades." This isn't true. I know exactly why Kody gets his balls tied in a knot—he's a perfectionist. "It's not like you're going to use your rocket science degree anyway. Once you get called up, you'll be making millions a year." I twist the cap off my own beer and take a long swig. Kody was a first-round pick. It's only a matter of time before he's playing for the NHL.

"Yeah, but my career isn't going to last forever, and when it's over, I want a solid degree under my belt so I can transition to my second career without any problems." Kody closes the textbook. "Or I could go back for a master's, and that's not going to happen if I don't have a good GPA."

"You got a lot of years before you're going to have to worry about that." I push up out of my chair and sweat drips down my back, thanks to the summer sun sitting high in the sky. I step out to the end of the dock, turn around, and do a backflip into the water.

I catch Kody's "Hey!" just before I go under.

I pull myself back out and drop down into my chair. Kody gripes about me getting his textbook wet as he slides it into a plastic bag and then into his backpack. I'll take his ire, though, because it means he's given up on studying. Kody and I have been tight since we were kids. Without me around to force him to relax occasionally, Kody would spend all day, every day either studying or on the ice.

"I'm kinda jealous that you two lucky fuckers are going to

be done at the end of this year." BJ drains half of his beer in three long swallows.

"Why would you be jealous? The two of us have to be responsible once this year is over." I motion between myself and Kody.

"I'm already responsible," Kody says.

"You know what I mean. We're already on the ice seven days a week with training. It's only going to get more intense from here."

College is fun. Unlike Kody, I don't worry all that much about my grades. As long as my scores are over seventy, I'm happy. Most of my energy goes into hockey. For the rest, I do whatever is going to keep me out of trouble with my parents, my professors, and my coach.

BJ's phone buzzes on his chair, and he checks the screen, one corner of his mouth turning up in a sly grin as he uses face ID to unlock it.

I nod in his direction. "One of your summer hookups looking for a beard ride?"

He snorts. "Nah. It's Lovey."

I arch a brow. Lovey's my cousin. She and her twin are super tight with my younger sister, Lavender, and we've grown up spending a lot of time together. We're basically one big extended family. BJ, however, isn't related to Lovey. "Oh yeah? What's going on there?" I ask.

He gives me the side-eye. "We're supposed to go shopping later. She's got a date, and she wants my opinion or whatever."

"Isn't she with my sister? Why wouldn't she go shopping with Lav and Lacey?" I glance over at Kody and am unsurprised to find him fidgeting uneasily. Any mention of my sister makes him antsy.

After living at home and going to a local community college last year, mostly to appease my parents who are overprotective as hell when it comes to her, Lavender wanted the real college experience, which included *not* living at home. So she's going to be moving in with me and River, her twin brother. Kody lives a few houses down the street with BJ and Quinn Romero, another of our hockey teammates. It should be interesting to see how things go since Kody won't be able to avoid my sister anymore. And I love the guy, but by *interesting* I mean really fucking awkward.

They had a bit of a codependency issue when we were kids, and things got messy for a while. The last time those two saw each other was more than two years ago, when Lavender was still in high school. And before that, I don't think they'd been in the same room since Kody and I were thirteen. Shortly after that, his family moved to Philly, but now we're all together again. It's good, but Kody's been in avoidance mode for a lot of years. He won't be able to do that anymore.

Kody glances at me and then away, his ears turning red, and the rest of his face following. He tips his beer back and chugs.

BJ glances between me and Kody, arching a knowing eyebrow. "Apparently my input is more valuable."

I shake my head. "You'd think between the three of them, they'd have enough clothes that a shopping trip isn't even required. Lav's been packing up her dresses, and there are boxes lining the hall. It's nuts."

BJ strokes his beard. "I almost feel bad for her."

"Why?" I frown.

"Uh, because River is like an overprotective, rabid guard dog, and you throw parties all the fucking time."

"Only at the beginning of the semester. Or when the occasion calls for it." I grin, though. I've been known to throw a lot of parties. For a while, I did it to force Kody to be social. He's pretty damn reclusive, and unless you know him well, he can be standoffish.

"Every day is an occasion for you," Kody mutters.

"As my Gram-pot would say, every day above ground is a good day." I move the conversation away from my sister, though, because I can tell it's putting Kody on edge, and I don't want to ruin the easy vibe. That he agreed to come spend the weekend in Pearl Lake is a freaking miracle.

My cousin's place on Pearl Lake is a twenty-minute drive from my parents' place in Lake Geneva. Originally, the Lake Geneva spot was their lakefront getaway, but when my dad retired from coaching, he moved out this way, and he and a bunch of his hockey buddies started a hockey-training program. Both Kody and I help coach kids in the summer, as well as attending our own training camp. The kids' camp ended last week, so we have a free weekend to relax, minus our own practices.

"There's supposed to be a beach party tonight. You guys up for it?" BJ asks.

"Dakota has a soccer game, and I told him I'd go," Kody says. "But maybe after, if it's not too late. And Coach added an early skate tomorrow at seven. I said we'd both be there."

"Right. Shit, I forgot about that." I might get a few months of freedom from studying, but hockey is all year round.

We shoot the shit for a while longer until BJ leaves to go shopping with Lovey and Kody heads to Dakota's soccer game, leaving me alone on the dock. I switch to water. Despite the beer only being two-percent alcohol, I still have to drive, and Pearl Lake is a small town with a tiny police force. My dad might be a former NHL star and a big deal around here, but that doesn't mean I'm irresponsible when it comes to drinking and driving.

The lake is calm today, so still it's almost like a pane of glass. It's late afternoon now, the sun starting to sink toward the horizon, the heat of the day beginning to settle. The muggy July nights have turned into cool August evenings, perfect for sleeping with the windows open.

I notice a paddleboard floating in the distance. It looks like someone is lying on it, sunbathing maybe? It continues to float toward the dock. It's close enough now that I can see it's a woman in a pale green bikini. Her dark hair fans out along the top of the board, and the paddle floats along beside her. There's something resting on her stomach, and a bottle is tucked between her arm and her side. She's wearing sunglasses, and her lips are parted. She's also a little sunburned.

I push up out of my chair and drop to one knee at the edge of the dock as the board bumps against it.

"Hey there," I say, but don't get a response.

Which is when I realize she's asleep.

I clear my throat and gently prod her shoulder.

She gasps and sits upright, sending the zippered baggie on her stomach flying, along with the hot pink travel bottle. The paddleboard tips. I grab for her to keep her from being dumped into the water along with her things, but it backfires when she latches onto me and pulls me in.

I release her right away, but she clings to me, grabbing my shoulders, kicking and flailing, almost nailing me in the groin. I grip the edge of the dock to prevent her from pulling me down, and we both pop up at the same time.

Her face is inches from mine, and despite her shocked expression, she's gorgeous. Her sunglasses are no longer covering her eyes, which are a stunning gray ringed in navy. Freckles dot the bridge of her nose, and she has full lips. Her face is heart-shaped, and her long, chestnut hair floats on the surface of the water, swirling around her arms.

"Holy shit!" She clutches my shoulders and looks around. "What the fuck? Who are you? Where am I?"

"I'm Maverick, currently your buoy and possible knight in a

wet bathing suit. As for where, you're in Pearl Lake. I think you must have fallen asleep on your paddleboard." I nod toward the board, which is now floating about fifteen feet away from us, but slowly heading back our direction. "I'm sorry I scared you."

"Pearl Lake? Oh crap!" She lets go of my shoulder and swims over to retrieve her paddleboard. While she does that, I grab the water bottle bumping the edge of the dock and the zippered baggie that contains a book. I think the sunglasses are probably a new addition to the bottom of the lake. I toss the items on the dock and swim over to help her with the paddleboard.

"Why don't you come on up and get your bearings?" I suggest.

She glances around. Two docks over there are a bunch of people still swimming. And several more are dotted with people drying off. "Yeah. Okay. Thanks."

I clip the paddleboard to the ladder and motion for her to go first. I try not to ogle her as she steps out of the water, shaking her head back and forth and twisting her hair around her hand, pulling it over her shoulder. But damn, she's smokin'. She's all curves and hips and long legs. Soft around the edges in the most appealing way.

I look up at the sky and mouth *thank you* as I follow her up onto the dock.

She runs her hands through her hair and then crosses and uncrosses her arms like she doesn't quite know what to do with them. And then she looks down at herself. Her hands go to her stomach. "Oh fuck me. I'm so burned! How am I going to get rid of this?" In the center of her stomach is a very obvious book-shaped tan line.

I bite my bottom lip and try not to laugh, but her expression is priceless. "I guess no crop tops for you this weekend, huh?"

"I'm too old for crop tops." Her gaze meets mine and then

drops, moving over me on a slow sweep. "I just pulled you into the water, didn't I?"

"I was planning to go for a dip anyway." I grab the towel from the back of my chair and pass it to her.

"Getting dragged into the water and willingly jumping in aren't quite the same." She drapes the towel over her shoulders. "I'm sorry. I think you introduced yourself, but I missed it because I was panic-flailing. I hope I didn't hurt you." Her gaze roves over me again. "You don't look hurt, but you do look like you could do a lot of damage in a fight."

I grin. "Should I take that as a compliment?"

She drops her head, hiding her smile. "If you want to, sure." She peeks up at me again. "Do you know what time it is? I have no idea how long I've been floating."

"It's closing in on five thirty, last time I checked."

Her eyes go wide. "No. You can't be serious."

I hold out my arm with my smart watch and tap the face so it lights up. "It's five thirty-eight."

"I've been floating for nearly six hours. I don't understand how I got here. I don't even know what side of the lake *here* is."

Pearl Lake is a lot smaller than Lake Geneva, but it's still a lot of water to cover on a paddleboard. "You're on the north side."

"The *north* side? Yeesh."

"Where's your cottage?"

"In Pearl Bay, on the south side of the lake."

"You wanna use my phone to call someone? A boyfriend maybe?" I'm totally fishing.

"That was subtle." She arches a brow and gives me a wry grin. "I don't have a boyfriend."

"That's excellent news. I don't have a girlfriend, in case you were wondering. And my name is Maverick." I extend my hand.

She blinks. "Maverick? Is that a nickname or a given name?"

"Given. And surprisingly, my parents aren't hippies."

"Did your mom like *Top Gun* or something?" She slips her hand into my palm.

I watch as goose bumps rise along both of our arms. "Actually yeah, she did. At least until Tom Cruise sort of . . . went out of style." I reluctantly release her hand.

"Ah, well, that's fair. I'm Clover." She dips her head, and if her cheeks weren't already pink with too much sun, I'd guess she was blushing. "And my parents were absolutely hippies. Please don't make a joke about four leaves and being lucky."

"I wouldn't dream of it, Clover-without-a-boyfriend."

We smile at each other for a few seconds. She's definitely older. Maybe mid-twenties. My size makes me look a little older than I am, and so does the fact that by the end of the day I have a hint of shadow on my cheeks, unlike my older brother, Robbie, who can still get away with shaving twice a week.

"Can I get you a bottle of water? Or a soda? You must be parched." I flip open the cooler and rummage around, setting cans on the arm of my Adirondack chair.

"Water would be amazing. Thank you." She plucks a bottle from between two cans of soda and then looks up toward the cottage set back on the hill behind us. "Oh wow. Are you renting this place?"

"My aunt and uncle own it."

"Wow." She lets out a low whistle. "What are they, movie stars or something?" She cringes. "Sorry, that was so rude."

"My uncle's a retired NHL player."

"Oh yeah? There are a lot of those guys on the lake, aren't there?" She drains half of the bottle in three long gulps.

"Seems that way. Do you watch hockey?" I ask.

She gives me a somewhat embarrassed smile and glances at

the dock where her book is sitting, slightly wet and still in the baggie. "I'm more of a reader than a TV watcher."

That's when I realize the cover of the book has a shirtless dude holding a hockey stick on it. "I play hockey," I inform her.

Her eyes flare. "Professionally?"

"No. Not yet anyway."

"You're very athletic. Hockey players have great stamina." Her eyes lift to mine. "At least that's what I've read."

"I'd say it's an accurate assessment." I nod to the chairs. "Do you wanna sit?" *On my face?*

She glances at the chair and then at the sun, which is slowly making its way toward the horizon. "I do. Absolutely. But it's probably going to take me a while to paddle back to my place."

"I can drive you, if you want. I've got a truck. We can put your paddleboard in the back."

She tugs on her bottom lip with her teeth. "That's nice of you to offer, but, uh, I'm sort of in the don't-take-rides-from-strangers camp."

"As someone with a younger sister, I can totally appreciate that stance. There's a beach party later tonight. Maybe I'll see you there?"

"Yeah. Maybe. I think I'd like that." She takes another long gulp of her water. "I should probably get going."

"Here." I pass her my T-shirt. "Why don't you take this? It'll keep you from turning into a beet."

"Are you sure? Aren't you going to need it?"

"Nah. I'm good like this." I run a hand over my chest.

"Not gonna argue with that." She pulls my shirt over her head. It's so long it hits her mid-thigh. She ties a knot on the side, presumably so she doesn't end up with another bad tan line.

I help her get back on the paddleboard and send her off, hoping I'm going to run into her again.

And I'm not disappointed, because a few hours later, I find her on the beach. Kody bailed on the party, and BJ is already being chatted up, so I take the opportunity for what it is. "You want to sit on the pier, away from the noise?" There's a huge bonfire, but it's loud and rowdy. The pier is quiet and calm.

"That sounds good." She takes a sip from her travel mug; it's a different one from earlier.

I tap my travel water bottle against hers. "What's in there?"

"Spiked hot chocolate; what about you?" She falls in step beside me.

"Just water. I have an early practice and I'm not much good if I'm hungover."

"That's very responsible of you." We reach the end of the pier and take a seat on one of the benches. "Do you go to a lot of the beach parties?"

I stretch my arm across the back of the bench. "It's not really my scene. How about you?"

"Not really mine either. I only came because of you." She glances at me out of the corner of her eye and sips her hot chocolate.

"You're the reason I came, too."

She smiles, her gaze fixed on the moon hanging heavy in the sky. "If beach parties aren't your thing, what is?"

"Hockey is a big one, but when I'm not on the ice, I like this." I motion to the lake, the moon reflecting of the surface. "And Scrabble and origami."

"Origami?" She tips her head, like she's trying to decide if I'm joking or not.

"Yeah, it's calming, and I don't do stillness well, so it helps keep my hands and my mind busy."

She shifts so she's facing me. "You're an interesting guy, Maverick."

"I'm glad you think so." I adjust my own position, and when I do, she reaches out and brushes something off my shoulder. Innocent flirting that speaks volumes about her comfort level with me. Which is good. "Now tell me what you'd rather be doing since beach parties aren't your thing either."

We spend the next couple of hours talking. But when the breeze coming off the lake cools, and Clover wraps her arms around herself, I suggest we take off.

She fiddles with the strap of her purse. "Do you want to come back to my place?"

"Not worried about stranger danger anymore?" I ask.

She shakes her head. "Not now that I've had a chance to talk to you. Just let me tell my friend I've got a ride home."

I wait while she checks in with a group of people before we leave the beach and make the short walk to my truck.

Once we're settled, Clover gives me directions to her place.

"Are you renting, or . . ." I let it hang, wanting to keep the conversation flowing.

"It was my parents' place," she says. "But they moved to Florida a couple of years ago. They were going to do the snowbird thing, but then they decided to stay there, so it's mine now. It's a small, two-bedroom cabin. Nothing like the places on the north side of Pearl Lake."

"Eh, they're more like houses on a lake than actual cabins. I kinda love the smaller places on the south side, where all the locals live."

"Me too, it's a little more . . . laid-back."

A few minutes later, I pull into the driveway and park the truck beside a dark blue Prius. The cabin is exactly what I expected it to be: cute and sweet and like something that belongs in a fairy tale. There's a small, covered porch with two

Adirondack chairs off to the right. Hanging baskets of flowers flank the entry.

"This is one hundred percent you, isn't it?" It matches the woman I got to know on the pier.

She smiles and ducks her head again. "It really is. I've spent a lot of time here this summer."

"It's too bad this is the first time we've crossed paths." I feel like I should give her an out in case she's having second thoughts. "You sure you want me to come in?"

She nods once. "Yeah. I'm sure."

"Okay." I cut the engine, and we open our doors at the same time.

I meet her at the hood and follow her across the driveway to the front steps. She unlocks the door and ushers me in, closing it behind her and flipping the lock.

I take in the small space. It's perfect—the kind of cabin that instantly feels like home. "This place is great."

"I like it." She tosses the keys on the counter and turns to face me. "Do you want to see my bedroom?" Again, if her cheeks weren't already pink with sunburn, I'm sure she'd be blushing.

"Straight to the point. I like it. Do *you* want to show me your bedroom, Clover?"

She arches a brow. "Are you going to answer every question with a question?"

"Only the ones I feel require verification and confirmation." My body is already responding to the idea of seeing her bedroom—and getting her into bed—but one step at a time. She may decide she's not as into me as she thought after the clothes come off.

"Maybe, before you show me the rest of this place, our lips could introduce themselves to each other." I tap my own. "Just a little warm up. See if the spark hits us the way I think it could."

She bites her bottom lip through a grin and takes a step closer. Her warm palms settle on my chest and smooth over my shoulders. I rest my hand on her waist and dip my head down but wait for her to make the first move. She pushes up on her toes and brushes her lips over mine. Then she comes back again, this time lingering for a few seconds before she strokes along the seam with her tongue. I part my lips.

Her fingers slide into the hair at the nape of my neck. It's longer than it should be, but I've been too lazy this summer to care. She makes a low, throaty sound, and her soft body presses against mine as our tongues meet and tangle.

Heat moves through my veins, and electric want zings down my spine, my erection swelling behind the fly of my jeans. I don't know how long we stand here kissing, but when we finally come up for air, we're both panting, and I'm really fucking hard.

"I absolutely want to show you my bedroom," Clover says breathlessly.

"Okay." One-word answers are about as good as it's going to get since half the blood in my body has rerouted itself to my far-less-evolved head.

She laces her fingers with mine, and I follow her across the living room, taking in the tiles on the Scrabble board as I pass, and then we're in her bedroom. It's feminine and pretty, every-thing in soft shades of yellow and cream, with pops of vibrant green. On her nightstand are several books and magazines, including an old copy of *Psychology Today*.

I don't have much time to process more of my surroundings because Clover leads me over to the bed and turns me so the backs of my calves hit the frame. She lifts her shirt over her head and drops it on the floor.

I bite my lip to suppress my grin when she looks down at her stomach and tries to cover the book-shaped outline.

"I would feel a whole lot sexier without this."

"You're sexy with or without a book tan line," I assure her.

She rolls her eyes, but she's fighting her own smile.

"Don't worry, Clover. The last thing I'm worried about are your tan lines." I sit down on the edge of the bed and part my legs, inviting her to stand between them.

She steps into the empty space and tugs my shirt over my head, discarding it on the floor before she runs her fingers through my hair again. "God, you are beautiful," she whispers.

"So are you." I drag my fingertips along her side and settle my hand on her hip.

She reaches behind her and unclasps her bra. I groan as the straps slide down her arms, revealing pert nipples and perky breasts.

My fingers flex on her hip. "I would really like to touch you."

A slow smile spreads across her full lips. "I would like that too."

I skim the swell of her right breast with gentle fingertips, circling her nipple, watching it pucker further, and then I lean in, taking the taut skin between my lips, sucking softly.

She climbs into my lap and when her fingers skim my belt buckle, I pause. "Just to be clear, I don't have any expectations here, so if at any point you need to call a timeout, tell me and we can dial it back, okay?"

"Okay." She nods.

When she goes for the button on my pants, I move back on the bed and flip us over. "Can I focus on making you feel good for a while?"

"You're already making me feel good."

"I'm aiming for orgasmically good." I kiss my way between

the valley of her breasts and down her stomach. "You okay with me taking these off?" I tug at the belt loop on her jeans.

"Yes. Absolutely."

I fold back on my knees and pop the button, then drag the zipper down. "Like unwrapping an early birthday present."

She laughs, and it's a little breathless. "How old are you? Wait. Don't tell me. Mid-twenties? Or maybe early? But definitely over twenty. You must be. That's the only way you could have the body you do. Years of training."

"Do you want me to answer that or not?" I kiss below her navel and drag her pants down her legs, tossing them over the edge of the bed.

"Yes. No. Yes." She shimmies out of her panties, and they join the rest of the clothes on the floor. "You don't have to be specific. But you're in your twenties right?"

"Yeah, I'm in my twenties." I place another kiss below her navel and stretch out between her thighs.

"Okay, that's good." Her toes curl against my side. "Are you being honest?"

"I wouldn't lie. It doesn't do either of us any good if we're feeling guilty." I turn my head to the right, kissing the inside of her thigh, sucking lightly on the skin.

"You are such a tease," she groans.

"Just building anticipation." I drag my tongue along the length of her, and she bows up off the bed.

"Oh fuck, yes, please." Her legs fall open, and she grips the hair at my crown.

I make her come with my mouth, and then a second time with my fingers, because watching her come is damn well addictive. She's gorgeous and sexy, and it's so much more gratifying than when I'm with someone closer to my age, where everything is tentative and they're worried about losing control.

As soon as Clover regains control of her limbs, she pushes on my shoulders. I flip over so I'm on my back, and she straddles me. Our mouths connect in a hungry kiss, her long hair tickling my skin. She pulls back and braces her hands on my chest. "I'm so glad I fell asleep this afternoon and floated into your dock."

I laugh. "Me too. And here I thought tonight was going to be another boring beach party."

She shimmies back, and suddenly the lightness of the moment disappears. Her excitement is overshadowed by my anxiety as she pops the button on my jeans. I shimmy out of them and toss them on the floor, leaving me in black boxer brief. Clover tugs the waistband down and frees my erection.

For a few seconds, I'm met with stunned silence. The look on Clover's face says it all.

It's better than the nervous laughter I sometimes get—or worse, the slack-jawed head shaking or the *"there's no way that'll fit."*

It didn't matter how much my dad drilled into my head that lube would forever be my best friend when it came to sex, it never fully prepared me for the realities of being exceptionally well endowed.

I'm not packing in the boyfriend-dick, fits-so-nice kind of way.

More in the this-might-be-uncomfortable-even-with-all-the-foreplay way.

"Holy wow." Her eyes flare. "Sweet baby Jesus riding a unicorn." Her gaze flips between my face and my cock, which is now lying on my stomach.

I say the first thing that pops into my head. "I have lube."

Her eyebrows rise, and she nods slowly. "Yes. Yes, I bet you do."

"But we don't have to have sex."

Her fingers circle the shaft. "Now I understand your attention to foreplay and why you were trying to get your entire hand in my vagina," she muses.

"Foreplay is the best part of sex," I offer. "And essential."

"I can see why you feel that way." She shifts forward, pressing the length against her stomach. The head covers her navel by half an inch. "I hope you have condoms, because I don't think the ones I have are going to be the right . . . fit. You're definitely way above average."

"I have some in my wallet."

It's on the bed beside us. I flip it open and pass her one, pulling out the small packet of lube as well. She plucks the foil packet from my fingers, tears it open, and rolls it down my length while I open the lube and squirt a little onto the tip.

"Just take it slow," I warn her as she braces a hand on my shoulder and lines my cock up with her entrance.

"I don't think there's any other way to take you," she murmurs as the head disappears inside her. She pauses.

Her gaze stays trained on the place where our bodies meet, and she keeps up with the slow hip rolls until her ass meets my thighs. Her fingers trail past her navel, going lower to skim over her clit, stopping at the base of my shaft. "It's almost obscene how full I am."

"Just tell me if you're uncomfortable."

"I'm not, but if that changes, I'll let you know." She rises a few inches, and her mouth drops open, head falling back when she lowers herself. I hold her hips, helping her find a rhythm.

She urges me to raise my hands and presses hers to mine, palm to palm. She laces our fingers together, leaning into them as she chases down her orgasm. Her rhythm falters for a beat before she starts to move again, long, slow strokes that tip me over the edge too. It's fucking bliss.

"You want to stay the night so we can do this again?" She presses her lips to mine.

"Ab-so-fucking-lutely."

We make a snack, and then have sex again in the kitchen. We shower and make out. Wake up in the middle of the night for round three. Try for round four with her condoms but end up sixty-nining instead.

At six in the morning, my alarm goes off, signaling skate practice. Clover is passed out beside me. For a moment, I consider waking her up to say goodbye, or leaving my number, but it's obvious she's got some years on me—in the best possible way—and I don't want to make it awkward for her. Besides, I'm heading back to college soon, and she's got a life to live.

Instead, I write a note on a piece of paper, fold it into an origami crane, and leave it on the nightstand. I walk out of her life twelve hours after I walked in. Maybe next summer, when I'm en route to a professional career in hockey, we'll cross paths again. Whether or not that happens, I've now got a sweet memory tied to this place.

2

It Was Good for a Minute There

CLOVER

Five weeks later

The beep of the house alarm being disarmed wakes me. I bolt upright in bed, breath caught in my throat. The wisps of my dream fade out slowly. I've been having the same one for over a month—more like a memory than a dream. My cheeks heat, and every muscle below my waist is clenching. My summer fling refuses to stay in Pearl Bay. He's followed me here, to Chicago, and every night I have the same dream, where instead of leaving behind an empty pillow and a paper crane, I wake up with him next to me.

"Wakey wakey, eggs and bac-y!" my best friend, Sophia, calls out from down the hall. She lives on the top floor of the duplex, and I live on the bottom. I lucked out that the tenant who previously lived here moved at the beginning of August, giving me the opportunity to take over the lease and live close to my best friend again.

"I'll just be a minute!" I call back and roll out of bed, sad to leave behind the dream, but excited about what the rest of my day is going to look like. I shrug into my robe as I pad down the hall to the kitchen.

Sophia is already pulling plates out of the cupboard.

"I lied about the bacon and eggs. We're having muffins for breakfast. And they're not healthy in the slightest. They're full of butter and sugar and blueberries," she tells me.

"Sounds like exactly what I need on a Tuesday morning, and blueberries are healthy." I head for the coffee maker, which is set to brew at 6:30, so there's a full, fresh pot waiting for us. Back in July, I was offered an incredible job opportunity at the college where Sophia works—a one-year contract to teach two first-year English and semantics classes—and I couldn't turn it down. While teaching at the college level full-time hadn't been something I planned on, the salary was too good to refuse. And it's a great addition to my resume.

Last week, things got even better when I was offered the opportunity to take over a creative writing seminar course from a professor who had to go on leave for back surgery. He's off for at least the rest of the first semester, if not the entire year. He passed over the course syllabus, and today I take over the class.

Up until now, I'd been teaching courses as an adjunct professor and writing for several online publications. It paid the bills, but it didn't leave much left over for savings. A one-year position teaching at a prestigious school definitely pays better. And the addition of the seminar will not only help pad my bank account, but it's the cherry on the sundae of this experience.

I pour two cups, feeling my phone buzz against my hip. I ignore it for now. I'm pretty sure I already know who it is.

"How are you this morning? Excited? Nervous?" Sophia asks as I set her coffee in front of her and take the seat across the table.

"Both, I guess? I have a feeling tonight's class will be a lot of fun to teach. All these young minds learning how to create worlds. It's amazing."

The English 101 courses are fine, but the classes are huge, and the material is fairly general. The second-year seminar course is much more intimate and the content inspiring. And it should be full of keen minds.

"I'm glad you're excited for it." Sophia separates the top of her muffin from the bottom, and despite it being full of butter and blueberries, she slathers more butter on both sides.

"What about you? How are the students handling it now that the honeymoon period is over?" I ask.

"The pressure is really starting to hit a lot of the kids, especially since midterms are coming up and the deadline to drop courses has passed. We advertised a stress management group last week and it's already full, with a waiting list."

"Oh wow, can you add a second session?"

Sophia is a counselor for the college, dealing mostly with students who are struggling with the demands of college.

She nods. "I think we'll be able to get approval for it."

My phone buzzes again, and I pull it from my robe. I already had a few unanswered messages last night. I finally look at it and groan, because in addition to the message from my mother wishing me luck today on the seminar class and confirming a phone call later in the week, there's one from my ex-husband. Or he would be my ex-husband if he would sign the divorce papers I served him back in August, which incidentally coincided nicely with my end-of-summer fling. The unanswered message tally is up to six.

Gabriel and I have been unofficially separated for a year,

which is longer than our marriage lasted. After we walked down the aisle, the charismatic man I'd come to know changed. And when he moved us across the country with no warning, taking me away from my support network, I put my foot down. Well, I packed a bag and left. For nearly twelve months after that, I was off the grid. Only my parents and Sophia knew where I was and how to find me.

But I couldn't stay married to Gabriel forever. I didn't want to be married to him at all. So I contacted my lawyer and had the divorce papers drafted and served last month. Of course, now that Gabriel can contact me again, he wants to reconcile.

Which is ridiculous. There's nothing to reconcile.

"Do you want me to check it for you?" Sophia asks, obviously aware of my trepidation and frustration.

I make the go-ahead motion.

She snatches the phone and holds it up to my face, activating facial recognition.

We're closer than sisters. She has my banking password. Sometimes I'm too reactive to deal with messages from Gabriel, especially this early in the morning.

She swipes, and her mouth turns down as she reads the message. "Oh, for fudgsicle's sake."

"What now? Do I even want to know?" I can feel myself deflating, which is a terrible way to start what's supposed to be an excitement-filled day.

"He wants to have the cabin on Pearl Lake reassessed. He thinks it's undervalued. He also wants to know if you've given any further consideration to seeing a therapist with him. Seems convenient that he's pushing the 'get back together' angle while also trying to squeeze more money out of you."

"Oh, fuck him. Of course he wants to have it reassessed." I cross my arms, my heart rate spiking. The hairs on my arms stand on end, and a zip of energy travels up my spine and wraps around my throat, creating phantom pressure. It's a sensation I've grown entirely too used to when dealing with Gabriel. "He went there all of once when we were married, and now he wants to make it impossible for me to keep it. I need him to sign the papers so I can move on with my life."

My parents handed over the deed to the cabin after I married Gabriel, sort of as a wedding present. Unfortunately, instead of keeping the cabin in my name only, they added his too.

Gabriel never had any interest in the cabin until I told him I wanted a divorce. Then he seemed to realize it had some value that wasn't just sentimental on my part. I have no interest in giving it up, but I'm not in a great financial position to buy him out. While the seminar course helps, it doesn't cover the cost of half the property.

"Do you really think he wants to reconcile?" Sophia says gently.

Another message comes in.

"What else has he added to the list?" I snap, immediately feeling bad because Sophia does not deserve my wrath.

"He said he's been talking to a therapist on a regular basis. And that he sees now why you two didn't work. And that it's his fault you felt compelled to run away and hide. Those are his exact words."

"I was afraid he was going to lock me in the basement and keep me like a pet!" I run a hand through my hair, shaking my head. I hate that he's still trying to control me. At least his motives are transparent to me now in a way they weren't when we were first married. "I'm sorry. Maybe I should look later, after I've finished teaching. I don't need to start my day in a bad mood, and you don't need me unloading on you."

Sophia gives me a sympathetic smile. "It's okay. I get that you're frustrated. You've been moving on for a year, and he's been stewing about you escaping his clutches. He's good at holding things over your head."

"I hope he gives up sooner rather than later, or the lawyer bills are going to eat my entire salary," I gripe.

"I know it sucks right now, but at least at the end you'll be free."

"I need to be patient and not reactive. It's hard, though, especially with the way he pushes my buttons on purpose." It's clear that's his intention with his most recent messages. He's trying to use what's important to me to bargain for another chance.

"Do you want me to respond for you?"

I shake my head. "Leave it for now, and I'll come back to it tonight. Now that he has my attention again, he wants it all the time, just like always." Is it passive-aggressive on my part? Sure. But he's being a manipulative ass.

"Okay." She checks the time. "I need to get ready for work."

"Me too. I won't be home until late since my seminar ends at ten, but I'll check in with you when I get back."

"Sounds good." Sophia kisses me on the cheek and heads for the front door, locking it behind her while I head down the hall to the bathroom to get ready for work.

My English 101 course starts at nine. The sheer number of students was a bit intimidating at first—there are three hundred freshmen in the class—but I've gotten used to the sea of bodies. I also have a TA to help grade assignments.

After my 101 class, I spend the afternoon in my office reviewing my lecture notes for the creative writing seminar this evening. It's much smaller, with only forty students. And the class is three hours. I'm a little nervous about taking over for such a seasoned professor, but with my background in library science and a creative writing minor, it's in my wheelhouse.

At six thirty, I lock up my office and head to the seminar

class. I arrive fifteen minutes early and find a handful of students already waiting at the door. They've been informed of the change, but I still get some curious looks.

I let them in, and they murmur hello, taking their seats and setting up tablets, laptops, and notebooks on their desks.

When seven o'clock arrives, I introduce myself and explain that I'll be taking over for Professor Connelly. I field a few questions and reassure the students that he's okay. I also brought in a get well soon card for them to sign. I pass it to the student directly in front of me, then pull up my attendance list and start calling names.

The door opens when I'm halfway through, and a student straggles in. It happened in my English class earlier, but in a class of three hundred students, it's easier to slip in the back door and quietly find a seat. That's what I expect this student to do.

Except his phone starts ringing. And it's not a normal ringtone. It's a song blaring through the room at full volume.

"Fuck. Shit." He's standing in the middle of the room, facing the back of the class, every single student staring at him in wide-eyed horror.

He rummages around in his pocket and pulls out the offending device as Justin Bieber croons "I'm so fucking lonely" to the entire class. Instead of silencing it, he answers the call— on speaker.

A male voice that sounds like an angry father starts yelling. "Why the hell am I getting calls about you being late for practice, you're—"

He spins around, gaze moving over the class as he takes in their looks of horror. He's wearing a baseball cap, and the lights above cast a shadow over his face. "Oh, fuck me," he mutters. "Hey, Dad, I'm in the middle of class. I'll call you back later." He rushes the words, so it all sounds quite garbled. Then he drops into the closest empty desk and slams his elbow on the edge on his way down. He sucks in a groan.

I give the student a look that I hope conveys how unimpressed I am. "Are you quite done?" I'm ready to go off on him, but he raises a hand and knocks his hat off his head.

"Uh, sorry, Professor. I think I might be in the wrong class." His eyes dart around the room. "Or maybe not?"

"Professor Connelly is out for back surgery. Professor Sweet is taking over the class," the student beside him says.

"Oh shit." His vibrant green gaze, ringed in hazel, meets mine.

All the air leaves my lungs on a *whoosh*. The room tilts, and I'm suddenly light-headed. I can tell instantly that he recognizes me, and the silence in the room is deafening. Fortunately, he fills it by rambling out an explanation.

"Sorry about the phone call. And for being late. Coach kept me after practice and my dad's on my ass because I had a bad game. I'm so sorry, Cl—" He clasps his hands in front of him and bites his lips together.

"Don't let it happen again."

My mouth feels like it's full of cotton, and the rest of me feels disconnected from my body. Because this student, sitting in the middle of my sophomore class, is my summer fling.

My one-night stand who left behind an origami crane and a lot of memories I wish I could now erase.

Fuck my life.

3

Not the Best Day

MAVERICK

Six weeks later

Forty-eight percent.

That's my grade on my most recent creative writing assignment. I tried to get out of this class—went straight to the registrar's office after Clover took over as the professor and begged them to change my schedule. But I'd missed the deadline by a week, and I needed the elective to graduate, which meant dropping it wasn't an option either.

So, I had no choice but to ride out the semester and hope to hell I could eke out a passing grade. I probably would have managed if Professor Connelly had been the one grading my papers since he's a hockey fan. It didn't seem to matter that the last time I'd written a creative anything was probably in high school.

But Clover taking over the class changed things. In theory, sleeping with my hot professor sounds awesome, but in practice, it's really fucking awkward.

And now I'm sitting here with a forty-fucking-eight percent because I'm 2500 words shy of the minimum word count. That's like ten fucking pages of words. Also, according to my mental calculations on my other assignments, I'm at risk of failing the course. My initial grades were decent, but since the professor swap, it's gone downhill, and my midterm grade was trash. And now I only have a handful of weeks to bring it up.

My dad is going to shit a brick if I fail a class. He was pissed enough when he saw I was skating on thin ice with two of my courses at midterm. I got the whole speech: *"Just because a team owns your rights doesn't mean you're going to get called up. Everyone needs a backup plan."*

He's not wrong.

Not having a backup plan is stupid. And at the end of the year, I'll have a kinesiology degree. With hockey seven days a week, school, and my part-time job at the gym, which includes teaching self-defense, I didn't want to overload myself with difficult classes. This course was supposed to be an easy C. And maybe it would have been if the woman who replaced Professor Connelly hadn't been on the receiving end of my orgasm delivery before the semester started.

I spend the rest of the class trying to find a way to appeal to my professor that doesn't entail sexual favors. Though I would willingly provide those, because hot damn, Clover Sweet—her last name has become a bit ironic—is incredible between the sheets. But considering the way she's avoided any and all contact with me, I don't see her jumping at the opportunity. Also, it would be considered bribery.

So I need to find a way to dig myself out of this hole. And I'm not exactly sure how to do that.

At the end of class, I take my time packing up, watching student after student approach her to talk about their creative writing assignment.

"You going to the pub, Mav?"

The girl sitting to my right is twisting her hair around her finger and snapping her gum. She looks a lot like my cousins Lovey and Lacey Butterson—they're identical twins and only people who know them well can tell them apart. I think this girl's name might be Sandy or Suzy or something. I'm pretty sure it starts with an S. Despite the gum snapping, she's damn well brilliant. She always has an entire monologue prepared on whatever we're discussing in class, and it makes Clover—Professor Sweet—absolutely glow. Which makes me hard. In turn, I don't have very fond feelings toward Sandy-Suzy.

"Not today. I got a few things I need to take care of."

Her face falls fractionally before her smile widens and she twists more of her ponytail around her finger, pulling her head to the side. "Maybe next week."

"Yeah. Maybe. Have a good time tonight." I force a polite grin and wait for her to leave with one of the other girls in the class.

I pack up my books and hang back until I'm the only one left. Then I head for the front of the room where Professor Sweet is busy packing up her worn leather bag. She's wearing a white blouse with a loose, droopy cardigan, and a pair of dress pants. Her dark hair is pulled up in a tight bun, and her black-framed glasses hang perilously close to the end of her nose.

I adjust my backpack as I amble her way. She glances up at me over the rim of her glasses, then focuses on the papers scattered across her desk, tapping them into a neat pile before sliding them into a folder. "How can I help you, Mr. Waters?"

She always addresses me this way. Never by my first name.

Maybe because she screamed it a lot that night we had together at her cabin. I need to *not* think about that right now.

I lean my hip on the edge of her desk. It's been a weird kind of torture, sitting in her class, listening to her smart talk about books and literature, knowing what she looks like naked. How she tastes. What she sounds like when she comes. It's been a lot of weeks of awkward, three-hour hard-ons. I'll blame the fact that half of the blood in my body is pooled in my dick for the words that come out of my mouth. "You look nice today, Professor Sweet."

She pauses in her mission to get her laptop into her bag, and her gaze flicks up to mine. Slate gray eyes—piercing and shrewd and not at all impressed.

I flash her my most winning smile and basically shovel my own grave by saying more stupid shit. "I like your cardigan."

Her lips flatten into a line and her back straightens, shoulders rolling back. "I don't have time for this, Mr. Waters. If this is about your assignment, I suggest you follow the instructions. Your piece was more than two thousand words under the minimum word count."

I hold up a hand, not to stop her, but in apology. Unfortunately, my mouth is my nemesis. "I meant no offense, Professor Sweet. I think you already know this, but I'm on the school hockey team. We have practice every day, and games—"

I have no idea why I'm leading with this. Maybe because I'm an idiot? Professor Sweet doesn't give a shit about my games or practice.

"I'm aware of your athletics involvement. It's not an excuse for handing in an incomplete assignment."

"I know. And I'm sorry. I just, I have a lot on my plate, you know?" This is better. I can appeal to her sympathetic side. I know she can be soft. I've experienced it.

"There's a lot of pressure for me to do well—in hockey, I

mean. Since there's a good chance I'll be playing pro next year." *Nope.* I can see immediately that this isn't working, but I can't seem to shut up. The words just keep coming out, not helping my case at all.

"I'm not sure if you know this, but my dad donates to the school's mental health foundation." *Because my sister mentioned that donating to a sports team I played on was nepotism, so he should put his donations elsewhere until I graduate.* She's needed a shit ton of therapy, so it seemed logical.

Professor Sweet plants her fists on her desk. Her right eye twitches. "Is this some sort of backwards blackmail because you refuse to take responsibility for your lack of effort?" she growls.

I bet angry sex with her would be amazing.

I shake my head. "Of course not, Professor Sweet. I'm just explaining—"

"Explaining what, exactly? That your father's donation should excuse you from following the rules like everyone else? You're a fourth-year student in a second-year class. You know what the expectations are. Maybe your other professors let you get away with this kind of laxness, but I'm certainly not one of them. You are skating the edge, Mr. Waters, and I will not be giving you a passing grade if you haven't earned it. And you certainly have *not* earned it thus far. Now, unless you'd like me to report you to the dean for trying to blackmail your way to a passing grade, I suggest you put in the time and earn the grades you're capable of. If you would like to resubmit your piece with the minimum required word count, you're free to do so. However, you will be penalized for handing it in late. Now, if you'll excuse me, I have other things that need my attention." She shoves her folder into her ancient bag and slings it over her shoulder. Then she spins on her heel—she's wearing flats—and storms out of the room.

That did not go nearly as well as I'd planned.

I CHECK my phone on the way out of the building, and of course, because this day isn't already a giant shitstorm, I have messages from one of the guys on the team saying he's at the pub and Carly is there, asking about me. I semi-hooked up with her early in the semester. Mostly as a way to get Clover out of my head. Not realizing that she would end up taking permanent residence in my brain by becoming my professor.

Since then, I've been trying to shake Carly, and I thought things were good—she's stopped showing up at parties, like she did at the beginning of the semester—but evidently, she's still going to be a challenge.

Going home *or* to the pub means the possibility of running into people I don't want to see. Home will have my family and Kody. It's not that I don't like my family, or my best friend. I need to get in a better headspace before I deal with them, though. Now that Lavender and Kody have sorted themselves, they're perpetually all cozy-cozy, and it's awkward. As much as I'd been waiting for them to figure their shit out, I'm finding I don't like the way it changes the dynamic.

So I go to the school's athletic facility instead. I don't want to risk running into my teammates and getting sucked into a conversation about our upcoming game. So I avoid the facilities dedicated to division one athletes, in lieu of the regular gym where the normal students work out.

On the way, I call my dad, who has texted a bunch of times. Apparently, the coach from Nashville called my coach, which isn't unusual. They're always checking on their investments, but it sucks that my dad is actually friends with Nashville's coach, and that means there are conversations being had. My dad is going to be relentless about messaging me until I answer.

"What's this I'm hearing about you being late for practice and distracted again?" is his greeting.

"I'm sorry. It won't happen again." It sounds like lip service, even to me.

His silence makes me want to fill the space, but I bite my tongue.

"Please tell me you weren't late for practice because of woman problems."

I can't tell if it's disappointment or frustration in his voice. Or both. "I'm not dating anyone. I'm focused on getting to the end of the year and being called up."

What else can I tell him? That I'm back to following his advice to remain uncommitted until my career is sorted out? For a few weeks, I needed the distraction from being stuck up in my head, and Carly seemed like a good way to do that. Except that backfired on me in spectacular fashion.

As soon as Clover took over as my professor, I officially went on a total dating hiatus. It needed to happen anyway. I've spent most of my college career making sure I don't get attached to anyone so I don't have to worry about things like breakups.

For someone who has involved parents, a financially easy ride, and hasn't had to work particularly hard for anything in my life—apart from hockey—I'm kind of a hot mess.

"Maybe I'm wrong. Maybe a girlfriend wouldn't be the worst thing in the world," he muses.

"Are you serious?" I cannot believe these words are coming out of my dad's mouth. "Girlfriends are drama and energy. I don't have time for that."

"I played my best hockey after I met your mother."

"Yeah, but as you've told me probably a thousand times, you also met Mom when you were done with college and so was she. The whole point of waiting until I'm in the NHL to settle down is so I don't end up meeting someone and get all attached and then have to get over it when the long distance is too hard."

I don't even want to think about what it's going to look like in June when Kody gets called up and might move to Vancouver, which would take him away from my sister. Again.

He sighs. "I don't want you to do something that's going to have a negative impact on your future aspirations, son. You're smart and talented. You have a lot going for you, and you're almost where you want to be."

"I know." Or at least I think I do. This hasn't been my best season so far, but the whole I-slept-with-my-professor thing has been a bit of a mindfuck. "I promise I'll get it under control. You don't have anything to worry about. And I won't be late for practice again." I say all the things I know he wants to hear.

I'm almost at the gym, and I'd really like to spend the next hour purging all the demons in my head and wearing my body down enough that I can sleep without dreaming. They've been vivid lately. And not entirely pleasant.

He sighs. "Okay. Your mom and I will try to come down for a game in the next couple of weeks."

"Sure. That'd be great, Dad." Most of the time I love having my dad at games, but I've been off the last couple. And the pressure of having my hockey-legend dad watching me can be a lot to handle under the best of circumstances.

We hang up, and I push inside the building. The regular gym is pretty quiet at this time of night—only a few girls on elliptical machines and a couple of hardcore dudes whose entire life seems to revolve around lifting weights, based on their thick necks and massive shoulders.

I'd prefer as much solitude as possible. I'm not in the mood for people, particularly not my teammates. Or socializing. I open the locker-room door and make a face at the smell. This happens on very rare occasions. There's some kind of issue and the showers back up. It makes it super rank—a combination of urine, smelly sneakers, body odor, and dick cheese. But I'll deal if it means I can avoid running into guys I know.

I pull on a pair of compression shorts followed by a pair of running shorts—because no one needs to see the outline of my junk while I'm running—and my tank. Then I shove my feet into my running shoes, grab my towel, and toss my stuff into a locker.

I head down the hall to the main gym, passing the pool as I go. I pause, considering. A swim might be good. We closed our pool in September, and I miss doing laps. This one is overly chlorinated, but it's better than nothing. And I could swim in my running shorts, if I had to.

I think I'm in luck and it's empty, but as I reach for the door handle, a head pops out of the water and arms pinwheel in slow, deliberate strokes, legs kicking without making a splash, propelling the person forward. I watch as they reach the end and flip over onto their back. It's a woman, based on the black one-piece meant for laps.

I shake my head. "Don't be a creeper." I let go of the door handle and continue to the main gym.

I hit the treadmill, running off the pent-up energy and the frustration over everything that happened today.

As far as my creative writing assignment goes, I should have put in more effort than I did. I figured I'd get a slap on the wrist for it being short, though, not a failing grade. Professor Sweet called me on my bullshit, which isn't something most of my professors would do. Many of them know who my dad is, and that I've been drafted to Nashville. And sometimes I do use that to my advantage. It's shitty, but then, a lot of people use their connections, so why shouldn't I? There's a good chance I'll never use this degree anyway, at least not if I get called up after graduation. Eventually I'll be making high six figures a year, or more. I doubt I'll earn what my dad did, because I'm not as good as he was, but I'm decent. Good enough.

Not the best, though.

Not like Kody, who seems to be naturally good at everything. He makes hockey look effortless, although I'm aware he nearly kills himself to be as good as he is on the ice. And when he fucks up, he punishes himself with workouts and drills. He's an interesting guy. We grew up together, but sometimes I wonder if he's my best friend just because we're both in hockey, and maybe also because our friendship kept him close enough to get to my sister.

I don't know that his brain is wired to use people like that, though.

I mean, he spent nearly a decade self-flagellating over Lavender and thinking he wasn't good enough for her. I don't know that he could handle the mental and emotional toll it would take to straight-up use me.

He's another reason I don't ever want to get attached to anyone.

Not him specifically, I guess, but the way he carries around the burden of loving someone. It's like a noose waiting to tighten and snap the life right out of you. Or worse, suffocate it out. It's fucking terrifying.

I'm all up in my head, not paying attention to the time, so at eleven, the kid working the front desk comes over and tells me he has to shut things down. I end my run and leave him to lock up. I know him from parties, so he lets me take my time getting out of here.

I nod to a couple of stragglers in the locker room and make small talk with one of the guys who always seems to be here at the same time as me. Eventually, the locker room empties, and I wait until everyone else is gone before I head for the sauna. I open the door and gag. There must be a backup for sure. It smells like baked urine and ball sweat in here.

I could head to the team's facility, but then I'd have to get dressed and risk running into my teammates. Or I could go home and use the hot tub, but there's a chance there are people over, using it already—maybe River and his football buddies, or my cousin BJ and our friend Quinn. They have their own hot tub and live two doors down, but they're always over at our place, using ours instead. Kody doesn't invite people over because he generally doesn't like them—people, that is.

The later I get home, the less likely it is that anyone will be awake, looking to talk or hang out. I rummage around in my bag, checking for the master key to the athletic facility that I found last year. It was lying on the floor outside the locker room, so I tried it, and it worked on the door. I found out pretty quick that it opened more than the men's locker room; it works on all the doors in the athletic facility.

Whoever lost it never reported it, because the locks haven't been changed. I've only ever used the key for after-hours locker room access. And I haven't gotten caught.

I grab my towel and the master key and poke my head out into the hall. It's quiet, and I know the guy who locks up never checks the locker rooms before he leaves. It should be a couple of hours before the cleaners arrive.

I pad down the hallway, still wearing my running shoes. There's no way I'd go barefoot in the guys' changing room. I did it once a long time ago and spent three years with plantar warts.

I knock on the door to the women's locker room before I slide the key into the lock. I crack the door a couple of inches and call out "cleaning," then wait to make sure I'm in the clear. The lights are still on, but it's empty.

My heart rate kicks up a notch as I steal across the room to the sauna. I keep the light off as I step inside, not wanting to draw unnecessary attention to myself. And then I inhale deeply. "It smells so fucking good in here," I say to the empty space. Soft and feminine. Way better than ballsac and piss.

I feel my way across the room and spread my towel out on the bench seat.

Dudes are disgusting. They're always sitting around bare-assed on the benches. Women, on the other hand, generally have some modesty. At least that's how I spin it in my head.

Besides, even if they do sit in here naked, I'd much rather put my ass where a bare vagina has been than a set of sweaty nuts.

I stretch my arms across the bench and let my head fall back, relaxing. Or at least I'm trying to. But my head is all over the place.

I need to resubmit that assignment for Professor Sweet. It's worth 15 percent of our final grade, and my average isn't high enough to take a fail. But filling in the holes in that story isn't going to be fun. And it's probably the reason for all the fucked-up dreams I've been having lately. Another confirmation that the past should stay where it is, hopefully buried under a ton of other shit.

Now that I have time to reflect on it, it was a stupid thing to write about. But as Clover—Professor Sweet—said, I was lazy and looking for an easy out. At the time, it seemed to fit the criteria for a creative piece meant to explore a childhood memory, especially since it's one that never seems to go the fuck away. Now I wish I'd picked something else. The first time my mom made me buy condoms would have been a good one, and far less difficult to write.

Whatever. I'll add two thousand words, get the passing grade, and make it through the rest of the semester, hopefully without pissing Clover off again.

4

From Bad to Worse

CLOVER

The student who works the desk had to come in and tell me, apologetically, that he needed to lock up the pool. It's already quarter past eleven by the time I'm done in the shower, and the women's locker room is completely empty. This isn't the first time I've been the last person here. I pause as I pass the sauna. There's no one left but me. It wouldn't hurt to spend ten minutes in there relaxing before I head home. And if someone should come knocking, I can feign that I lost track of time.

The lights are off, so I step inside and feel around for the switch on the wall, flicking it on as I let my towel drop to my waist. It takes me a moment to process what I'm seeing—and for me to register that I'm not nearly as alone as I believed myself to be.

A naked, hulking man stretched out along the bench lifts

his head and blinks. A very familiar man, who I've seen naked before.

Who is now my student.

My student.

My *naked* student.

I scream in both shock and surprise and feel around for the door handle. "How the hell did you get in here?" I shout.

Maverick Waters is a big man. A very big man. I hate that, despite my shock, I can still appreciate the way the thick muscles in his arms and chest flex and bunch as he shifts his position, sitting upright. His abs actually ripple as he drops his hand to shield himself. Not that it matters—I know exactly what he's trying to hide because I've had my hands and mouth on it, and it's been inside me.

I'm so busy with my internal freak out and trying to find the doorknob that seems to have magically disappeared that I lose my grip on my towel, and it hits the floor.

"Shit." Maverick lifts one hand to cover his eyes and scrambles to wrap his own towel around his waist. It's small, one of the ones borrowed from the gym. And it doesn't cover much of his mammoth body.

I snatch my towel from the floor and wrap it around myself, trying not to think about the countless feet that have walked across this tile all day. The alternative is being completely naked in front of Maverick, and while that was fine in August, it certainly isn't now. I'll take the possibility of gross feet.

"What the fuck are you doing in here?" My voice is too loud, and the only thing I seem capable of doing is speaking at an inappropriately high volume.

Maverick starts to stand, but he doesn't secure his towel, so I get another eyeful of his junk.

I finally manage to find the doorknob and wrench it open,

taking a quick step out into the locker room. "Oh my God. Did you *wait* for me?"

He shakes his head, eyes wide and flitting around the sauna. "No, Clo—I mean Professor Sweet—"

"Did you *follow* me here?" My voice is high-pitched and strained, but also appropriately incredulous. "You can't offer me your dick in exchange for a better grade!" *There are so many better ways I could have phrased that statement.*

His eyebrows climb his forehead, and I swear for a moment I can see the wheels turning in his head. But his cheeks flush red and he swallows, shaking his head with vehemence. "That's not . . . I can explain."

"Explain what exactly? You need to get the hell out of here!" I take another step back and point toward the door at the other end of the locker room.

He follows the order, turning sideways as he moves past me, but his arm still manages to brush mine. He mumbles an apology and fists the towel at his waist. His free hand grips the back of his neck. "I honestly thought I was alone, and no one was here. Some asshole pissed in the rocks in the guys' sauna or something, so it smells horrible in there, like dirty ball sac and feet. It smells nice in here—not like any of those things—so I thought I'd sneak in for a few minutes and unwind. I wasn't waiting for you. And I didn't think I could offer my dick in exchange for a passing grade, even though it's gotten rave reviews from you in the past." He cringes.

"Are you fucking serious right now?" I whisper angrily, glancing around the room, paranoid that someone is going to catch us in here and jump to conclusions. He might be correct about the rave reviews but bringing it up now certainly isn't going to win him any damn points.

He closes his eyes for a moment. "I'm sorry. I'm really sorry. I don't know why I said that. Sometimes I open my mouth and stupid shit comes out. But you know that already since I do it regularly in your class. I didn't even know you came to the gym."

He definitely puts his foot in his mouth. He does it on a weekly basis, in between adding meaningful points to the class discussion. It's both infuriating and sometimes mildly entertaining. However, him showing up in the women's sauna is the opposite of entertaining.

"I should call security! I could get you expelled for this!"

His eyes flare, and he points to his bare chest. "I could get you in trouble for sleeping with your student."

Heat, the kind associated with blind rage, courses through my veins. There is no way I'll allow myself to be manipulated like this. "Are you trying to blackmail me?"

His eyes bulge again. "No! That's not—I'm just saying—"

"You need to leave. Right now!" I point to the door.

"You're right. Okay. I'm sorry, Professor. I'm going." He makes a beeline for the exit, head down, broad shoulders rolled forward. He trips on his way and stumbles, hitting the door with a grunt. He pushes it open, and I wait a few seconds, my heart thundering in my chest, before I rush across and turn the lock.

I'm shaking and on edge as I gather my things and quickly dress in one of the stalls that locks from the inside. I half expect him to be waiting outside the locker room again, but I slip out into the darkened hallway and manage to leave the building without running into anyone else.

It isn't until I'm in my car on the way home that I finally feel like I can breathe again. I don't know what to make of that entire situation—or whether I should believe him when he said he didn't follow me.

The second I'm in the door at home, my phone dings with a message from Sophia. I scan the first line and ping her back right away. I'm much later than usual, and she's been worrying for the past half hour. She doesn't like the way Gabriel keeps calling and messaging me. She's afraid things will escalate.

He's a control freak and good at manipulating situations, but I don't think she has to worry about him seeking me out here. I haven't told him where I'm working, and the only address I've given him is a PO Box in Pennsylvania. The mail goes there first before it's forwarded here.

I'm aware I can't keep my location a secret forever, especially if I plan to finalize the divorce before my contract with the college ends, but if I can get through this semester, so my one-night stand is no longer in my class and stops being a constant reminder of my bad decision-making, that would be great.

A minute later, Sophia is at my door, letting herself in and locking it behind her. "Is everything okay? I figured you'd be home an hour ago."

"I'm sorry if I made you worry. I stayed at the gym longer than I meant to."

"It closes at eleven, and it's almost midnight," Sophia points out.

I motion for her to have a seat. It's not as though I'm going to keep what happened to myself, and I feel like *not* reporting Maverick to security right away was on brand for me. I don't love conflict. It's part of the reason it's taken this long for me to serve Gabriel with divorce papers.

"I closed down the pool and thought I'd sneak into the sauna for a few minutes after hours."

She arches a brow. "For a rule follower, that's pretty un-rule-followy."

"I know. And I should have come home and used the hot tub, but I was the only person in there, or so I thought."

Sophia is the only person I've told about Maverick. She

advised me to ignore and avoid him as much as possible and to pass his assignments over to my TA, which is exactly what I've done. And while it's been awkward having him in my class, it seemed to be working fine until tonight.

I explain what happened, starting with Maverick's failing grade, him trying to smooth talk me after class, and me being less than accommodating. Then I add in Gabriel's insistent messages this afternoon that we need to talk, and me needing to decompress with a swim. I end with stepping inside the sauna and finding Maverick there, naked and sprawled out on the bench seat.

Sophia asks all the same questions I did—did he think he could sleep his way to a better grade?—and then the one I've been fighting with ever since I left the gym.

"Did you report him to security?"

I shake my head. "I should have. But I was in there after hours when I shouldn't have been." Regardless, the smart thing would have been to go directly to security and tell them. "I'm sure there's even video footage of him entering and leaving the women's locker room." I hadn't thought about it at the time. I'd been so panicked, discombobulated by how cavalierly he lay there, as unaware of my presence as I was of his for a few seconds before I managed to hit the light.

"Did you feel threatened?" Sophia asks, her expression full of earnest concern.

I consider that. I was shocked, and I reasonably questioned what he was doing there and why, but he seemed as surprised to see me as I was him.

I've proven to myself already that I'm not always the best judge of character when it comes to men, though. It wasn't until I was out from under Gabriel's thumb that I could see exactly how bad things had been.

"I don't trust my instincts," I tell her. "But he seemed contrite—and genuinely horrified."

She nods. "Maybe you need to have a conversation with him?"

I run my fingers over my lips. "Maybe." But emailing him to request a meeting would be opening a whole different can of worms. And if I don't go to campus security, what kind of message am I sending? "Probably."

It would have been easy enough to tell security I'd lost track of time. It's true. I did. But I willingly snuck into the sauna after hours, and now this is what I'm contending with. And if I say something to security, Maverick can turn around and out our past relationship to my superiors. I feel like I'm trapped.

I shake my head. "I don't understand what he was thinking."

"He's a twenty-year-old student. He wasn't thinking," Sophia points out.

"Twenty-one," I correct, scrubbing my hands over my face. It was the first thing I checked after he showed up in my second-year class. I'd been relieved that he was a fourth-year student who happened to end up there. "I just need to get through the rest of the semester. Then he's out of my class, and I can close the door on that chapter of my life."

5

Sinking Ship

MAVERICK

I'm in full-on panic mode as I bust my ass out of the athletic facility and into the parking lot. I think I may have threatened to blackmail my professor, which is a total asshole move. But man, the idea of my entire future going up in flames because I was in the women's sauna after hours seems like a pretty shit way to go down.

I've always checked to make sure it's empty. Always. And this time it backfired on me spectacularly.

I pull into my driveway and pray like hell no one is in the living room so I can sneak upstairs and hide. Of course, that's not what happens. BJ is passed out in the recliner, which is common. Half the time we leave him where he is. Sometimes he's still there in the morning; sometimes he's gone. He often has balls-early skate practice, like me and Kody when we want to get in extra ice time.

Kody is sitting in the middle of the living room floor, surrounded by very organized pieces of paper with what look like math equations written all over them while a hockey game plays on the TV.

"Where's Lavender?" I ask.

He startles, and a few of the pieces of paper he's shuffling slide out of the pile and onto the floor beside him. "She's upstairs."

Kody would probably surgically attach himself to my sister if he could. The only time they aren't together is when we're at hockey practice or she has class. "Why are you down here?"

His cheeks flush. "Uh, because she has an assignment due in the morning and said she needs to concentrate, and I'm too much of a distraction and I'm not to come back up until she messages me." He thumbs over at BJ. "We were playing Xbox until he passed out half an hour ago, and I decided to organize my math notes. I figured you'd be at the pub tonight with some of the guys."

"Nah, not tonight. I got a warning from Treble that Carly was there, and I didn't want to risk running into her."

"You guys haven't been a thing for a while. What's the deal there?" He starts putting the math sheets back into his binder, one stack at a time, adding those divider things.

"I don't know how much of a thing we ever really were, but she's having trouble letting go."

"She was here a lot at the beginning of the semester. Didn't you take her on a date to a movie? Or am I remembering that wrong?" He scratches his forearm, then pulls his shirtsleeve down to cover his wrist.

I sigh. "The whole movie situation was supposed to be a group thing, but it ended up being the two of us. She keeps showing up wherever the team is, so my go-to tactic is avoidance." And has been since Clover took over the creative writing class. Being involved with someone feels wrong for whatever reason. "I'm not dating right now. Gotta stay focused." Kody knows about my end-of-summer hookup, mostly because I was late for practice the next day. But he doesn't know she's currently my professor.

"I thought you were low-key seeing someone after the Carly thing ended," he muses.

I did make an offhand comment about seeing someone who wasn't into the party scene back when him and Lavender first started dating. It was a bit tongue-in-cheek since I was stuck on the Clover situation and the fact that I was seeing her on a weekly basis. "That ran its course," I sort of lie.

"Oh, that makes sense." He nods. "You wanna hang out for a bit? I'm watching replays of our last game against Illinois State."

I should go upstairs and work on that creative writing assignment, but I haven't had a lot of opportunities to hang out with Kody since he started dating my sister, and I could use the distraction. Being alone with my thoughts isn't very alluring. "Yeah, sure. Want me to grab you a beer?"

"Yeah. Great. That'd be awesome."

I leave my gym bag and backpack at the bottom of the stairs and stop by the kitchen to grab a snack and two bottles of beer. But the second I return, Lavender comes barreling into the living room.

"Vaginaland is open for business!" She makes a *V* in front of her crotch and then stops mid-thrust when she realizes I'm standing there. "Oh hey, Mav. If you can pretend you didn't see or hear that, that would be great." Her face turns red in patches that also cover her neck.

"You're not worried about BJ?" I thumb over at him.

"He's asleep."

"That's what you think." BJ cracks a lid. His eyeball shifts from Lavender to Kody—who's frozen like a statue, eyes comically wide with horror—over to me. He reaches for the lever on the side of the chair and pulls the footrest down. "Way to make things awkward, Lav."

"I thought Kody was alone—or mostly alone! And what's awkward is when Maverick's past flavors of the month stop by looking for him, and I have to be the one to give them the bad news that he's having a herpes flare up!" She pinwheels her arms like a drunk octopus.

"Wait! What? You don't seriously tell people I have herpes, do you?" While I can deal with rumors, that sure isn't one I want to contend with.

Lavender rolls her eyes. "Of course not. I'm not that much of an asshole. But I did tell a girl at one of your parties that you broke your dick when you tripped over some dirty underwear on the way to the bathroom. I also told her you probably wouldn't be back in the saddle until next semester. I was doing you a favor, because she seemed a little obsessed with you. Like, she knew all your stats and could list every single girl you dated last year. She did stop by with a card and some chocolates, which I told her I would give to you, but I threw them out because it seemed a little too, 'Tag, You're It,' circa Melanie Martinez's *Cry Baby* album. You're welcome for saving you from that potential stalker nightmare."

"Did you get her name?"

"No. But I think she hangs out with Bethany." Lavender's eyes slide Kody's way for a second.

None of us are surprised when he purses his lips and grumbles, "Can we treat her like Voldemort and never say her name again?"

"You, of all people, should know you can't run away from your past," Lavender says. "Anyway, like I said, I'm done with my assignment, so you're allowed back in my room whenever you're done bromancing." She makes a circle motion to the room and spins around, heading back the direction she came from.

"Now that the entertainment is over, I gotta head home." BJ pushes out of the chair, pats Kody on the head, and gives my shoulder a squeeze. "See you guys when I run out of food or I get bored, whichever happens first."

Kody's phone pings. He glances down at the screen and gives me a sheepish look. "Sorry about that." He motions to the space where Lavender was standing.

"Eh, it's Lavender. She inherited the same faulty filter as I did." I let him off the hook. "Why don't we take a raincheck on the beers. I need to work on an assignment anyway."

"Maybe we can go for a late lunch after practice tomorrow or something?" He gathers his things and unfolds his legs.

"That works."

"Cool. See you in the morning." He rushes up the stairs, leaving me alone.

I put the beers back in the fridge and head for my room, glad my sister's is on the third floor, in the attic, and that it's not directly over mine.

Now that I'm home and not in quite the same panicked state, I realize all over again how bad my situation with Professor Sweet could be. She has every right to report me.

My dad will 100 percent shit a brick if I get expelled. There will most certainly be lectures. That will suck, but it won't be nearly as bad as his disappointment—not to mention the highly negative impact it could have on my career if word gets out that I was in the women's locker room of all places.

I know better than to take risks like that. Even after hours.

For a split second, I entertain what that would look like: an expulsion, or worse, the NHL future I've been preparing my whole life for slipping through my fingers.

What would it be like to have a normal life? To not have a dad who's a hockey legend. To not follow in his footsteps. To not have the pressure. To be like my older brother, Robbie, who's a brainiac. Or like my younger brother, River, whose mission in life seems to be stewing in a pit of rage and anger he made for himself and hiding who he really is because he thinks . . . I don't know what he thinks, but he seems pretty determined to be miserable.

And more than my brothers, I wonder what it would be like to be Lavender. Traumatized, yes. Forever changed by what happened to her as a kid, definitely. But strong, resilient, and the most forgiving, compassionate person I've ever met.

She'd be so disappointed in me right now if she knew what I'd done tonight. That I hadn't taken into consideration the impact my actions might have on someone else, especially being where I was.

I open the door to my room and want to turn right back around. It's a fucking mess. The bed is unmade because I had to rush this morning. Clothes are strewn all over the floor and draped on my chair. It smells ripe in here, like my sheets need to be changed and there's probably a pair of running shoes that need airing out.

My room seems to match my internal mental state: chaos and filth.

I spend a few minutes cleaning up and then jump into the shower. Despite the cluster of today, as soon as I step under the spray, my body responds by giving me an annoying, persistent hard-on. This is my preferred location for such activities, and my bedroom shower elicits a Pavlov-like response.

Normally, I wouldn't have a problem taking care of my situation. Most days I fantasize about Professor Sweet telling me she needs to see me after class to discuss extra credit. But tonight, that feels wrong. Instead, I turn the temperature to cold. That does the trick.

I cut the water and nab a towel, drying myself off roughly as I cross to my dresser. I find a pair of clean boxers and some sweatpants, an old T-shirt that used to belong to my dad, and a hoodie. Then I sit my ass down at my computer and try to come up with two thousand more words. I'd start over entirely, but I've already got more than half of it done.

It's closing in on two in the morning by the time I'm finished. I'm sure I'm going to get crap marks on the grammar, but at least I made the word count.

As exhausted as I am, I'm on edge, and my brain won't shut off. I get in bed and stare up at the ceiling, watching the shadows shift and move as cars pass by slowly, thumping bass. A few hollers come from down the street.

My eyes have adjusted to the dark, and I notice my closet door is closed. I stare at it for a while, debating whether I can handle it being left like that all night. It's a weird thing. I always keep it ajar. Doesn't matter if my room is neat or a sty like it is today, or if my closet is overflowing with dirty laundry, I always leave it open a crack. Otherwise it reminds me too much of the past. Of other mistakes I've made.

I roll out of bed and amble across to the closet, without tripping on anything this time. Logically, I know the only thing in there are my clothes, my laundry basket, and a few old high school photo albums, but I flick on the light and check to make sure. A flash of memory hits me.

Lavender's split lip.

River screaming bloody murder.

Kody's accusing glare.

Dad taking me to his office and yelling so loud he was a sonic boom.

Choking on the guilt.

I flick off the light and pull the door closed.

When I finally fall asleep, it's not peaceful. I dream I'm locked in a room that gets smaller and smaller, and the door to escape doesn't have a knob, so all I can do is bang on it until my bones break and pierce the skin. And still, no one saves me from myself.

6

I'm so Sorry

MAVERICK

I check Professor Sweet's office hours first thing in the morning. Luck seems to be on my side since she's scheduled to be there at nine. I'm crossing my fingers that she's the kind of professor who shows up early, because I need to deal with this situation.

My palms are sweaty as I make my way to her office on the twelfth floor of the English building. I'm beyond nervous. The nightmares were next-level shitty, and I couldn't eat breakfast, my stomach a churning mess. I feel like a dick for the way I behaved, and it didn't occur to me until after I'd gotten home how much I'd probably freaked her out.

I need to know what I'm facing.

I walk down the hall, glancing at the nameplates on the doors until I reach the one that reads PROFESSOR CLOVER SWEET.

55

It's ironic that her name happens to be some kind of nature, flowery thing. She could be a character in a Disney movie.

If I believed in signs, I might think it was one.

I can smell her before I see her, which sounds creepy, and maybe it is. But her perfume is distinctive. It's not floral, as her name would suggest. It's like . . . cinnamon and something sweet, maybe with a citrusy bite.

The clicking of her fingers on the keyboard and the low tones of music filter into the hall. At first, it sounds like classical because of the violin, but an electronic beat follows—a marrying of two very different types of music. I stand there for a moment, listening. It's an emotional piece, a journey through a river with everything from raging rapids and deadly waterfalls to the serene warmth of a bubbling sulfur spring.

I pull my hood down and hunch my shoulders, hoping it will make me less imposing. The last thing I need is to scare the fuck out of her again.

I take a deep breath and knock on her door. Her office hours start in twenty minutes. Hopefully that's long enough to sort this out.

She doesn't pause her typing as she calls out, "It's open. Come on in."

I push on the door, allowing it to travel slowly toward the wall, and I make sure I'm standing off to the side so I'm not blocking the exit. There's nothing I can do about my size, not a thing I can do to make myself less physically intimidating, apart from how I position myself and my body language. I tuck my thumbs in my pockets and tilt my head down, so I have to look up at her, aiming for submissive as I take in her office. There's a desk, facing the wall so it's not a barricade between her and her students. A vase of daisies on the windowsill. A half-eaten Godiva chocolate bar next to her keyboard. A small jar of individually wrapped Lifesaver mint candies sits next to the single empty chair, along with a box of tissues and a coaster with BOOK NERD printed on it.

I aim for contrite when I finally speak. "Good morning, Professor Sweet. Can I talk to you about last night?"

Her eyes go wide, and she glances over my shoulder to the empty hallway as she rolls her chair backwards. The office door across the hall is closed. She's wearing a mint-green cardigan and a pair of black pants. Her shoes are flats. Her hair is pulled up into a tight bun, and she pushes her black-rimmed glasses up the bridge of her nose with her index finger. Her nails aren't painted. They're naked and carefully filed. The nail on her middle finger is shorter than the rest, like maybe it broke.

She looks different than she did in the summer, although a bikini shifts the focus. Still, it makes it tough to guess her age.

Her full lips thin as she rolls her shoulders back, sitting up straighter in her chair as she narrows her eyes at me.

"I should report you to the athletics department. Or your coach," she whispers angrily.

I nod my agreement. "You absolutely have every right to do either or both of those things. And if you choose to, I will deal with whatever the consequences are."

Her brow furrows, as if she's confused by my response. I'm sure she expected me to come here and threaten to blackmail her again because we slept together.

"You could be expelled," she adds.

"I know." It's one of the reasons I'm here, but not *the* reason, I realize. I nod to the chair beside her desk. "May I sit?"

I can practically feel her unease like another body in the room, and I wish I could do something to assuage that.

Eventually, she motions to the chair. Then she crosses her legs and her arms. Closed posture. Defensive. She also rolls her chair slightly toward the door. Maybe to get a better view of the hall, maybe so she has an easy escape route.

I set my backpack at my feet and clasp my hands together, propping my elbows on my knees.

I keep my eyes down and notice that her socks have little bunnies on them.

"I'm not here to plead my case with you, if that's what you're thinking," I say quietly. Before I walked in, I was, but now . . . not so much.

"Then what's the purpose of you coming here? I'm aware of who your father is, and how much money has been donated to the school over the past four years. Are you here to tell me everyone is going to look the other way on this?"

"I sure as fuck hope they wouldn't."

Although I'm aware there's a possibility that this could get swept under the rug, should she decide to bring it forward, the thought makes my blood boil. And honestly, there must be video footage of me going in there that some lazy security guard is too busy jerking it to internet porn to be bothered keeping up with. It pisses me off to think that if she did stand up for herself in this instance, she might very well be brushed off, and I could get no more than a slap on the wrist.

I look up at her a moment. "I'm actually here to make sure you're okay."

If she crosses her arms any tighter, she might crack like a walnut. "Make sure I'm okay? Why?"

I glance into the hallway as a pair of students walk by. I wait until their voices fade before I continue. "You were in a place where you should have felt comfortable, and I had no right to be there. At all. If I'd known you were in the locker room, I wouldn't have stepped foot inside, Professor."

"I still don't understand how you got in there in the first place," she whispers and fingers her collar, tugging it nervously.

"I found the key a while back, and since it was after hours, I thought it wouldn't be an issue," I admit, unable to stop myself from coming all the way clean. "And the sauna in the guys' locker room had a funk. Women are better at keeping things clean, and I'm less likely to end up with plantar warts or a rash I can't identify."

She scoffs and looks away. "That's a stereotype."

"It smells a lot better in there." I run my hands down my thighs. "Anyway, that's not really the point. When I got home, I realized I might have made you feel vulnerable. And I shouldn't have said I could report you for . . . what happened in the summer. That wasn't right, especially under the circumstances. So if you want to report me, I completely understand, and I will corroborate your story." I wait for the sinking feeling, the panic now that I've laid it all out for her, but it doesn't come. I know I'm doing the right thing, regardless of the cost.

"Corroborate my story?" She fingers the buttons on her cardigan.

"If you want to tell them I was in the women's sauna and shouldn't have been, that you were alone and I made you feel unsafe, I won't deny that it happened, and I will take full responsibility for my actions. Even if it means facing an expulsion." Or losing my potential career.

She clasps and unclasps her hands. "You're telling me you're willing to risk an expulsion because you might have made me feel unsafe?" Skepticism laces her words.

I glance toward the door and blow out a breath. I don't want her second-guessing my reasons for doing this. "I can imagine that having me in your class this semester hasn't been easy for you." I tap on the arm of the chair. The semester ends in five weeks. She's a visiting professor. Whatever I tell her isn't going to matter in the grand scheme of things.

So I give her more truth than I probably should.

"My younger sister goes to school here, and she lives with me. If some guy surprised her like I did you, I'd kick his ass.

Maybe even worse. No." I shake my head. "I'd definitely do worse than an ass kicking. But since I can't kick my own ass, I wanted to at least tell you I'm sorry. And that it won't happen again." I set the key on the edge of her desk and add my printed-out, revised creative writing assignment that meets the minimum word count.

"The key works in the athletic facility and nowhere else. Thank you for hearing me out, Professor. I'll see you in class on Tuesday. Unless I'm expelled. But if I'm not, I promise I'll keep my mouth shut, and I won't approach you again."

I grab my bag and leave her office before she can say anything else.

7

Down the Rabbit Hole

CLOVER

I sit there for a minute after Maverick leaves my office, trying to understand what his motive could be. It almost seems like he *wants* me to report him. That doesn't make a lot of sense—not from what I understand about his potential career trajectory. While I've tried my hardest not to pay attention to him—other than being annoyed when he shows up for class late or checks his phone messages while I'm teaching—I am aware, based on what I've read in the school paper, that he shows real promise, along with a few of the other students on the school hockey team.

I'm also aware that for every student who thinks they're going to get called up to a professional sports team, there are another dozen whose dreams are going to be crushed. I don't know enough about the sport to be able to say which category Maverick fits into. Not that it should matter.

I pick up the key and flip it between my fingers. It could be any key. The only way I'll know if he's lying or not is if I take it to the athletic facility and see if it works. And there's no way to know whether he's made copies.

The question remains: Where did he find it, and how long has he had it? How many offices or changing rooms has he snuck into? Would it give him access to personal files? His own? His teammates'? As soon as I think it, I brush the thought aside. He seemed so contrite.

I remind myself that my feelings about this could be skewed. Particularly since I'm still dealing with the man I married and his attempts to pull me back into a relationship I don't want to be in. It makes sense that I don't have a lot of faith in the authenticity of the opposite sex.

I put the key in my purse, so it's out of sight. I'll take it with me the next time I go to the athletic facility and find out how honest Maverick was.

My phone buzzes on my desk, startling me. *MOM* flashes across the screen. Normally, I would message back right away, but this morning is throwing me for a loop, so I leave it for now and turn my attention to the revised paper sitting on my desk. I leaf through it. The font hasn't been enlarged to make it seem as though it fits the word count, and the spacing doesn't look off, but it seems awfully convenient that he's handed in a paper copy.

I log into my computer to check for an emailed version. I notice a message from Maverick received about ten minutes before he showed up at my office door. I read through the first few pages of the paper, aware that I need to pass it over to my TA for a revised grade, but it doesn't hurt to have a look.

Students were supposed to write the story of a childhood memory from the point of view of someone other than themselves. As I read through the first few pages, my stomach rolls and sinks, because the story is about a little girl who goes missing at a carnival.

I perform a search with *Waters + carnival + abduction*, and a slew of headlines appear.

Most of the articles chronicle the brief abduction of a little girl at a local carnival more than a decade ago. They don't name her, but they do name the family. The case seems to have been high profile mostly because the girl's father is hockey legend Alex Waters.

Maverick's father.

And the pieces start to fall in place.

Based on the dates, Maverick would have been seven or eight years old when his sister was abducted. According to the articles, she was only missing for an hour, and the man who took her suffered from mental health issues. He'd lost his own daughter in a tragic accident he caused not long before the abduction, and he'd suffered a psychotic break.

Understandably, there's little information detailing what happened to the girl while she was missing. And although they found her relatively quickly, the trauma was clearly real. Based on the story Maverick decided to write for this assignment, it's something that still affects him deeply.

I have to pause my research when a few students stop in to discuss assignments. But when my office hours end, I close my door and fall down a rabbit hole of information related to the abduction of Lavender Waters.

It forces me to see Maverick in a different light. And makes me believe he was sincere when he came in here this morning and said he would corroborate my story if I chose to report him.

It isn't until the alarm goes off on my phone that I realize I've been scouring articles for hours, and I have a class in less than twenty minutes. I turn off my computer, gather my things, and rush off to teach my class.

I DON'T HAVE my gym clothes with me, and I feel extraordinarily conspicuous as I make a stop at the athletic facility before I head home for the night. It's a few minutes out of the way, but I need to know whether this key does what Maverick said it would.

When I reach the women's locker room, I peek inside. There are a couple of women at the mirrors, but no one is paying attention to the door. I slip the key in the lock and turn. The deadbolt appears. I quickly reverse the motion, sliding the key free.

My hands are shaking, and a fine sheen of sweat covers the back of my neck as I move down the hall toward a darkened corridor—the one that leads to the physical therapy offices, which are currently closed. The door to get into the hallway is locked, giving me an opportunity to test the key a second time. And once again, it turns in the lock.

"He was telling the truth." I close my fingers around the warm metal, feeling the bite of the teeth against my palm.

"Ma'am? Can I help you?"

I startle and spin around. "Oh!"

A man wearing a blue Facilities Services shirt, pushing a rolling bucket and mop, stands about ten feet away. He takes a cautious step back. "I didn't mean to startle you. The PT clinic closes at seven on Wednesdays."

"Oh, it's fine." I wave a hand in the air and clutch my purse. "I wasn't paying attention to where I was going and got turned around. I, uh, a student turned in a key today. It might be an important one. Maybe I could pass it over to you?"

His eyes flare. "Oh yeah, you can give it to me. I'll pass it to my boss. Did the student say where they found it?"

I shake my head. "No, he seemed like he didn't know what to do with it." I drop it in his hands.

"Right. Okay. And you're a professor here?" He flips the key over in his palm, and his eyebrows lift.

"I am. Visiting. Anyway, thank you. We wouldn't want it in the wrong hands."

"You're right about that." He slips the key into his pocket.

"Have a good night." I start down the hallway, but he stops me.

"Uh, ma'am, you wouldn't happen to know which student passed over the key?"

I force a polite smile and shake my head. "Some of my lectures have a few hundred students in them. He might play for one of the school teams, though?"

"Okay. Thanks. Have a nice evening."

I rush down the hallway toward the main entrance, not entirely comfortable with my lie. I push through the front door and step out into the cool evening air. It's dark already, the sidewalks lit by overhead lamps.

As I drive home, I pull up my mom's contact. I should have called her earlier. She has a tendency to worry, in part because of the situation with Gabriel. At first, she and my dad couldn't understand why I didn't want him to know where I was. Because they'd moved down to Florida, they only met him a handful of times. So they hadn't seen the other, less-polished side of him. But eventually, they understood my perspective, and for that, I could not be more grateful.

"Hi, Mom. Sorry I didn't get back to you sooner. It was a busy day," I say when she answers the phone.

"It's okay. I just wanted to check in and see how things are going."

Mom tells me about the various friends they have dinner plans with this week before she asks the question that comes up at some point in every conversation lately. "Have you made any progress with Gabriel?"

I grip the steering wheel tighter. The mere mention of him makes my throat feel tight. "No, Mom. No progress. He has the papers; he just needs to sign them now."

She makes a sound. "I'm sorry this isn't easier for you, honey."

"Thanks."

I shift the subject away from Gabriel, and we chat for a few more minutes before I let her go with a promise to call again later in the week.

I pass a row of student houses in one of the nicer neighborhoods. I live about three blocks over from here, far enough away that I don't have to put up with the noise or the parties, but close enough to the pub district that sometimes drunk and disorderly college students stumble down my street in the wee hours of the morning, hooting and hollering.

I pull into the driveway beside Sophia's Beetle. We have dinner together most nights of the week, except Tuesdays, when I have my night class, and Thursdays, when she counsels students until nine. I'm half an hour later than usual, but I sent her a message saying I was running behind, so I'm unsurprised to find her in my apartment, dinner already started, when I walk through the door.

I drop my purse on the side table and round the corner, stepping into the kitchen. She's standing in front of a pot on the stove.

"Everyone should have a best friend like you," I tell her. I cross to where she's standing and peek over her shoulder. "What smells so good?"

"I'm trying a new recipe for mushroom risotto," she tells me. "But it might be my first and last time. The stirring component to this is a lot more work than I anticipated."

"Want me to take over?"

"Please. I'm halfway to carpal tunnel."

We switch spots.

"Whatever you do, don't stop stirring." She goes to the fridge and pulls out a bottle of wine, uncorking it on her way to the cabinets.

"Wine on a Wednesday?" I arch a brow.

"I needed it for the risotto and figured we might as well have a glass while we're cooking—or more than one." She tops off her glass and pours a fresh one for me, dropping in two ice cubes because I like my wine a little watered down, at least the white stuff. She passes me the glass. "You got a gift basket today."

"A gift basket? From who? For what?"

She points to the top of the garbage can, where a gift basket sits awaiting its fate. "You have one guess."

I can tell by looking who it's from. "How the hell did he get my address?"

"I guess you'll have to call him if you want to find out. I was going to toss the whole thing, but some of your favorite treats are in there, so I figured I'd let you make the decision."

I take a hefty gulp of my wine and set it on the counter—otherwise I'm going to chug the entire thing. Today has been a day. "I hate being wasteful."

"Is there anyone at work who might appreciate it? Maybe you could leave it in the lounge and people can pick at it?" Sophia suggests.

"Maybe. Are there chocolate-peanut-butter pretzels in there?" I ask.

"And movie theater popcorn." Sophia makes a sympathetic face and pats me on the shoulder. "Don't feel bad about wanting to keep it."

"I hate it when he plies me like this. He's trying to butter me up."

"Literally with the popcorn," Sophia jokes.

"I'm not going to let my guard down. Then he'll come in and try to plead his case. Thank God he lives far enough away and can't show up on a whim." I continue stirring the risotto with increased vigor.

"Let's hope it stays that way," Sophia says.

"There's no reason for him to move to Illinois. He travels too much for work." But as I say it, I wonder how true that is. Gabriel seems to be ramping up his attempts to get back into my good graces, rather than acquiescing and signing the divorce papers. He's proven that he makes important life decisions on a whim—like the way he proposed and how quickly we got married.

He also took a consulting job after that, and secured me a position at the same company without asking. At first, the surprises seemed impulsive, and mostly well-intentioned, but over time it got to be . . . too much. After a while, I started to see that he wasn't doing it to be nice. He was doing it so he could keep tabs on me.

Sophia makes a noise, neither in agreement nor disagreement. "Let's worry about the basket after dinner. How was the rest of your day?"

"Odd, to say the least. Maverick came to my office first thing this morning," I tell her.

She pours a healthy amount of white wine into the pot of

creamy rice and mushrooms. "No! What happened? Did you report him?"

I shake my head, and Sophia gives me a disapproving look.

I hold up a hand, the one that isn't busy stirring in the wine. "Hear me out before you judge my lack of action." I detail how he came in looking all contrite, that he was apologetic and adamant about wanting to make sure I felt safe. "It almost felt like he *wanted* me to report him."

"Then maybe you should. Maybe it's a cry for help."

"I considered that, until he passed over the key and his revised paper."

"What if it's a copy? And why would his paper change your mind?"

"Because he wrote it based on a personal experience. His younger sister was abducted when she was six, and he was there when she went missing." I explain what happened, informed by both the articles I read earlier today and his paper.

"Oh, God. I can't even imagine." She presses her fingers to her lips and shakes her head. "And she's okay? His sister?"

"She's a student here at the school. And she lives with Maverick. When can I stop stirring this?" My hand is starting to cramp.

"Let me test it." She grabs a spoon and dips it into the pot, blowing on it for a few seconds before she tastes it. "Probably five more minutes. I'll take over again. You grab the wine."

I do as she asks and pour until she tells me to stop. I cork the bottle and lean against the counter. "How would I even know if the key was a copy?"

"You can take it to a locksmith. They'll likely be able to tell you if it's an original."

"Really?"

"Yeah, but it doesn't mean he hasn't made copies and doesn't have a whole stack of them at home."

"I already turned it over, so I can't get the answer to that."

"Who'd you turn it over to?"

"Someone who worked in the athletic facility."

"Okay." She nods pensively. "Well, from what you've told me about Maverick, making copies doesn't seem to fit his profile."

I swirl my wine, and the ice cubes clink against the glass. "How do you mean?"

Sophia rubs the space between her eyes. "I'm looking at this through a psychology lens, so bear with me. After you first slept with him, before he was your student, you talked about how sexy you found it that he consistently asked for permission before you engaged in—"

"Do not say intercourse."

"Do you like *relations* better?" She gives me a cheeky grin.

I make a gagging noise. "*Relations* sounds like what people in retirement homes do."

"Apparently people in retirement homes get it on all the time. They have very high STI rates."

"Why are we talking about grandparents and STIs?"

"We're not. We're talking about the sex you had with Maverick."

"Can we move this along?" I make a go-on motion. "I've been actively trying not to think about what the sex was like, and I was doing great until I saw him naked again."

"I'll get there. In a minute. There's a purpose to my bringing this up. You used words like *patient*, *attentive*, and I believe *fucking magical* was also thrown in there. You called him a unicorn."

"I didn't know he was going to be my student then."

"That's not the point. The point is that during the short span of time when you fucked like bunnies, he was all those things. And now you're telling me he came to see you, apologized, gave you the key to the athletic facility, and expressed concern for your well-being and feelings of safety."

"But last night he threatened to blackmail me for sleeping with him."

"After you told him he could be expelled?"

I cross my arms. "Yes."

"Okay. So he reacted to your reaction. And then apologized for saying that at all. Now we have another layer to add. A man you have been intimate with handed in a paper *before* the sauna incident that indicates he's experienced a very serious trauma. His whole family has."

"Because of what happened to his sister."

"Yes, exactly." Sophia turns off the burner and moves the risotto to a trivet on the counter.

"Can you help me make all the connections here?"

"Today, when he came to see you in your office, his primary concern should have been an expulsion and the possibility of losing his entire future as a result, but it wasn't. He was concerned about how he made you feel, about your safety."

"He said there should be consequences for his actions."

Sophia nods. "Exactly. It's not what you would expect from someone in his position. His father is a hockey legend, and he seems to be on the same path."

I grab my phone from my purse, ignore the messages from Gabriel that have appeared over the past couple of hours, and search *NHL + Waters + career*. An image of a man who looks very much like an older Maverick pops up on my screen, and his stats and earnings while he was a player are also public. "It says at one point his father was the highest-paid player in the league." It also says that Maverick was picked up by Nashville as a first-round pick when he was eighteen.

Sophia arches a brow. "Those are quite the shoes to fill and quite the interesting family profile."

I drop my phone on the counter, remove my glasses, and scrub a hand over my face. "Do you think I did the right thing then by not reporting him?"

Sophia sighs. "Yesterday I was all for reporting him, but with this new information . . . It's more complicated than a jock being entitled. These are unusual circumstances, and your judgment is clouded by your history with him. You've done the right thing by turning in the key. It might be a good idea to let things lie now and do your best to avoid him for the rest of the semester."

8

Knife's Edge

MAVERICK

I've never suffered from anxiety. Not really. At least not the way my sister does, or Kody.

When Lavender was little, even before she disappeared for what was the longest single hour of my entire life, she was always quiet when we were out in public places, a silent observer—and especially with people she didn't know well. But inside the walls where we lived, she was different. Herself. Full of life and giggles and smiles.

Kody's anxiety is different and layered with his obsessive tendencies. He still pukes before almost every single game, like he did when we were kids. Our freshman year, the older players made fun of him for it—until they saw him play. He has the grace of a figure skater and the speed of someone half his size. And he constantly worries about everything. It can't be easy to deal with the shit that goes on in his genius head all the time.

Between Lavender and Kody, I'm pretty used to dealing with *other* people's anxiety. But until this week, I'd never experienced it myself to such an extreme level, and it gives me a very different perspective on what those two battle. My every waking minute is consumed by thoughts of Professor Sweet. I keep waiting for a call from the dean, or my coach, or the head of my department, or the athletic facility manager, asking me where I got a key to the building and why I never turned it in, and what was I doing in the women's freaking sauna.

So, on Sunday night, when the athletic facility manager stops by the locker room to talk to us right before the game, I nearly shit my pants. But he doesn't single me out. Instead, he tells us a key was turned in this week, and that there'd better not be any more of them floating around out there, or some of us will be looking at game suspensions.

Unfortunately, my relief over not being expelled is over-shadowed by the questions I don't have answers to—like, did Professor Sweet intentionally leave my name out, or are they just going to let me get away with this?

As a result, my head is a mess during the game, and I'm playing like garbage. It's the beginning of the third period, we're down one, and Kody and I are sitting on the bench, waiting to be called back into the game.

"You all right tonight, man?" He taps rhythmically on his thigh.

"Yeah. I'm good." I nod once, and my knee bounces a couple of times.

"You sure? You've been . . . off all week." He raises his hand, as if he's going to rub his bottom lip, but his cage is in the way, so it drops back into his lap.

"I failed an assignment in one of my classes." That's only a small part of the reason, but I'm not going to tell him the truth.

"I thought you'd pulled your grades up. Can you do something for extra credit? Or redo the assignment?"

The idea of failing something gives Kody hives.

"I dunno, but I resubmitted it, so I'm hoping I get a passing grade. I don't want my dad to have another reason to sit me down and lecture me, you know? But my professor isn't my biggest fan, so who knows how that's going to go."

"Why does he hate you?"

"He's a she. And because I'm me."

Kody frowns and opens his mouth to ask a question, but we're called back to the ice, ending our conversation. A few minutes later, Kody scores a goal, and I manage the assist, which is better than me continuing to shit the bed for the rest of the game. My dad often watches the replays, so I'm glad there's something semi-positive for him to focus on. I hate it when he struggles to find something good to say about the way I played.

"Nice goal, Bowman." Cooper, one of the rookie forwards, pats Kody on the shoulder as he passes him on the way to the shower.

"Thanks, man," Kody mumbles as he grabs his towel from his locker.

"We're all going to Eddie's for something to eat. You guys wanna join us?" Treble, a junior, asks.

Kody looks to me before answering.

I shrug. "Better than reheating that lasagna from two nights ago."

"I think BJ ate that for breakfast anyway," Kody says.

I roll my eyes. "Don't you guys have food at your place?"

"Yeah. But we don't have you or Lavender at our place. And she can make a mean lasagna." He doesn't even have the decency to sound apologetic about it.

I look to Treble. "We're in."

Half an hour later, ten of us are sitting around a table at Eddie's, an off-campus restaurant and bar, rehashing the game. Eddie's is not far from where Kody and I live. The food is better here, and the chances that I'll run into one of the girls I've formerly dated is lower.

Normally I'm a social guy, but I'm exhausted from all the freaking worrying, and my head is still all over the place, so I find myself zoning out, watching the hockey game on the TVs above the bar and plowing through my plate of wings while everyone else picks apart tonight's game and speculates on how our next game is going to go.

When the game on TV goes to commercial break, I hit the bathroom and stop our server to tell her we're celebrating a birthday. I ask her to bring out one of those brownie sundae things and put it on my tab. I need a reason to smile.

On my way back to the table, a flash of pale green catches my attention. I glance over at a woman wearing a long cardigan, sitting in a booth, with another woman seated across from her.

Professor Sweet.

She doesn't notice me as I pass her table, but when I return to mine, I realize I have a perfect view of her from my seat.

Her hair is down, falling in loose waves around her shoulders, like it was when I met her in Pearl Lake. She looks younger with her hair down, and if she traded the cardigan for a hoodie, she'd probably look like a student.

"Should we get the bill?" Kody asks when I take the seat next to him.

"In a minute." I drag my attention away from my professor.

At that moment, a gaggle of servers comes down the aisle, heading for our table.

"Ah, fuck." Kody tries to slouch down in his seat.

"Like I was going to pass up an opportunity like this." I put my arm around his shoulder—in part to keep him from bolting —and whistle loudly, pointing at him. "This guy right here. He's the birthday boy!" I shout. Kody's birthday is in April, but they don't know that.

The servers break into an off-key rendition of "Happy Birthday," and I join in. But that's not the best part. It's the sparkler in the middle of the sundae that looks like a mini firecracker, shooting sparks three feet into the air.

"I'm gonna get you back for this. I hope you know that," Kody gripes.

"You have to get used to the attention, my man. You're going to be breaking NHL records in a matter of months." I give his shoulder a squeeze and drop my arm as the sparkler sputters and dies out.

He gives me a sidelong glare, but a hint of a smile pulls up the corner of his mouth. Even though Kody is one of the best players out there, he still needs the praise. Sometimes I think he needs it more than most.

"You're gonna be right there with me," he replies, grabbing one of the spoons left by the servers. "It would be so awesome if one of us gets traded when we're called up and we play for the same team."

"It would," I agree. But I'm aware that the chances of that are slim, and it's more likely that I'll be playing against him next year, not with him.

I glance over at Professor Sweet's table, and for a moment, our gazes lock. She averts her eyes quickly, untucking her hair from behind her ear so it falls forward as she leans in. The woman across the table leans in too.

My stomach has been off since the whole sauna thing, but I still dig into the sundae. When Kody and I have eaten as much as we can, we pass it down the table.

I use the fact that my hands are sticky with chocolate sauce as an excuse to go back to the bathroom. It also means I pass Professor Sweet's table again.

Like me, she ordered the wings, which I can appreciate. Wings are messy, and it's hard to eat them with manners. As I'm passing, she sucks the barbecue sauce off her thumb and tosses the bone in the discard bowl. I should *not* find that sexy, but I do. Her gaze shifts as I come into her line of sight, and her cheeks turn pink.

I nod, but don't acknowledge her otherwise. On my way back from the bathroom, I spot the server that's taking care of her table and pay her bill on a whim before I settle Kody's and my tab. When I get back to our table, he's already got his jacket on, ready to go, so I leave, sparing Professor Sweet one more glance. She's frowning at the server who motions to our table, but I'm not there anymore. I don't know if I just nailed my coffin shut or what.

It's nearly eleven by the time we get home. Kody disappears upstairs to Lavender's room.

I mentally berate myself for paying my professor's dinner tab, like I'm trying to buy my way out of my previous fuckup, as I sit down at my desk and pull up my school email. I've been obsessive about checking it, hoping for a revised grade on my paper.

I scroll past a couple from my coach about training and practices, and my mouth goes dry when I see one from Professor C. Sweet. Her TA is cc'd, and it was sent four hours ago. Before dinner at Eddie's.

Dear Maverick,

Based on the resubmission of your assignment, your grade has been updated. There is a twenty percent penalty for late work, as outlined in the class syllabus. Please ensure that you include all

components prior to the deadline on future assignments to avoid such penalties. Your revised grade is attached.
Please feel free to email me with any concerns or questions.

Best,
Professor Sweet

I check the comments. I managed to get a seventy-two, even with the penalty and my crappy grammar. It looks like it was marked by the TA again, based on the comments in the margins. I read through the email twice more, searching for a hidden meaning or some kind of . . . sign, maybe? Does this mean she's not going to report me to anyone other than the athletics facility manager? That she believed me when I told her I was sorry? I don't even know if she named me or not.

I debate sending her a reply to tell her I've just seen this now, but I'm not sure if that's going to make the situation worse or better. So I leave it.

TWO NIGHTS LATER, I arrive to class early. Today we're talking about story structure, which is something I admittedly know very little about. My older brother, Robbie, always had a book in his hand, where I generally had a hockey stick.

At the end of class, I take my time packing up my stuff, and as expected, Sandy-Suzy asks if I'm going to the bar.

When I say no, her right foot rotates back and forth, and she does that ponytail twist thing, exactly like my cousins do. "Maybe you want to get coffee instead?"

The awkwardness of being asked out by one of my peers is magnified by the fact that it's happening in front of someone

I've slept with, and made that much worse since she's my professor—whose good side I'm trying to get back on.

"It's cool of you to offer, but I've got a lot of stuff going on, and I need to keep my focus on school and hockey this year."

"Right. Yeah. Of course. That makes sense." Her expression screams dejection, and I hate that I've made her feel like that. "I'll see you next week." She rushes for the door and ducks out of class.

I shoulder my bag and push out of my chair. Professor Sweet glances around the room, maybe realizing we're the last two people here.

She crosses her arms. "What exactly were you trying to accomplish at Eddie's?"

I take a step back. "It was me trying to apologize for my thoughtlessness, but I didn't see how it could have been taken differently until after I left the restaurant. And I didn't see the revised grade until I got home, which is when I realized how shady that probably looked to you."

She stares at me for a few long seconds, saying nothing. Her throat bobs with a swallow, and she tips her chin up, looking down her nose at me. "You're no longer failing the course, but there's still one more independent assignment and the exam, so I wouldn't suggest using your athletics involvement as an excuse to shirk your educational responsibilities again."

"I won't." I tuck a hand in my pocket. "I'm not trying to be a pain in your ass, but, uh . . . Are you planning to report me to anyone else?"

She mutters under her breath before her gaze shifts my way —not *to* me, exactly, but in my direction. "Can you just be grateful I didn't name you and leave it alone?"

Well, that answers that question. "I am grateful. I just . . . Thank you."

She lifts her ancient bag. "Do not make me regret this decision. I didn't do this because you're on a sports team, or because of your family or their influence. Or because of what happened before. I did it because I see potential that's being wasted, and I did not want to be the person to derail your future. I'm hopeful the lesson has been learned and the behavior won't be repeated. Ever again."

"It won't. I swear."

She nods. "I'll see you next week." She turns and stalks out of the classroom.

I should be glad this semester is almost over, but for some reason, the closer I get to the end, the less I want it to get here.

9

Turn a Corner

MAVERICK

When I get home, the living room is empty. I grab a beer and head upstairs, running into my younger brother, River, in the hall. He looks surprised to see me.

"Hey." His brows pull together in his customary furrow.

"'Sup? You heading out or grabbing something from the kitchen?"

"Uh . . ." His gaze darts around. "Going to a friend's house."

River has always been the emo-kid in our family. He carries the weight of the world on his shoulders—wants to fit in, but hates everyone except for Lavender, sometimes me and Robbie, and our parents. Also, he desperately wants our dad's approval, but chose football over hockey when he hit high school.

I nod once. I know better than to dig with River.

"You by yourself?" He looks over my shoulder, as if he's expecting someone to magically appear behind me.

"Yeah. I came from my night class. Is Lavender home?"

He pokes at his lip with his tongue. "Yeah. She and Kody are upstairs."

"Everything okay there?" River hasn't ever been Kody's biggest fan.

"With the two of them? Fine, I guess. She seems happy and like she's got him by the balls, which is how it's always been."

"That's accurate. But I meant is everything okay with you, in respect to them." I point to the ceiling. River had a pretty epic meltdown when he found out Lav and Kody were dating. Since then, things seem okay, but sometimes it's tough to tell with River.

He rubs his lip. "I think it took me a bit to come to terms with how different it is now, and that Lavender doesn't need to be protected. Back when we were kids and Kody was always coming to the rescue, I used to feel like I was failing as her twin, because *we* were supposed to have that bond." His eyes lift to the ceiling. "Those two have this connection that's impossible to compete with, and Kody has always been all-in when it comes to Lav. It's easier now, because it's obvious she's the one in the driver's seat, you know?" He runs a hand through his hair. "Gotta be kind of weird for you, though."

"Eh. We all knew it was coming. And you're right about Lavender being the one running this ship. I mean, I think she probably always was, but now she's aware." It's clear she's learned how to stand on her own.

River nods thoughtfully. "As much as she hated staying home last year, I think she needed it—not necessarily the being-at-home part, but the not having us all watching over her."

"It's like she aged a decade in a year," I muse.

He smiles, and it's full of pride. "She's pretty badass, isn't she?"

I laugh, thinking about the stunt she pulled in a white thong bikini, and the whole talking to Clarke to piss Kody off. And then her brief stint in the dorm before she moved back in with me and River. "Yeah, she really is."

River claps me on the shoulder, his expression turning serious. "I'm glad you pushed for her to live here. I don't know whether it would have happened if I'd been the one to suggest it."

I poke him in the side. "Shh . . . . That's not something I want her to know. At least until I'm out of here."

"Dude, I'm implicated as much as you are because I went along with it. I'm taking that to the grave—or at least until their wedding, because that would be a fun bomb to drop then."

We fist bump, and he heads down the stairs, off to wherever.

I spend the next hour trying to work on an assignment, but my brain is on overdrive, and I can't settle. It's approaching midnight, but there's no way I'll be able to sleep at this point. So I decide to go for a run.

I pull on my running shorts, then layer on a T-shirt and a hoodie, grab my baseball cap, and head downstairs. My running shoes are shoved into the corner. I shake out the deodorizer balls, jam my feet in, and tie the laces.

Once I'm outside, I tuck my earbuds in and blast my running playlist, taking a right on the first side street, then another right and a left until I'm out of the student housing section and into the regular subdivision—houses owned by people who manicure their lawns and care about curb appeal.

When I reach Hackett Street, I make another left. I don't usually take this route, but then I don't often go for a midnight jog either. Halfway down the block, I notice a gaggle of guys approaching someone putting out their recycling. It's a ballsy move to do that now. I always wait until morning, because putting it out at night is a crapshoot as to whether some drunk dickbag is going to kick it all over the road.

The guys down the street are so loud I can hear them over my earbuds. I click the pause button, so the music no longer drowns them out.

From the sound of it, these guys are drunk and looking for trouble. And the person putting out their recycling seems to be on the receiving end of that. When the three of them spread out, circling the person at the end of the driveway, I speed up.

"Come on, baby, show us what's under the robe! I wanna see those titties!"

I see red as I realize they've surrounded a woman in a bathrobe. My throat tightens as they close in on her, and I pump my arms and legs faster, eating up the distance between me and them.

"Hey, assholes!" I shout, hoping to draw their attention my way.

I push through their circle toward the woman, who is currently holding her garbage can like a shield, her recycling strewn across the sidewalk. She doesn't seem to know where to focus or what to do as she spins around, searching for a way out. One of the guys yanks the garbage can out of her grasp. She stumbles back and lands on her butt on the sidewalk, then tries to crab walk backwards, losing a slipper. A bunny slipper. Her long hair covers most of her face.

"What the fuck is wrong with you?" I step in front of the woman, turning myself into a human shield as I shove the guy holding the garbage can. He stumbles and loses his balance when he steps off the curb. The garbage can lands on top of him, and he smacks his head on the concrete.

The other two step forward, but one is distracted by his

friend on the ground. They look like they might be in their forties, and like maybe life hasn't been the easiest.

"You need to mind your own business, kid," the one closest to me snarls, revealing missing teeth. He smells of booze and cigarettes.

None of them is in particularly good shape, but they're definitely wasted, and that means they're not thinking clearly and may be looking for a fight. Which is fine. It would give this woman plenty of time to get inside, and they're making enough noise that hopefully a few of the neighbors will hear the ruckus, even if they can't see it through the large trees lining the sidewalk.

"So you and your loser friends can go back to harassing some poor woman trying to put out her goddamn garbage? I don't fucking think so." I glance down at the guy's jacket and notice a company logo on it. And I know the place. It's where I take my truck for servicing, and I've talked to the owner a few times because he knows my dad. "Don't think Hank would be very happy to find out his employees are sexually harassing random women." I flick him in the chest, and he comes at me, which I anticipate. I block his shot and go low, shoving my shoulder into his stomach, setting him off balance too.

The guy who ended up on the ground is struggling to his feet. The third one, who looks like he hasn't eaten a good meal in weeks, takes a couple of steps back, maybe realizing his odds aren't great.

He raises his hands in the air. "I don't want no trouble."

"Too fucking bad, 'cause you're in a heap of it."

The guy who tried to take a swing at me manages to get up on one knee, huffing and wheezing. He struggles to his feet and mumbles something about fucking me up, but his skinny friend grabs him by the shoulder. "Marty, man, we should get out of here."

I pull my phone out of my pocket and start snapping photos.

The big guy lunges at me and basically runs right into my fist. It's almost comical the way he stumbles back, again, and this time knocks over both of his friends. The three of them struggle to right themselves.

"I'm calling the cops," I warn.

They scramble to their feet and rush down the street, HANK'S AUTOMOTIVE REPAIR in big red letters across the guy named Marty's shoulders.

"What a bunch of fucking idiots." I turn back to the woman, who has managed to pick herself up off the sidewalk.

One side of her hair is tucked behind her ear now, so I can see half of her face.

Clover.

Professor Sweet.

I try to catch her eyes. "Hey, it's Maverick. Are you okay, Professor?"

She nods once, obviously shaken, clutching the front of her robe as her eyes dart around.

"I'm gonna help you clean this up, okay? Are you hurt at all?"

"I-I don't think so. Just . . . unnerved."

She exhales a tremulous breath but doesn't move as I right the garbage can and pick up the bag that fell out. Then I collect all the discarded papers and empty Quaker Oatmeal packets and put them back in the recycle bin.

She's still missing her bunny slipper. So I grab that and kneel in front of her, tapping the top of her foot. "Just lift an inch, okay?"

"Oh. Yes. Of course." Her voice is soft and breathy.

When she lifts her foot, her hand comes to rest on my

shoulder. The contact is jarring, sending a wave of goose bumps flashing over my skin.

She slides her bare foot into her bunny slipper, and as soon as it meets the ground, she removes her hand from my shoulder. I rise slowly, keeping my head down. "I'd like to walk you to your door and make sure you get inside safely. Is that okay, Professor?"

"Um . . . I think . . . I think that would be okay."

It sounds more like a question than a statement without any certainty or ease behind it. "You're safe with me. I promise. But if you would prefer I stay here, on the sidewalk, I can absolutely do that. I'm worried, though, because you're shaking, and I feel like maybe you're a little rattled and you need a minute to process."

She looks down and lifts one of her hands, the tremor visible even in the inky darkness. She turns her hand faceup, and I get a load of her palm, which is missing a layer of skin at the fleshy part near her thumb. "I must have gone down harder than I realized," she whispers.

"I think you did. Do you trust that you're safe with me?" I ask again.

"Those men could have hurt you."

"They could have, but it would have given you time to get inside. And I play hockey, remember? I'm used to taking a beating. You, not so much." I give her a gentle smile. "Do you live on your own? Do you have a roommate? Or a boyfriend?"

"Boyfriend?"

"Who lives with you? Is there someone else inside who will make sure you're okay and taken care of?" When we hooked up back in August, she didn't have a boyfriend. But that doesn't mean things haven't changed since.

"Oh. No. My best friend lives in the apartment above mine, though."

"Okay. That's good. Do you want to call her?"

"She sleeps with earplugs in. She only wakes up when her light alarm goes off."

"Light alarm?"

"It simulates the sunrise."

"Oh. Got it. I can help you with your hands and make sure you're okay before I go, then?" I don't want to leave her on her own, not when she's still in shock.

She looks up at me, eyes searching my face in a way that makes me feel exposed, but I remain still, giving her the time she needs to make a decision about what she's comfortable with.

"I trust that I'm safe with you," she says softly.

I nod once and exhale the breath I seemed to be holding. I place a hand on the small of her back, then realize the contact might be too intimate and shift to her elbow so I can guide her along the walkway and up the front steps. Her slippers slap the concrete. I look away as she keys in the code to the front door and opens it.

I leave my shoes on the mat inside the door and follow her into the kitchen, waiting until there's enough space before I skirt around her and pull out a chair. "Why don't you have a seat, and I can have a look at those hands."

"I'm fine. It's just a few scratches," she says, but she sinks into the chair. She's wearing a pale green bathrobe. The bottom is dirty now, because the ground was damp, likely from the rain we got this afternoon, and there are dark reddish-brown spots on the lapels, where she was holding it together.

"I still wouldn't mind taking a look, if that's okay with you." I crouch in front of her.

"It's really not that ba—" She flips her hands over so they're palm up, resting on her thighs. "Oh. I didn't realize . . ."

In the kitchen light, the damage looks a lot worse than it did outside in the murky night. As I suspected, she's skinned her palms pretty good—enough that it's going to scab over and be uncomfortable for a few days. "Do you have a first aid kit anywhere?"

"In the bathroom. It's down the hall."

"Okay. Great. Do you have any juice in the fridge? A little sugar would probably help with the shakes and all the adrenaline."

"I'm really okay."

"It's the fight-or-flight response, all those endorphins rushing through your body. It sends the body into survival mode."

"Right. Yes. That makes sense." Her tongue sweeps across her bottom lip. "There's lemonade in the fridge, second shelf on the right."

"And the glasses?"

"Cupboard to the left of the fridge."

"Okay." I push to a stand and wash my hands in the sink before I open the cupboard to reveal a mishmash of glasses with different cartoon characters on them, all of them faded with age. They've probably been around since long before Professor Sweet was born. I pick a mug that has a cute cartoon of a waffle on it. Then I read the cursive text underneath: *Don't be a twat-waffle.* I grab the handle and move over to the fridge. I find the lemonade exactly where she said it would be, shake it up, and pour her a glass.

"Do you have any straws?"

"Second drawer from the sink. Right side," she says softly.

I find a package of bendy straws in there and pull one free, dropping it into the mug. I turn around and find Clover staring at her scraped, bleeding palms. I grab a couple of paper towels, wetting them with cold water in the sink and squeezing so they're not dripping before I bring them and the juice over to her.

Her hands are still shaking, so I don't try to pass her the mug. Instead, I bend the straw and bring it to her lips. Her gray gaze lifts. And for the first time, I realize she's not wearing her glasses.

It reminds me of the first time I met her. Her eyes are slate gray, ringed in deep blue. Her hair falls around her shoulders in thick, dark waves, so long it nearly reaches her waist. I remember what it felt like to have my hands in it.

Stop thinking about that, asshole.

"I can hold the mug on my own." There's bite in her tone.

"If you want." I turn it so the handle is facing her, and she takes it gingerly. But I put a single finger under the bottom when her shaky grip causes the lemonade to slosh to the rim and nearly over the edge. She stabilizes the mug with her other hand before she takes a long sip. And then another and another until she finishes the entire cup.

She sets it on the table, and I pass her the damp paper towels. "You can put this on your palms, and I'll be right back with the first aid kit, if that's okay with you."

"I can get it." She holds the sides of her robe together with her fingertips, making a move to get up.

I stand and take a step back, giving her space. "I know you can, but I'm here to help, if you'll let me."

She drops back into the chair and closes her eyes, swallowing a couple of times. "I'm not weak."

"I know you're not. I can grab that first aid kit?"

She nods once. "Down the hall, second door on your right. In the second drawer of the vanity."

I walk down the hall, taking in the art hanging as I pass— stark, black-and-white photos of derelict houses, beautiful despite their dilapidated state. I pause for a moment, staring at a hauntingly gorgeous photo of a woman in an elaborate dress, kneeling amidst the chaos and debris. A shiver runs down my spine, and I remember I have a purpose and continue down the hall.

I pass the first door without glancing inside and keep going until I reach the next one. I flick on the light and step in. The room itself is white, but the shower curtain boasts a cityscape in cartoon figures and bright colors, making the room feel sunny and personal.

I'm hit with a more potent version of Clover's perfume, or body wash, or whatever she uses or wears to make her smell the way she does—like cloves and cinnamon and lemon and something that reminds me of comfort and holidays. The space is neat and tidy, towels folded and hanging on the bar, and the vanity free of clutter, apart from an electric toothbrush and one of those foaming hand soap pumps.

I glance in the mirror, my reflection staring back at me. *Help her, set her at ease, keep the flirting to a minimum, then get out.* I look past myself and realize I can see directly into her bedroom. It's different from the one at her cabin and nothing like college-kid bedrooms, with posters and laptops and clothes strewn over the floor. Everything is color-coordinated, sophisticated, and organized. I drop my gaze, aware I'm in her personal space and seeing parts of her life she hasn't invited me into.

But I can be helpful. I can smooth over some of the hard edges I've created with the whole sauna incident, with the awkwardness of this semester.

I open the second drawer down on the vanity and find several rolled washcloths in a variety of colors. On the right side is a small first aid kit. I turn on the tap, letting the cold water run, and wet a dark washcloth, wringing it out before I carry it and the kit back to the kitchen.

Clover is sitting exactly where I left her, dabbing at her palms with the now-pink-tinged paper towels.

"I brought a washcloth. They were in the same drawer as the first aid kit," I explain as I set them on the table and pull out another chair. "I made sure to pick one that wouldn't show the stains."

"That was very thoughtful."

I shrug. "When you play hockey, you get used to dealing with blood."

"Hockey is an aggressive sport," she murmurs.

"It can be, if you're playing with emotions and not your skill set."

"How do you mean?"

"It's a lot of testosterone and competitive personalities, especially when we're all trying to impress the coaches and scouts, which breeds aggression." I position myself at an angle, so I can reach her hands, but I'm not invading her space as much as when I was crouched in front of her. I flip the lid, remove a couple of iodine pads, and tear one open.

"Have you had many injuries?" she asks, her gaze going to my right eyebrow.

When we were together in the summer, we talked, but mostly it was light stuff. Easy conversation. We avoided personal details and focused on orgasms and the intense chemistry we seemed to share.

"Enough. I've gotten slashed with a stick and fractured my wrist once, and I got a puck to the head and needed stitches." I tap the eyebrow she's looking at. "We were playing street hockey, and I'd taken my helmet off for a minute. My best friend hit a slap shot. It ricocheted, and the result was this and a mild concussion."

"How many stitches?" She reaches out and smooths her finger across my eyebrow.

I clear my throat before I reply. "Seven or eight, I think."

"I've never had stitches." She drops her hand back to her lap. "Have you had many concussions?"

The concern in her tone is a little surprising.

I'm used to the lecture from my dad about the dangers of head injuries, so I know better than to get into it on the ice, for the most part. But sometimes it's hard not to drop the gloves and throw down when I know I could beat the hell out of the guy.

"Nah. Just the one. My dad had a bad accident once, though—took him out of the game for the rest of the season, and he missed the playoffs that year. When he woke up in the hospital, my mom was there, and he couldn't remember who she was. They were engaged at the time, and all he knew was that he loved her. He tells me that story every time I get into a fight on the ice about something stupid." I take one of her hands in mine.

Her fingers are long and slender, delicate, like they're made for playing the piano. I focus on the injuries, and not the fact that I know what they feel like on my body. The pad of her baby and ring finger are both missing skin. I give those my attention first, using the iodine to clean them of whatever dirt is left and then blowing on them, like my mom used to do with Lavender whenever she would fall and scrape her knees, which was often. Lavender isn't known for her gracefulness. Neither is my mother.

"You're going to need bandages on these two fingers for a day or two." I pluck the clear ones from the kit, which will be a lot less obvious.

"That's probably for the best," she agrees. "You have younger siblings, right?"

I offered up a lot of personal information in that short story for her class. I know she didn't grade it, but likely she read it . . .

If she did any research at all, she knows it wasn't embellished. "Yeah. My sister Lavender and my brother River are twins. They're a couple years younger than me."

"What about younger cousins?"

"My parents have a lot of close friends who are part of our hockey family, and some of them have younger kids. Why?"

"You're exceedingly adept at first aid. And gentle."

My gaze flicks up to hers and then back to her hand. "Lavender had pretty bad anxiety as a kid. Sometimes when she got really upset, her fingernails would dig so hard into her palms that she'd break the skin."

"Oh no. That's . . . not good," she says softly.

"It wasn't. And whenever it happened, my mom would get upset, and so would River, so Lav started coming to me. I would help her clean them up and use liquid bandage on them, which stings, but works well and was a lot more inconspicuous than wrapping her hands in gauze."

"That must have been hard for you, having to keep that from your parents."

I frown. Maybe she *hasn't* read my story. "When Lavender was little, she was taken. Not for long, but it scared the shit out of us—my family, I mean. So Lavender had enough shit to deal with. She didn't need my parents hovering more than they already did. And I got it. I mean, the shit that happened when we were kids was fucked up. But she'd get so upset with herself whenever she got anxious, and then things would sometimes spiral. I just . . . I owed her, so hiding it from our parents seemed like the only option. At the time, anyway." I make sure Clover's palm is free of dirt. They've stopped bleeding now, which is good.

"What do you mean things would spiral?"

"Nightmares, bed-wetting, that kind of thing. But I took care of those for her whenever I could too, so we could keep the peace." I pull out the liquid bandage and unscrew the cap. "This part is gonna sting."

I work from the outside to the middle, blowing on the liquid as I go, the smell making my nostrils sting. Clover remains still and stoic while I apply it, making sure the whole wound is covered. "This will last for a day or so, and then you don't have to worry about it bleeding on your clothes." I move on to the other hand.

She hums in acknowledgment. "You're so different right now than you are when you're in my class."

I lift my gaze for another second, then refocus on her injuries. I want to address the elephant in the room, but I don't want to invite more awkwardness. "I've probably been a dick in your class. It hasn't been intentional. Mostly I didn't know how to manage the dynamic, and sometimes I don't think before I do and say things. It's hereditary. I get it from my mom."

Her expression is wry. "Which part is hereditary?"

"The verbal diarrhea. Digging myself into a hole and not being able to get out without making an ass of myself. Out of all my siblings, I think that's what she passed on to me. My mom has it way worse, and she got it from my Gigi, who is the queen of inappropriate conversations. I love her, but her overshare filter is totally blown. And apparently so is mine tonight, since I'm telling you my entire life story."

I swipe the liquid bandage along Clover's other palm. This one isn't nearly as bad. Just a few small scrapes.

"I appreciate the distraction," she says, the tremor in her voice not quite so obvious anymore. "It makes it easier to focus on the present."

"I get that—the trying to stay in the now. It's how I try to live my life, because looking back can be a minefield." I need to shut up, but I feel compelled to keep talking, to keep her from focusing on the fears that might be lingering in the periphery of her thoughts, the things that rule mine.

"Because of what happened to your sister? What you wrote about in your story?" Clover asks.

I nod. "Sometimes I can go weeks without thinking about it, but sometimes it's a constant loop. And I wonder what it's like for *her*. Because she's the one who went through it, not me."

"That's why you stepped in today." It's not a question.

"Women are to be revered, not abused—verbally, emotionally, or otherwise." My jaw cracks. "Those guys were assholes, and we should call the police and file a report. Plus, I know the garage they work at. I'll call their boss in the morning and let him know what happened. He won't be happy about it."

"How is your hand? I think you punched one of them?"

I glance down at my knuckles. There's a small bruise forming, but otherwise it's fine. "It's nothing to worry about." I close the first aid kit. "Anyway, your hands are all taken care of. You fell pretty hard, though, so I wouldn't be surprised if you're a little sore all over tomorrow. A hot bath would probably be helpful. Also, sometimes the shock takes a while to wear off before the emotional weight of it hits, and it's nice to have a friend around when that happens."

Clover blows out a breath. "Thank you for being so . . . compassionate."

"I want to make sure you're okay," I tell her.

She nods a few times and gingerly laces her fingers together, as if she's unsure what she should do with them now.

"I teach a self-defense class at one of the gyms off campus," I add. "It's free for anyone who wants to take it, and I run it twice a week, usually on Monday evenings and Saturdays, unless I have a game, and then one of the other trainers subs in for me. Maybe you'd want to come check it out? You don't even have to participate, just watch or whatever. It teaches you the basics. It's a real mixed bag of people who come out, sometimes moms and their daughters, lots of students from the college, sometimes a group of friends. It's kind of empowering, you know?"

She cocks her head to the side, and this time when she looks at me, I feel it on a visceral level, like she's trying to see her way inside me. I avert my eyes and scan the kitchen. There's a magnetic notepad stuck to the fridge with a pen attached to it. I get up, feeling a little restless and like I probably need to get the hell out of here.

I tear a piece of paper free and scribble down the name of the gym, the address, the time the class starts, and my cell number because I can't remember the number of the gym off the top of my head. When I have my wallet with me, I also have cards for the gym with the class times on the back of it.

"Anyway." I turn back to her. "Here's the info, if you want to think about joining us. Or observing. You can even bring your friend." I point to the ceiling. "Some of the women who take the class have had negative experiences with men, kind of like what you've been through, and there's always a female trainer with me so we can make sure everyone is comfortable." *Yeah, it's time to get the fuck out.* I set the paper on the table.

She stands up, adjusting her robe, maybe finally registering that she's not dressed in real clothes. Like she does with her cardigans, she pulls the sides over each other. "Thank you. I'll think about it."

"I should go. Unless you need anything else."

"I think . . . I think I'm okay."

"You're sure?"

She nods, somewhat hesitantly, but when she doesn't offer anything else, I nod again. "Okay. I, uh, I put my cell number on that paper. I wanted to do that in August, but I didn't want to put pressure on you." I tap the edge of the chair. "Anyway, you don't ever have to use it, but if you're feeling unsafe, or you need to talk it out or whatever, all you have to do is send me a message and I'll run by. No questions asked."

She glances at the paper, her teeth sliding over her bottom lip. "Okay. Thank you. Hopefully I don't need to do that."

"Better safe than sorry, right?" I couldn't make this more awkward if I tried.

She gives me another tremulous smile and nods.

I head for the hallway, and she pads along behind me.

She stands a few feet away while I struggle to untie the stupid fucking knots in my running shoes. There's a little bench, one with hooks behind it like we have at my parents' house in Lake Geneva, so I sit on that to avoid taking up 90 percent of the confined space.

"Thank you again," she says. "For everything."

I finally manage to get the knot untied and jam my foot into my shoe, quickly tying the laces. "You gonna be okay?" I ask the floor.

"Yeah. I, um . . ." She clears her throat, and I look up to find her chewing on her bottom lip, struggling not to break down and losing the fight.

She lifts one hand, her fingertips touching her lips. "I didn't even scream. I didn't make a s—" She chokes on the word and shakes her head. "I should have done something."

"It's okay. You're okay now. You're safe. And those guys were drunk assholes. They were out of it and not thinking clearly." I feed her all the lines meant to help calm her down, even though my head has already gone through scenarios I don't want to entertain. Memories I try to keep buried float to the surface . . .

Lavender's ripped dress.

The deep cuts on her palms that left scars.

Her haunted eyes.

"I don't know what would have happened if you hadn't run by." Her voice is a wavery whisper.

I stand and lift a hand, letting it hover in the air for a second before it falls back to my side. "But I did. And the important part is you're safe. A little banged up, but safe."

She brushes away a tear. "This is so embarrassing."

"Hey, hey." I want to offer her comfort, but I don't know where the lines are anymore. "It's okay. This is a lot. And it's layered with other stuff. I'd be more concerned if you *weren't* visibly upset by this." I take one of her hands in mine. "I don't know if this is out of line or not, but I give a pretty mean hug, if you need one."

She presses her bandaged fingers to her lips and nods. "Please? I'm sorry."

"No apologies necessary." I open my arms, and she steps forward, eyes on my chest. I envelop her small frame. She's familiar in a way that's hard to explain. I've spent a handful of weeks sitting in a classroom listening to her insightful commentary about the craft of creative writing. And I've slept with her. It's a strange position for both of us.

She inhales a shuddery breath and exhales on a soft sigh as I give her a squeeze. "I got you. You're safe."

She makes a little humming sound and turns her head. Her cheek comes to rest against my hoodie-covered pec, and she wraps her arms around me.

We stand there like that, just breathing, for long seconds. My heart thuds in my chest.

"You really are a great hugger."

I chuckle. "I wasn't lying. Careful though, they're addictive."

She laughs and steps back, but her hands slide around my sides, and she rests one palm on my chest for a few seconds.

Her eyes lift, and her tongue sweeps along her bottom lip. "It's good I don't get addicted to things easily, then, isn't it?"

"Good for you, I guess. Not so much for me." *Watch yourself, Waters.* "You okay?"

"Much better now. Thank you." She smiles softly.

"Good. Remember, you have my number, so if you need anything—hugs, self-defense lessons, someone to take your garbage to the curb, more hugs—I'm a few blocks down, and I can run pretty damn fast. Especially when it's a hug request." I wink, and she laughs again.

"You are a relentless flirt, aren't you?"

"Totally." I nod somberly. "Seriously, though, think about coming to my self-defense class. If nothing else, it's a great opportunity to beat the crap out of me."

"I'll think about it," she says again.

10

Teacher's Pet

CLOVER

Three days later, I'm in the middle of dinner prep when there's a knock on my door. I assume it's Sophia and her hands are too full to manage the door. While we eat dinner together more nights than not during the week, Friday happens to be our dinner-and-movie date night. I wipe my hands on my apron and head for the front door, opening it with, "You better have the red wine!"

I stop short when I realize it isn't Sophia at all. It's Maverick.

He's dressed like he's ready for a date: black dress pants, crisp white button-down, tie with the school hockey team logo on it, and a sharp black blazer.

He runs a hand through his hair. "I can hit up the liquor store and be back in ten with some red wine. But you'll need to give me an idea of what kind, because I only drink it at weddings when they shut down the bar during speeches."

I chuckle. "Are you even old enough to buy wine?" I know the answer to that, but I don't think it hurts to remind him there are some lines we can't cross.

"Ouch. That hurts, Professor." He presses a hand to his chest and stumbles back a step, then gives me a dimple-popping half smile. He glances over my shoulder, likely checking out the most recent gift basket that arrived sometime this morning. "Am I interrupting? Smells like you're cooking."

I smooth my hands over my hips. "I'm just getting dinner ready. Sophia is coming over—my friend who lives upstairs." Why am I suddenly awkward? And why do I feel compelled to explain?

"That's good. You gonna watch a movie and chill out tonight?"

"We are."

"Good. That's good." He folds his hand behind his back. "You doing okay? How are your hands?"

"They're good. Healing."

"Any other bruises? Sore spots?"

"I've got a decent bruise on my hip, but I've been using the hot tub out back in the evening, so I'm almost back to normal." I thumb over my shoulder.

He nods and taps his temple. "Sleeping okay?"

"Yeah. It helps that Soph is right above me." I point to the ceiling. "Thank you for coming by to check on me, and for your help the other night."

"I didn't want to email about it, you know, since they monitor those things." He taps on the hand railing. "It's good you ended up filing a report."

I blink in surprise. "How do you know that?"

"I talked to the guy who owns the mechanic shop."

"Right." I vaguely remember him mentioning that he knew the automotive shop.

"Two of the guys have been fired. He wasn't real happy when the police showed up at his shop looking to talk to them." He rubs his jaw. "Anyway, I wanted to make sure you were all right, and to bring you a little something. It's nothing big." He reveals a gift bag that's been hidden behind his back.

"Oh no. No. Nope. You can't bring me gifts, Maverick. It's inappropriate."

"I'm not trying to buy my grade. I noticed that your slippers got—"

I shake my head. "However well-intentioned you may be, I can't accept a gift. You just can't."

Besides it being inappropriate, it reminds me too much of Gabriel.

His eyes widen. "Shit. I didn't mean to make you uncomfortable. I just wanted to replace some of the things I know got damaged. I'm sorry, Professor."

"It's the optics of it, especially with our history."

He gives me a lopsided grin, gaze moving over me on a slow sweep. "Okay, message received."

He's about to take a step down when Sophia comes around the side of the house. She's holding a bag of fresh bread and a bottle of wine. Her gaze flits from me to Maverick and back again.

"Uhhhh . . ." Her improv isn't the best.

"This must be the bestie." Maverick throws one of his dimpled smiles her way. "Have a fun night with my favorite professor. And try to convince her that it's a good idea to come to my self-defense classes."

Sophia raises one eyebrow at me. "Hi, Maverick Waters."

Maverick's grin widens as he passes her on the front steps, and he turns and walks backwards down the driveway.

"You're talking about me, huh? That's good. I can work with that."

"Have a good night, Maverick. Try to stay out of trouble."

"I'll do my best." The monster truck parked in front of my house beeps, and he climbs into the cab, turns over the engine, and waves as he pulls away from the curb.

Sophia whistles. "What was that all about?"

"He was checking in on me after what happened the other day."

She pats me on the shoulder. "It's a good thing the semester is almost over."

"Yes, it is."

THREE DAYS LATER, I'm standing outside Pump It Up with ten minutes to spare before the self-defense class starts. When I talked to my mother earlier today on one of our biweekly chats, I mentioned I was thinking about taking the class. I didn't tell her what happened with the drunk hecklers, and I was right not to, because just the mention of the classes put her on alert. I assured her everything was fine—even though that's questionable—and used Maverick's words, saying I thought it would be *empowering*, which seemed to appease her.

A familiar black F-150 pulls into the lot and parks beside my Prius. My heart rate picks up. It's a reaction I've been fighting since Maverick showed up in my creative writing class. But the warm feeling in my chest is new, and I attribute it not only to the things I now know about him, but also to the way he came to my defense, and his continued concern for my well-being.

I stand in the shadows, against the side of the building as

Maverick opens the driver's side door and climbs out, hood pulled up over his head and the brim of a hat peeking out. I went back and forth about whether I should come to this class, all things considered, and decided it would go a long way toward making me feel more confident in my ability to defend myself.

He closes the door and tugs his hood down, then pushes the driver's side mirror in and angles his body so he can maneuver around my car without grazing it.

He stops short when he reaches the front of the car and sees me standing there. "Professor?" His eyes light up. "I thought I recognized your car. I was hoping I'd see you tonight."

My stomach flutters, and I internally roll my eyes at my body's reaction to his admission. "Were you?"

"Yeah. When you didn't show up for the Saturday class, I wasn't sure if I'd pushed it when I stopped by to check on you. I worried I'd made you feel uncomfortable. But it's good that you're here. Hopefully you'll learn some helpful stuff." He gives me a hopeful smile. "I gotta get inside 'cause the class starts in less than ten. You wanna come with?"

"Sure. Yes. Okay."

He motions for me to go first, since the sidewalk is narrow, but when it widens enough, he falls into step beside me. "How are you? How are your hands?"

"Mostly healed now. That liquid bandage is a miracle. And the bruise on my hip has faded a lot. It's still a bit sore, but otherwise I'm fine."

He nods. "I'll keep that in mind when we're practicing some of the moves tonight. How about emotionally? You feeling okay? How was movie night with your bestie?"

My cheeks flush at the memory—how suddenly the emotion had swept over me when he'd been about to leave the night of the attack. All the what-ifs creeping in and pushing me to the edge. How I'd accepted that hug from him and how easy it was to find comfort in it. "Movie night was good, and thank you for stopping by to check in."

He opens the door, stepping aside to let me go first. "No problem. I just wanted to be helpful. We're over there, in the room on the right." His fingers graze my elbow as he guides me.

We pass everyone from college students to grandmothers sprinkled throughout the expansive space—running on treadmills and stair climbers, riding recumbent bikes and reading books, lifting weights in pairs.

I follow him into one of the fitness studios. Close to a dozen women are already standing around, chatting quietly with one another. There's a woman instructor at the front of the room, and her face lights up as soon as she sees Maverick. "Ah, there you are! We're almost ready to get started."

There's a mother with her daughter who looks to be in her late teens, a pair of women in their mid-thirties, a trio who look to be in their forties, and a pair of younger women who are closer to my age, or maybe a few years younger.

"Should I have brought a friend with me? I'm the only one on my own," I whisper.

"You don't need a partner." He gives my shoulder a gentle squeeze, then drops his hand and steps back. "You'll be okay. You've got this, and I'll be here to help the entire time."

He heads to the front of the room. "Evening. I'm Maverick." He lifts his hand in a wave, expression open. "I'm here to teach you how to beat the crap out of me."

The group laughs nervously, and the two younger women and the teen daughter openly check him out.

The other trainer's name is Laura, and for the next few minutes, they explain the purpose of the class and the basic moves they'll be showing us.

Maverick puts a pouch over his waist, clearly to protect himself, and then he and Laura start by demonstrating a basic arm grab and how to get out of the hold. Then they move around the class, allowing each of us to give it a shot.

When Maverick reaches me, he gives me an encouraging smile. "Are you okay to try this with me, or would you prefer to work with Laura?"

"I'm fine to work with you." I wipe my hands on my thighs. At this point I've watched several people perform the move.

He nods. "Okay. I'm going to walk you through it, and we'll do it a few times until you feel like you've got it. Sound good?"

"Yup." I nod, feeling irrationally nervous about the whole thing.

"If you're uncomfortable at all, or you feel like it's too much, let me know."

"Okay."

At my affirmation, he shows me how to perform the move, giving me step-by-step instructions, repeating it several times until I have it down. "Nice work, Professor. You'll be kicking my ass in no time." He gives me a fist bump, which seems to be his go-to with his students.

This whole situation is weird, but his praise gives me all the warm fuzzies.

"You don't have to call me 'Professor' when we're out of class." Even as I say it, I don't know how I feel about it, but having him call me Professor when we're in a setting like this feels awkward.

"Okay, Clover." He gives me a wink before he returns to the front of the class. We learn to escape from three more holds: being lifted off the ground, a chokehold, which is intense to say the least, and a hair grab. At the end of the hour, we review all the defense moves we've learned, and Maverick and Laura answer any questions and tell the group that they hope to see us next week so we can build on our defense skills. Their final suggestion is that if we have a friend we can practice with, it helps cement them.

Maverick stays behind to talk to a few of the women in the class, but when I shoulder my purse, he holds up a finger. "Give me a minute, and I'll walk you to your car."

I hang back, waiting for the last of the class to leave. Maverick pulls his hoodie on and shoulders his gym bag. "See you on Saturday, Laura."

"Have a great week. You were fantastic as usual tonight."

"Thanks, so were you." He puts his ball cap on. "How was that for you?" he asks, shifting his attention to me. "You picked up the moves quickly. Do you think you'll come back next week?"

"I might." It was eye-opening, and empowering, like he said it would be. It's also . . . a little conflicting.

"Better than a flat-out no. Is it weird for you? Being my student instead of the other way around?"

I chuckle and glance at him from the corner of my eye. "A little, but you're very good at teaching, and putting everyone at ease."

"It's important to make everyone feel comfortable, otherwise it's hard to be effective."

"I can see that."

He holds the door open for me, and we walk across the parking lot where his giant truck and my little car sit under one of the floodlights. When we reach our vehicles, I clutch the strap of my bag and turn to him. "Can I ask why you do this?"

Maverick spins his keys on his index finger, catching them in his palm before he releases them and spins them again. "I do it for my sister."

I'm unsurprised by this. From what I've learned recently, it seems Maverick does a lot for the people he cares about. "Did you teach her self-defense?"

"She and my mom took classes together when she was a teenager. I let her practice the moves with me. Eventually I decided I wanted to teach them to other people, so they'd know what to do if they ever ended up in a situation like Lavender did. I mean, she was six when it happened, so it wasn't like she was old enough to take those kinds of lessons, but I never wanted her to feel helpless like that again. Or anyone I cared about."

"You mean when she was abducted at the carnival when you were kids?" I'm trying to follow his train of thought. The story he wrote seemed to be from an outsider's perspective, looking in, but now I wonder if it was his adult self, looking at that childhood trauma.

"Yeah. If things had been different, she never would have gone missing." He's still spinning his keys, around and around, but he loses his rhythm, and they fly out of his hand, landing on the ground at my feet.

I scoop them up. There isn't much space between his truck and my car. Only a couple of feet separate us, and when I straighten, my shoulder brushes his chest. Again, goose bumps flash over my skin, but this time they're hidden by my jacket. "How do you mean?"

"We were supposed to wait for her." His jaw works. Sharp angles and soft eyes. Haunted. "But we didn't. None of us were ever the same after that." He swallows, gaze bouncing from my hand to my face and back again. "Do you think maybe we could go for coffee or something? I can fill in some of the gaps in that story I wrote."

"I don't know if that's a good idea, Maverick."

"It's coffee, Clover. Lots of professors have coffee with their students. I, uh, I just . . . Writing about that has kind of made it feel fresh again, if that makes sense? And I don't have a lot of people I can talk to about this kind of thing."

He seems so earnest, and like he could really use someone to listen. He's not wrong about professors having coffee with students. It happens on campus all the time, especially with graduate students. The difference is most of those professors haven't slept with the student in question.

"Just a quick coffee?" He gives me what can only be described as puppy dog eyes.

"Okay. We can go for coffee."

"There's a place a couple of blocks over, unless you'd feel better about going somewhere on campus. Like the café?"

"A couple of blocks over is fine. I can follow you?"

"Sure. Yeah. That'd be great." Maverick holds my door open for me. "It's called the Coffee Emporium. Have you heard of it?"

"I've been there before."

"Okay. Drive safe. See you in a couple." He closes the door and hops into his truck, pulling out of the lot before I can rethink this decision.

11

What the Hell Am I Doing?

MAVERICK

I climb into my truck and shake my head as I turn the engine over and pull out of the spot, waiting for Clover to do the same before I leave the parking lot. I don't really know what I'm doing. Or why I'm trying to get my professor to go on a coffee date.

All I know is that writing that freaking story for her class seems to have unearthed a bunch of memories I can't shove back into a box. I can't talk to my family about this, and I sure as hell can't talk to Kody. Clover already knows the basics, so telling her the whole story makes the most sense, and then maybe once it's all out, I can stop having the weird dreams, and the invasive memories will chill.

The coffee shop is quiet this time of night, so there are lots of empty spots in the lot next door and only a few occupied tables inside—a couple in the back, a man reading a paper, and two women who look to be in their thirties having a serious discussion.

We approach the counter, and I order a sugary latte and a piece of cake. "What can I get for you?"

"I can get my own. Thanks, though."

Her smile is a little stiff, so I don't push it. She orders a tea, and we take a seat at one of the empty booths. It's strange to be sitting across from Clover and not in a classroom. I've gotten used to the invisible wall that went up as soon as I became her student, but it seems to have developed a few cracks recently. Otherwise, she wouldn't be here.

I'm close enough to see the smattering of freckles across the bridge of her nose. They've faded since the summer. Without her glasses, she looks closer to my age—mid-twenties maybe. "How old are you, anyway?"

"Seriously? That's your first question?" She quirks a brow.

"You know how old I am."

"My age isn't relevant under these circumstances. You need to keep in mind that I'm still your professor."

"For a handful of weeks. I want to say you're twenty-six or twenty-seven, but that would make you a child prodigy. Were you?" I curl my hands around my mug, feeling the heat seep into my fingertips.

"No. And I'm older than twenty-seven."

"By how much?"

She rolls her eyes and purses her lips. "I'm almost thirty."

"Almost? So you're still in your twenties, like me."

"For a few more months, yes." I can tell I'm making her uncomfortable.

I don't want her to get up and walk out, so I shift gears. "By the time my dad was in his mid-thirties, he was retired from playing hockey."

"That's very young." She tucks her hair behind her ear.

She has three earrings in the right one. Two up near the top of the shell, as though maybe she had an industrial at one point and didn't quite want to give up the rebellion. It's a bit at odds with the bunny socks and cardigans and thick-rimmed glasses.

"He played for more than a decade. Professional hockey careers are short compared to the way most people will stick with the same thing for decades. Some players only get a season or two on the ice before their career is over." I rest my elbows on the table. "How old were you when you finished your PhD?"

"Twenty-six."

"That's faster than most." For reasons I'm unsure of, I want to know how she got where she is. "Why were you in such a rush to get through college? It's kinda the last hurrah before you have to start taking life seriously."

"Are you saying you don't take life seriously?"

"It's not that I don't take it seriously. It's that I know it's full of slap shots and chippy plays, so you gotta enjoy the good stuff when it happens."

"Is that why you half-ass your assignments in my class?" She arches a challenging brow.

"I half-ass a lot of things. I don't think I realized how intense your class was going to be."

"Did you think it would be an easy A?"

"More like a moderately effortless C. I probably should have paid closer attention to my advisor when I was signing up for classes. My first professor seemed to like me well enough, but that obviously changed. I tried to switch out after you took over, but I'd passed the deadline, so you were stuck with me."

She laughs, and her smile does something to me, makes my chest all warm. It's stupid. She's a professor. Educated. Established. She's done everything she can to put distance between us this semester, but for whatever reason, the universe seems pretty determined to keep pushing her back into my orbit.

"Do you have a boyfriend?" She said there's no live-in boyfriend the other night, but that doesn't mean there's no boyfriend at all. Plus, there was a gift basket in her foyer when I checked in on her on Friday.

She focuses on her tea. "I thought we were going to talk about your creative writing assignment, not my personal life."

"We are. I'm just curious. You're beautiful. Smart. Funny. Kind. Strong. Independent. Someone has to have noticed that besides me."

She leans back in her seat and crosses her arms. "You can't flirt with me, Maverick."

I bite my thumbnail and give her a half grin. "It's a compulsion. I can't help myself."

"Does that mean you flirt with everyone?"

"Not everyone. Just women I find attractive, and I'm a single Pringle, in case you were wondering."

"I wasn't." She shakes her head and picks up her mug. She's still smiling, but it's stiff now. "Keep it up and I'm leaving."

"I'm sorry." I hold up a hand. "I'm nervous and deflecting."

"It's fine." She sips her tea and sets it down on the table. "And why are you deflecting?"

I focus on my mug for a moment. "For all these years, we've never really talked about what happened to my sister. A creative writing piece isn't the same as a conversation, but putting it on paper . . . I don't know. I didn't expect it to sit with me the way it has."

"*We* as in you and your sister?"

"*We* as in my family. We talk *around* it most of the time. I mean, it happened more than a decade ago—almost a decade and a half—so it makes sense that it's not a huge topic of conversation. And Lavender doesn't want to be defined by something that happened when she was too young to really remember." I take a sip of my latte, wishing I'd gotten water, or that they served beer here instead.

"You were both quite young, weren't you?"

I nod. Part of me wants to reject going back to that day, but the other part wonders whether purging this information will make things better.

"But old enough to remember," she says softly.

I set my mug down. "I guess. Lavender says she remembers it mostly in smells and sensations, not what actually happened."

Clover nods thoughtfully. "Do you think that's because she was so young?"

"Maybe." I pull a napkin from the dispenser. It's thin and easy to tear, but it'll keep my hands occupied. I start folding it into a square, following the pattern that's engrained in my brain from doing it so often. "That's the part I probably have the hardest time with—the never really knowing what happened. And it's not like she hasn't had loads of therapy. She's gone not just because of what happened, but because she has pretty bad social anxiety. Even before the abduction, she was quiet whenever we were with people she didn't know, or in large crowds. After, though, there were times we'd have to leave someplace because it was too much for her."

"What would happen? What made it too much?"

"I don't know really." I run my tongue over my eye tooth for a few beats. "But she'd shut down. Like her body was there, but she was trapped in her head. It always freaked me out. I was scared she was going to stay like that. But she always came back. Eventually."

"You said in the parking lot that you were supposed to wait. What did you mean by that?"

"We ran ahead of Lavender and River, and we shouldn't have."

"We?"

"Me and Kody. My best friend. He's Lavender's boyfriend now." I set the finished crane on the table and pull another napkin free. I feel restless, like there's an itch under my skin that I can't get to. I want to get up and run—hit the ice and do skate suicides until my legs and lungs are burning. Until I puke. I do that sometimes, push my body so hard that I make myself throw up. Those nights I sleep almost peacefully.

"That sounds complicated. And you said your sister lives with you? What about Kody? Does he go to school here too?"

"Yeah." I fold another crane, the piece of cake I ordered sitting untouched in front of me. "He and I play hockey together. He lives two doors down, with my cousin, but he's obviously at our place a lot now too. He's the reason I didn't wait for my sister that night at the carnival."

"I don't understand. He didn't want to wait?" Clover's expression is pensive, like she's trying to reconcile the story I wrote with what I'm telling her.

"No. He did. That's why I didn't." I wish I could shut the hell up. There's a reason I don't talk about this. I don't want everyone to know how fucking awful I really am. "Kody's been in love with my sister since he could say her name. Even as kids, they had this untouchable bond. Lavender's like that. She radiates goodness."

"And you don't think you do?"

I huff a laugh. "I'm not a good person."

"From what I've witnessed, you're pretty selfless."

"I'm not, though." I shake my head and lean forward, resting my chin on my fingers. "Sometimes I'm really fucking selfish."

"How do you mean?"

I scrub a hand over my face as long-buried memories surface. "All I wanted to do was run through the funhouse one more time with Kody and then ride the roller coaster and get a funnel cake. But we spent what felt like a freaking hour—and was probably more like five minutes—convincing Lavender it would be fun if she came with us. I knew ninety percent of the reason she wanted to come was because Kody was going, and she idolized him."

"And Kody is her boyfriend now?" I can see her trying to piece it all together.

"Yeah. They started dating this year."

"Is that hard for you?"

"It was inevitable. Those two have been destined to be together their entire lives. Kody just needed to have his shit together first." I poke the slice of cake with my fork. "Anyway, that night I was trying to be patient, but everything with Lavender was kind of an ordeal back then. She needed a lot of coaxing and coaching, even to do normal things. Anyway, she started to shiver, but she'd left her coat in the car on purpose. Our mom had made it for her, and it had this ruffle thing around the neck that made her itchy. Our mom was going to go back to the car to get it, but I didn't want to wait, so I told Kody to give her his hoodie."

"I'm guessing he did?"

"Yeah. I knew he would because he had a real soft spot for Lavender. Has, present tense, obviously. So finally we get to go into the funhouse, and River, Lavender's twin, is holding her hand. Our older brother went on ahead of us, because he was in the middle of a book he wanted to finish and he didn't give a shit about the funhouse. He wanted the funnel cake." I swallow down bile as I remember what happened next. "Kody wanted to wait for Lavender and River. He even stopped me from running on ahead at one point. But I figured they'd be okay. I mean . . . I didn't think she'd get lost or anything bad would happen to her. So I made him come with me instead of waiting for them."

I feel like there's a weight on my chest that won't lift, but I keep talking, unable to stop now that I've started. "Robbie, my older brother, was already waiting for us when we came out, but when River and Lavender didn't appear right behind us, I checked around at the entrance to see if maybe Lavender got scared and decided she didn't want to go through, but she wasn't there. And when I came back to the exit, River was there, but Lavender wasn't." My stomach churns as I remember the way he looked, his panic. "He was crying so hard he didn't even make sense. And then when we realized she was missing . . . Kody went with my dad to look for her, but I was convinced she was going to come out of the funhouse. They even sent people in to look for her. Turned on all the lights and everything." I press the heels of my palms against my eyes. "But when they found her. . . *fuck*. I'll never forget it. Her hands were all bloody because she'd screamed into her skin."

"Screamed into her skin?" Clover's fingers flutter around her throat.

I pinch the bridge of my nose. "I overheard my mom and dad talking about it after. I guess the guy who took her told her if she screamed, she would never see her parents again. So she dug her nails into her palms until she broke the skin."

"You told me about that before, when you helped me with my hands."

"That's right." I nod. "She dug her nails in so hard, it broke the skin. It happened once in a while after that, when she was really upset or scared."

Thankfully she grew out of that. And Mom kept her nails short to prevent it from happening after the first couple of times, but man, it sucked when she came to my room in tears, asking me to help fix it so Mom wouldn't see and get upset.

"You see now, though, what I mean when I say I'm not a good person. I forced Kody to come with me, and we left Lavender behind. If I'd waited, she wouldn't have gone missing. I'll never know what happened to her. I'll never know how bad it was."

12

Pieces of the Puzzle

CLOVER

This was such a bad call. Going to the self-defense class seemed like a good idea—until I ended up here. I don't know what to do. I want to offer comfort. I want to offer him the same hug he gave me last week.

But that's . . . not appropriate. I probably shouldn't have accepted *his* affection last time. But I was shaken and emotional, and the connection we seem to share made it hard to say no—and is likely a big part of the reason I'm sitting here.

And I'm so torn.

These are the missing parts of his creative writing piece. The darkness that permeated his writing made me question whether it was really his story at all until I read the news articles. The weight of it still cloaks Maverick in sadness and other emotions I'm trying to understand, even though what I should be doing is getting the hell out of here.

121

Now I understand better his reaction to what happened in the sauna, his focus on my feeling unsafe, coming to my rescue when those men were heckling me, taking care of me, wanting me to attend his self-defense classes. Maverick blames himself for what happened to his sister. He wears the guilt like a crown of thorns.

"Do you really believe you're the reason she went missing?" I ask.

"I believe it because it's true." His voice is sharp and gritty. "We didn't wait, and she went missing."

"What about your older brother? Wasn't he supposed to wait too?"

"Robbie was ahead of us."

"But you don't blame him for not waiting, so why are you blaming yourself? It seems like you're taking responsibility for something you didn't have control over."

"I wanted to prove that Kody was my friend first."

"You say that now, but then you were just a child. Maybe you were frustrated and annoyed with the situation, but that doesn't make you responsible for what happened. Just like Lavender was a victim, so were you and the rest of your family. The only person who deserves blame for this is the man who took her." I wish I could press pause on this conversation and call Sophia for advice. I think about what she would say. How would she approach this?

He shakes his head and slides out of his seat. "This was a bad idea. I shouldn't be talking about this, especially not with you."

"Maverick, wait!" I want to reach out and stop him, but I realize that's a problem, *and* that I don't have the background to really help him with this. "I have a friend who might be able to help. She works in the counseling department—"

He sneers. "I don't need therapy. I need to bury the fucking past and leave it there." He rushes out of the café, and I don't try to follow. He's too agitated, and I'm too confused to make good decisions where he's concerned.

After a minute, I shrug into my coat and bring my mostly full tea and his slice of uneaten cake to the counter. I don't know how I could have made that go differently, but I feel horrible that he ran out, and that I couldn't offer the comfort I wanted to.

Before I leave the café, I grab one of his napkin cranes from the table. Then I head home. And if today hasn't been overwhelming enough, there's another new basket waiting for me on my front porch. I don't even need to look at the card to know it's from Gabriel; the contents tell me that. I set it in the corner in the front hallway, unprepared to deal with it now.

Despite it being almost eleven, and both of us needing to be up early, less than two minutes later, Sophia is at my door, wearing her pajamas, tea mug in hand. "You're home exceptionally late. How was self-defense class?"

"The class was good." That part isn't a lie. I learned a lot, but my decision-making after the class was over is another story. I motion her inside.

She pauses when she sees the basket sitting in the corner beside the coat closet. "Good grief, another basket?"

"Yup."

"Garrett's popcorn? Godiva chocolates? Wow. Gabriel's really bringing his snack A game, isn't he?"

"Seems that way." It annoys the hell out of me that now, after I've handed him divorce papers, he wants to ply me with gifts. He's not taking this seriously.

Sophia follows me into the living room and sits on the couch. I take the spot in my usual chair, pick up a throw pillow, and set it in my lap.

"You look antsy and guilty. What's going on?"

I blow out a breath. "Maverick asked me to go for coffee after the class."

She gives me a worried look. "He's still your student."

"I know, and before you lecture me about boundaries, he wanted to talk about his creative writing story and what happened to his sister when he was young. What was I supposed to do? Tell him no? He's never opened up to anyone about it before—not until he wrote that piece for my class."

She doesn't jump on me. Not yet anyway. "That must have been a heavy conversation."

"He blames himself for what happened." Sophia has read the story and some of the news articles on the abduction. "I pushed too much, though, and he got upset and left."

"What did you say that made him so upset?"

"I told him it wasn't his fault that his sister went missing. That the only person to blame was the man who took her, and then I suggested he talk to someone other than me about it. He didn't like that idea, and he left." I put my hands over my face. "I should have shut up and listened."

"I'm going to ask you a question, and I want you to keep in mind that I'm your best friend and I know your history with him—"

"All we did was talk. It was coffee in a public place. Professors have coffee with students all the time."

Sophia takes another sip of her tea and sets it on the side table. "I don't want to psychoanalyze you, but I do think we need to address the fact that you're already defensive, and I didn't even have a chance to ask the question."

I give her a look. "I already know I shouldn't have said yes to the coffee."

"Which speaks volumes, don't you think? What's going on between the two of you? He's stopped by to check on you, you went to his self-defense class, and then, despite knowing it was a bad idea, you went out for coffee with him."

"To *talk*. He wrote that story for a reason. He needs someone he can talk to about this. I think it's been eating him for years." I still sound defensive, but Sophia doesn't call me on it.

"Considering your history with him, and your current role as his professor, do you think that person should be you?"

"Well, I did suggest someone else . . ." And then he bolted. "I didn't want to shut him down. I don't know what I'm supposed to do. How do I handle this?"

"You need to tread very carefully here, Clover. This is a lot more than being a friend and a listening ear. You're still in a position of power. And it sounds like he *could* probably use therapy, but he might not be in a place yet where he's willing to consider that. Regardless, you two have a very layered history, and he's still your student for a few more weeks."

"I need to keep the lines with him clear."

"And with yourself. Do whatever you need to to keep the boundaries in place—at least until he's not your student anymore."

13

Extra Credit

MAVERICK

The TV is on when I get home, which means there are probably people hanging out. I cross my fingers that it's BJ passed out on the lounger, but instead, I find my sister and Kody. It's not a surprise, but the position they're in is irritating.

Kody is stretched out on the couch, feet hanging over the end. Lavender is straddling his hips, and his hands are on her ass.

"Whoa! This is supposed to be a safe space!" I bellow, causing them both to jump. "Why can't you do that in your damn bedroom?"

"Oh shit." Kody basically tosses Lavender to the floor, then sits up in a rush and grabs the closest pillow, putting it over his lap. "Hey. Sorry, man. We didn't hear you come in."

I ignore Kody and glare at my sister, who's sitting on the

ground, her face beet red. "You have a TV in your room. Why are you down here dry humping my best friend when you can do that behind a closed door? Like this whole thing isn't already awkward enough!" I motion between the two of them.

"The TV in my room is tiny, and this one has better sound. And we lost track of time. At least we have all our clothes on," Lavender says.

"Lav, baby, not helping," Kody mutters.

I can't even with the fucking pet names. "No making out in the living room," I tell them sternly. "And no sex in the hot tub either."

Kody makes a face and a gagging sound. "Hot tubs are filthy. I would never have sex in one."

"Just like your mind," I fire back. "Those are the new house rules. If anyone is in violation, they have a week of dish duty. I'm going to bed."

"Sorry, Mav," Kody calls after me.

I don't bother responding. It's bad enough that they're always in each other's pockets these days. I don't need to witness their make-out sessions.

I lock my door as soon as I'm in my room and head for my bathroom. I need a shower to wash away all the bad memories. Now that I'm no longer freaking out, I realize it was pretty shitty of me to walk out of the café and leave Clover on her own.

I want to make sure she got home okay, but running by her house at this time of night would be a high level of creepy. Emailing could raise flags. She gave us a cell number in case of emergency situations, but I'd put messaging her at the same level of creeper as emailing and running by her house. So I let it be.

But that means I have shitty dreams. The kind where bad

things happen to the people I care about. And apparently one of those people is Clover now.

I SKIP creative writing class the following evening, trying to find a little perspective. It doesn't do much good, though. I feel a lot like I'm going through withdrawal. I've grown accustomed to the three-hour lectures and the uncomfortable hard-on that accompanies listening to Clover.

On Wednesday morning, I wake up to find that the remaining leaves have blown off the trees, thanks to the storm we had last night. The remnants of it color the sky gray and make the day feel dank and dreary.

Despite the crappy weather, I pull on my running shoes, throw a hoodie over my T-shirt, and head toward the park for a run. I might also be planning to run by Clover's place. Not that I expect her to be standing in her driveway, but I still feel like crap for the way I left things on Monday. If there's even a remote chance I could run into her and apologize, I'll take it.

Luck seems to be on my side today, because as I jog past her house, I notice a ladder propped up against the siding and a familiar figure, wearing a black cardigan, standing precariously on the second step from the top, feeling around in the gutter.

The house is a story and a half, dormers at the front, presumably so all the ceilings aren't slanted on the second floor. The roofline isn't particularly high at the front of the house, but still, it's a good twelve feet up at the lowest point.

I slow to a stroll as she reaches in again and tosses a handful of muck-covered leaves to the driveway below. She's wearing yellow rubber kitchen gloves, and her face is a mask of disgust.

She looks down and blows out a breath, grabbing the ladder with both hands, as if she suddenly realizes how high she is.

"Hey, Clover, what are you doing up there?" I call out.

She startles and flails, and I rush to hold the ladder steady so she doesn't set it off balance.

"Whoa! Careful. Can you come down before you break your neck, please?"

"You scared the crap out of me!"

"I seem to be really good at that. You shouldn't be on a ladder without a spotter, though."

"I didn't realize how high I was. Am." Her voice is pitchy as she clutches the ladder with both hands and lowers one foot, tapping the air until her toes find the next step. She repeats the process until she's low enough that I can reach her foot.

"I'm gonna guide you down, all right?"

"Okay. Yes. That would be great."

She's wearing a pair of flats, the soles of which are worn, and the ladder is wet, making it slippery. I wrap my hand around her bare ankle and guide her foot to the next rung, then do the same with the other until she's low enough that I can grab her by the waist and lift her to the ground.

She spins around. "You shouldn't yell at people on ladders."

I cock a brow. "Like I said, you shouldn't be on a ladder without a spotter. And based on how uncomfortable you seemed up there, you shouldn't be on a ladder at all."

"I was fine until you scared me."

"Really? Because you didn't look fine with the way you were flailing around. And your face is all red. Are your hands shaking? Are you afraid of heights?"

"No. Yes." She blows a loose tendril of hair out of her face, and when it falls right back into place, she tries to swipe it away with the back of her gloved hand. "Maybe a little."

"What were you doing up there?" I motion to the ladder.

"The gutters are clogged, and there's a leak in my bathroom. I think it's coming through the wall, but I can't be sure. The landlord is away, so I figured I could climb up there and get whatever was blocking it out, and then the leak or whatever is going on in the wall would stop. But it's a lot harder than I thought it would be."

"Want me to climb up and look? I can check out your bathroom too." I have zero experience with plumbing and leaks, but Kody and my cousin BJ recently had their entire kitchen redone because of an electrical issue, so I can probably call the guys who did the work over there if I need to.

"I'm sure you have better things to do with your time—like working on the assignment you missed because you skipped my class last night." She gives me a pointed look.

"Sorry about that. I needed to work out some personal stuff."

"Would that personal stuff be related to our conversation on Monday?" She clears her throat. "I didn't mean to upset you."

"I shouldn't have left like I did. I felt like an asshole. Feel like an asshole, still. I'm the one who brought it up in the first place, not you. I didn't know how to handle the conversation, so I bailed. I apologize for that." I motion toward the ladder. "Now can I help you with the gutters?"

"Is that you closing this discussion?"

"For now, yeah. You gonna let me take care of this?" I tap the ladder.

"I was fine."

"If you mean fine in the sense that you're hot as hell, then yeah. But if you mean you're a pro on a ladder, I'd be inclined to disagree." She crosses her arms, and I grin. "Do you happen to have gardening gloves handy?"

She shucks off the yellow rubber kitchen gloves. "Maybe in the shed."

"Let's take a look, then." I motion for her to lead the way.

We walk down the driveway, between Clover's car and her bestie's, parked side by side, past a deck with a hot tub, and a set of stairs that lead to the second-floor apartment. We cross the lawn to the back fence where a small, rusted-out garden shed sits. The flowers around it have been trimmed back, dormant until spring. I step in front of her and put my hand over the handle before she can reach it.

"Let me go first." I try to open the door, but it's locked.

"There's a key. Just under here." She steps in close, her shoulder brushing my arm as she pushes up on her toes to retrieve it.

I hold out my hand, and she sets the small key in my palm. My skin is suddenly clammy, and a shiver runs down my spine as I push the key in the lock.

The smell of gas.

Dad's bruised hand.

Lavender's cut palms.

Kody's accusing glare.

Lavender's screams in the middle of the night that lasted for months.

The dreams that wouldn't go away.

"Maverick." Clover's palm comes to rest on my forearm.

"Huh?" I look down at her, seeing the concern in her gaze.

"Are you okay?"

I shake my head to clear it. "Oh yeah. Fine. I'm fine. Sometimes raccoons make nests in sheds, and they're pretty vicious when they feel threatened." I turn the key and then the handle, pushing the door open.

A small lawn mower is pushed into the back corner, along with a gas can. To the right are tomato cages, empty planters, a couple of small bags of fertilizer, and an assortment of gardening tools. I find two pairs of rubber-palmed gardening gloves that are made for hands a lot smaller than mine, but they'll do.

I get Clover to hold the ladder for me while I climb up and check the gutters. She was right about it being clogged. There's an old bird's nest in here damming up the water, making it impossible for anything to get past.

Clover keeps calling up to me about being careful, and I make sure I toss the crap I'm pulling out in the same direction the wind is blowing—away from Clover. Once the gutter is clear, I climb back down the ladder, peel the gloves off, and help her put everything away.

"I can come in and have a look at the bathroom, if you want," I offer.

"You don't have to do that."

"I don't mind—unless it makes you uncomfortable."

She bites her bottom lip, her gaze darting to the house.

"I'll just go." I thumb over my shoulder and take a single step toward the sidewalk, not wanting to make this awkward.

She grabs the sides of her cardigan and pulls them over each other. "No. It's okay. You can have a look. Just let me make sure the bathroom isn't a mess."

Instead of leading me to the front door, she takes me around the back, to the deck with the hot tub. A sliding glass door opens to a formal dining room that doesn't look like it gets much use. On top of the table are two gift baskets full of treats.

"You celebrate a birthday or something?" I nod to the baskets.

"Or something." Her cheeks flush.

"Secret admirer?" I toe off my shoes and leave them on the mat at the door.

"Also no."

"How come I'm not allowed to bring you replacement slippers but this gift giver is allowed to send whole freaking baskets?" I ask.

"Because you're my student. And if you must know, these are from my ex. If I could send them back, I would." She waves a dismissive hand toward the table.

"Your ex, huh? Does that mean he's trying to get you back?"

"Trying and failing. Give me a second." She disappears down the hallway, leaving me alone with the baskets.

I round the table, checking to see if there are cards attached, but they've either been removed or they didn't exist in the first place. One of the baskets has been opened, with a few items missing. I wait at the threshold of the room until she gives me the all clear. Then I head down the hall.

I've been in this bathroom once before, when I retrieved the first aid kit after she hurt her hands. Just like that time, it's neat and tidy, smelling of Clover's distinct perfume, or body wash, or whatever it is.

She points to the wall with the window that faces the driveway. It's one of those frosted-glass jobs, so no one can see in, but it still provides light. There's an obvious wet mark on the drywall. I press around the area, and it feels damp and spongy. "So, I'm gonna be totally honest with you."

"That doesn't sound good." She clasps her hands.

I knead the back of my neck. "I don't have a lot of plumbing experience, apart from knowing how to fill and drain a pool and how to use a plunger on a toilet. But you're right that there's water coming in from somewhere, and I'm guessing it probably has something to do with the gutters, like you thought. So, if it dries up, you know you're good, but if it doesn't . . . Well, either way, I'd call the landlord. And I have a few contacts for professionals if your landlord doesn't have anyone."

She nods. "Oh. Well, you're ahead of me on the plumbing

knowledge because mine begins and ends with knowing how to use a toilet plunger."

"I can give you a number, if you need one."

"I'll check with my landlord first, but I appreciate it."

"Okay." I nod, then rack my brain for something else to talk about that isn't plumbing. "Have you had a chance to practice the moves you learned in my class yet?"

"Not yet, no."

"Do you want to run through them? It's always good to practice them the week you learn them, so they stay fresh in your head." I thumb down the hall toward the dining room. "Seems like it might be good to have some practice if you've got a persistent ex who doesn't know how to deal with being dumped."

"He's harmless, just annoying." She taps her bottom lip, maybe considering it.

"It won't take long. We can run through them once, real quick. I promise I'll be on my best behavior."

She hesitates, but finally says, "Okay. We could do that. Should I change into something less constrictive?"

"Sure. Yeah. That works. I'll get the living room set up for us."

"I'll be right back."

She steps out of the bathroom, giving me room to leave, then disappears into her bedroom. I move the living room furniture around so we have space to practice the moves without knocking lamps over or shoving breakable things off the tables.

I pull my hoodie off and drape it over the couch cushion. I don't have any kind of junk protection, but I can improvise.

Clover appears a minute later wearing a pair of capri yoga pants and a *Stranger Things* T-shirt that slides off her right shoulder as she sets her glasses on the coffee table. She adjusts it, but it falls again almost immediately, so she leaves it where it is. Her long hair is pulled up in a ponytail that hangs down her back. Her feet are bare, her toes painted a pale green. I'm thinking that's her favorite color.

"You ready to kick my ass, Clover?"

She chuckles. "Never in my life did I think I'd hear those words leave one of my student's mouths."

"You're my student now." I wink just as I remember I'm supposed to ease off on the flirting. "Never thought I'd look forward to having my professor hand me my ass. Should we start from the top? Review the first moves and go through them a couple of times?" This I can deal with—teaching her things, keeping it light, not bogging it down with all my shit.

She rubs her hands together and nods. "Sounds good."

We run through the first move, which is the arm grab, and it only takes two tries for her to get it right. The next one we spend time fine tuning, with me showing her how to get out of the hold faster, depending on the position.

When I lift her off her feet, her head whips back. I don't manage to give her my cheek in time, which means her skull connects with my nose. I stumble back a step, and her heel connects with my groin. I can handle the headbutt to the nose, but the foot to the groin at the same time is a lot. So I land on my ass, still gripping her around the waist. That means I get another shot in the face, compliments of the back of her head.

We land on the floor in a heap, Clover sprawled on top of me. When she flips over, she ends up straddling my waist. "Is this some new move—oh! Oh my God! You're bleeding!"

I bring my hand to my nose and feel the wet, warm trickle of blood on my fingers, seeping out and dripping down my cheek. "Tissue would be good."

"Let me see! How bad is it?" She pries at my fingers, but stops when hers come away smeared with red. She looks around the room, maybe searching for a tissue. "Shit." She whips her top over her head, balls it up and shoves it into my hand. "Use this."

I don't argue. It's black, so at least the blood won't show, and this seems like a nice rug, and not one she'd like covered in my blood. I should sit up, so the blood doesn't run down my throat, but she's still straddling my torso, one hand splayed on my chest.

In that moment, the pain dulls enough for me to register that she's in nothing but yoga pants and a sports bra. And not one of those basic sports bras—not that there's anything wrong with basic. But this one has a thin, mesh-looking overlay on top of lime green cups.

It's fucking sexy, as far as sports bras go.

And her cleavage is right there, in front of my face.

I don't even feel the throb in my nose anymore. But I feel it below the waist as other parts of my body react to the visual stimulus.

"I'm so sorry. Is it slowing down? What can I do?" Her fingers drift along my cheek. Her face is only inches from mine. Her warm breath smells like citrus and cinnamon. Her ponytail brushes over my arm, and her hand hovers near my face.

"I should sit up." My voice is muffled by her shirt.

"Right. Yes. Of course." She moves back, except the way she shifts causes her to bump against my erection.

She shoots to her feet and launches herself across the room. "Oh God! Oh my God! What the hell, Maverick!" Her eyes are wide with shock as they bounce from my face to my very obvious erection. "How can you be . . ." She doesn't finish the question. Instead, she squeezes her eyes shut and covers them with her hands.

I bark out a laugh. "Are you serious? You weren't afraid of my dick the last time I poked you in the butt with it."

She purses her lips, and makes a small gap between her

fingers, revealing one glaring eyeball. "That was before! When I didn't know you were going to be a student in my class."

I roll up into a sitting position, smiling behind her shirt. "I'm bleeding over here. Help a dude out."

"I don't even get how you can be—" She flails a hand in my direction. "That!"

"Do you mean hard, Clover?"

She gives me the stink eye again before she closes it.

I snicker, finding this entire situation beyond hilarious. "You're wearing a sports bra. There's cleavage, and you just made me bleed. It's fuckin' hot. You want to grab me some tissues so I don't ruin this shirt?"

"Oh my God." She rushes out of the room.

I take the opportunity to rearrange my hard-on, tucking it into the waistband of my boxer briefs so it's not acting like a divining rod when I stand up.

Less than a minute later, Clover returns, wearing an over-sized, paint-covered shirt, and drops to the floor beside me. "Let me see." She gently pries my hand away. "Do you think your nose is broken?" She cups my face between her palms, inspecting my nose. Her bottom lip is between her teeth.

"It's not broken. I might have a sweet pair of black eyes tomorrow, but I'm fine."

"How can you be sure? Should you see a doctor? Maybe I should get you some ice."

I grab a few tissues from the box beside my hip. "I'd know if it was broken. Ice isn't going to do anything. You can kiss it better if you want, though." I smirk at her disapproving frown.

"I can't believe you're flirting with me while you're bleeding!"

"You're a sexy badass, and I already told you, it's a compulsion."

"This wasn't a good idea." She sits back on her heels. "I can't keep a level head with you."

"So why try?"

"You're my student."

"And you're *my* student until you're done with self-defense," I counter. "I'll even give you private lessons from now on."

"It's not the same, and you know it."

"Then what am I doing here, Clover?" I can see her pulse hammering in her throat, see the battle she's fighting.

She clasps her hands and drops her head, staring at her lap. "I'm in a position of power. It's unethical."

"I think that's semantics. We already leveled that field a while ago. Anyway, what happens at the end of the semester, when you don't have that excuse to hold on to?"

"You'll still be a student, and I'll still be a professor."

"I'm not asking for anything serious. And I'll probably end up in Nashville after graduation, depending on how things go. We already know we have chemistry. I feel it every time I look at you. And there's this pull. It's different. Not like anything I've experienced before."

"Because it's taboo. I'm your professor."

"What's going on here existed before, when we were in your cabin. If this was seven months from now, and I'm playing for whatever fucking team decides to try to replicate my dad's legacy with me, who would be in the power position then?"

"It's not that simple." She seems so torn.

"Isn't it, though?"

"This . . ." She motions between us. "I don't know how to handle it any better than you do. I felt awful on Monday, and then yesterday when you didn't show up for class?" She shakes her head, her expression imploring. "I need you to help me keep the boundaries in place, at least until the end of the semester, Maverick. Because I don't think I can do it on my own."

That piece of truth is more than I expected. I nod once. "Okay. I get it if you need to wait until I'm not your student. I'll stay inside your lines—at least until the semester is over and my final grades are handed in. Then we can reassess."

I push to a stand and bring the T-shirt back to my nose when I feel blood trickle down my chin. "I'm going to go. I'll hold onto this and give it back to you when it's not covered in my blood anymore. You can have my hoodie as collateral." I nod to the red hoodie with my team logo on it. "I'll see you in class. Hopefully mine before yours."

14

Slippery Slope

I stand in the middle of my dining room, staring at the sliding glass door. "What the hell am I doing?"

I'd been shirtless. Straddling his lap.

He'd been hard.

The walls I put up when he stepped foot in my classroom are turning into rubble. I drag a hand down my face. It smells like his cologne. Part of me wants to believe his fascination will wane, that as soon as I'm not his professor anymore, the allure will be gone, and he'll move on.

It's what I try to tell myself, *and* Sophia when she asks, again, what exactly I'm doing. But I don't know that I believe my own words. Or that I want to. Maverick isn't wrong. That pull between us exists. And the more I learn about him and get to know who he really is, the harder it becomes to deny that it's about more than just chemistry. So the only way I can handle it is to avoid him.

I don't attend the next self-defense session, and at nine forty-two that night, there's a knock on my sliding door. Maverick's hulking figure stands on my back deck, hands clasped in front of him, breath leaving him in white bursts.

"What are you doing here?" I'm dressed in leggings and an oversized shirt, hair pulled up in a ponytail.

"I'm here for your private self-defense lesson. And I have the shirt I borrowed." He holds up my Steve the Babysitter shirt. *Stranger Things* is a guilty pleasure for me. "Blood-free." He gives me that lopsided grin that makes it hard to turn him away.

"I don't think the lessons are a good idea anymore."

Most of his face is in shadow, but his bottom lip slides through his teeth. "I promise I'll be on my best behavior, Clover. What happened last time. . . It won't happen again. I'll absolutely stay in control. I really want to teach you how to defend yourself."

"It's not you I'm worried about. It's me," I tell him. "If you keep coming over here, offering me private lessons, I'm going to make decisions I can't unmake. And let's be real, you're terrible at the whole not-flirting business." I smile uneasily, hoping he understands that this isn't me trying to push him away. I'm trying to protect us both.

"As much as I want to disagree, you have a point." He lifts his hat, running his hand through his hair and revealing his face.

"Oh my God." I step forward and reach up, as if to touch him, then withdraw my hand and bring it to my lips. "Did I do that?"

He has two black eyes.

His smile widens. "You sure did."

"How can you even explain this?"

"I play hockey. Shit like this happens all the time. I'm fine. And super fucking proud that I'm such a great teacher." He winks.

"I can't believe you're joking about this! I feel awful." I poke at my cheek with my tongue. "Are you sure your nose isn't broken?"

"It's not broken. I promise. Stop worrying about my face and think about how badass you are that you're capable of doing this kind of damage to a guy my size."

I bite my lip and stare up at him. Even with two black eyes, he's still stunning. "It is kind of badass, isn't it?"

"It's totally badass. Are you going to let me teach you some more moves?"

"I don't know if it's a good idea for me to give you black eyes all the time."

"To be determined, then?"

"To be determined," I agree. "Will you be in class tomorrow?"

"Eh." He lifts a shoulder and lets it fall. "I'm not sure I can sit through a three-hour lecture with you and a bunch of sophomores who don't know how badass you are. It's torture."

"You've done it for the better part of the semester."

"Yeah, but that was before you got into my head and under my skin." He taps his temple. "Three hours with a hard-on isn't conducive to learning. It's too heightened a state. There have to be studies about it."

I sigh.

"That's one of my favorite sounds, Clover. Hands down. Want to make it again so I can record it and listen on repeat?"

"This is the flirting I'm talking about."

He thumbs over his shoulder and winks. "That's my cue to

leave so I don't go crossing more lines than I already have. See you in my dreams."

And with that, he disappears around the side of the duplex.

MAVERICK DOES SHOW up for class the following night, and leading up to exams, he stays true to his word. He doesn't stop by my house again, and the only time I see him is in class, or occasionally I pass him on campus. He nods and says hello but stays inside the lines I've drawn for us.

But at the end of every class, he leaves a paper crane, labeled with a number, on the edge of his desk. At first, I think it's a countdown to the end of the semester, but the numbers keep going up instead of down. Curious, I look up the significance of paper cranes and discover that a thousand cranes equal a wish. He's at five hundred now.

The week before final exams, I wake up to messages from Gabriel.

This isn't uncommon. I can see the pattern emerging again, thanks to talks with Sophia. It's what he did when things first started to go south in our relationship. He would try to take something away from me, I would fight against it, and he would do it anyway and then buy me something as a means to placate me. At first it worked. Then the things he took away became bigger, more important—essential even, to my well-being.

He continues to send gift baskets and call or message, asking when we can sit down and talk. He keeps bringing up the property in Pearl Bay, knowing it means something to me, but he doesn't realize it's about more than wanting to hold on to a little piece of lakefront property.

I continue to tell him there's nothing to talk about, and he assures me there is.

I scroll through the messages, suddenly on alert. Because he's in town. And apparently, he just happens to be passing by my house this morning. "Fuck."

I roll out of bed and rush to throw on the clothes I laid out last night. Sending baskets was one thing, stopping by with barely any notice is another.

I fire off a text to Sophia, but it's only six fifteen in the morning. She doesn't usually show up at my door these days until closer to seven. I could run up to her place and hide there until he leaves. But who knows how long Gabriel would wait. I'm just prolonging the inevitable, and I don't want to hide anymore. I want him to see that I'm just fine without him. That I'm actually better than I've ever been. That leaving him was the smartest decision I've made.

Even now, with all the complications, having Maverick in my life helps me see clearly, in a way I couldn't before, all the ways Gabriel was trying to control me.

Maverick is everything Gabriel is not—altruistic, caring, a champion for strong, independent women who can take care of themselves, and like me, a little broken by the things we've been through. I see our parallels, the way he's been changed by what his sister went through, and the ways I've been changed by marrying someone who wanted to keep me inside a box.

Still, I'm grappling with the stigma and my own feelings about the entire thing. But we have a connection—the kind that makes me wish even more that Gabriel would just sign the damn papers, and this semester would finally come to an end.

Eyes on the prize. I need to stay focused on my goal here. I've just shoved my feet into my shoes when a black BMW pulls into the driveway. And there he is. *Gabriel.* There's no way I'm letting him into my house. Not when there's a university hoodie hanging from the hook at my front door which my almost-no-longer student left here and still hasn't taken back.

15

Not-so-Friendly Competition

MAVERICK

I've been avoiding Hackett Street for the most part, but today I'm on autopilot as I take my morning run. Instead of bypassing the street, I make a right onto it. I'm about to adjust course when I spot a black BMW parked in front of Clover's place with an out-of-state license plate.

I slow to a stroll as I approach her driveway and notice a man standing in the middle of it. Another two steps and Clover appears. She's dressed in a pair of black pants, a white blouse, and the mint-green cardigan she's so fond of. Her hair still hangs loose around her shoulders.

In her signature move, she's gripping both sides of her cardigan and lapping them over each other.

I wave uncertainly and stop at the end of the driveway, trying to figure out the dynamic and her posture. "Hey, Professor, how's it going this morning? Everything okay?"

She startles and offers me a tight-lipped grin as I look between her and the man with his back to me. "Oh, hi, Maverick." Her hand flutters up to her throat and then back down to clutch her cardigan. "Everything's fine."

I take a couple of steps toward her, in part because I'm not entirely sure I believe her and because I want to get a closer look at this guy. "I noticed your garbage isn't out yet. You need a hand getting it to the curb?"

"It's okay. I'm about to put it out." Her smile is stiff, her expression remote. Indifferent.

"It's no problem for me to do it, if you're busy." I take another step closer.

The man standing in front of her turns around.

I hold out a hand and try to keep my expression open and friendly. It's the one I use when I'm at the gym, meeting a new group of women who've signed up for self-defense. Relaxed. Welcoming. "Hey, I'm Maverick, I live down the street." I thumb over my shoulder.

"Nice to meet you, Maverick." His smile mirrors mine, but his gaze is shrewd and assessing as he takes me in. "Gabriel Lockwood." His grip is firm, and he returns his attention to Clover. "I'm so glad my wife has the kind of neighbors who look out for her. Makes me feel a little bit better about the neighborhood she's living in." He stresses the word *wife*, and I doubt I imagine it when his grip tightens around mine for a moment.

I try to keep myself from reacting, but I'm pretty sure my eyebrows pop. Well, shit. When she said an ex sent her the basket, I figured she meant an ex-boyfriend, not that she was married, and apparently still is.

"*Ex-wife*," she counters. "And you really don't need to worry about the neighborhood. It's not as though I'm living next to a methadone clinic." She's definitely throwing out a hostile vibe.

"There's a lot of student housing around here, though. You should be on the other side of the university." He tucks a hand in his pocket and gives her a mischievous grin. "And I haven't signed the divorce papers yet, so I still have a chance at winning you back."

He winks at her, and I barely resist the urge to punch him in his smug face.

She returns his smile with a saccharine one of her own. "On a cold day in hell."

Gabriel's grin widens, and he turns back to me. "You can see why I'm trying my best to get her to give me another chance, can't you? Life is boring without this kind of sass on a daily basis. You said you live down the street? Are you a student of my wife's?"

I tuck a hand in the pocket of my hoodie, wishing I was dressed differently and hadn't called her professor. I glance at Clover, who's still holding the sides of her cardigan.

This guy is older, probably in his mid-to-late thirties. He's wearing name-brand everything, and not in a trying-too-hard kind of way, but in an I-make-a-lot-of-money way. There's an air about him, too, like he's used to getting what he wants. He's charming and established. Not a twenty-one-year-old with most of a degree and a part-time job at a gym.

"Yeah. Until the end of the semester anyway. Then I'm just her neighbor." I rock back on my heels.

His expression reflects amusement. "And which course is my wife teaching you?"

"Creative writing."

"Ah, yes, my wife is an excellent storyteller, aren't you, darling?"

That sounds like a shot if I ever heard one.

"*Ex-wife*, Gabriel," Clover reminds him, lips pursed, arms crossed.

"Not until the papers are signed, my love. And we need to schedule a dinner to talk about that." He gives me a conspiratorial smile. "Wish me luck getting her to agree to give me another chance."

"Professor Sweet seems pretty adamant about the ex part, so I guess you're gonna need all the luck you can get, huh?" He has to be the one sending her the baskets.

"Seems that way. It was nice to meet you—Maverick, was it?"

"That's right."

"Is that a nickname or your given name?"

"Given."

"Interesting. Well, Maverick, I appreciate you helping out Clover, but now that I'm in town, that probably won't be necessary."

"Right. Okay." I've got no less than a million burning questions, none of which I can ask. Like, since when did he move to town? "It was nice to meet you, Gabe. I'm sure I'll see you around." I turn to Clover. "See you on campus, Professor."

"Of course. Thank you for popping by."

"No problem. Anytime."

I walk backwards a few steps before I turn and head down the street, but at the end of the block, I go right instead of heading for the park and circle back toward my house. I don't mind a little friendly competition, but a husband who's trying to win her back is a whole different level.

And it makes me realize exactly where I am when it comes to Clover.

This isn't a game I'm playing.

I WALK BACK through the front door of my house to the smell of freshly brewed coffee. This could be a good or a bad thing. Good, because it means I'm not responsible for making it; bad, because I have no idea who's in the kitchen.

If it's Kody and Lavender doing their morning dance—Lavender wearing a smirk and Kody blushing like a twelve-year-old with his first boner—I'm probably going to punch someone. And that someone would be Kody.

Which wouldn't be fair, because it's not his fault I'm in a mood and can't deal with happy couples.

Not to mention that I'm over here pining away like an asshole for my professor who's still married—to a guy who has a career and a life and isn't still in college. In a handful of months, I'll be in a better position, but there's a good chance I'll also be in a different state. Or possibly out of country, depending on how ready they think I am.

Needless to say, my headspace isn't good.

There's no way to get back up to my bedroom without going through the kitchen, which seems to be a design flaw in this house. So I'm relieved when I find my cousin BJ sitting at the kitchen table, sipping a cup of coffee. He has one of Lavender's mugs, and it reads *You're Awesome, Keep that Shit Up.* Except it's a pretty, floral design, so you don't register what it actually says until you're close.

BJ glances up from the newspaper sitting in front of him and makes a circle motion around his face.

I stare at him a moment, waiting for him to say something in follow up. "Morning?" I offer when he doesn't.

"That it is." His eyes flick to the clock and back to me.

"That was an exceptionally short run, and you're not really sweating."

"How do you know how long I've been gone?"

"I heard you when you left, less than half an hour ago." He leans back in his chair, crossing one impossibly long leg over the other. He's a year younger than me, but his full-sleeve tattoo, man bun, and beard make him look a lot older. "And now you're back and looking all . . . angry. What's the deal?"

"There is no deal."

"If you say so." He makes a *hmm* sound and sips his coffee.

I give him my back and go in search of my favorite coffee mug. It's not in the cupboard, though, which means it's in the dishwasher. I check that, too, but it hasn't been run yet, so I go back to the cupboard and pick my second-favorite mug. It used to be my mom's, but I stole it. It reads *Mrs. Waters*, but the letters are made of penises. She doesn't know I have it, and I always keep it in the back of the cupboard, so they don't find it when they come visit.

I pour myself a cup of coffee, add enough sugar to cut the bitter and some cream to turn it tan, and set it on the table. Then I go back and grab two bowls, the gallon of milk that's half-empty, and three different boxes of cereal. I don't bother with the Lucky Charms since Lavender's hands have been in every single freaking box. She picks out all the fucking marshmallows. It drives me up the damn wall, especially since there are several boxes of cereal marshmallows sitting on the shelf right next to them.

I slide a bowl in front of BJ and keep the slightly bigger one for myself. Most of the time I make myself a real breakfast— eggs, bacon, whole grain toast, that kind of thing. But not today. Still, I start with the healthier cereal option. This morning I'm going with Frosted Mini-Wheats as course number one. I dump half the box into my bowl and pour milk over it, letting it sit for a minute before I dig in. Mini-Wheats are a particular favorite because they do such a good job of soaking up the milk.

"How are you handling things?" BJ asks conversationally, bypassing healthy options in lieu of Cinnamon Toast Crunch.

"Handling what things?" I shovel Mini-Wheats into my mouth.

He points to the ceiling.

I shrug.

"So, not well, then."

BJ doesn't pour any milk on his cereal. Instead, he picks at it like it's a bowl of chips.

"There's nothing to handle. They're together, like we all knew they would be eventually."

"There's a significant difference between knowing it's going to happen and it actually happening, though. And let's be real, for a while there it looked a lot like Kody was going to fuck things up permanently."

I let my spoon rest on top of my floating Mini-Wheats and take my hat off, running my hands through my hair and lacing my fingers behind my neck. "That whole thong situation was . . ."

"Very OOC for Lavender, but also badass." BJ strokes his beard and smiles.

I frown. "OOC?"

"Out of character."

"Oh yeah, for sure it was." I wasn't there to witness what happened, but I saw the pictures circulating after the fact. Kody threw Lavender over his shoulder like all his brain cells had died and he'd turned into a caveman. "Never in my life did I think I'd see Lavender in a thong bikini."

"She's good at making a statement when she needs to," BJ says, sifting through his cereal bowl.

For what, I have no idea.

"Agreed. Better than I realized, maybe."

"She's always had her own way of doing things." He pops another piece of cereal in his mouth. "It's like her star has finally started to shine. It's good. But it can't be easy for you."

"How so?" Having Lavender move in here was my idea.

BJ steeples his fingers and taps them against his lips. "Your friendship with Kody has always been . . . tricky."

"You mean because he's always been in love with my sister?" I don't mean for those words to come out with bite. Do I want my sister and my best friend to be happy together? Absolutely. But it digs at sore places.

BJ shakes his head. "It's more than just love, though. Those two." He takes a moment to think before he speaks, which is BJ's way of having conversations. Sometimes it takes an hour to get to the point, but most of the time, by the end, the picture is a lot clearer than when we started. "They're soul mates. They can't help but be drawn to each other. And Kody, man, he tortured himself for years over her."

"Because of the carnival," I mutter.

BJ's eyes shift to mine and spark. "That's part of it, yes. But there are so many layers. He lived to save her after that happened."

"And I've always been the tightrope he had to walk to get to her. But now that he has her, where does that leave me?" I don't expect the bitterness in my tone, or the way I suddenly feel even more . . . insecure maybe? Today is a bag of shit.

"Ah. And there it is. The real issue." BJ props his elbows on the table and leans forward. "I challenge you to look at it another way, Maverick. You were never the tightrope. You were Kody's anchor and Lavender's shield. You prevented him from getting to her before he was ready to deal with what it meant to have found the person he was destined to love more than any other. Because let's face it, Kody can't half-ass his feelings. He only experiences the world in two ways—full color or none at all. And Lavender, well, she's his fucking rainbow."

"I don't even know how to be his friend anymore. I feel like I've become a black cloud or something. Like I'm a reminder of all the ways things got screwed up when we were kids. I don't know. Everything has changed." I wish I understood why this whole thing makes me feel . . . like I'm mourning something maybe.

BJ leans back in his chair. "You're not a black cloud. You're the threat of lightning that can blow it all to pieces. The gatekeeper. And he needed you to be that. Lavender needed you to be her quiet shield. You never openly stood in their way, but you were there to keep watch. It's what you do, Maverick. Unconsciously, consciously, you protect everyone around you. Which begs the question, who protects you?"

I stare at him for a few long seconds, processing. He's more right than I want him to be. "Who the fuck are you?"

"Just a dude who keeps my eyes open even when they're closed."

"I don't think I'd ever want to spend a day in your head. I'd drown it's so deep."

"Don't think I haven't noticed that you're trying to change the subject." He pops another piece of cereal into his mouth and chews twice. "How many close friends does Kody have?"

"Is that a trick question?"

"It's not supposed to be. Who does Kody willingly spend time with? Lavender aside, obviously."

"Me, you, Quinn, uh . . ." I stall, thinking about who Kody gets messages from, who he makes plans with, which is limited to the guys he lives with, one of whom is BJ, and me. Sure, he'll interact with all the Buttersons, and our teammates when we're at practice or in the locker room, but he doesn't go out of his way to talk to any of them. "That can't be it."

"Can't it?"

"He has more friends than you and me." But now as I sit here, I have to ask myself if I have any friends besides him and Kody either. Because as much as I might go for beers with those guys, I wouldn't really call them friends. Acquaintances, maybe.

"Does he ever talk about the people he spent time with when he lived in Philly?"

I think about that for a moment. "Not really."

"Not at all," BJ corrects. "But when he moved, he stayed in contact with you, and me to some extent, but not to the same degree. And when you guys were applying to colleges, he's the one who started the group chat, making sure you were both applying here. You've never been his default friend, Mav. He doesn't operate that way. He either is or he isn't. He doesn't have an in-between. I know it has to be awkward as fuck for you to figure out where the new lines are in your friendship, but consider how it's been for him—never wanting to let you down and afraid he's going to fuck this up and lose not only his soul mate, but possibly his best friend too."

"He's never around anymore, and when he is, he's with Lavender," I argue. "I've tried to make plans with him, but it's like I'm an afterthought now. I feel like I've *lost* my best friend. Like outside of hockey, I'm irrelevant."

BJ leans back in his chair and laces his hands behind his head with a nod. "This is not me saying you don't have a right to feel the way you do. But I think you've also taken a big step back, consciously or not. Maybe to give them room to do their thing, or maybe to protect yourself because subconsciously you expect him to pick her over your friendship."

I scrub my hands over my face—carefully. It still kind of hurts. "Yeah, maybe you have a point. But the make-out sessions on the living room couch are more than I can deal with, regardless."

"That's fair. But also infrequent. And I bet Kody is struggling as much as you are with how this all should work. Just talk to him about it, man. You've been friends since before you were born. There's a balance here. You just need to find it."

"Have you ever considered becoming a therapist?"

BJ pops another piece of cereal in his mouth and chews before answering. "That's not my path right now. That's not to say it won't be eventually, but I have other things I need to do first."

"Such as?"

"Do what my mom wasn't able to."

Aunt Lily, BJ's mom, taught figure skating for as long as I could remember, but now she helps organize the schedules and takes her teams to competitions. "You want to be a professional figure skater?"

"I want to make it to the Olympics, like she almost did."

"Whoa, shit. Aunt Lily almost made it to the Olympics? Why didn't I know this?" My aunt Lily and my mom are half-sisters. They found that piece of information out when my Gigi drunk-blabbed about her one-night stand with a hockey player, who also happened to have a one-night stand with Aunt Lily's mom. It's a whole lot of six degrees of separation.

He taps his fingers on the table. "Most people don't talk about the dreams they don't achieve. She should have gone, but you know how expensive that shit is. The dream was right there, at her fingertips, and our loser, deadbeat grandfather wouldn't help out, so it slipped through her fingers. If she can't live the dream, I can do my damnedest to do it for her."

"What about what you want?"

"It *is* what I want."

"But you said you were doing it for your mom."

"I love skating, so it's not that hard to shift my goals around and put this one at the top of the list. I've got the rest of my life to do whatever the hell else I feel like."

"You could have gone the professional hockey player route, if you wanted." He plays pickup with us in the backyard all the time. He's good. Really good.

"But then I'd be in the same predicament as you and Kody. I like hockey, and maybe if I'd put my focus there instead of on figure skating, I could have been good enough to go pro, maybe not. But trying to make it to the Olympics? Sure, there's pressure, but it's not the same. My mom didn't get to go, so even if I don't either, I'll still know I tried. But if I do, well, that's the accomplishment, isn't it?"

"Yeah, I can see the logic in that, I guess. Sometimes I wonder what the fuck I'm doing."

"We all wonder that, Mav. And you've got some big shoes to fill. You and Kody are part of the reason I went the other direction. It's a lot of pressure to live up to an idea someone already has of you."

"Being an Olympic athlete is no less pressure."

"But a different kind. And I'm not trying for gold. I'm just trying to make it to the trials. And if I don't, that's okay, because my goal is trying. Anyway, back to what's important. When you first walked through the door, you seemed angry, and you weren't throwing out that vibe when you left this morning."

"How the fuck can you pick up on my vibe when you were asleep before I left?"

"I heard you rummaging around in the kitchen. You grabbed a granola bar. Actually, you grabbed three—ate two in the kitchen and stuffed one in your pocket. Then you took the garbage to the curb. And I know you were throwing out a different vibe because you were whistling, like you were looking forward to something."

"Yeah, well, that changed." I rub the space between my eyes.

"Your booty call didn't answer the door?" He smirks.

"She's not a booty call."

BJ nods slowly. "I knew it had to be a woman."

"It's not . . . even a thing, so you can stop right there."

"Uh-huh. If that's how you want to play it. Everything about your face tells a very different story." He pushes back his chair, unfolds his long, lanky frame, and grabs his half-eaten bowl of cereal, patting me on the shoulder as he passes. "I'm here when you want to stop lying to yourself, or you want to talk about the reason you've spent a lot of time dating girls you're not interested in, and now you're hiding whoever it is you're involved with."

"You don't even do relationships, so how the hell can you offer advice?"

He gives me a look. "I do relationships. They just last for one night most of the time. I'll see you later. I gotta head home and shower before skate practice."

And with that, he walks out of the kitchen. A minute later, the front door opens and closes.

As usual, I'm left wondering how my twenty-year-old cousin seems to be the wisest of everyone I know, despite the fact that he sleeps more than most newborns.

16

Caution Tape

MAVERICK

I spend the rest of the day mulling. I mull over what BJ said, especially the offhand comment about me dating girls I'm not interested in. And the fact that Clover is married to a guy who's probably fifteen years older than me.

I don't like the gnawing feeling in the pit of my stomach, or the tightness in my shoulders that I can't shake, or the way I'm grinding my teeth every time I think about the way her not-quite-ex dismissed me.

I also don't like that I'm over here telling her my fucking secrets, and Clover didn't even tell me she's still married. I feel like I'm being strung along, and I don't like it. I thought we were on the same page, that we were waiting out the semester until I'm not her student anymore. She said she's having trouble maintaining boundaries, but maybe I'm making this into something it isn't.

That thought reinforces all my insecurities, and I'm starting to realize I have a lot of those. Most of which I try to keep buried under smiles and jokes.

So when I hit the ice later that evening for our game, I'm in a sour mood that only gets worse when I miss a tap in during the first period. Luckily, Kody recovers the puck, scoring the goal I missed.

He takes his seat next to me on the bench and Quinn Romero, his roommate and our teammate takes the ice. He's working on his master's thesis and while he came here on a hockey scholarship, he wasn't ever drafted. It doesn't seem to bother him, though. He plays because he loves the game, not because he feels like he has to.

"You all right, man? You seem . . . tense tonight."

"Just having an off game." I can feel him looking at me, but I keep my eyes on the ice.

"You wanna run some drills tomorrow afternoon? Just you and me? Maybe we can grab a bite or something?"

"Why? My sister busy or something?" *Fuck*. I'm being a dick.

That conversation with BJ comes back to me. Maybe he's right. Maybe I'm the one making this harder on both of us. I turn to Kody before he has a chance to call me out. "Sorry. I'm in a mood. Yeah, sure, we can run some drills tomorrow afternoon."

"We could also grab something to eat after the game, if you want? I haven't seen much of you outside of practice and games. Is everything okay?"

"Everything's fine. Just trying not to fail my classes and get through exams, you know? And yeah, a bite to eat after the game would be good."

"Just keep it low-key? You and me?" He motions between us.

"Like a date?" I arch an eyebrow.

He grins, and then his expression sobers. "I kinda thought you were pissed at me."

I clap him on the shoulder, not wanting to put my shit on him. "I'm not pissed at you, just trying to figure this whole dynamic out, you know? It was you and me and the guys for three years. It sort of feels like shared custody now that you and Lavender are a thing."

"It's good the holidays are coming up. We'll have a break from all this." He motions to the ice. "And we'll have more time to hang out."

The refs blow the whistle, and Kody and I rush back out onto the ice for the faceoff. He's center, and I'm left wing.

Russo, the player across from me, taps the end of my stick with his. He gives me one of those chin tips. "First time on the new skates, Waters?"

"Fuck off," I snap.

"Must suck when even the rookie players are better than you," he goads.

The puck drops, and because I'm distracted, I miss the pass, and he steals the puck, shouldering me out of the way and racing down the ice.

I'm a second behind him, but the mistake has already been made, and I need to get the puck back into our team's hands. I panic and make a bad play, my stick sliding between his legs. He goes down, and they blow the whistle, giving me a two-minute penalty for tripping.

The next time we're on the ice together, he makes another comment about my shitty playing and shoulder-checks me. I shove him back, and he spins around, getting in my face, calling on the refs to give me another two minutes. And like an idiot, I give them a reason because I haul off and punch him.

It isn't until I'm sitting in the box again that I notice my dad four rows up at center ice. "Fuck," I mutter, and he cocks a brow at me.

He does this sometimes, showing up at a game without telling me. And of course there's a scout from Nashville here, too. As if I need the added pressure.

We end up winning by one goal, thanks to Kody.

"You still want me to hang around since your dad is here?" he asks when we're back in the locker room.

"Nah. It's cool. You don't need to see my dad rip into me about my shitty performance tonight." I blow out a breath. "And I really need to stop channeling my inner Eeyore."

He gives me a sympathetic look. "We all have off nights. He knows you usually play cleaner than this. And Russo was being a dick the entire game."

Quinn stops as he passes us and claps me on the shoulder. "Russo deserves more than a shot in the face."

"Still. I know better than to play with my fists. If there's a lecture coming, I kinda deserve it."

"We all know better, but when someone's grinding you like he was, it's hard not to react." He turns to Kody. "Whose bed you sleeping in tonight?"

Kody's cheeks flush. "Uh, probably not mine."

Quinn's gaze shifts from me to Kody and he smirks. "See you both at practice tomorrow, then. And don't beat yourself up too much, Waters, the pressure can be a lot to handle."

"Thanks, man." I know he's trying to be helpful, but he's not looking to make the pros, and that's been the goal my entire life.

Kody turns back to me after Quinn leaves and clears his throat. "We'll still run drills tomorrow afternoon? And we can go for dinner after that."

"Sounds good."

He heads for the showers, even though he'll take another

one as soon as he's home. I take off my gear, not paying much attention to the conversations going on around me.

"There's a party going on at Deever's. I vote we go. One of the sororities is there." A freshman holds out his phone, showing our teammates a video clip of two girls doing keg stands. "Waters, you wanna come?" He gives me a nod.

"Maybe. Send me the address."

I've been off the party scene for weeks now. But after this shitshow of a day, I might need to unwind with a lot of beer. Or shots.

The freshman, whose last name is Frenchie, sends me the details. I tell the guys I might see them later, then hit the showers, passing Kody on his way out.

He bumps his fist against mine. "See you back at home."

"Sounds good."

I take my sweet time in the shower and getting dressed. As expected, my dad is waiting for me outside the locker room. He's chatting with a couple of the younger players, and when he sees me, he lifts his hand in a wave.

They shake his hand and head for the door, glancing over their shoulders as my dad strolls toward me, one of his eyebrows quirked. I'm a carbon copy of him. Same build, same height, same hair, same everything—apart from the bump in his nose where it was broken more than once in his earlier years, and the fact that he's an infinitely better hockey player than I'll ever be.

"I didn't realize you were coming tonight." My shoulders are already tight, bracing for what's to come.

"I had a dinner meeting in the city with one of Aunt Sunny's clients, and I figured I'd check out the second half of the game." He pulls me in for a back-pat hug.

Aunt Sunny works for a nonprofit organization that helps kids with terminal cancer meet their favorite hockey players.

It's awesome, but also tragic. They'll never experience a broken heart before theirs gives out on them.

Dad and I make small talk on the way to his truck. "You drive here?" he asks.

"I got a ride in."

"Want to grab a beer?"

"Maybe a coffee would be better. I have an exam I need to study for when I get home." It's not a lie, although I don't plan to study tonight. And this is my way of cutting this visit as short as possible.

"Coffee it is, then." My dad's truck beeps, and I toss my backpack in the back seat, then climb into the passenger seat and buckle up.

"You want to tell me what happened out there tonight?" he asks as he slides the key into the ignition.

I knead the back of my neck. "I don't know. Just played like garbage, I guess."

He glances over at me. "Are you okay?"

"Yeah. Just . . . exams and games are a lot to juggle. I don't want to shit the bed."

"Your grades are okay, though?"

"Yeah. They're up."

"Okay. That's good. One more semester and you've got a degree under your belt, and I have a feeling you'll get called up. Just keep your eye on the goal. You're almost there."

"What if Nashville decides they don't want me?" I give voice to the fears that plague me after games like this.

"There's another team that wants you if Nashville doesn't." He says this with such conviction, as if it's a given.

"But what if there isn't?"

"There will be. Trust me. The scouts are talking. That's all I can tell you, though." He pulls into the drive-thru of an independently owned coffee shop and rolls down the window. He gets a black coffee, and I get one of their latte things that are full of sugar and caffeine.

I wait until he pulls ahead before I say, "What if I don't want to get called up?"

A crease forms between his eyes. "You've been working your entire life for this, Maverick. Why would you want to walk away now? What's going on? I'm worried about you, son. This isn't like you."

I lift my hat and run my hand through my hair before replacing it, adjusting the brim. "I know. I'm being stupid. Tonight, I played like a rookie, and it put me in a shit headspace. I'll be fine next game."

He squeezes my shoulder. "You will. It's normal to have doubts after a rough game. We all have them. I had lots of bad games. And I got lots of penalties when I was a rookie and playing with my emotions and not my skill set. I don't ever expect you to be perfect. You know that, right?"

"Yeah, Dad, I know. Thanks for the pep talk." But part of me wonders if I'm so focused on hockey because it's the one thing he and I have in common, and I don't want to give that up.

We pull around to the window, and my dad pays for the coffees before the college-aged girl passes them over. Once we're back on the road, my dad says, "You know I'm always here if you need to talk."

"Yeah, I know. I appreciate it." But telling my dad what's going on in my head isn't something I can do.

"How's everything else? You dating anyone new?"

I shake my head and take a sip of my overly sweet coffee. "Nah. Gonna focus on exams and getting through to the holidays. Doesn't make sense to get involved with someone when I don't have the time for it."

"Okay. But, uh, in case something changes, you all stocked

up on condoms and lube? You know I can always call in a favor and get you what you need if you're running low."

"I'm good, Dad. Still going through the liter of lube Mom put in my stocking last year." It was the *only* thing in my stocking. She wrapped it in festive paper with penises wearing little Santa hats and beards. I have no idea where the hell she found the paper, but I made origami cranes out of it and put one on each plate at the table when she had her friends over for a New Year's dinner party.

"Good. Good." He taps the steering wheel. "Remember, foreplay isn't a suggestion, it's a necessity if you're a Waters man."

"I'm super aware of that, Dad, but thanks for the reminder."

Thankfully, my dad stops both the sex lectures and the hockey talk. He makes a right down Hackett Street, and my heart does this weird thing in my chest, as if it stops beating for a second before catching up again. It's just after nine, and Clover's front porch light is off. As we pass, I notice a pair of figures in the kitchen.

And that black BMW is parked in front of the house. Still. Again. I grab the door handle.

"Mav?"

"Huh?" I tune back in, my throat tight. The automatic locks are on; otherwise, I'd already be out of the vehicle.

"You're coming home for Christmas and staying for a bit between games?" Dad asks. "You've got almost two weeks off, according to the schedule. Everyone's going to be up at the lake. Your aunts and uncles, the Bowmans and Westinghouses too."

"Yeah, I might have some shifts at the gym, though."

"Is that still working out for you? Do you think you're taking on too much with your final semester coming?" He pulls up in front of the house.

"Nah, it's only a couple shifts a week. I can handle it."

"Okay. I just don't want you to get overwhelmed." He gives my shoulder another squeeze.

"You gonna come in? I don't think River's home." His car isn't parked in the driveway, and he's been sleeping somewhere else a lot.

Dad shakes his head. "It's late. I should head home, and I saw your sister earlier this afternoon before my meeting. We had a late lunch. She seems like she's really settling in here. It's good that she has you to watch out for her."

"She's different than she was when we were kids." I pinch the bridge of my nose as memories pop like bubbles in my brain. It's been like that a lot lately. It makes it hard to stay focused on any one thing.

"Mav? Is something going on with Lavender?" My dad's hand is still on my shoulder.

I shake my head. "No. She's fine." I reach for the door handle, but blurt, "Do you ever think about what happened at the carnival?"

"Of course." He clears his throat, his voice gruff. "More often than I'd like."

I nod, but don't look at him. "It's been coming up a lot for me lately."

"Is your sister talking about it? Do you think she needs to talk to her therapist more?" There's an edge of panic in his voice.

"Lavender isn't talking about it," I reassure him. "And she seems like she's handling college fine."

"Then what's going on? Is it Kody-related? Does it have to do with their relationship? Do I need to talk to him?"

I hold up a hand. "No, Dad. You don't need to talk to Kody. It's not about that. Just forget about it."

"You're a good kid, Mav. Impulsive, but good."

I want to stab myself in the eye. I nod again, my mouth dry, my stomach unsettled. I swallow down the bile and force a smile. "I should hit the books. I've got an exam to study for."

"Yeah. Of course." My dad's expression is pinched. He looks like he wants to say more but isn't sure what or how. "If you ever need to talk, about anything, all you have to do is call. Your mother and I are always going to be here for you, no matter what."

"I know, Dad." Except I'm not sure he would say that if he could see inside my head.

"Tell River to call when he gets a chance. Your mom thinks he's dodging her messages because it takes him more than twenty minutes to respond." Dad shakes his head.

"I'll try, but I haven't seen much of him lately." I hop out of the cab and grab my backpack from the back, waving as he pulls away from the curb.

I drop my bag in the front foyer, grab an Uber and head to the freshman party, needing something to distract me. The driver takes Hackett Street, which seems to be a shortcut to a lot of places. The black BMW from this morning is still parked in her driveway. It's closing in on ten. I guess if the car is still there in the morning, I know what the real deal is.

I can hear the thump of bass as soon as we turn onto the car-lined street. It's mostly student housing and apartments around here.

I saunter up the driveway, not really sure what the hell I'm doing here. The house is small and run-down, a true student home—unlike the one I live in with my siblings. Inside, there's a keg in the middle of the living room, along with a handful of rookie players and some freshman girls who are questionable jailbait. The whole scene is one I've avoided for the most part since my freshman year. There's a reason all the parties were at my house, where I could control who came and went, and I could disappear when I didn't feel like dealing with drunk idiots anymore. I spent most of the time making sure people didn't get so hammered they could no longer make good decisions.

And now here I am, in the middle of everyone's bad decision-making. I've only been here for two minutes, and I'm already regretting it.

"Waters! You showed, man! Guys! The legend is heeeeeeeeeere!" shouts Deever, the freshman throwing the party.

And suddenly I have a lot of attention. One of the guys hands me a shot. And as the group around me grows, more drinks come my way. I accept them, wanting to drown out everything that's happening in my head. I expect the alcohol to take the edge off, but it seems to be doing the opposite.

After a little while, I can't stay focused on the conversation. Especially since a group of freshmen, most of them *not* on the hockey team, want to talk to me about my dad and his awesome career, and how cool it is that I'm carrying on tradition and going to the NHL, and blah fucking blah.

It gets worse when a few girls slide into the group, and one links her arm with mine and asks me if I came alone.

"I'm actually seeing someone," I lie, for reasons that don't make a lot of sense, other than the fact that being here feels wrong on a lot of levels, even if Clover lied about her ex. And right now, he's in her house. Maybe in her bed. Maybe he's been there all day.

"Oh." She makes a pouty face. "Are you like, exclusive?"

"Sure." If by *exclusive* she means I exclusively whack off in the shower to images of my professor, then yes. We're absolutely exclusive.

"But she's not here?"

"No." I scrub a hand over my face. "I gotta get out of here." I push my way out of the group, shaking off the girl.

I realize I'm pretty damn drunk when the floor feels like it's moving under my feet. I have to use the wall to keep me from falling over. I need water. And maybe to puke.

I stumble my way through the living room and out the front door. I trip down the front steps and around the side of the house and relieve myself in a bush. I call an Uber, my stomach twisting uncomfortably.

When the Uber arrives, I cram myself into the back seat. As I'm sitting there, I pull up the introductory email for Clover's class. Her cell number is at the bottom. A lot of professors do that—give a contact number outside of the university.

I compose and send a single message:

17

The Breaking Point

CLOVER

Today has been a test of my patience. It started with Gabriel stopping by at stupid o'clock in the morning, thinking if he caught me early enough—and half-awake—he would get me to agree to sit down and talk.

I managed to send him on his way. However, my class schedule and office hours are easy enough to get a hold of from the school, which meant he was waiting at my door when I arrived home from work—with flowers, dinner, and paperwork. If I hadn't let him in the house, he would have made a scene. And that's about the last thing I need.

Three hours later, my dinner remains untouched, along with my full glass of wine, and the paperwork remains unsigned—it wasn't the divorce papers, it was the assessment of the cabin.

"I don't understand why you're being so rigid, Clover. I'm

willing to negotiate fairly, but you haven't given me a chance here." He crosses one leg over the other and steeples his hands, leaning in, his voice soft. "Let me take you out. Let's go for dinner. Tomorrow night. Let me show you I've changed."

"You haven't changed, though, Gabriel. You're doing all the same things you did when we were married."

"We still are married."

"And why is that?" I hate how smug he looks, like he's already won.

"Because I believe we can work this out. I'm waiting for you to see that too."

"And I keep telling you, I don't want to work this out. Marrying you was a mistake."

He leans back, expression shifting. "Your mistake was running away and hiding for a goddamn year. It's childish and dramatic, Clover."

"You cut me off from my family and friends!"

"That's untrue and unfair, and you know it." He gives me a disapproving look. It makes my blood boil. "You know I couldn't pass up that job in Rhode Island. It was too good an opportunity."

"That's not how it went, Gabriel. You can't keep turning things around on me and making yourself the good guy in this. You isolated me, changed my cell phone provider without me knowing, tracked me through my phone, blocked my friends from calling me—"

"That tracking app was meant to keep you safe. There had been a rash of break-ins in the area."

I rub the space between my eyes. "You're always going to have an excuse for your behavior and your actions. These gifts? They're not going to win me back. In fact, they're going to do the opposite. You keep telling me you want to reconcile, but you have no regard for my feelings. And how am I supposed to believe anything you say when in the next breath, you're telling me you want the cabin? You've only ever been there once and hated it!"

"Look at you, getting yourself all worked up, and over what? A shack in the woods. This is ridiculous. I am trying my best here. Your hysterics are unnecessary." He inspects his nails, as if I'm boring him.

"You need to leave before I call the police."

He gives me a look. "Oh, come on. Look at yourself, Clover. What do you think the police are going to do? You're a train wreck. No one is going to love you the way I do. If you can't make it work with me, who can you make it work with?"

"Get the fuck out now!" I shout, hating that I'm giving him exactly what he wants—my emotions, my tears, my frustration.

He raises his hands in supplication. "No need to shout. I'm only two feet away from you, my love." His chair scrapes across the floor as he pushes away from the table. "I'll come back when you're calmer and capable of having a rational conversation."

I follow him to the front foyer and wait until he has his things. He tries to forget his scarf, but I make sure that doesn't happen. As soon as he leaves, I lock the door behind him. Tonight, Sophia is out with a few of the therapists from her office. I should have gone with her when she invited me, but with the last few finals coming up, I thought it would be better to stay home.

I fill a glass with water and take an Advil to offset the headache knocking on my temples. I need Gabriel to sign the divorce papers, so I can be done with this and move on.

I consider tossing the glass of wine down the drain, but it's my favorite, and it seems like a terrible waste. Dinner already went in the garbage. The flowers will go to my neighbor across the street in the morning.

The moment I retrieve my phone from my purse and take it off silent, it pings with multiple missed messages. There's an excited one from my mother, wanting to plan out meals for my holiday visit. But the one that catches and holds my attention is from a vaguely familiar number.

Only a few students have reached out via my cell this semester, and usually because they needed clarification on an assignment that was due before I had office hours.

I stare at the screen until it goes blank. I have a feeling it's Maverick, especially after everything he witnessed with Gabriel this morning. I check the piece of paper with the gym information he left for me and confirm my suspicions.

I don't even know what I'm doing anymore. Gabriel thought it was cute that my student clearly has a crush on me. I brushed it off, but it left me with an uneasy feeling that's carried through the day.

I debate whether I should check the message or let it be. The final paper for the creative writing course is due in a week. After that, I have an additional week to submit final grades, but I'm aware that as soon as those exams are in my hands, I'll be passing his and several others to my TA to be marked.

After two gulps of wine, I open the message. I can't read the tone, but I imagine he's either hurt or angry. Probably both. And this is my fault.

I shouldn't have gone to the self-defense classes. I shouldn't have said yes to the coffee. I'm the one who turned this into a complicated situation.

I don't want to respond by text, so I hit call instead, unsure if I'm about to make this better or worse.

He answers on the second ring. "I can't decide if it's a good or bad thing that you're calling me." His words are heavy and a little slow.

"I felt a call would be better than a text, all things considered."

"Why didn't you tell me you're married? Why lie?"

I sigh. Sophia would probably tell me to hang up. But Maverick deserves an explanation. "We've been separated for more than a year. He's refusing to sign the divorce papers. I'm not married to him willingly anymore. I haven't been for a long time. He's holding me hostage by withholding his signature." I close my eyes. "I have office hours first thing tomorrow morning. Why don't you meet me there and we can talk? I think this is a better discussion in person."

"I have a morning skate at six thirty. I'll be there for about an hour."

"I'll be in my office before eight."

"You sure you want me to come to your office for this conversation?"

"Gabriel is being difficult and unpredictable. So yes, my office is best."

"Are you safe there?"

"I'm safe."

"Okay. If that changes, I'm a phone call away."

"I'll be fine. We'll talk tomorrow."

"Okay." He ends the call with a quiet click.

I'm already in so deep, I don't know if there's a way to dig myself out of this hole anymore.

18

The Last Straw

MAVERICK

I wake up with a splitting headache. I remember the Uber ride home and sending a text message, and I have a very vague memory of a phone call.

I grab my phone from the nightstand and check my recent messages. I sent one at eleven thirty last night, and not long after, I received a phone call from the same number. I think I'm supposed to meet Clover at her office.

Drunk texting is never a good idea.

I drag my ass out of bed and get ready for morning skate. I'd back out, but I could use the extra ice time, even though I feel like a bag of shit, and I don't play much better. At least it's just a few guys looking to run drills. Kody asks if I want to grab breakfast with him, but I make up an excuse and tell him I'll catch up with him later, like we planned.

I head directly to the English building and take the elevator to Clover's office. Her door is ajar, and she's already at her computer. It looks exactly the same as it did the last time I was here. But everything was different then—the boundaries hadn't shifted yet. The cranes I've left in class are now sitting on the windowsill. I don't want to read into that, but it's hard not to.

Her hair is down, falling in loose waves around her shoulders. She's wearing black pants and a long, tunic-style shirt, topped with a pink cardigan. She looks gorgeous. And tired.

I knock on the door, my stomach in knots.

"Come in." She rolls her chair back as I step into her office.

"Morning, Professor." I'm on the fence as to whether it's a good one or not.

"Why don't you close the door and have a seat?" She motions to the chair beside her desk.

I do as she asks, glad I left my backpack in my truck so I feel less like her student and more like her equal. "I'm going to be totally honest and let you know my memory of last night's call is pretty foggy." I grab a tissue from the box on her desk and start folding it even though it's not great for origami. "Did I do or say anything I shouldn't have?"

"No." She shakes her head, and her gaze shifts to the side. "Why is your memory foggy?"

"I might have had a few drinks." I tap the arm of the chair. "Did you say anything you shouldn't have?"

She circles the rim of her coffee cup with a single finger, her focus there. "I called you, and I probably shouldn't have."

"Because I'm still your student."

"Yes."

I don't think it's worth pointing out that I won't be for much longer. It's a sticking point with Clover, and while I'd like it to be different, I get why it's not. "I probably asked this last night, but as a refresher, why weren't you honest about your ex not actually being your ex?"

She folds her hands in her lap, and her bottom lip slides through her teeth. "I'm waiting for him to sign the divorce papers. We haven't been a couple for almost a year and a half, so I don't consider us together, or married, even though he does."

"Is he someone I should be worried about?"

"In what sense do you mean?"

"He was at your place yesterday morning and again in the evening. I saw his car when we drove by on the way home from my game last night—not on purpose either." *At least that time.* I set the finished crane on the side table and grip the armrests. "And I'm sorry I ran by yesterday. I was on autopilot and not thinking about the route I was taking, not consciously anyway."

She nods, as if she's putting together the pieces of last night's puzzle. "He said he wanted to talk yesterday morning, and I wouldn't make time for him, so he took it upon himself to show up again in the evening. I had hoped he would sign the papers, but that wasn't on his agenda. I became frustrated, and so did he. He enjoys playing mind games, but I'm not concerned for my safety. My annoyance level is another story."

"What kind of mind games?"

She picks up the crane and settles it in her palm. "He likes to twist words and actions. He's very good at manipulating."

"It doesn't make me happy that he's showing up at your house unannounced, then."

"That makes two of us. If I felt unsafe, I would say something, but I'm more frustrated than anything else."

"Okay." I don't know that I feel any less on edge than I did before I walked through the door, just for different reasons now. "I'm not big on playing games, Clover, so if I'm waiting on the end of the semester for no reason, just tell me."

She's quiet for a few seconds before she says softly, "I don't play games either."

"Okay." I push out of the chair. "Not long now, and we can stop doing this dance."

She smiles faintly, even as her throat bobs with a nervous swallow. "Good luck on your finals."

I open the door and check to make sure the hall is empty before I leave her office. I guess we'll see how it all plays out once my grade is handed in.

A FEW DAYS LATER, I'm sitting at the kitchen table, reading over my final story for my creative writing class one last time and shoveling cereal into my mouth when Lavender walks in. I expect Kody to be two steps behind her, but he isn't.

"Where's your boyfriend?" I ask as she opens the cupboard and pushes up on her toes, trying to reach the Lucky Charms. I've intentionally pushed them back so they're hard for her to get to.

I also put the stepstool on top of the fridge. Is it a dick move? Yup. But it's entertaining to watch my pint-sized sister get irritated on occasion.

She glances over her shoulder and gives me a look. "You mean your best friend?"

"Who is now your boyfriend." I shovel another spoonful of cereal into my face.

She turns around, crosses her arms, and gives me her unimpressed look. It's the same one our mom gives when I dress up bananas in the costumes she makes and leave them around the house. Lavender doesn't say anything. Just keeps staring.

"He *is* your boyfriend."

"He's been *your* best friend since you two could make spit bubbles."

"He's been in love with you since he understood the concept," I fire back. I don't know why I'm in super dick mode, other than I'm stressed.

"I thought you were okay with this." She pokes at her cheek with her tongue. "You're the one who invited him to live here when their kitchen blew up."

"I *am* okay with it."

She climbs onto the counter, nabs a box of cereal, a bowl and a spoon, and crosses to the table, dropping into the chair across from me. "You two need to spend more time together. Without me around."

"We play hockey together every day." I can feel my ears going red, though, because this is the same conversation I had with BJ, and Lavender picking up on it too means I'm the common denominator in the problems here.

"That's not the same. The whole team is there. He says you're hardly around anymore. And every time he tries to do something with you, you bail on him."

I'm about to argue, but then I realize he *has* been making an effort. Like the other day when he asked if I wanted to have breakfast after our morning skate, and then I ended up blowing off our plans that afternoon. We were supposed to run drills in the backyard, but I wasn't in the right headspace for it, and I couldn't be honest about why. "It's finals" is my lame excuse.

She pours cereal into her bowl and tops it with milk. "I get that maybe you two can't talk about"—she makes sexual hand gestures—"or whatever anymore, because that would be really fucking weird, and we already have enough of that with Mom and Dad and the banana costumes and Gigi and her always giving me sex toys, but it doesn't mean you can't or shouldn't hang out together." She pokes around in her bowl of cereal, dunking marshmallows. "If you're upset that we're dating, say something to him about it. Deal with it. He and River have managed their issues, as much as they can anyway. Punch each other in the kidneys if you need to but avoiding him and me isn't going to fix the damn problem. He *misses* you." There's a sadness in her eyes I don't expect.

I frown. "He said that?"

"It's been implied a lot lately. I don't know if you've noticed, but Kodiak isn't the most socially adept human being on the face of the planet. His friend group is pretty damn limited. And as much as I love him and love spending time with him, I need some balance too. And I actually can't deal with the hockey talk." She sighs. "So please, deal with whatever your feelings are and spend some time with your best friend so I don't have to listen to a forty-five-minute breakdown after every single game."

I make a face. "He does do that, doesn't he?"

"Yeah. He does." She rolls her eyes. "Most of the time I try to shut him up by sitting on his face, but it doesn't always work."

I choke on a mouthful of cereal, spraying it across the table and my notebook. "I did not need to know that, Lav."

"Whatever. That's for all the times I've had to deal with the sound of your flavor-of-the-month banshee-screaming her love of your cock when I'm forced to walk by your room. Although . . ." She lifts a finger. "I haven't heard that for a while. Like, a really long while. So you're either dating someone exceptionally quiet in bed, or you're on a hiatus. Or whoever you're seeing has her own place."

I stuff more cereal into my mouth instead of answering.

"Or *his-their* own place," she adds.

I give her a look.

"Just checking. River's finally learning to accept himself. You never know."

I've recently come to find out that Lav's friend Josiah has

been low-key sucking face with River for most of the semester. None of us was surprised to learn River was gay. It was the fact that he'd been secretly dating one of Lavender's friends that was the shocker.

"Do you think he'll come out to Mom and Dad over the holidays?"

Lavender lifts a shoulder and lets it fall. "I don't know if he's there yet. I guess we'll have to wait and see, and give him some nudges to help him get there."

She shoves her hand into the box of Lucky Charms and withdraws a handful, picking out the marshmallows and dropping them in her bowl. "Anyway, back to you and Kodiak needing to spend more time together. Last week, he made me put on goalie equipment so he had someone to practice with."

"He lives with Quinn and BJ. Either of them can shoot the puck with him."

"Eh." Lavender makes a face. "I think you're the only one who will put up with his super Type-A-ness. Anyway, over the holidays, you two need to spend some time together so I can hang out with Lovey and Lacey without it being awkward."

"Why would it be awkward?"

"Because Kodiak has been tagging along on our girl adventures, and it's hard to shop for some things when he's with us. Plus, we can't talk sex tips when he's there either."

"Right. Okay. Noted. Spend time with Kody over the holidays. Why isn't he here right now?"

"Because he needs too many rewards when he's studying, and I don't want lockjaw or a broken vagina going into exams. You're welcome for the overshare. I have several more years of this before we're even Stephen." She pushes back her chair and stands, ruffling my hair on her way past me. "Love youuuuuu!" she shouts as she skips up the stairs.

I consider how absent I've been lately, the way I've been

brushing off Kody, the way I'm always hoping no one's around when I come home. Lavender's right. I've been scarce.

Kody isn't big on confrontation, especially when it comes to me. Mostly because he's felt a lot of responsibility for how messed up Lavender was when they were kids.

Maybe we're more alike than I thought.

My story isn't due until tomorrow, but I want to hand it in early, if possible. So after I finish my read-through, I get myself together and head out. I don't usually have much in the way of test anxiety, but today is different. Once this story is handed over, I'm in the final stretch of being Clover's student. The invisible barrier that's been between us in the form of her ethical dilemma should cease to exist soon. I've sent her an electronic copy, but I'm handing in a paper one as well. I have it time-stamped by the English office before I drop it in Clover's mailbox.

And then the wait begins.

That afternoon, I shoot the puck around in the driveway with Kody when we need a break from studying, and I play video games with River, BJ, and Quinn when my brain can't handle more information. But time feels like it's moving backwards.

I have two more exams, and I'm aware that final grades aren't due until after the exam period has finished. I know better than to reach out before the grades have been submitted.

THANKFULLY MY LAST exam happens to fall on final exam day, which means I have a reason to stick around campus right to the end. On Friday afternoon, when exams are done, I fight the urge to stop by Clover's place. Instead, I end up at the bar with a few of the guys from the team. Even Quinn shows up for a bit, but he's scarce this semester, only around for hockey, and otherwise locked in his room studying. He had a breakup awhile back and I don't think he's getting over it. His one mistake in the form of Bethany early in the semester seemed to be the beginning and the end of things on the dating front from what BJ tells me.

I order a beer and nurse it, watching the clock. Since I passed over my final creative writing paper at the beginning of the week, the grade should be in by now, even though the deadline isn't until tomorrow.

I glance around at my teammates to make sure none of them are paying attention to me as I pull Clover's contact up on my phone. I don't know what protocol is here. Do I wait for her to reach out? Is she waiting on me?

I open the thread and see humping dots, indicating that she's composing a message. I wait for something to come through, but the dots continue to hump along the screen until it goes blank again.

I send a message of my own:

I don't know if this is a standoff or what, but I'm tired of waiting. And really, I can't see her being the one to step over the line. It has to be me. I throw a twenty on the table and leave the bar.

19

No More Walls

CLOVER

Two hours ago, my TA emailed the final story grades for my creative writing class. Ninety minutes ago, I submitted them. I've been sitting in my living room ever since with my phone in my hand, text message composed, my finger hovering over the send button. The screen goes blank every five minutes.

Fifteen minutes ago, Maverick sent a question mark.

I know I should decide one way or the other. But now that I'm here, at the end of the semester, I don't know what the right choice is anymore.

The knock on the door startles me, and for a moment I worry that Gabriel is showing up unexpectedly again. It's late, though, and the knock is coming from the back door, not the front.

Maverick's last exam finished hours ago. And I haven't seen him since he left my office last week.

I push out of my chair and cross the living room on unsteady legs, phone still in my hand. He stands on my back deck, wearing dress shoes, black pants, a gray button-down, and a black wool jacket—the kind someone would wear for a nice dinner out. He looks older. Refined. Not like a student.

He tucks one hand in his pocket and quirks a brow.

I hit send on the message:

> Submitted.

He pulls his phone out of his pocket, and the right side of his mouth tips up in a questioning half grin that makes my stomach flutter. He taps the door handle, and I drop my phone on the dining room table and open it for him.

Snow swirls in the air, melting in his hair as he steps in out of the cold. "When did you submit them?"

"Ninety-seven minutes ago." I try to smile, but my nerves make it feel strained. "And I had my TA grade your final, just like everything else."

I won't jeopardize his chances at a future, or my own. This tells me everything I need to know about where I am with him, even if I've been trying to weave a different narrative until now.

"So I'm not your student anymore." He shrugs out of his jacket and hangs it over the back of a chair.

"You're not my student anymore, but you're still *a* student." It's a weak argument, but I'm struggling with what it means if I do this.

He tips his head fractionally. "You need to do this dance with me one more time?"

I bring my fingers to my lips and drop my head.

"It's okay if you do." He strokes my cheek with the back of his hand. The contact is all too brief. "I'm only a student for one more semester. I looked into the guidelines. As long as I'm not *your* student, we can do whatever we want."

I grab the sides of my cardigan and pull them over each other. I've been through the school's code of ethics. I know it's not grounds for termination for me to be involved with him at this point, but the optics are something else. "I'm thirty, and you're twenty-one."

"You're twenty-nine, and I'll be twenty-two soon enough."

"I turn thirty first. You should be dating girls your own age. *Students* your age."

He rubs his jaw. "I've never dated girls my own age, and I'm sure not going to start now. They're not who I want. They're not *you*."

"Maverick." It's just his name, but I feel the weight of it in my heart. Because it's not a plea or an admonishment, it's filled with longing and desire. With need. With defeat. It's been more than three months since we were together, and the memory of that night is as clear as if it were yesterday.

"Sitting in your class has been a torture I willingly endured. I'm not imagining that there's something here." He motions between us. "You wouldn't have let me in if we weren't on the same page. You keep saying it's because I'm a student, but you didn't have a problem with this back in August."

"I didn't know there was eight years between us then, and we were acting on attraction. Things are different now," I whisper.

This is what I've been telling myself this entire semester.

My role made it easier, not wanting the power dynamic to be unbalanced.

He lets me voice my fears before he continues, "I get that you were worried about the risks, but now that I'm not your student, there aren't any. I understand that it's complicated for you, being in the position you are. But it's temporary. You're going to move on after this year, and I'm going to get called up to the NHL." He bites the corner of his lip. "No one has to know. This can just be ours." He runs his hands down his face and brings them palm to palm, his index fingers touching his lips. "I know my being a student is a sticking point for you, but I'm so fucking old inside, Clover. No one my age gets what this is like, how the things I've been through have changed me. But I feel like maybe you do."

I will my body not to react, but no matter what, when Maverick is close, I warm to his proximity. My heart rate quickens, my palms grow damp. It's so much easier to ignore when he's dressed in jeans and hoodies, looking the part of the student—harder when he's dressed for business and looks very much like the man I know him to be.

"Clover. Look at me." His voice is a gritty whisper.

I swallow and lift my gaze.

"Tell me you don't want me, and I'll leave."

"It won't work between us," I whisper.

"That's not what I asked. And I'm not asking you for long-term anyway. I'm asking you for now. Tonight. A week. A month. Until your contract is up, or you get tired of me, whichever comes first. I can be your rebound. I'll be the in-between guy until someone you can get serious with comes along. But if this is too much for you, all you have to do is tell me I'm alone in this, that my feelings are misplaced. Doesn't matter if it's true or not. I'll go. I'll walk away. I don't deserve you anyway."

It's that final sentence that crumbles what's left of my defenses.

I put my hand over his to stop him when he reaches for his coat. My action speaks louder than any words, but I say them anyway. "You're not alone."

He exhales slowly and flips his hand over, bringing us palm to palm. His fingers curl gently around mine. "I'm losing my mind over you. This semester has been fucking torture."

"I agree. But I still don't think it's a good idea for us to get involved." *For so many reasons.* However, that doesn't mean I have the willpower not to give in. My feelings have been building since he walked into my office, apologized, and handed over the key to the athletic facility. Probably even before that.

His eyes lift, grin rueful. "It feels a lot like we're already involved."

I lick my lips, my mouth dry. "I don't want either of us to get hurt," I admit.

With his eyes still on mine, he raises our clasped hands and drags my knuckles down his cheek. "I promise I will never do anything to intentionally cause you pain. So if you need me to leave, I'll go."

I close my eyes, warring with myself. I *should* tell him to go, but it doesn't mean I want to or that I will.

Because he's right. Despite all the reasons we shouldn't be together, there's something here. He's an old soul, whether from experience and trauma or because he's lived his entire life in everyone else's shadow while still being forced into the limelight. He's wise beyond his years.

"I don't want you to go." It's more breath than words.

He squeezes my hand. "I'm sorry I'm making this so hard for you. I wanted to leave you alone, to step back and fuck off. But being close to you calms me in a way I can't fully explain."

"Like you said, if I didn't want you here, I wouldn't have let you in the door." This is the honesty he seems to need.

His lips hover over my knuckles. "Can I kiss you?"

I give myself permission to submit to the wanting. "Yes."

"Are you sure, Clover?"

I lift my gaze to his. "I'm sure."

He holds it for several long seconds and then reaches out and sweeps his fingertips from my temple to the edge of my jaw. "We're not doing anything wrong. It's okay to want."

I'm not sure if he's reassuring me or himself. He flips my hand over and presses his warm lips to the inside of my wrist. I smile as a slight grin turns up one corner of his mouth.

"I didn't say *where* I was going to kiss you." His expression turns serious as he lifts my hand and wraps it around the back of his neck. "Is this okay?"

The way he seeks permission is unbearably sexy. "Yes, it's okay."

"Good. That's good." He nods once as he drags a fingertip along my cheekbone. "Can I kiss you here?"

"Yes, please," I whisper.

His lips brush my cheek, and his thumb sweeps along my bottom lip. "What about here?"

"Yes."

"You're sure?" He murmurs the words against the corner of my mouth.

"I'm sure." I start to turn toward his lips, but he cups my face in his palms, expression so earnest, it nearly breaks my heart.

"I don't want to take what you don't want to give, Clover."

"I want this, even if I've been trying to convince myself otherwise." I tug on the back of his neck, and his lips meet mine, soft and tentative.

Until I take the last step and close the space between us.

It's been months since I've been this close to him without barriers. I've been trying to keep boundaries, mental and otherwise. Now, though, I can feel every ridge and angle, the soft and hard of him.

A low groan leaves him, and he pulls my bottom lip between his, sucking gently. His hand comes around my waist, pulling me in tighter as we angle our heads, lips parting, accepting each other in.

I push aside my fears and give in to the heady desire. Our tongues tangle in languorous, drugging sweeps that make my knees weak and awaken primal need. He breaks the kiss, and his mouth moves along my neck, all soft lips, wet tongue, and a hint of teeth. "So fucking sweet. I've missed the way you taste." When he reaches the hollow behind my ear, the fingers of his free hand sweep down my side and settle on my hip. "Will you let me take you to bed?"

"Please."

He backs up until he can see my face and I can see his. "Unless you're good. I mean, we can chill out, drink tea, play a round of Scrabble." He thumbs over his shoulder to the living room, where the Scrabble board is sitting on the coffee table. "Whatever you want."

"You did not come here to play Scrabble." I grab the front of his shirt and try to pull his mouth back to mine.

He tips his head back so all I can reach is his chin, and he smirks down at me. "It might not have been my primary reason, but it could have been *one* of them."

"You've been talking a big game for a while now, Maverick. You getting performance anxiety on me?"

His smile widens. "You're my favorite fucking person, you know that?" He runs his hands down my back and cups my ass, lifting me off the floor and wrapping my legs around his waist. "Bed first. Scrabble later." He holds me up high, his lips on my neck as he carries me down the hall to my bedroom.

"I hope the only thing I have energy for after this is a glass of wine and some pillow talk."

"I can deliver on that." He pushes the door open and kicks it shut behind him. "Well, not the wine, unless you have some, but I'd be willing to drive around and see if there's an all-night liquor store later."

He sets me on the edge of the bed, and I shrug out of my cardigan, tossing it on the floor before I move back on the mattress, giving him room to climb up after me.

He settles one hand on my ankle and smooths his palm up my shin, over my knee and along the outside of my thigh. "It feels like it's been two lifetimes since I've been with you." He drops his head, and his mouth finds mine again.

We stay like that for long minutes, hands roaming, mouths locked in a lazy kiss. I tug his shirt free from his dress pants and slide my hands up his back, the fabric bunching. He's so broad, and the muscles in his back tense and flex as he holds himself above me, careful not to put his weight on me, except where he's nestled in the cradle of my hips.

I wrap my legs around his waist and hook one foot over the other, tipping my hips up, feeling his thick ridge pressing between my thighs. I clench at the memory of what it was like the last time we were together like this.

He pushes up on one arm, bottom lip caught between his teeth as he fingers the hem of my T-shirt. "Can I take this off?"

"Please. Yes."

He shifts his position, kneeling between my thighs, both hands easing up and under the shirt, exposing my stomach. When he grazes the underside of my bra, he pauses, dips down to press a soft kiss above my navel, and then keeps going.

I raise my arms to make it easier, and he carefully pulls it over my head, tossing it onto the floor.

"Yours too." I start unfastening the buttons of his shirt with unsteady hands. When I've managed to get the top two undone, he reaches behind him and pulls it over his head.

We've been naked together before, more than once. But it's different this time. So different. We're not two strangers with chemistry. It's so much more than that. We spent weeks avoiding each other, and then everything shifted. It stopped being about what *had* happened and started being about what *could*. Now every touch is steeped in intention and desire.

He dips back down toward my mouth, but I put a hand on his chest. "Let me enjoy the view for a moment, please."

He chuckles and skims my cheek with the back of his hand. "You're excellent for my ego and very welcome to cop all the feels you want."

I laugh and bite my lip, running my fingers over his chest, following the smattering of dark hair, skipping over the dips and ridges of his abs to the fine trail that disappears into the waistband of his dress pants.

"You really are incredible, inside and out," I whisper.

"So are you." His muscles jump and flex under my touch. And like always, his skin flashes with goose bumps, and so does mine. I smooth my hands back up, thumbs sweeping over his nipples and along his collarbones.

I tug, and he drops his head, lips brushing over my cheek. His gentleness seems so at odds with his formidable size. His tongue strokes out to find mine, and I melt into him. There's nothing hurried in the way Maverick kisses me. And all the while, his fingers trail up and down my side, skimming the edge of my bra, smoothing over the swell of my breasts, but never going under the fabric.

I run my hands down the broad expanse of his back. When

his mouth disengages from mine and he kisses a path along the edge of my jaw, I slide a hand into his dress pants and under his boxer briefs, pushing down while I lift my hips. The thick ridge of his cock glides over my clit through layers of fabric.

He groans into my skin and parts his lips. His tongue sweeps out, warm and wet and soft, followed by the gentle press of his teeth. I push my fingers through his hair, grip the strands, and tilt my head. "Do that again."

"Do what again?" His voice is a gritty rasp.

"Use teeth."

He parts his lips, tongue sweeping along my skin, followed by the soft press of teeth. I arch and tighten my hold on his hair. "More, harder."

"I don't want to leave marks." He presses a tender kiss to my skin.

"I have scarves and turtlenecks. You're not going to hurt me." I stroke my thumb down the back of his neck. "Again, please."

He exhales a slow, heavy breath and repeats the sequence: gentle kiss, warm tongue, and the delicious, too-brief sting of teeth. He trails more kisses along the side of my neck and over my collarbone. "You." His lips move along the edge of my bra. "Are." He bites the swell through the fabric. "Stunning." He slips a hand under, fingertips gliding along the edge of my breast. "Can I take this off?"

"Absolutely. Yes, please." I arch to give him more room, and he frees the clasp with one flick.

He tucks his finger under the strap at my shoulder, tugging down to expose a nipple.

His eyes lift to mine as he lowers his head and circles it with his tongue before covering it with his mouth. And my hands are back in his hair. I tighten my legs around his waist and grind against him, desperate for more skin-to-skin contact, more sensation, just . . . more.

But it's very clear that Maverick has plans, and they don't include rushing. My bra ends up on the floor with our shirts, and he cups one breast, thumb grazing the nipple while he sucks and licks the other, alternating back and forth until I'm a writhing, moaning mess.

My clit throbs from all the grinding, and I swear if he keeps it up, there's a chance I'll come without him touching me below the waist. I'm right at the edge when he kisses between my breasts and starts to head lower. His hair tickles my stomach as he passes my navel. He pushes up, folding back on his knees. His fingertips skim the waistband of my leggings. "Is it okay if I take these off?"

"I would love that, yes." The less I'm wearing, the better.

I lift my hips, and he hooks his fingers into the waistband, dragging them down my legs.

I start to push my panties over my hips to be helpful, but Maverick covers my hands with his. "I'd like to do that, if it's okay with you."

"You getting me naked is absolutely okay," I assure him.

He grins and bends to kiss the space below my navel.

"Now?" I ask, annoyed that I sound all breathy and desperate.

"Soon."

20

A Little Patience, Please

MAVERICK

When she groans my name, I laugh. "Patience, Clover. I've been waiting months to get back into bed with you. You can wait a few more minutes before I take your panties off."

"A few minutes? Don't you mean seconds?"

"No, but it can be longer, if you keep trying to rush me." I stretch out between her legs, getting comfortable.

"I need you to touch me."

"I will. I promise." I kiss the inside of her right thigh, then lift my gaze as I press my lips against the fabric between her thighs. Parting them, I press my tongue against the cotton, then catch it between my teeth, right over her clit, and pull, releasing it with a quick snap.

Clover sucks in a shocked, needy breath, and I loop my arms around her thighs as I lick up the seam, teasing her for long minutes, enjoying her soft sighs and pleas for more. I hook a finger into the crotch of her panties, and my knuckle glides over her clit.

She bucks and moans. "You're driving me crazy."

"The feeling's mutual." I bite the inside of her thigh.

"Just, *please*," she gripes.

"Please what, Clover? Tell me what you want." I splay a hand over her stomach when she tries to lift her hips off the bed.

"I want your tongue on me. I want you to make me come with your mouth."

"You mean like this?" I pull her panties to the side and lick the length of her, tongue flat against her clit before I cover it with my mouth and suck.

"God, yes." She shoves her hands in my hair and holds me there—as if I'm planning to move anytime soon. I taste her, lick and nibble and suck, relishing every last gasp and sigh.

Her toes curl against my sides, and a low, guttural moan escapes as the first orgasm sweeps over her.

"Fuck, I missed this," I murmur against her skin.

"Me too," she whispers.

I give her a minute to recover before I start again, tongue swirling and stroking, dragging up and down the length of her, dipping inside before I latch onto her clit, alternating soft suction with gentle teeth until she comes again.

I swipe a hand across my mouth and sit back on my knees. I rid her of her panties, then shuck off my pants, leaving me in a pair of black boxer briefs. My erection nudges the inside of her thigh as I tuck my knees under hers and spread her legs wide.

"You are fucking gorgeous." I brush a thumb over her clit. "Every inch of you." I drag my fingers lower and ease a single one inside, pumping several times before adding a second.

When I curl them forward, Clover's eyes flutter closed for a moment.

"There it is. That's what I was looking for." I withdraw, sucking my fingers into my mouth, groaning at the taste of her. "I could eat you all night."

"I'd rather you fuck me all night."

She reaches out and tries to pull me on top of her, but I ease my fingers back inside. "I *am* fucking you."

"With your cock, not your fingers." She groans when I curl them again.

I shake my head. "Not yet. We've been here before, Clover. You're not ready."

She stops arguing as I hover over her and drop to my elbow, the fingers of my other hand still moving inside her. Instead, she clutches my wrist and rides my hand to yet another orgasm.

Her hips drop back to the mattress, and she flops against the pillow. "You're a master at multiples."

"Anytime you're looking to stockpile orgasms, all you have to do is call. I'll drop whatever I'm doing and let you ride my hand or my face."

She laughs and then groans as I curl my fingers again, easing them out one at a time, my lips brushing over hers with each withdrawal.

"And then your cock, obviously." Clover pushes on my chest and I shift so I'm on my back.

I lift my hips, shoving my boxer briefs down my thighs. Once I've kicked them off, Clover moves to straddle me, settling over my erection on a soft sigh. Her tongue peeks out to run along her top lip, and she rolls her hips.

She leans down, sucking my bottom lip between her teeth, her long hair sweeping across my chest. "I can't wait to have you inside me again. Filling me up," she whispers against my lips.

I reach over to the nightstand where I set my wallet and flip it open. I free the gold-foil square and the small packet of lube, and Clover plucks the condom from my fingers. She shifts back on my thighs, tears open the wrapper, and pops out the latex circle. She rolls the condom down my length, and I get the lube ready.

"Just remember to take it slow." I sit up so we're chest to chest as she positions me at her entrance and starts to sink down.

"Don't worry, I haven't forgotten how hard it was to walk the next day."

I laugh, and so does she, but it turns into a mutual groan when she lowers herself another inch.

I put a hand on her hip and watch her face. Her eyes aren't on mine, though. They're trained on where she's stretched around my cock. Her fingers dip between her thighs, running over the still exposed shaft. "It's almost as thick as a soda can," she muses.

"The circumference is, like, an inch and a quarter less, which doesn't sound significant, but it is."

She throws her head back and laughs. I love how much fun she is in bed; how different it is to be with someone whose sexual appetite matches mine.

She settles her palm against my neck, her smile full of amusement. "Should I assume you've taken all the comparative measurements, then?"

I shrug. "Sort of helps to have a basis for comparison when you're in my position."

"I can see that." She lifts up and lowers herself a couple more inches, taking more of me inside. She exhales a shuddery breath.

"You okay?" I tighten my hold on her hip, keeping her

steady, breathing through the sensations, tamping down the urge to just . . . thrust.

"Mmm . . ." she hums and presses her lips to mine. "Better than okay." Hip roll. "So much better than okay." Slide down. "So full." Rise up.

She keeps rolling her hips, taking in more of me until her ass finally settles on my thighs. She adjusts her position and wraps her legs around my waist, curving her palm around the nape of my neck.

Clover presses her lips to mine, tongue stroking. I part and let her in, groaning as she starts rocking in my lap. The gentle friction makes me want more, but I let her set the pace.

She moves faster, sliding up the length of my cock, before dropping back down on a low moan. "This is even better than I remember."

I grip her hips to still her. "Go easy."

She shakes her head and repeats the same sequence, sucking in another gasping breath. "Oh my . . . fuck." Her eyes roll up and then return to mine. "Right there. Every time, you hit the spot." Her nails dig into my shoulder. "I'm going to come again." She drops one hand between us, fingers dragging up the shaft as she rises. "So fucking incredible." On the down slide, she circles her clit.

"Let me do that." I take over, mimicking her movements as she rides me.

She keeps moving, bouncing on my cock, faster, harder, groaning low in her throat every time her ass hits my thighs.

She drops her hand to cover mine. "More pressure. You're not going to break me." She moans.

"Like this?" I circle harder and faster, but she presses down, showing me exactly what she wants and how she wants it.

"Just like that," she says between labored breaths. "So good. Right there. So close." Her mouth drops open and then clamps shut, body going rigid as the orgasm rolls through her. I feel her clench around me, and I have to focus on her so I can keep myself in check the way I need to. I keep circling until her fingers curl around mine and her head drops to my shoulder.

I run a hand down her spine. "How you doin'?"

She chuckles, and her lips sweep along the side of my neck. She nips at my jaw and kisses her way back to my lips.

"I thought maybe I'd imagined how amazing the sex was. Or romanticized it, but clearly, I didn't." She sucks my bottom lip. "It's even better."

21

A Lot to Handle

"I want you on top of me." I start to shift, but Maverick's hand settles on my hips, and his fingers dig into the fleshy part of my ass.

"I don't know if that's a good idea."

"I think it's a great idea."

His hold tightens when I try to move. "I'm really jacked up, Clover."

"How do you mean?" I roll my hips, loving the way it feels to have him inside me again.

"I don't know if I can stay in control the way I need to if I'm on top." His jaw works, teeth grinding together, though not from anger. He's embarrassed . . . uncomfortable, maybe. "It's better for you like this."

I think about the sex we had back in August. It was incredible. The first time was in my bed, the second on the kitchen counter, and the third time was in the middle of the night. I'd pulled him on top of me, but he shifted us so I was straddling him again. Even when we ended up sixty-nining after the shower, I was on top—which makes sense considering his size and me needing control. But this is different.

"Okay." I nod my understanding. "What are you afraid will happen if you're not in control?"

"I'm too amped." His eyes fall closed when I shift again. "I could hurt you. Not on purpose, but I could."

I skim the edge of his jaw. "How would you hurt me?"

"I'm a lot to handle, which you already know."

"Mmm . . ." I follow the ropy muscles in his shoulders. "I've handled you fine so far, wouldn't you agree?"

His gaze shifts to mine, hot and desperate. "You've been on top. You're in control."

"So why don't I stay on top for now, and you can help guide me?"

"Okay." He laces our fingers together. "But if it gets to be too much, tell me, okay?"

"Of course, and you'll do the same?"

He nods once. I have to wonder what his past experiences have been like to make him so worried about hurting me. But it seems to be part of who he is. Even back when we were two people acting on attraction and nothing else, my pleasure was paramount. His self-awareness makes him an exceedingly conscientious lover—maybe more than he realizes, and maybe to his own detriment.

I move over him, taking him in deep and rising again, watching his expression, the tightness in his jaw, the strain in his neck. He's holding back.

I unlace our fingers and drag mine down his cheek. "You

always take such good care of me," I whisper, leaning in to kiss him. "I want to do the same for you."

He makes a sound, somewhere between a groan and a growl, but one hand settles on my hip and the other rests on my thigh, fingers flexing.

I lace my hands behind his neck. "Show me how you want me to move."

"This is good. You're good like this."

I suck his bottom lip between mine. "Show me, Maverick. I'll tell you if it's too much, but I already know this isn't enough for you."

He drops his chin, forehead coming to rest in the crook of my neck. Eventually he cups my ass and starts to lift and lower me, slowly at first, gently, but a dozen strokes in, his rhythm begins to falter.

"Don't stop." I bite his earlobe. "I want more of you. I want to feel you for days."

His hold on me tightens, and I brace my forearms on his shoulders, telling him how good he feels, that I want him deeper, that I need him to fuck me harder.

"I don't know . . . It feels too fucking good. I can't—"

I grip his chin in my palm and encourage him to meet my gaze. "I'm not made of glass, and you're not going to hurt me. Let go so I can too. I'm greedy for another orgasm, and I'm so close, Maverick."

I watch the shift happen behind his eyes, the uncertainty usurped by need and desire.

"I want to be under you." I bite his bottom lip and let it slide through my teeth.

He flips us over, his huge body hovering over me, hips sinking into mine, but he's still holding back.

"This is exactly what I needed." I wrap my legs around his waist and dig my heels into his ass, pulling him deeper on a low moan.

His forehead touches mine. "If it stops being good, tell me."

I pull his mouth down. "It won't, but if it does, I promise I'll tell you."

He nods once and slides his forearms under me, hands curling around my shoulders, arching my back and pushing my hips into the mattress. If I thought I was full before, it has nothing on the way I feel now.

He moves in long, slow strokes that hit deep and make my body sing. His gaze stays locked on my face, cataloging my expression, paying attention to my moans and sighs and gasps.

I run my fingers through his thick, damp hair, pushing it back, but it falls into place again, cutting across one eyebrow. A fine sheen of sweat breaks across his forehead as his thrusts gain speed and momentum. With every fill and retreat, he goes deeper, his hands anchoring me under him, preventing me from sliding up the bed and into the headboard, which incidentally, is hitting the wall with a repetitive *thump-thump-thump*.

"Just tell me if this position is too much." In one smooth surge, he folds back on his knees, me clinging to his shoulders as he adjusts his hold, cupping my ass so he can lift and lower me, faster and harder.

I can feel the orgasm building as Maverick's lip curls, and he makes a feral sound. "I'm gonna come," he warns.

"Yes, please." I caress the edge of his jaw. "Let me see you."

His hands curl over my shoulders, his hips lifting one last time as he holds me in place. His eyes fall closed, and I brush my lips over his. "Maverick, look at me."

His lids flip open and lock on me. "Just let go, so I can too."

His mouth drops open and then clamps shut with a snap. He shudders violently, and I rock my hips, chasing down my orgasm as I watch his wash over him. I feel him, not just around me and inside me, but on a deeper level—the kind of connection I've never experienced before. I suddenly understand it's what every relationship I've been in before now has been missing. It's always been just sex, but this is transcendental.

I feel simultaneously whole and broken. I can't and don't want to un-experience this, but even though this is supposed to be temporary, it's going to hurt like hell when it ends.

I have to enjoy it while it lasts.

Maverick takes my face in his hands and kisses me softly, indulging in a few strokes of tongue before he releases my lips.

"That was . . . intense. I haven't come like that since . . . I don't know." He shakes his head, and his eyes dart away. "The last time I was with you."

"You want to talk about why you don't like to be on top?"

He arches a brow. "You really want to talk about my sexual history when I'm still inside you and we're both rocking afterglow?"

"Is that your way of saying you don't want to talk about it?"

He looks to the side. "It's not my favorite topic."

"Your sexual history as a whole, or why you're so afraid of losing control?" I trace the outline of his collarbones.

"Both, I guess." His fingers trail up and down my spine.

"Should I assume that in the past you've caused one of your partners some discomfort and that's stuck with you?"

"In a nutshell, yeah." His gaze goes to the ceiling.

I caress his cheek. "Sex is a two-way street, and it requires a lot of communication. I love that you're careful and considerate, but whatever happened in the past, it's not all on you to be the one making sure everything is okay. It goes both ways. So, in the future, unless I tell you otherwise, you're more than welcome to pound me into the mattress like you're exorcising demons out of my pussy, okay?"

He laughs and cups my face in his hands, pressing a gentle

kiss to my lips. "Noted. Does that mean you're ready for round two?"

"Absolutely."

He wraps his arm around my waist, rolls us over so he's on top, and drops his mouth to mine. And we start again.

22

Space I Don't Want

MAVERICK

I wake up the next morning to the feel of something tickling my stomach. I blink a few times, my brain slow to come online—especially since I'm not in my own bed, or my house.

It only takes a few seconds before last night comes rushing back. Me showing up at Clover's unannounced. The sex. So much sex. I figured after the first time she'd need a break, or some pillow talk, or maybe some sleep. But no.

All those months of avoiding, then dancing around each other made us voracious.

And she's currently naked, kneeling beside me, hair sleep-messed and sex wild, her tongue pushing at her top lip. She runs a finger along my cock, which isn't quite awake yet either, but will be soon.

"What are you doing?" My voice is raspy and thick with sleep.

She startles and gasps. "Oh my God! I thought you were still asleep." Her cheeks flush with color.

"I was. Why are you creeping on my business?"

"Your business?" She arches a brow.

"Less-evolved head, penis maximus, Thor's hammer—pick your preferred name for my favorite appendage." I point to my cock, which is lying on my stomach, angled toward Clover.

She grins. "Thor's hammer? Is that what you call your fuck stick?"

I bark out a laugh. "Fuck stick?"

"It's actually more like a fuck log, but that doesn't roll off the tongue quite so nicely." She strokes a single finger from the tip to the base. "You know, this is like false advertising."

I fold an arm behind my head. "How so?"

"Your soft is someone else's generous hard."

"I'm a grow-er who should be a show-er, is that what you mean?"

"Yes!" Her eyes light up. "That's it exactly. Like, this should stay basically the same size and get hard. But it gets harder *and* bigger."

"It's the Waters curse," I tell her.

She hums distractedly. "Curse?"

"Yeah. Apparently stupidly huge fuck sticks run in my family."

"There must be a story that goes along with this." She keeps petting my cock, stroking up and down the length with her fingertip, and every time she does it, it grows.

"There is."

"Are you going to tell me?"

"Depends, I guess."

"On?" She runs her finger around the crown and over the slit, where it's weeping already.

"What you're planning to do when I stop growing."

She gives me a cheeky grin. "Log ride?"

I laugh, and my cock kicks under her touch. "Then I'll tell you the story after. I need to get you ready." I tap my lips. "Bring that pretty pussy up here so I can eat you before I fuck you."

FORTY-FIVE MINUTES LATER, I'm standing in Clover's kitchen in my dress pants and nothing else because she's wearing my button-down. The first thing she did was adjust the blinds so no one can see in. I pour myself a glass of water and down it, then fill it again and down another. It's nine in the morning. The holiday break has officially started. I have one last self-defense class to teach in a couple of hours, and then I'm supposed to head home for Christmas with my family. That's usually something I enjoy, but this year I'm not as excited to be in Lake Geneva when the person I want to spend time with—mostly naked—is standing right here.

Clover pushes up on her tiptoes, trying to snag the canister on the shelf second from the top. She's not particularly tall. I could grab it for her, but instead, I pick her up by the waist, lifting her a foot off the ground so she can reach it.

"You could probably bench press me," she says when I set her back on her feet.

"Oh yeah. You weigh what? A buck ten, a buck fifteen?"

"One twenty-five."

"I could press you for sure."

"I can lift a bag of potatoes over my head no problem." She

flexes her biceps with a grin and starts measuring out ingredients for pancakes.

I lean against the counter. "You know they have boxes of the stuff that only needs water, right?"

"Sacrilege." Her eyes are wide with horror. "Please tell me your diet doesn't consist solely of things like mac and cheese and pizza."

"Nah, we eat pretty good. My sister can cook, but she could also live off Lucky Charms. I need large quantities of carbs and protein, and my dad didn't want me or my brothers to be those guys who couldn't follow the directions on a package of pasta, so he used to take us to a cooking class once a month when we were kids. And when we were teenagers, we all had to take a night a week and make the meal, which we were happy to do, because my mom basically burns everything. She tries, but she cooks pork chops until they resemble shoe leather."

"What's your favorite thing to cook?"

"I like to barbeque in the summer, but I make a mean pot of chili. I'm also a fan of crockpot meals because I can throw everything together before I leave in the morning, and it's ready when I get home. And sometimes there are leftovers, unless Kody and my cousin come for dinner, which is often."

She dumps a teaspoon of baking powder into the mixing bowl, sets it on the counter, and turns to me. "You are very untwenty-one. When I was your age and in college, I lived on ramen and peanut butter sandwiches."

I shrug. "My mom eats like a ten-year-old. She'll eat candy for breakfast. But when you grow up in a house with an elite athlete for a father, you learn a lot about feeding your body for your sport."

"You've had to be responsible from a young age, haven't you?"

"I'm not always responsible. See my shitty midterm grades

this semester for details. And I'm pretty sure my advanced physiology exam didn't go all that well."

"Why do you think that?"

"Because I was busy working on my creative writing story and studied the wrong things. I'm sure I still passed, but not with the grade I'm capable of."

"I still don't understand why you picked a second-year creative writing class when you're in your final year of a kin degree, anyway." She cracks an egg and drops it into a measuring cup, whisking it to break the yolk.

I bite the inside of my cheek. "I needed an elective, and I'm pretty decent at essays, so I figured that would come in handy for the class. Although, essays and creative writing aren't the same at all, which I now know. I thought about taking an abnormal psych class, but it was at eight thirty on Monday morning, and creative writing was a night class."

Clover arches her brow at me.

"I also wasn't so sure I wanted to look all that closely at the darkness I carry around with me."

"I think the darkness comes from your family's trauma, but what I see more of is your kindness and selflessness."

"I think you're looking at me through rose-colored glasses, or orgasm-tinted ones, maybe." I try to brush it off with a joke, but Clover doesn't let it go.

"You put other people before yourself all the time."

"That's because when I put myself first, the people I care about get hurt." I sip my coffee.

"Do you mean what happened to your sister at the carnival?" Clover stops mixing batter to focus on me.

"That's one instance, yeah. Lavender needed people to look out for her, and sometimes I resented that. And it frustrated me that my best friend was in love with her before he even understood the concept," I admit.

"Those are normal, human emotions. We all have thoughts we shouldn't, Maverick, feel things we're ashamed of. Especially when we're young."

"I just wish I could take it back. If I hadn't acted selfishly, everything might have been different. Lavender wouldn't have endured all that trauma."

"You *all* endured the trauma, Maverick. Every member of your family was a victim, including you." She places a hand on my cheek, offering comfort I don't think I deserve, but I want it all the same.

"It's the what-ifs that are the hardest to deal with, you know? And now I have to go home, and the memories that float around up here . . ." I tap my temple. "Sometimes it's more than I know what to do with." I take her hand in mine. "The night I texted you, I tried to talk to my dad about it."

"Was that a first?"

I nod.

"What did he say?"

I shake my head. "He jumped to the conclusion that something was wrong with Lavender, so I dropped it."

"Oh."

"I can never tell him the truth, Clover—that it was my fault. Never. He can't know I left her behind on purpose. He'd never forgive me."

Her expression turns sad. "I wish you could see the man you are, instead of the boy who made a mistake. I see you, all of you—the good, the bad, and the broken. You are kind, Maverick. You are sweet and gentle and selfless. You will do anything in your power to protect the people you care about, even if it means you shut yourself off from them. I hated not being able to be there for you when we talked about this the last time, but I was so scared of the way I felt and all the lines I was afraid to cross. I'm glad I get to be someone you can talk to now."

I fold her in my arms and rest my chin on top of her head. "Can we stay here in this bubble for the holidays and forget the rest of the world exists?"

"I wish I could, but I'm flying to Florida this evening to see my parents."

I let her go and lean against the counter, glad to have a reason to change the subject, even if this one doesn't make me feel any better. "How long will you be gone?"

"I'm staying for two weeks. I planned it months ago." She sounds apologetic as she drops a pat of butter in the frying pan. "What about you? You're going home? I don't even know where that is."

"My parents live out on Lake Geneva. It's about a twenty-minute drive from your cabin in Pearl Bay. At least in the summer it is. We've got a lot of family out there. My dad's former teammates are like extended family, so there are a lot of get-togethers."

"They live there? I thought you were visiting your cousin." Clover's eyes flare as she pours batter into the pan.

"I usually spend part of my summer there, coaching kids' hockey camp with my dad and Kody. That'll end after this summer, though. Will you be back before New Year's?" I don't want this to be the only night I get with her, and I worry that two weeks is a lot of time to think.

"I will, yes." She flips the pancakes and turns the burner to low.

"Do you have plans?"

"Nothing concrete."

"Maybe you want to spend New Year's with me? I could come back here, or we could meet up at your cabin?" I tuck her hair behind her ear. "We could have a naked weekend—or longer, depending. Just you and me, before the winter semester starts."

Her hand comes up to cover mine. "I would like that."

"Good. Me too." I'm about to kiss her again, but the doorbell rings, and we both startle. "Is that your bestie?"

She glances at the clock and shakes her head. "She works Saturday mornings until eleven thirty, unless someone canceled a session." She crosses over to the kitchen window and peeks out the blinds. "Shit. What the hell is he doing here now?"

I don't like the tight feeling in my chest, or the sudden panic in her voice. "Is it your ex?"

"Yes. Dammit. I can't answer the door like this." She looks down at herself, wearing my shirt and nothing else, her hair a mess, smelling like me and sex.

"Do you want me to handle it?"

She presses her fingers to her temples. "No. Definitely not. He knows you're my student."

"I'm *a* student. Not your student anymore."

"Still. The optics are terrible. Fuck."

"Won't he leave, eventually?"

"My car is in the driveway. He knows I'm here. Or that if I'm out, I can't have gone very far." She grabs my hand and pulls me through the living room, checking to make sure the back deck is empty before dragging me into her bedroom.

"What do you want me to do?" She's right. The optics are bad. And her divorce is already complicated. While I don't care if her not-quite-ex knows I'm sleeping with her, I can see why *she* doesn't want him to know.

She pulls my shirt over her head and rushes to her dresser. She drags a pair of cotton panties up her thighs and grabs the mismatched bra from the floor while I put my shirt back on.

The doorbell rings again, followed by knocking. She pulls a sweater over her head and throws on discarded leggings she nabbed from the floor. "Can you leave through the sliding door?"

"Are you sure you want me to go?"

She pushes up on her toes and gives me a hasty peck on the lips. "He can't know you were here. The implications are just too . . . I'm sorry, Maverick. I'll call you later, okay?"

23

Close Call

"For the record, I don't love that this guy keeps showing up like this," Maverick says.

He doesn't fight me, though, letting me guide him toward the hallway. I go first to make sure the back deck is clear before I usher him out.

"Noted. Me either. We can talk about it later." I reach for the sides of my cardigan, but I'm not wearing one, so all I can do is cross my arms.

He jams his feet into his shoes, grabs his jacket, kisses me on the cheek, and slips out the sliding door. I'm grateful the snow from last night has already melted, otherwise it would be a lot harder to hide his hasty exit. I rush back down the hall, pulling my bedroom door closed on the way. My bed is a rumpled mess, and there are condom wrappers and empty lube packets littering the floor and the night table—all things I don't need Gabriel to see.

My plan is to tell him that continuing to show up at my house uninvited and without warning isn't appropriate, and that if this continues, I'm going to get my lawyer involved, and he can go through her. Do I want to spend four hundred dollars every time Gabriel feels he needs to reassess our division of assets? No. But I'm tired of the bullshit, and this was too close a call.

It's one thing for Gabriel to find out I'm sleeping with another man—and I'm entirely within my rights to do so, since we've been separated for nearly a year and a half. But finding out I'm sleeping with one of my former students? That's a recipe for disaster I don't want to learn how to make.

"What are you doing here?" I ask as I throw the door open.

Which is the moment my smoke alarm goes off.

I try to close the door in Gabriel's face, but he grabs the handle before I can shut it all the way. I debate my very limited options and let him into the house, because the alternative is my kitchen going up in flames and him seeing Maverick trying to steal his way down the street.

The pancakes are charred on the edges. Two plates sit on the counter. I quickly dump the pancakes into the sink, turning on the water. I hit the button for the fan on the stove and rush over to the window to let in some fresh air and get rid of the smoke.

Gabriel leans against the kitchen doorjamb, his arms crossed. His expression is passive, but he scans the room, eyes landing on the empty plates, then moving to the pair of coffee cups on the counter, and the full pot of coffee that's been sitting for more than an hour now, because of a distraction in the form of sex.

My stomach flip-flops. If the timing had been different, this could have gone very wrong.

"Am I interrupting?" Gabriel sweeps his hand out.

"Sophia's coming over for brunch." It's not a complete lie. Usually after her Saturday morning sessions, we have a late breakfast or early lunch. Like me, she's flying out to see her parents later today. We scheduled our flights so we could go to the airport together.

He makes a noise but doesn't comment otherwise.

"Why are you here anyway? I've already told you I'm not giving up the cabin. It's not up for discussion, and you don't even like it there."

"It has sentimental value for me now." He crosses over to the kitchen table and pulls a chair out. It scrapes loudly across the floor. "Aren't you going to offer me coffee?"

"No, because I'm not inviting you to stay. This needs to stop, Gabriel. You can't keep coming over unannounced and expect me to drop everything for you. If this is part of your strategy to win me back, it's pretty piss poor."

He drops into the chair, his expression remote. "I see you haven't calmed down since I was here last. I thought giving you some time to think would be enough, but apparently *elevated* is your new favorite state when I'm around. You know what might help?" He steeples his fingers under his chin and smiles serenely.

"You leaving would do the trick," I snap.

He pushes out of the chair and crosses the room in two quick strides. I take a step back and end up against the fridge. Gabriel grabs the handle and boxes me in with his other hand.

"What the hell are you doing?" My heart slams around in my chest. Gabriel was a lot of things when we were married—controlling, subversive, mean, spiteful, and at times verbally abusive—but he was never violent.

"You seem nervous, Clover. What are you hiding?" His expression shifts, and he leans in.

I duck out from under his arm and spin away from him, putting distance between us. "How else am I supposed to feel when you keep showing up uninvited?"

He plucks something from the counter.

A crane.

"This is an interesting new hobby."

"Stop touching my things."

He leans against the counter and inspects the paper crane. It's made from a Scrabble score sheet. Thankfully the number on it is not particularly visible. "When exactly is Sophia going to be here? I didn't see her car in the driveway."

"It's in the shop. Your welcome is worn out, Gabriel. I need you to go. Now."

"Why must it always be a fight with you?"

"Why must it always be mind games with you?" I shout.

"I don't deserve this anger. Everything I did, I did for you."

"Everything you did, you did so you could *control* me."

He sighs and drops his head, shaking it slowly. "I love you, Clover. But you are making it exceedingly difficult to be nice. I gave you space for a year. I didn't come after you, and I could have—*should* have, even. The only person you're making this harder on is yourself." He takes a step forward, and I pick up the closest heavy object, which happens to be a ceramic gnome I painted when I first moved to Pearl Bay.

They have a little store in town where you can paint and cure things. I don't really want to ruin it because it marks the beginning of me reclaiming my life, but I'm starting to feel like Gabriel is losing his mind, and I could end up in the trunk of his car if I'm not careful.

He sets the crane on the counter and gives me a disapproving look. "What are you doing?"

"You need to leave. Now."

"Good God, love, have you lost your mind?" He has the audacity to force his expression into a worried frown. "What are you honestly going to do with that?"

"Lob it at your head if you don't leave, after which I will call 911 and tell them that my estranged husband is in my house and refusing to leave."

His jaw clenches, and his nostrils flare. "Fine. Have it your way. But remember, this is on you when you realize you've made yet another mistake. When you eventually come to your senses, and you will, I may not be so nice about taking you back."

"The bullshit that comes out of your mouth is astounding." I hug the stupid gnome to my chest and follow him to the foyer, needing to see him leave so I can lock the door.

He pauses in the front entryway, gaze stopping on the red hoodie hanging from the hook—the one Maverick left here.

His eyes narrow. "Red isn't your color."

"It's the school color." Not untrue.

"It looks awfully big for you."

He reaches out to touch it, but I smack his hand. "Keep your hands off my things. And oversized hoodies are all the rage. Please don't stop by again unannounced. Or at all, really, unless it's to drop off the signed divorce papers."

He opens the door and pauses. "Aren't you going to visit your parents over the holidays?"

"It's none of your business."

"Of course not. Well, have a merry Christmas."

When I don't respond in kind, he steps over the threshold. It looks like he's about to say something else, but I close the door before he can and lock it.

I lean back against it and glance at Maverick's hoodie hanging on the hook. What a stupid place to leave it, for anyone who comes to visit to see. It's gigantic. It's more like a dress on me. Thank God the lettering on the back spelling out HOCKEY wasn't visible. I pluck it from the hook and carry it back to my bedroom, where I hang it in my closet.

I still need to pack for my flight tonight.

And clean up my bedroom.

My thighs are already sore, and my butt hurts like I did a million squats.

As I'm picking up the discarded wrappers and tied-off, cum-filled condom bombs lying on the floor beside my bed, my phone pings.

I have a message from Maverick. His name isn't applied to his contact, still coming up as a phone number because I didn't want to make it conspicuous. Or maybe it's more conspicuous without a name attributed to it.

> Checking to make sure you're okay

I respond right away.

> Everything's fine. He's gone and Soph is coming over

He offers to come back, but I'm aware he has to teach self-defense this morning, and that it would be better to wait a bit, just to make sure Gabriel isn't going to return. I tell him I'll be fine, but to message when he's done with his self-defense class.

I bring my phone with me to the kitchen so I can work on cleaning up that mess. On the upside, the smell of burned pancakes, while unpleasant, does a lot to help cover the smell of sex, latex, and Maverick's cologne, which I can still smell on myself.

Sophia shows up half an hour later. "Why does it smell like burned food in here?"

"Because I burned food."

She sets the takeout cups from our favorite local coffee place on the table and scans the kitchen, eyes narrowed. I drop down in the chair, and she takes the one across from me while I fill her in on everything that's happened, from Maverick coming over last night, to the mind-blowing sex, and then Gabriel showing up without warning and Maverick having to sneak out the back door. "I slept with my student, Soph," I conclude. "Again."

"Well, technically you slept with him before he was your student and then again when he became your *former* student, so this can't come back on you as professionally or ethically damning."

"But morally." I press my fingertips against my eyes. "How will this look?"

Sophia sighs. "If you were planning on making a career as a professor, I would be concerned, but you're covering a sabbatical, and you have a PhD in library science. This job was a stopgap and a way to pay for this divorce. Nothing more. I guess the question now is, are you planning to *keep* sleeping with him?"

"It's not a good idea."

"That's not a no."

"He wants to spend New Year's with me." I tap my lips.

"What did you say to that?"

"Yes, but I probably shouldn't have."

"Because you think he's too young, or because he was your student?"

"Both. I don't even know what I'm doing anymore, Soph."

"You're having hot sex with a hot jock who you have incredible chemistry with. The age difference is irrelevant. There are lots of people who end up in relationships with their former students. Lots."

"Usually it's female students and their much-older male professors. And how many times have we passed judgment on those professors?"

"It's the married ones who cheat on their wives that I judge."

"I'm married." I point at myself.

"Not because you want to be. Gabriel has been dragging this out forever, and that's not on you. Maybe it's good that you're going to see your parents for a couple of weeks. Weigh the pros and cons. But your job here is temporary, and Maverick has a career in professional hockey ahead of him."

"I know. This whole thing is temporary—my job *and* what's going on with him."

"Enjoy it while it lasts, then. Lord knows you've spent the last two years in and then trying to escape a relationship with a serious power imbalance. You deserve to have some fun."

"Do you think that's why I'm attracted to him? Because he's younger and not established?"

"You're attracted to him for a lot of reasons. One of them being that he's hot as hell. He's also built like Adonis and apparently has the dick of the ages. Plus he's proven to be a caretaker and a protector. And he's experienced some trauma of his own that you can empathize with. You connect. And maybe it helps to know it doesn't ever have to be something serious. I've known you for a lot of years, Clover. You're a good person. You married the wrong man, and he threw your world into upheaval. Maverick is nothing like him, and I'm sure that's very appealing." She reaches across the table and squeezes my hand. "Try not to overthink this too much. But if you can't handle the guilt that comes with it, that's okay. You have the next couple of weeks to breathe and figure things out."

After Sophia and I have a non-burned brunch, she heads upstairs to her apartment to pack, and I return to my bedroom to do the same. While I'm looking forward to seeing my parents, what's going on with Maverick weighs heavy on my mind. Twenty minutes before Sophia and I leave for the airport, he messages.

I stare at the message for long seconds before I respond.

His response is immediate.

My heart keeps skipping beats, telling me how much of a mess I am over this man.

The dots appear and disappear a couple of times, and then there's a knock at the patio door. I rush down the hall and open it, letting in the cold winter air along with him. His gaze moves over my face on a slow, assessing sweep. "How are you?"

"Okay. You?"

"Worried you're going to do a lot of thinking over the next two weeks, and it's not going to be in my favor."

I smile, but it's strained, and I drop my head, struggling with the emotions that have been plaguing me all day.

Instead of saying more, he wraps his arms around me and pulls me against his chest. "Whatever you need from me, I'll give it to you."

"It was a close call this morning."

"You're freaked out, huh?" I feel his lips against my temple.

"Nothing about this is simple," I murmur against his chest.

He releases me and takes my face between his warm palms. "Well, one thing is simple. We share some pretty wicked chemistry." He slants his mouth over mine, and I grip his wrists, allowing myself to stop thinking about all the ways this could go wrong. Instead, I get lost in the kiss and wish we had more time.

"Okay! I'm all set to go. Oh! Hey now." The sound of Sophia's voice has Maverick releasing me and stepping back, elbow hitting the door, his expression full of concern and questions.

"She knows," I assure him.

He looks back and forth between us, tips his chin in my direction and asks Sophia, "She say good things about me?"

"Says you're the best she's ever had."

He grins. "The best, huh?"

I give Sophia an incredulous look. "Seriously?"

She shrugs. "That's what you said."

"Like he needs his ego inflated." I poke Maverick in the chest. "Wipe that smirk off your face."

"Sorry, Professor Sweet . . . as pie." His grin widens.

I purse my lips. "We need to leave for the airport."

"I know. I'm heading to Lake Geneva soon. Open this on Christmas Day." He tucks a small box into my purse. "I'll be thinking about you. A lot. Mostly while I'm in the shower. And bed." He tucks his finger under my chin and angles my head so he can kiss me. Chastely this time. "Call me when you land."

"Okay."

"Later, bestie." He winks at Sophia and slips out the back door.

"So, just a fling, huh?" Sophia says as I lock the door and follow her down the hall.

"I'm in the middle of a divorce. It can't be anything more than that."

She's undeterred. "You're in deep already, aren't you?"

I sigh. "I think so."

"Well, no matter what, you deserve to have this. Better to have lusted and lost than never to have lusted at all, right?"

I laugh, but it's already so much more than lust, even with all the boundaries I had in place until now. I have no idea what condition my heart is going to be in by the time it ends.

As much as I'd like to be able to cut ties and walk now, to not come back for New Year's, my body misses him already. And my head? Well, it's a mess.

24

Home for the Holidays

MAVERICK

As I arrive in Lake Geneva late on Saturday night, a full day and a half after my siblings, I get a message from Clover telling me she's made it to Florida and that she needs a little time to think things through.

That gnawing feeling that settled in my gut when I had to sneak out of her house this morning like a sordid secret grew all day long. Even when I had a chance to drop off a Christmas present and say goodbye, it didn't ease up.

And now I know why.

I can't blame her for needing time—not when she's still trying to get out of her marriage and her ex is showing up whenever the fuck he wants. While there isn't anything wrong with what we're doing, I get the issue. I'm sleeping with my hot former professor. She's sleeping with a former student.

Six months from now, she'd be sleeping with a professional hockey player.

Timing is a real jerk.

I park my truck beside my sister's car and send a single message in return:

> Backing off. I'll wait to hear from you.

The humping dots appear and disappear several times.

So I send one more message, to alleviate as much guilt as I can for her.

> You don't need to placate me. I know there's more at stake for you. I'd rather you say nothing at all than give me lip service. I think I've already proven I can be patient.

My finger hovers over the button for almost a minute before I press send.

Twenty seconds later, my phone rings. I blow out a breath, nerves making my throat feel tight. I wonder if this is how any of the girls I've ever dumped have felt. And if it is, I owe a lot of apologies.

I answer on the third ring. "Hey."

"Don't let me off the hook like that," Clover says. "I knew what I was signing on for when I opened the door and let you into my house and my . . . life."

"You set boundaries, and I kept trying to push them over."

"And I let you." She sighs. "I'm trying to sort out my feelings. And my motivation. I just need some time."

"I get it. Try not to overthink things too much." I flip the paper crane I keep on my dash between my fingers.

"That's not my strong suit, but I'll do my best. Enjoy your time with your family."

"You too."

I end the call feeling worse instead of better, which is something I'm not used to. This isn't like my usual casual flings, where I can put my feelings in a box and leave them there. With Clover, I finally got what I'd been wanting since I walked into her classroom. Or even before that, when I left the crane at her place in Pearl Lake. Only now that I've had a taste of what it could be like, I want more. I feel the physical distance in more than just the states that separate us. I don't know how to define the emotion, but the usual warmth I feel when I think about Clover has been replaced with a tightness in my chest that I don't know how to alleviate.

I grab my bag from the back seat, half-hoping everyone is in bed already, but I can see the glow of the TV from the living room as I make my way up the front steps of the wraparound porch.

I stand there, breath leaving me in cold bursts, psyching myself up to deal with whoever is awake and shoving down the worry that over the next two weeks, Clover is going to decide the risks outweigh the orgasms.

There's nothing I can do about it.

Considering how much of a mess my head is already, I should probably cut and run—tell her it's not a good idea to keep doing this. For her sake. But I don't want to.

I open the door and step inside the front foyer. Lavender and River's shoes sit on the mat next to the door, and I toe mine off too, putting them beside River's and hanging my coat in the closet. I set my bag at the foot of the stairs.

I'd avoid everyone, but that will raise red flags, so instead, I grab a beer from the fridge and a bag of chips from the pantry—my mom has stocked up on all our favorites—and cross through to the living room.

My sister and mom are curled up on the couch, watching a Marvel movie, a bowl of popcorn on the cushion between them. A glass of white wine—probably a Riesling, if I had to guess, since that's my mom's favorite—sits on the side table beside her. Lavender has some kind of cooler. She's not legal to drink yet, but my dad is Canadian, and the drinking age in Canada is nineteen in most provinces, so that's always been Lavender's defense. Besides, she likes the sugary drinks you'd have to consume in mass quantities to even get a buzz, and she usually limits herself to one or two.

"Hey! My favorite second-born son is finally home. I was starting to worry about you. I'd thought you'd be here for dinner." Mom throws off the blanket and opens her arms.

I set the beer and bag of chips on the side table beside my dad's lounger and fold my mom into a hug.

"Sorry, my shift at the gym ran a little longer than anticipated, and I had a few things I needed to take care of at the house before I left."

"It's okay. You're here now. Did you eat dinner? Can I heat something up for you? Lavender made shepherd's pie. I can make a plate for you."

"I'm good. I grabbed dinner in Chicago. Where's Dad?"

"He was snoring, so we sent him to bed," Lavender says. She tosses a piece of popcorn in the air and tries to catch it with her mouth, except she misses and it rolls to the floor.

"He had an early morning and a busy day," Mom adds. Her

gaze moves over my face, and her hands rest on my biceps. "You look tired, honey. Lots of late-night studying?"

I nod. "Yeah. I'll catch up over the break."

She *hmms* and picks a piece of lint off my shirt. "Some of the boys are planning to go to the arena early tomorrow morning, so be prepared for a knock on your door first thing. And then your dad and I are taking off for a couple of days with the rest of the old people."

"Another one of those last-minute vacay deals Dad couldn't resist organizing?" They do this almost every year—disappear for a couple of days with their friends right before the family descends for the holidays.

"Mmm . . . You know what he's like. We'll only be gone for two nights. Then the grandparents will arrive. I'll leave all the details for you."

"Okay. Sounds good." At least it gives me a couple of days to shake the funk I'm in. Hopefully.

The final credits start to roll.

"I'm going to bed, but you two are welcome to watch whatever you want." She kisses me on the cheek. When she pulls back, her expression is questioning. "What's the smell?"

I sniff my shirt. "Laundry detergent?"

She shakes her head. "It's citrusy and festive? Like, cloves, maybe?"

"Dunno. Soap or something probably." I force myself to maintain eye contact. I know exactly what the smell is. Clover's body wash, shampoo, and hand soap are all the same brand.

She pats my shoulder. "Well, whatever it is, it smells nice. See you two in the morning." She crosses over and kisses Lavender on the cheek, then heads down the hall.

I drop down on the other end of the couch from my sister.

"You're arriving rather late." She pops a piece of popcorn into her mouth and doesn't miss this time.

"I had shit to take care of."

She gives me the eye, sets her popcorn on the table, and leans across the couch until she's only a couple inches away from me.

"What are you doing?"

She grabs my shirt and sniffs loudly. "You smell like . . . a woman."

"I ran out of my body wash and had to use what was available."

"Why didn't you tell Mom that?" She sits back, eyeing me with suspicion.

"Why does it matter?"

She nods several times, slowly. "Answering a question with a question. I'll let it go for now, but I think you're hiding something. Or someone."

"Whatever. Where's River?"

"Probably sexting Josiah. He should tell Mom and Dad he's gay already, and then Josiah could come here for New Year's or something."

"I don't understand why he's dragging his feet on this."

"Probably because he doesn't want to have an awkward conversation with either of them about safe anal."

"Well, that's legit." I make a face. "I can't even imagine what that conversation would look like with Dad. I feel like he'd be all concerned about Josiah with the Waters curse and all." I point to my crotch unnecessarily.

Lavender spit-sprays her cooler and swipes the back of her hand across her mouth. "Oh my God. The conversations with Josiah are way TMI."

"What do you mean?"

"Sometimes Josiah forgets River is my twin and there are things I don't want to know about his sex life." She gives me an arched eyebrow.

"Ah. Well, here's to awkward conversations with best friends." I clink my beer bottle against her cooler.

"You don't have plans tomorrow, do you? I mean besides the ice time with Dad in the morning." Lavender changes the subject.

"Nope, not that I'm aware of, why?"

"I'm supposed to hang out with the twins. Just girls. It'd be great if you spent some time with Kodiak and the rest of the guys."

"I was planning to text him. Where is he anyway?"

"He had some thing with his mom. He wanted me to come with, but he needs time with his family, and I needed to hang out with Mom so she could ask me a million questions about how things are going. She was asking about you, FYI, and how I thought you were doing. I think she's worried, so don't be surprised if she corners you at some point and digs for information."

I rub the back of my neck. "No one needs to worry about me."

Lavender rolls her bottle between her palms. "That's their job, Mav. And until this year, I've taken the front seat for all the worrying, but now that I'm handling college away from home, and I have a steady boyfriend, they get to shift their focus else-where, and you seem to be the target. I thought you'd like a heads-up."

"Thanks. I appreciate it." I sigh. "It must have been a pain in the ass, always having them watching over you like that."

Lavender shrugs. "Sometimes it felt like I lived inside a bubble. I get it, though. I'm the only girl, and things were kind of messy when I was a kid. The overprotectiveness was their way of dealing with what happened at the carnival. The reality is, bad things happen to good people every day, and at the risk of sounding cliché, what doesn't kill us makes us stronger. I'm me because of what I've been through, and I know every single person in this family holds their own bag of guilt over that night, including me."

"You didn't do anything wrong."

"Didn't I?" Lavender tips the bottle back and swallows the last mouthful of her cooler. "The only reason I wanted to go in the funhouse was because everyone else was going." Her teeth run over her bottom lip. "And Kodiak. Everything was always about him." She rolls her eyes at herself. "It still is. And it always will be. I knew I should have stayed put and waited for someone to come get me, but I panicked. If I'd stayed where I was, that lunatic wouldn't have taken me. Or if I'd stayed with Mom and Dad, Robbie wouldn't have felt bad for rushing through the funhouse so he could keep reading. You and Kodiak wouldn't feel bad for going on ahead. River wouldn't feel bad for losing his grip on me.

"So many things might have been different. Our lives might have been different. But I can't go back and change things. I can't undo what's already been done." She sighs and extends her arm, hand palm-up on the couch cushion between us, most of the pale, crescent-shaped scars are barely visible. "I don't know what your bag of guilt feels like, Mav. But I think sometimes it's heavier than it should be."

I set three fingers in her open palm, and she curls hers around mine. "I just wish we would have waited. The hardest is not knowing what happened while you were missing."

Lavender rests her cheek against the cushion, and her expression shifts, sadness passing through her eyes and then understanding. "The memories are really spotty, and mostly I was just scared. He kept calling me Cali. And I think he was drunk or high, or both. He wasn't in his right mind. I don't know that I could comprehend that at the time. It seemed like he thought I was his daughter. He didn't make a whole lot of sense. I remember trying to dig my heels in and trying to scream, but all the sound got stuck." She taps her throat.

"You don't have to talk about this," I tell her, suddenly not sure this is making anything better at all. "I don't want you to relive all this shit." And part of me is scared to hear it, because what if my worst nightmare is true? What if all the bad things I worried about did happen?

She squeezes my hand. "It doesn't help any of us to pretend like it didn't happen. And maybe part of the problem is that we've tiptoed around it so much and it's left a lot of holes for you to climb into."

"I know what that hour looked like for me, but I don't know what it looked like for you." And maybe the not-knowing was a punishment I inflicted on myself for letting her down the way I did.

She nods. "He kept telling me not to scream and that if I did, I'd never see my mom again, which is why I did that stupid thing with my nails. I was just . . . so fucking scared. Kodiak had those candies in the pocket of the sweatshirt he gave me—Jolly Ranchers—so I kept tossing them on the ground, hoping it would make me easier to find. Then he brought me to that shed or whatever it was. He told me to stay put and stay quiet, and then he locked the door and left me in the dark. I stayed there until Dad and Kodiak found me. But he didn't hurt me, if that's what you're worried about." Her voice is soft but strong. "I mean, I had bruises, and he wasn't exactly gentle, but he didn't *do* anything to me. Mostly the whole thing just scared the shit out of me."

It's so hard to swallow. "He didn't . . . ." I can't even finish the question, can't get the words out, and I wonder if this is what Lavender felt like as a kid, choked by her own voice.

"No. He thought I was his daughter. He didn't hurt me like

that. He was out of his mind, but he wasn't a monster. He was broken."

I drag a hand down my face, relief warring with the guilt that still slices through me. Knife wounds that never seem to heal. "Fuck. I'm sorry. I just . . . I didn't know."

"I wish I'd known how much you were struggling with this. I would have told you all of this sooner." She slides over and wraps her arms around me, and I hug her hard, probably harder than I should, but she squeezes me back fiercely.

Eventually I release her, and she sits back. "It's not just my trauma, Mav. It happened to all of us. Our whole family suffered because of it. I've spent a lot of time talking about it in therapy, working through it all, but I think maybe it's been different for you because you hold your cards close to the vest."

I grit my teeth against the emotions climbing my throat. "Sometimes I fucking hate myself for not waiting."

"Oh, Mav, no." Her eyes soften and shine with tears. "You've always been my biggest ally, and I know that can't have been easy for you. You've lived in an impossible situation your entire life. You've had to play so many roles. I see it. I know the lengths you went to in order to keep me from being more over-protected than I already was." She squeezes my hand again. "You're an awesome older brother."

I shake my head. "I'm not awesome. I've done a lot of selfish things."

"You've done more selfless things. Shift the focus forward. We can't live in our pasts, or they'll drag us down and keep us locked up." She smiles softly. "It was never your fault. It was a fluke. A terrible one, and the only person truly at fault is the man who took me. Stop punishing yourself for being an eight-year-old boy who wanted to run through a funhouse with his best friend."

"How the fuck did you get this wise?"

"Fifteen years of therapy and a lot of reading. I'm worried about you," she says softly.

"I'm okay. I promise." I squeeze her hand. "Thank you for this, though. It helps a lot."

"Anything for you, big brother." She releases my hand and pushes to a stand. "I need to pee. And go to bed. And so do you because Dad will get you up stupid early. He was giddier than a toddler jacked up on sugar about the fact that he would have someone to play hockey with."

The abrupt shift jars me, but when she holds out her arms, I stand and accept another hug.

"I love you. Take it easy on yourself." She pats me on the back and disappears down the hall, leaving me alone with her words and my thoughts.

And I feel . . . good. Lighter. For the first time ever, I have a tiny seed of hope that maybe I'll be able to let go of the past and start living in the present.

"RISE AND SHINE! Get your ass out of bed. We've got ice time in an hour!"

"Seriously? You need to knock before you bust into my room in the morning, Dad!"

"I did knock. And I texted you and called four times. You have the rest of the holidays to sleep in. We rented the arena for three hours, we're playing dads versus kids before your mom and I take off for a couple of days. I have those fritters you're so fond of waiting downstairs."

I glance at the clock on my nightstand. It's seven in the morning, which is considered sleeping in during the regular hockey season. We often have practice at five thirty. "You drove to Pearl Lake to get fritters?"

"No, they have a new location here. You have fifteen minutes to get dressed. Meet me in the kitchen." He closes the door behind him.

I roll over and pick up my phone. I have a bunch of messages. A group text that includes BJ, the Butterson twins, Kody, and Quinn, and several messages from my dad telling me to get my ass out of bed. There's nothing from Clover. I should expect this, but I don't love it.

I take care of my morning wood, get dressed, and head downstairs to the kitchen. The smell of fresh fritters makes my mouth water. Two travel coffee mugs sit on the counter, along with a box of fritters, and next to that is River, who clearly hasn't bothered to brush his hair and is about as awake as I am.

He, however, is shoveling fritters into his face and gripping his coffee cup.

"Morning, sunshine." I try to reach into the box, but he swats the back of my hand with his fork and wraps his arm protectively around the fritters.

"These are mine." He points to a second box. "Those are for you."

"You're in a good mood."

"It's the fucking holidays. I'm supposed to be sleeping." He stabs another fritter and takes a huge bite out of it, groaning. "These are so good." His phone buzzes on the table, and he glances at the screen before quickly flipping it over.

Dad appears in the kitchen a few seconds later. "We're all set. Grab your coffees and your breakfast and let's roll."

"I don't know why I have to come. I play football, not hockey," River grumbles, but he pushes back his chair, grabs his box of fritters, and heads for the door. I do the same, minus the grumbling.

We pile into Dad's truck, River claiming the back seat. His phone is in his hand almost immediately. Mine keeps buzzing in my pocket, but the only person I want to talk to is Clover. And she needs space, so I get to talk to my dad, instead.

"What time did you get in last night, son?"

"It was late. I had a few things to take care of after my shift at the gym."

He nods a few times and taps the steering wheel. "Would one of those things you had to take care of be a girlfriend?"

"No, Dad. No girlfriend. I told you, I'm taking a break from the dating scene. Besides, next semester is going to be heavy. I have bio-chem, which isn't my favorite subject."

"Kody could probably help you with that."

Talking about school makes me think about Clover, which makes me wonder what's waiting for me after the holidays, so I change the subject. "Maybe. When is Gram-pot coming down?"

"Him and Grandma Daisy are supposed to be here the day after your mom and I get back. And Grandpa Sid and Gigi should arrive on Thursday."

"Cool, cool." I love it when my grandparents come to visit. Gigi tells us all kinds of cringeworthy stories about my mom, and Gram-pot is a weed scientist and always has the best edibles. During the season, I don't partake, but he sneaks me a couple of low-dose brownies when he visits.

When we arrive at the arena, the entire Butterson clan, minus the twins, is already there, as well as Kody, his younger brother, Dakota, BJ and Quinn, and their dads. Darren Westinghouse, my dad's long-time best friend and former teammate, is also there, plus Ryan Kingston and Bishop Winslow, two of the guys my dad used to coach back in the day. They're tight with Kody's parents and ended up buying property on Pearl Lake too. They're retired from the league now, and my dad invited them to be part of the not-for-profit hockey training program he and my uncle Miller set up several years back.

We spend the next three hours playing hockey. It should be fun, but I'm hyperaware of how awesome Kody is on the ice, and how much I feel like I'm struggling to keep up these days—especially with all these former NHL players skating circles around me. And River, despite having picked football as his sport of choice, can keep up with the best of them. And then there's BJ, doing fucking leaps and twirls and still managing to get the puck in the net.

I fumble an easy pass from Kody and follow it up by shooting wide and missing the net. Instead of keeping my shit together and laughing it off, I throw my stick across the ice.

My dad calls a time-out and picks up the stick, then skates me over to the bench. "You don't need to be so hard on yourself. There aren't any scouts watching."

"I'm underslept, stressed about my grades and shit." I tip my head back and squeeze some water into my mouth.

He puts a hand on my shoulder. "You don't have to be perfect, Maverick. Sometimes we're just playing to play."

I nod, biting back an asshole retort. I don't know why I'm being like this. He's just trying to be positive. "I know, Dad. I'll get it together."

But I don't. I keep missing easy passes and fumbling the puck. It's embarrassing. And I hate it even more that every single dad/former NHL pro keeps trying to give me positive feedback, telling me we all have bad days on the ice. What they don't realize is that I'm starting to have more bad days than good. While Kody keeps gaining confidence, I keep losing it.

Afterward, we go for brunch, and Kody and I end up beside each other, our dads talking pros and what we can expect with the new draft class this spring. Kody is excited, but it makes me stressed. BJ's dad, my uncle Randy, is sitting next to Rook, Kody's dad, half paying attention to our conversation. BJ is at the other end of the table with Quinn and the rest of the Buttersons. Even Laughlin, the only Butterson with dark hair and a black-cloud personality to match, is down there laughing and joking around.

Uncle Randy, who is sitting almost across from me, strokes his beard, gaze bouncing between Rook, my dad, me, and Kody. "You know . . ." He grabs the last breadstick. "It's gotta be rough for you boys, always listening to these two wax poetic about hockey like it's the only sport in the world."

Both Rook and my dad frown.

"That's not true," my dad says.

"We played hockey for three hours, and you've been talking about hockey since we sat down at the table. These boys live and breathe it, and it's only December. They've got a whole semester before they need to worry about this stuff. Give them a break."

That seems to do the trick, and we shift topics, talking about holiday plans and mundane shit, like how Kody's sister, Aspen, is handling high school and how she broke up with her boyfriend because her robotics program was taking up too much of her time.

Eventually we head back to the house, and I'm grateful when our parents finally leave to catch their flight, getting me out of any more talks with my dad—at least until they return from their getaway.

25

The Inside Out of It

MAVERICK

The next couple of days are low-key. I hang with Kody and the guys, not playing much hockey. I need the break.

Then when my parents get back, I'm immersed in family time. That means lots of time on the ice rink my dad has in the backyard. I miss having my older brother, Robbie, around. He's been out in the wilderness of British Columbia for the past year with his girlfriend, doing pot research and living the life. I don't think he's going to be back this way anytime soon, other than a yearly summer visit. That's unfortunate, because he's good at occupying my dad's time with things like Scrabble. Ironically, I also love Scrabble, but my dad's default with me is always hockey.

I want to be in a better frame of mind, especially after that conversation with Lavender. I should be able to put the parts of my past that haunt me back in their coffins, but with everything that's currently going on, I still feel like I'm skating at the edge of a cliff.

On Wednesday, Gram-pot and Grandma Daisy arrive, and on Thursday, Gigi and Grandpa Sid show up. The house is full of family and festivities, but I can't seem to get into the holiday spirit.

Even with all the awesome food in the house, my appetite is for shit, and I can't get a decent night's sleep. I keep dreaming about getting lost, and when I find a staircase, it goes down, down, down, getting darker and darker. But I can't go back up, because every time I turn around, there's a wall behind me.

I want to reach out to Clover, but I don't know if I should.

She's all I can think about. From the moment I wake up in the morning to those semiconscious minutes before sleep pulls me under, she's on my mind.

And I miss her.

I feel like I'm coming down with something. Food tastes wrong. Life seems like it's shrouded in a gauzy film of gray.

I watch the way my sister and Kody are together, stealing secret glances and furtive touches, sneaking off when they think no one is paying attention and returning twenty minutes later, Lavender wearing a smirk and Kody looking even more jacked up than usual.

The night before Christmas Eve, we have a big dinner, which is basically the only kind of dinner we have around here during the holidays. But since my mom can't actually cook, and Lavender, me, and River can't be responsible for making a meal for thirty-plus people, we have it catered.

Gram-pot and I are playing a game of Scrabble—again, normally Robbie would play against him. Gram-pot glances around the living room to make sure no one is paying atten-tion to us before he rummages in his pocket and produces a baggie. He slides it across the table. "You look like you need this."

I glance down at the bag. Inside are two double-chocolate cookies.

"I'd only eat one of those, though. Otherwise, you'll be drooling on the floor in an hour."

"You speaking from experience?"

"Your grandma was not impressed when I passed out in my lounger so hard that I peed myself."

I'm in the middle of a sip of scotch—I mixed it with ginger ale when my dad wasn't looking because I can't stand the taste of the stuff—and I start choking. I slam my fist into my chest a few times and cough, clearing my throat. "Are you serious?"

"As a heart attack."

"You're almost eighty, Gram-pot. You should probably stop using that phrase."

He waves a hand around in the air. "Ack, we all go some-time. I hope my end is swift like a reaper in the night." He makes a circle around his face. "What's eating at you, Mav? You're not your usual happy-go-lucky self."

I focus on my tiles. "Just got a lot on my mind. Final semester of my degree, contract talks coming, and all that."

"What about woman problems? You got any of those?"

"Nah. No woman problems." I open the baggie and pop a cookie into my mouth.

"Not ready to talk about it, then."

I give him an arched brow. "There's nothing to talk about."

"I remember what your dad was like when he messed things up with your mom by being a grade-A jackass. He wore the same mopey expression you're sporting. Walked around like Eeyore, moaning about how he lost the best thing that ever happened to him. And over a fucking endorsement campaign. It was ridiculous." He shakes his head. "Lucky for him, your mother is an understanding woman. I don't think the good genetics hurt him much either." He starts laying tiles and spells the word C-U-S-H.

"Those two are a couple of weirdos."

"Well, the apple doesn't fall far from the tree. And when you're looking at the same kind of career as your dad, if that's still your plan . . ." He gives me a somewhat skeptical look. "You need someone who's going to stand beside you and keep you grounded. Your dad found that in your mom, and when he realized what he had, he was pretty relentless in his pursuit. I have a feeling you'll be the same."

"I guess in time we'll see." I tally his points and huff a laugh when I realize what the letters I have will spell if I use the C from Gram-pot's *cush*.

Even when I try not to think about her, there she is.

By the time we're called for dinner, I'm feeling the cookie I ate. My mom asks me to fold the napkins, like I always do for events like this, but I keep messing them up, so they look like a bunch of cranes that have flown into the sides of houses. It also takes me way longer than usual. And I eat an entire bowl of olives in the process, leaving oily fingerprints on all the cranes.

On the upside, I have an appetite. I eat enough to put myself in a food coma.

My mom stops me on my way up to my room. "Gram-pot gave you one of his cookies, didn't he?"

"How'd you know?"

"Your eyes are all bloodshot, and you ate an obscene amount of scalloped potatoes at dinner."

"I love scalloped potatoes."

"I know. But you're definitely high."

"Are you going to tell Dad?" He'll be pissed if he knows I ate a cookie. The team does random drug tests, and after the winter holidays is prime testing time. Same with after spring break. Everyone knows it. Me included.

"Of course not."

"Are you going to make me tell him?"

She shakes her head. "No, but don't think I haven't noticed that you and River have switched roles. He's all happy and chatty, and you're all . . . morose and reclusive."

"I'm fine, Mom. I promise. But I need to lie down."

"Okay. I guess I'll have to take your word for it." She steps aside. "But I will be pinning you down over the next few days to have a chat. Don't think you'll get to leave without at least one mother-son bonding sesh."

"They're my favorite anyway." I lean down and kiss her on the cheek as I pass.

I climb the stairs to my bedroom, close the door, and shut the lights off. I nap hard for a couple of hours but wake up around ten thirty and can't force my brain to shut back down.

I grab my phone and peruse the messages from the guys. An hour and a half ago, they messaged to ask if I was coming out. At this point, there's zero chance I'm leaving the house. Besides, I don't feel like doing the whole social thing.

I hit the bathroom, relieve myself, and dig through the vanity for some eye drops.

Then I lie back down and scroll through social media. Kody's feed is full of hockey pictures and Lavender. Mine is full of . . . nothing. The last thing I posted was hockey practice a few weeks ago.

Clover has an IG account, but obviously I've never followed her because that would be stupid as fuck. But it doesn't mean I haven't creeped on her a couple of times. Most of the time she posts pictures of flowers or dinner, and occasionally a selfie of her and Sophia hanging out. But there's no consistency. Weeks and months can pass between posts. I fight not to give in to the urge to creep on her, but I lose the battle after a minute.

This week she's been a lot more active, with several new posts popping up on her feed. There are pictures of her with her family in Florida. There's another couple too, closer to Clover's age, if I had to guess. I can tell the man is her brother. I wonder what it would be like to meet her family—not that it would ever happen, but still . . . How would they react to me, eight years her junior and still in college? Would it be different once I'm playing professional hockey?

By the end of next semester, a lot will be different.

I scroll to the next picture. She's wearing a beach cover-up, but it's sheer, and it shows off the bikini-clad figure underneath. That I've had my hands and mouth on. That I've been inside.

It was posted today.

I squint and use my thumb and finger to enlarge the photo. Around her neck is a thin gold chain with a familiar charm dangling from it.

I flip back to the previous picture and zoom in, but her neck is bare in that one. Back one more image, two days ago, and again, bare neck.

Which means sometime between yesterday and this after-noon, she opened the gift I slipped her before she left for the holidays. And if she's wearing it, that means she's thinking about me like I'm thinking about her.

I could call her out, see what happens.

It'd be a hell of a lot better than sitting in this limbo.

I'm not used to doing the pursuing, which I realize is how this has been the entire time. It makes sense, considering her position versus mine—me with nothing to lose, her with a career and a life and a reputation. Usually, I can count on whoever I'm dating to message, ask when we're hanging out next. The role reversal takes some figuring out.

Before I can talk myself out of it, I fire off a message:

> You were supposed to wait until Christmas Day.

I leave my phone facedown on my bed and look around in my desk for some paper, needing to keep my hands occupied. I find origami paper in the bottom drawer. It's faded with time and age, but it'll do the trick. I start folding, my mouth going dry as I wait for a buzz.

It takes five minutes.

I flip it over and find a message from Clover.

My stomach does a few somersaults and a swan dive, but I'm committed now. I open the message and smile.

> Are you creeping on me?

It's followed by that gif of Homer Simpson disappearing into the bushes.

I send her back a shifty-eyed gif in response.

> I couldn't wait any longer. It was taunting me every time I looked in my purse. I love it. It's beautiful and beyond thoughtful. Thank you.

There's a pause before the dots appear and then a second message comes in:

I stare at the message, trying to read between the lines. But all I can do is hypothesize. I hate being in the dark, not knowing where I stand. I've always made it clear with anyone I was dating that I wasn't boyfriend material, that I couldn't do long-term. The truth is, I was never invested. BJ was right. I've only dated women I wouldn't get emotionally attached to. They were fun, and they usually had the same MO I did. They wanted hot sex and no strings, something temporary so they could keep their focus on what really mattered: their grades and their friends. I was something to do in their spare time.

For the first time in my entire life, I don't want to be the afterthought. But I've already set the parameters, and I don't know how to undo that. Except maybe by being honest with her and seeing if things shift and change over time.

Another message appears thirty seconds later.

I stare at those three words, wondering how hard it was for her to type them when I'm thinking the same thing.

It takes nearly three minutes for her to respond.

I tuck my noise-canceling wireless earbuds into my ears and hit the video chat icon. A few seconds later, Clover appears on the screen. She's sitting on a bed, wearing a pair of shorts and a tank. She's definitely not wearing a bra. Her hair is pulled up in a topknot, strands hanging around her face. One knee is pulled up to her chest, chin resting on it.

"Hi."

"Hey." I set my phone in the holder attached to my bedpost so I can recline against my pillow without having to hold the phone. It's great for watching movies in bed. Among other things.

Her eyes roam over my face, and she takes in my surroundings as she fingers the charm around her neck.

"I miss you too, in case you were wondering," I tell her. "And I could practically feel your guilt knocking against my screen from that one message. You been up in your head the whole time you've been with your family?"

She drops her forehead to her knee, then peeks up at me. "How am I that transparent after one message?"

"It's not just what you say, Clover. It's what you don't say and your actions that give you away."

"Like opening the gift early," she supplies.

"It was sort of a tip-off that maybe you were thinking about me the way I've been thinking about you. I know you asked for time to think, but, uh, it's making me pretty crazy over here, not knowing whether I'm coming or going." I swallow my nerves, nab a piece of paper from my nightstand, and start folding it.

"I'm sorry for that. I wish this were . . . less complicated."

I want to say it's only complicated because we're making it that way, but that would be untrue. "You on the fence about New Year's, then?"

She sucks her bottom lip between her teeth, releasing it slowly. "I should be."

I tuck an arm behind my head. "Does that mean you're leaning in my favor?"

She lifts the charm and runs it over her lips. "I can't stop thinking about you."

It's not a direct answer, but it's not a no. "Does that mean you've been *trying* to stop thinking about me?"

"I've been watching hockey with my dad."

"Don't think I haven't noticed that you're not answering my questions."

"I don't know how to explain it, but it's as if when the semester ended, the imaginary wall I tried to create to keep us from doing something we shouldn't suddenly didn't have a foundation anymore. And now that it's gone, I have permission to want things. To want you," she says softly. "And I do. A lot."

"Can I be honest with you?" I ask.

"Of course." Her expression reflects nervousness.

"I haven't tried not to think about you. In fact, I've been

thinking about you a lot, Clover. Do you want to know what kind of thoughts I've been having?"

"I'm pretty sure I can guess." I love the way her cheeks flush and she bites back a smile.

"You want me to tell you anyway?"

She nods once.

"I doubt it's much of a surprise that I've been thinking a lot about what you're like in bed."

She grins and turns her head, eyeing me from the side. "And what am I like in bed?"

"Sweet, just like your last name implies. And sassy, and so fucking sexy. And the way you taste." I make a low, appreciative sound. "So fucking good." I ease a hand down my stomach and grip my erection through my jogging pants. "And then I start thinking about what it's like to be inside you, the way you sound, how fucking phenomenal you feel, and I don't want to stop."

She uncrosses her legs, folds the right one over the left, and runs her palm down her shin. "I think about all the same things."

"But you try not to?" I ask.

"I should. I used to, but I can't anymore." She tilts her head to the side. "What are you doing over there?"

"Missing your hands and your mouth and your sweet, sweet . . ." I grin. "Disposition."

She laughs and shakes her head. "I mean, what are you doing with your hands? And don't answer my question with a question."

My smile widens. "Would you believe me if I said I was making cranes?"

"No."

"You ever had phone sex before?" I circle the crown with my thumb and grin when her cheeks turn pink.

"No, have you?"

"Nope." I shake my head. "Wanna get off with me?"

Her tongue peeks out. "I don't have a lot of privacy here."

"You don't think you can be quiet?" I taunt.

"I'd like to suck that smirk right off your face."

"I'd like you to suck something else off."

She barks out a laugh, then slaps a palm over her mouth. "Give me a second." She moves out of view of the video, and less than a minute later, she returns and drops a bunch of stuff on the bed, pushing it to the side.

"What's all that?" I ask.

"Props." She holds up a small bottle of lube and waves it in front of the camera. She drops it on the comforter and grabs the hem of her tank, lifting it over her head. "Get naked with me."

Boxed in

Even though I miss Maverick, I have New Year's with him to look forward to, and it's nice to spend time with my family. Everything is going great until Gabriel shows up on Christmas Day—conveniently an hour before dinner. And in true Gabriel fashion, he arrives laden with gifts and flowers.

My mother ushers him into the kitchen, where I'm busy pouring holiday sangria into glasses. I'm so shocked—though I probably shouldn't be—that I drop the glass I'm holding, and it shatters on the floor.

I also lose my filter. "What the hell are you doing here?"

My mother rushes over to help with the glass, mouthing *I'm sorry*, but I put up a hand. "It's all over the floor. I don't want you to get hurt."

The room is suddenly tense with the awkwardness of the

situation. My mother hates to be rude, and I'm sure she has no idea how to handle this—not to mention still wrapping her mind around it.

When I first left Gabriel, my parents thought it was temporary, but I made them promise not to tell him where I was or give him any information regarding my whereabouts. I know my parents support my decision to leave him now, even if it took them a while to fully understand how awful my marriage became.

But none of that changes the fact that he's currently in their home.

I cross the room, heading for the closet where we keep the broom, but Gabriel stops me. "Stay where you are, love. I wouldn't want *you* to end up hurt."

I ignore him and bend to pick up the bigger shards, setting them carefully on an empty plate on the counter. I'm about to bend again, but his arm encircles my waist, and he lifts me off my feet. Gabriel fireman-carries me around the island, then sets to cleaning up the mess.

My mother and Nicki, my brother's girlfriend, stand off to the side, seeming unsure what to do. Nicki hasn't been around long enough to know Gabriel, and he's generally not a topic of conversation. He dumps the pieces in the garbage, then grabs a fresh glass from the cupboard, all while chatting with my mother and Nicki like it's totally normal that he's showed up out of the blue.

"Are you visiting your parents?" my mother asks, trying desperately to be polite.

"I am. I have some business in town, so it made it easy to spend a few days with them."

"How are Sylvie and Jacob? I haven't seen them since we ran into you in the fall."

I glance between my mother and Gabriel, tugging at the

collar of my shirt. It's suddenly hard to breathe. "When was this?" I ask.

My mother waves a hand in the air. "A while back. Early October, maybe. We were at the same restaurant. They invited us to join them." Again, there's apology in her voice.

I wonder if that's how Gabriel found out I was in Chicago. It would make sense, timeline-wise. As upset as I'd like to be, I'm aware that Gabriel is very good at getting information out of people and then using it against them. "Why didn't you tell me?" I ask my mom. I could really use that drink now.

"You weren't being very reasonable at the time, were you, now, love?" Gabriel cuts in. "I was still hoping things would change." He crosses the room and folds my hands around the glass, his gaze dropping to my throat. He reaches out and fingers the crane charm on my necklace, and it's everything I can do not to throw the wine in his face and slap him.

"Don't touch me," I grit through clenched teeth.

The right side of his mouth quirks up in a smile as he lets it drop back into place. "Is that new?"

"It was a gift from Sophia." I clasp it between my fingers.

"Hmm . . . Interesting. Seems a very intimate gift from a friend."

"We'll give you two a minute," my mother says.

"I'll be right out to join you," I call after her. As soon as I hear the door to the back porch close, I take a step back.

"Where did that necklace really come from?"

I ignore the question. "You need to leave. Now."

"That would be rude, considering your mother invited me to stay for a drink." He picks up his glass of scotch, ice tinkling as he takes a sip. "She's very worried about you, you know."

"You need to stay the hell away from my family." I remind myself that he likes to twist words, and that he's likely trying to stir up shit and make me question my parents' loyalty. "And me."

"Darling, you need to calm down. I came here because I wanted to wish you a merry Christmas. It's the holidays. I'll have this one drink and leave."

He doesn't give me a chance to respond, just turns around and heads for the back porch. And he doesn't stay for one drink. In fact, he stays for dinner, because his parents celebrate on Christmas Eve and they're out with friends tonight, he explains. And he doesn't really give my parents an opportunity to say no.

During dinner, Gabriel presents as the charismatic man I naively fell in love with, and it's infuriating. The only person who seems to see him clearly at the moment is my brother, Blaine, but when his girlfriend ends up sauced before dessert, they head back to their hotel, leaving me with Gabriel and my parents.

I help my mother clear the table, and my dad, ever oblivious, invites Gabriel out back to look at his new lawn tractor. It's the first time since Gabriel arrived that he hasn't been glued to my side—apart from the two minutes I was in the bathroom.

My mother looks over my shoulder, making sure we're alone, but I shake my head and grab her hand, pulling her down the hall to her bedroom. I close the door behind us, lock it, then continue to the bathroom, putting the barrier of extra doors between us and prying ears.

I hate how paranoid I am right now.

"What's going on?" Mom asks as I press my back against the door.

"He makes me feel like I'm losing my mind."

"Honey, are you okay?" Her hands come to rest on my shoulders. "What is happening right now? I thought you two were getting a divorce. Did you change your mind?"

I'm relieved to hear that the optimism her voice once held during conversations about Gabriel is no longer there. I shake my head. "No! Gabriel showing up out of the blue seems to be his new go-to tactic. Why didn't you tell me you ran into him in the fall?"

She drops her hands and clasps them in front of her. "You were so happy about your position at the college, and I didn't want to upset you. It seemed coincidental. I'm sorry I didn't say anything."

I nod. "It's okay."

Her fingers go to her lips. "I shouldn't have invited him in for a drink. I was just surprised, and I thought . . . I don't know. He acted like you were expecting him. I'm so sorry, Clover. I didn't realize he was making this so difficult."

"It's not your fault. He's good at manipulating people and situations and turning on the charm when he wants to."

"Do you want me to get your father to ask him to leave?"

I shake my head. "It's fine. I can tell him."

But when Gabriel finally does leave, he returns a minute later to report that he has two flat tires and needs to call AAA. It's another three hours and going on midnight before the tow truck finally comes. I end up having to tell Maverick I can't call and not to message until I contact him.

By the time Gabriel is gone, it's after one in the morning. And then I can't find my phone, so of course I start panicking. My paranoia reaches new heights when I find it in the driveway, the screen cracked. Did I drop it, or did it end up under Gabriel's tires on purpose?

The next morning, I drop my phone off to be repaired, but my mom has a day planned for the two of us, and by the time we're done, the store is already closed, so I'm not able to pick it up until the next day. It puts me on edge because it means I can't reach out to Maverick to let him know what's happening.

I fake exhaustion early that evening and disappear into the bedroom so I can finally call him.

I'm on the fence about telling him what happened, worried about his reaction, but feeling very much like I could use his support. If there wasn't a flight between us, I'd want to go to him right now. As it is, my heart skips like a scratched record when his face appears on the screen. "I'm sorry for the cryptic messages, but there were some issues." I check to make sure my door is locked. I've been paranoid over the last two days, worried Gabriel is going to show up again.

"What kind of issues? What's going on that all I got was radio silence for almost three days?" He rubs his bottom lip, and while his voice is even, I can see the hurt in his eyes.

"Can we talk about it when I see you?" I start biting my nail but realize they're going to be stubs if I'm not careful.

"Is this going to be one of those situations where you want to see me so you can tell me we're done?" he asks softly.

"No! That's not—I don't want to upset you." *Of course that's where his head has gone.* It's where mine would go if I received the same message from him.

"Hey. What happened that's got you so rattled?"

I bite the inside of my cheek, knowing I can't keep this from him. "You're not going to like this."

"I'm going to like *not* knowing less," he counters.

"Gabriel showed up at my parents' place on Christmas Day, and he invited himself to stay for dinner." I feel like now would be a good time for Maverick to teach me how to make those origami cranes.

He nods somberly. "Yeah. You're right. I'm not happy about that. What was he doing in Florida?" He cracks his jaw. "Should I be worried?" He taps his lips, clearly stressed by the situation. I don't want to make that worse for him.

"His parents live here, and he was visiting them for the

holidays. And no, I don't think you need to be worried. I'm just . . . frustrated and paranoid. I want to see you for New Year's, but I'm concerned he's going to show up at my house back in Chicago."

He nods slowly. "Then why don't we go to your place in Pearl Bay?"

"They don't plow my road very often in the winter."

"What about snowmobile access? Could we get in that way?"

"I think so, but I don't have one."

"I do. Can you give me the address? I'll get everything ready. And I can even pick you up at the airport."

I hesitate. "It's a lot of driving for you."

"I'd drive halfway across the country for a night with you at this point. Back and forth to the airport is nothing."

My heart skips a beat and warmth floods my body. This feels so much better than the mind games Gabriel plays. "Okay. New Year's in Pearl Bay it is."

27

All the Ways to Fall

I'm a mess on the flight home, even though I changed it so I fly into Milwaukee instead of Chicago, which will put me closer to my cabin on Pearl Bay. My paranoia is ridiculously high, and I'm afraid Gabriel somehow managed to get my flight information and is going to show up at the airport.

My stomach is a twisted knot when I get off the plane and text Maverick that I've landed. As soon as I have my bag, I head for the exit, scanning the area, still worried that Gabriel is going to show up and ruin my plans.

I'd been struggling with what I should do before he showed up at my parents' place, but once he came in and turned my holidays upside down, I decided I'd had enough of playing by everyone else's rules.

I want what I want. And that's Maverick.

If all I can have is a few months, I'll take it and not regret it.

My breath catches when I see him walking toward me. He's wearing a peacoat, black dress pants, and a white button-down. His shoes clip across the tiles, the floor gritty with salt and wet from snow.

He's refined, put together, and gorgeous. He doesn't look like a college student. He looks delicious. And I'm standing here in a pair of leggings, an oversized sweatshirt—I almost wore his hockey one on the plane—and my hair in a messy ponytail.

He stops when the tips of our shoes touch—his black and polished, mine scuffed—and his eyes take me in with a hot sweep. "How do you feel about PDA?"

"What?"

"Public displays of affection. Are you for or against them?"

"Most of the time or right now?"

"Right now."

I glance around, reminding myself that we're not in Chicago and no one here knows us or that up until a few weeks ago, I was his professor. "Right now, I feel reasonably good about them."

He grins, that dimple in his left cheek appearing. "I was hoping you'd say that." He cups my face in his palms and covers my mouth with his. I grip the lapels of his coat and sink into the kiss. One hand leaves my face and pulls my hood up to shield me, and the other drifts down my arm and wraps around my waist. He pulls me tighter against him and angles his head to the side, deepening the kiss for several mind-bending strokes of tongue.

When he finally breaks away, he holds the edges of my hood and backs up only enough that his beautiful face is clear. "I missed you more than I wanted to," he admits.

"Me too."

"At least we're on the same page. Want to get out of here?" He inclines his head toward the door.

"Absolutely."

He takes my suitcase in his free hand, and we head for the exit. The blustery cold of winter has me tucking my chin to my chest. Maverick puts his arm around me and pulls me against his side, protecting me from the wind until we get to his truck, parked in the short-term valet.

He opens the passenger door, hands me the keys, and puts my suitcase in the back seat before he rounds the hood and takes his place behind the steering wheel.

He leans over and kisses me again, and I wish I could snap my fingers and we'd be in Pearl Bay. Our kiss lasts until someone honks their horn behind us. Maverick unlocks his lips from mine and sighs. "To be continued."

He shifts the truck into gear, and we leave the airport. He places his hand on the center console, palm up, and I slip mine into his. It's snowed over the holidays, the landscape blanketed in white.

"How was the flight? How are you?" he asks.

"The flight felt longer than usual, but anticipation does that. And I'm . . . better now that I'm here with you," I answer.

He gives my hand a squeeze. "That's good. I'm glad to hear that."

"How are you? How were the holidays with your family?"

"I'm better now too. The holidays were okay. I'm not used to having someone I miss, and my family picked up on that."

"Oh?" It comes out pitchier than I intend it to.

He glances over and gives me a tight smile. "Don't worry. They don't know about you. I won't say anything, not even to Kody. I won't put you at risk like that."

My heart clenches at the way his jaw tightens. "Thank you

for understanding. I'm sorry I made the holidays difficult for you."

"You didn't make them that way. I'm the one who pursued you. I understand the limitations and restrictions."

I wonder if part of the allure for both of us is that this has the added bonus of being not only taboo, but secretive too. We're only real in the cosmos we create with each other.

I internally berate myself for going down that rabbit hole mere minutes after I've gotten what I want, which is time with Maverick.

I bring our clasped hands to my lips and kiss his knuckles, finding myself wanting to know about all the things I've missed over the past two weeks and wishing I could have seen him with his family. He's clearly close to them the same way I am to mine. Or as close as I can be when they live in Florida.

"Tell me what you did," I say. "How'd you spend your time? I want to know more about your parents. Did you play hockey with your dad? Tell me about your mom and her filter-less antics."

"I played some hockey and spent time with Kody, which was good. Lavender and I had a heart-to-heart, I guess you could call it."

"Was that a good conversation? What did you talk about?"

His jaw ticks. "Yeah, it was . . . helpful, I guess. We talked about what happened at the carnival when she went missing. I've never wanted to bring it up with her, because she'd already lived through it. Why make her do it again, you know? But it's been weighing pretty heavy on me lately, as you know. Anyway, she set some things straight for me, and that was good."

I squeeze his hand. "That's great. Do you feel better now? Less like it's yours to own?"

He blows out a breath. "I think so. Or at least it's starting to feel that way. I think I also didn't want to ask because if her answer had been different, all that guilt I've been holding on to would've been even heavier. But I'd been spinning all these worst-case scenarios, and it felt like they were eating me alive. *Fuck.* This got heavy real fast." He shakes his head. "Anyway, things are better, and that's what's important. And now I'm here with you, which is the icing on the cake of this holiday."

I let it go for now, not wanting to push him, but relieved that there's finally been some healing for him where his sister is concerned. "What else did you do? Did you spend a lot of time with the rest of your family?"

"Oh yeah, my grandparents came to stay with us for a while, so the house was basically a zoo. My Gram-pot is pretty awesome."

"Gram-pot?" I must have heard that wrong.

"Yeah. He's a chemist. Spent his career developing medical marijuana strains. He snuck me a couple of cookies without my dad knowing—you know, 'cause they perform random drug tests when you play on the school teams."

"And your dad wouldn't like that, obviously."

"I could get cut from the team if they found out, and potentially lose my shot at the NHL. Weed is pretty tame, but they still don't want us putting that stuff in our bodies."

"But you took the risk?" It's a bit shocking how cavalier he is about it.

"I needed the escape from my head and drinking myself into oblivion didn't seem like a good alternative. One cookie isn't going to stay in my system that long. It's more if it becomes a habit that it's a problem. My younger brother smokes a lot, but he's not interested in a professional football career, so he's not too worried. And he needs something to mellow him out."

"Should I be worried that you needed a cookie to escape your head?"

He gives me a sidelong glance. "Wait until after we've fucked each other into next week before you start psychoanalyzing me, Clover."

I bite his knuckle.

"You wanna use those teeth anywhere else, you know you're more than welcome."

I glance at his crotch, which has a prominent bulge. "I'm sure there are places you don't want me to use teeth."

"Well, not like—" He gnashes his together a couple of times. "But a light, teasing graze is always welcome—more like when I nibble on your clit."

I groan and cross my legs, the memory of his mouth between them causing everything to clench. "How much longer until we're in Pearl Bay?"

"About twenty minutes." A smirk tips the corner of his mouth. "The center console is a pretty crappy obstruction. Otherwise, I'd offer to stick my hand down your pants."

I bark out a laugh, then bite my lip and glance between Maverick's face and his crotch. "I could stick my hand down your pants, though."

His top lip curls. "I appreciate the offer, sweetheart, but I need to keep my attention on the road, and if my cock is in your hand, I'm going to be hella distracted. You could put your hand down your own pants."

"Hmm." I tap my lip. "Now that's a good idea. Then maybe we can skip some of the extensive foreplay and get to the good stuff faster."

Maverick makes a face. "The foreplay is the good stuff."

"You trying to pound the demons out of my vagina is the best part, though."

He cringes. "That sounds awful."

"It doesn't feel awful. In fact, it feels the opposite of awful.

Orgasmic, even." I use my phone to light up the center console. "Where's your wallet?"

"In my pocket, why?"

"Because if I'm going to fuck my own hand, I'm going to need that little packet of lube you always carry around with you."

"How do you know I always carry it with me?"

"I'm assuming. And while I don't normally do things like that, based on how much time you spend on foreplay, I sense that you probably restocked your wallet as soon as you got home."

"I actually didn't restock it right away. In fact, I didn't restock at all until yesterday when I realized I was running out of time to pick up all the things I needed for tonight."

I hold my hand out.

"You're serious?"

"Pass me your wallet and find out."

He digs in his jacket pocket and passes it over. I flip it open. He has a credit card and a few other cards, in addition to his driver's license, which tells me his birthday was in early September—just a few weeks after we hooked up in Pearl Bay. In the money pouch is a row of three condoms and a small packet of lube. I fish out the lube and fold his wallet, setting it on the console between us. I kick off my flats and lift my butt, pushing my leggings over my hips and down my thighs. I remove them the rest of the way and drop them on the center console as well, so they don't get wet from the snow I tracked into the truck.

Maverick pulls off the freeway and follows the darker, lesser-traveled roads that lead to Pearl Bay. I shift around in my seat and set my phone in one of the cupholders, making sure there's enough illumination from the screen that he has a semi-decent view of my bare legs, without it lighting up the entire interior. I settle in the seat so my back is to the door and my knee rests against the glove box. The other foot I prop up on the center console.

Maverick glances at me out of the corner of his eye. "You still got your panties on, sweetheart."

"I know." I slide a hand down the front of my underwear, skimming over my clit.

"I can't see what you're doing."

"I know that too."

He huffs a laugh and refocuses his attention on the road. But every few seconds he looks back over—just a glance. I run my finger up and down my slit, slipping it in up to the first knuckle, then using my wetness to circle my aching clit. I let my head rest against the window and hum softly.

"Tell me what's going on over there?"

"I'm getting ready to be stretched by your fat cock."

His jaw ticks, and his grin turns lascivious. "I can't wait to fuck all those dirty words out of your sweet mouth."

"Me too." I ease my hand out and glance at the road as we pass a sign for Pearl Bay. Only ten minutes away now. I push my panties to the side and ease two fingers in on a low moan.

His gaze darts between me and the road, gripping the steering wheel so tight his knuckles are turning white. "Fuckin' hell, Clover," he groans.

"Having some regrets about this suggestion?"

His gaze drops between my legs. "Not hardly."

"Eyes on the road, sweetheart," I mock.

His lip twitches, but his eyes return to the road. He has to brake a little harder than it seems he expected when the GPS announces our turn is in three hundred feet. The back end of the truck skids, but he regains traction and makes the right-hand turn. We're just a few miles away now, but the drive in from here is slower, the roads narrower and not lit up at all.

"I'm not going to have a lot in the way of self-control when we get there," he grinds out.

"Good. I don't want you to have self-control." I add another finger, my gaze bouncing between Maverick and the windshield as we slowly make our way over the snow-covered road, down a hill, and around three bends before we reach the driveway to my place, which has been plowed. The cabin comes into view, and I notice the snow has also been shoveled off the front porch, and there are lights on.

As soon as the truck is in park, Maverick hits the release on his seat belt, cranks the back of his seat flat and reaches over to undo my seat belt as well. He hits the interior light, illuminating us. "I want you to finish what you started."

"The cabin is right there." I nod toward the front windshield, but push my fingers deeper, lifting my hips, stroking inside, trying to reach my G-spot, but the angle is all wrong.

"I know. I want to watch you fuck your hand right here, before I take you inside and keep those fingers, that mouth, and that sweet, sweet pussy busy for the next few hours."

"You've already watched me fuck my hand." I stretch my other leg over the dashboard.

"Not the same through a screen." He runs his hand up my shin and along the inside of my thigh. "I want my truck to smell like you for the next month. Every time I get in here, I want to remember the way you look right now. So fucking sexy." He leans in and kisses the inside of my leg. Then he bites the skin. "My sweet, dirty girl."

I shudder, grinding down on my hand, but I know it's not going to be enough. "Maybe you can help me?"

"What kind of help you looking for?" He kisses the inside of my thigh and sucks.

"Whatever you're willing to give. I can't hit the spot the way you can."

"That must be frustrating."

I bite my lip and nod.

"I could make it easier for you." He grabs me by the hips and lifts so my ass is resting on the center console. His hands glide along the inside of my thighs, thumbs brushing over the place where my fingers disappear inside me.

"Look at you. So fucking perfect." He drops his head and bites his way up the inside of my thigh, then licks along the edge of my fingers, still buried inside me. I suck in a sharp breath as he eases a finger in alongside mine.

He pauses and lifts his head. "Too much?"

I shake my head. "No. I need more."

He keeps going, and I feel his finger moving along the back of mine, curling over my middle and ring finger, sliding past them. He presses against them, and I moan loudly, bucking my hips up. "There it is. You almost had it."

"I know. So close, but not quite enough."

He flutters his finger, using just the right amount of pressure, and the hot edges of an orgasm start to burn through me, lighting me on fire from the inside. It goes on and on, wave after wave of intense pleasure, dragging me under and sending me skyrocketing into bliss.

"I need in you." Maverick cuts the engine. "We'll come back for everything else later."

He nabs his wallet and clamps it between his teeth, opens his door and slaps the interior light off, then jumps down, grabs my ankles, and pulls me onto the seat. For a second, I think his plan is to have sex outside in the freezing cold, but he wraps my legs around his waist and hoists me up, hits the lock button, and uses his elbow to close the door.

The snow crunches under his feet, and I nab the wallet from his mouth. My teeth chatter, and a shiver rips through me as the cold air hits my bare legs. A few seconds later, he pushes through the front door of the cabin. A fire, all embers now, glows in the fireplace, which means he found the spare key I keep hidden in the garden shed and managed to let himself in.

He closes the door behind him, shutting out the cold, and carries me over to the wooden island, setting me on the counter. I tear a condom free and rip the foil package open, then realize Maverick is still fully dressed.

I set the condom beside me, push his coat over his shoulders and start on his shirt while he unbuckles his belt. He yanks his shirt over his head when I've managed to get the top three buttons open. I shimmy out of my underwear and pull my shirt over my head, tossing it on the floor. My bra is next as he kicks off his pants and boxers.

His erection stands at attention, thick and long and hard. I wrap my hand around the velvety shaft and sigh as I stroke him a few times.

"Fuck." He plants his fists on either side of me, watching my hand moving over his cock. He lifts his head enough that I can see his eyes. They roll up once, and he exhales a shuddering breath. "I'm probably not going to last very long the first time."

"That's okay. Me either."

He huffs a laugh.

I pick up the condom and free the latex from the foil square. "And I know you can go all night, so I'm not worried."

"You're probably going to have to tell me when you've had enough, because I'm feeling pretty insatiable."

"We match." I roll the condom down his length and guide him to my entrance. "Now show me that you missed me as much as I missed you."

The head slips inside, and he pauses, eyes lifting to meet mine. "I needed to hear that from you."

I wrap my hand around the back of his neck. "And I needed to tell you."

He eases in, one slow inch at a time. Our eyes drop, and I lower a hand, my fingers grazing his shaft as he pushes in, stretching me, filling me. I drag my fingers over my clit, and everything clenches.

"Don't do that again, please."

I clench. "You mean this?"

"Fuck, Clover. You're killing me. I'm going to embarrass myself."

I take his face in my hands. "Kiss me."

He presses his lips to mine, soft and sweet as always. We tilt our heads, allowing the kiss to deepen—tongues stroking, bodies connected, but unmoving, apart from his fingers running up and down my spine.

When we finally come up for air, his eyes search mine. "Why is it like this?"

"Like what?"

"I don't know how to explain it. I want more of you. I feel like you're as much inside me as I am inside you. I feel seen. Whole. Like nothing matters but you and me."

I smile softly and settle my hand on his chest, right over his heart. I'm in so much trouble with this man. But at least we're in trouble together.

"I feel it too, this inexplicable draw. You're more than a craving; you're a need." I wish we were in different places in our lives. I wish this wasn't so complicated.

He nods once. "I didn't mean to get in this deep."

"I know. Me neither." I wrap my legs around his waist.

I pull his mouth to mine and get lost in the feel of him and the connection that draws me deeper into the web of desire, now tangled with emotional weight.

28

Inside the Bubble

The next morning, we don't get out of bed until close to noon, having stayed up ridiculously late because of our mutual insatiability. When our stomachs start rumbling at each other, we make our way to the kitchen, put on a pot of coffee, and get started on breakfast.

I find the fridge fully stocked. "You thought of everything, didn't you?" I set a carton of eggs and a package of bacon on the counter.

"I wanted to make it easy for us." He opens and closes cabinets, pulling out the things we need. Then he turns to look at me. "Not to put a damper on the morning, but would you be willing to fill me in on this ex of yours?"

We managed to avoid talking about Gabriel last night, but I knew this conversation was coming, especially after the shit he pulled on Christmas. "What do you want to know?"

Maverick grabs a package of shredded cheese from the fridge. "How you met. How long you were together. Why you married him. Why you want a divorce. I just want to get an idea of what that relationship looked like for you."

I nod. It makes sense that he has questions. "I met him at a conference during the final year of my PhD. He was a speaker, and I was enamored. He's very charismatic and good at telling people what they want to hear. He was married once before, when he was younger, but it didn't last. I learned why after we were married. He's a manipulator, and he changed after the wedding. I didn't like who I was becoming when I was with him, or how little say I had in my own life choices, so we separated."

"What do you mean by that? How little say you had?" Maverick stops laying strips of bacon in the frying pan to focus on me for a moment.

"He made it so I was dependent on him. Right after we were married, we moved away from my family and friends. I stopped feeling like my own person." I pause a moment, needing to breathe. I hate how lost I became. How hard it was when I realized he was all I had. I'd felt trapped.

Maverick rests his hip against the counter. "How old were you when you got married?"

"Almost twenty-seven. We were only married for six months before I left." Gabriel had upgraded my phone, and in the process, erased all my contacts and started tracking me. He'd been adamant that he was trying to protect me. That had been the last straw.

"Did you date a lot before him?" Maverick cracks an egg in a measuring cup and dumps it in a bowl, then grabs another one.

"I had a few long-term boyfriends between high school and

my PhD." I start beating the eggs with a fork as he adds the second one.

"What do you consider long-term?" he asks.

"Over a year." I give him a sidelong glance. "What's the longest relationship you've had?"

He almost fumbles the next egg. "I had a few girlfriends in high school. Most of them didn't last more than a few months, though. I did date one girl sophomore year for almost an entire semester."

"What happened that you broke up?"

"She started to get attached, and I wasn't emotionally available the way she wanted me to be. I needed my focus to be on hockey, so I broke it off. She ended up dating one of my teammates after that. I think they might still be together, actually."

"That couldn't have felt good for you."

"I wasn't going to be the boyfriend she wanted me to be. They were good together. They fit. She and I didn't. We looked good in pictures, and that was it. I couldn't see a future with her. I couldn't see past the next day. Most of my relationships have been like that."

"Because you've been afraid to get attached?"

"Because I was afraid to care about someone and potentially hurt them." He settles a finger under my chin. "I didn't want to see past tomorrow." He presses his lips to mine. "And I didn't want to break someone's heart, or my own."

"Has that changed?" I ask softly.

"I'm here, aren't I?"

WE SPEND our time at the cabin in a bubble of bliss. We have sex, sex, and more sex. We shower together, sleep together, nap together. But we also cook meals side by side, working in domestic comfort. Maverick is considerate, patient, and fun. His soul is old, and he carries the weight of the world on his shoulders, but at the same time, he has the most infectious laugh and a beautiful smile I can't get enough of.

When we're not naked, we talk, or cuddle on the couch and read the *Psychology Today* magazines Sophia always passes on to me when she's done with them, discussing the articles. We play Scrabble, and Maverick wins four out of every five games because he cares more about points than he does the words themselves. We bring in wood whenever the fire gets low, build a giant snow penis after a snowfall, and Maverick tries to teach me how to shoot a hockey puck. I keep missing the makeshift net, and the pucks disappear into the snow, some of them so deep in the banks that I won't be able to find them until spring. One of my not-so-terrible shots lodges the puck in the shaft of our snow peen and nearly takes it out.

Being with Maverick makes me wish I could turn back time for me, or fast forward it for him, so the gap between where he is in his life and I am in mine wouldn't seem quite so vast outside the walls of the cabin.

As the end of the holidays inches closer, it becomes harder to ignore the reality we have to face when we return to Chicago. I've told Gabriel he's to contact me only through my lawyer, and I blocked his number, but I can't avoid dealing with him altogether if I want this divorce to be finalized.

This afternoon, Maverick is stretched out on the couch, me between his legs, my back against his chest. I'm reading an article on addictive personalities. He keeps kissing my neck, which is distracting, but also welcome affection. It also means I've been on the same page for a solid ten minutes.

I tip my head, giving him access to more skin.

His phone buzzes on the coffee table. It's been doing that

all day, and he's been checking it periodically, but not responding.

"You should answer," I tell him. "Your friends are probably worried about you."

"It's just my sister, digging for information. I already told her I was with a friend and wouldn't be back until tomorrow." He drags the tip of his nose along the column of my neck and bites my earlobe. "I guess we should talk about what this is going to look like when we're back in Chicago, huh?" He wraps his arms around me. "And don't answer that with a question."

I grin and turn toward him, kissing the bottom of his chin. He has a scar from when he split it open as a child in a hockey accident. "I was going to ask if there's a way you want this to look."

"If I had it my way, we'd keep doing exactly what we're doing. But I'm aware that's not possible. I guess I want to know where you stand. Does this end here?"

I'm silent for a long moment.

Maverick picks my hand up and brings it to his lips. "It's okay if it does. I'll understand. I don't want to make things harder for you, and I know this puts you in a difficult position."

"Are you trying to give me an easy out, or yourself?" I ask.

I feel his lips turn up against my knuckle. "Both, probably. I don't want to fuck up your career, and I get that this could be a stain you can't wash away. We always knew it was temporary. Maybe it's better to end on a high note than to wait until the bottom falls out."

I can't tell if he's saying this because he's gotten what he wanted or because he's honestly trying to protect me. Or himself. "Why are you being so logical?"

"Because I care about you. I don't want to do damage, if it's avoidable." He presses his lips to mine. "Let's enjoy the time we have left here. We don't have to make any decisions right now."

That night, I barely sleep at all, in part because my brain won't shut off, but also because we spend half the night alternating between making out and slow, unhurried sex.

In the morning, we make breakfast, both of us quiet and introspective. I want to stay longer, but I have courses I need to prepare for and so does Maverick. And he has hockey practice early tomorrow, so staying another night isn't possible, or reasonable.

But still, I drag my feet, packing slowly, wishing I could pause the world. I stand at the end of the bed, my suitcase open. I packed sexy things, even though I was supposedly on the fence about spending New Year's with Maverick. Every item I drop back in the suitcase now has a memory associated with it—mostly of him peeling me out of my clothes and us picking them up off the floor later.

I swallow past the lump in my throat, fighting the prickle behind my eyes. I promised myself I wouldn't get emotional, not in front of Maverick.

"You want me to bring anything out to the truck?"

I turn to find him standing in the doorway, forearm propped against the jamb. He's wearing a long-sleeve white Henley and gray sweatpants. What is it with men and gray fucking sweatpants?

"You're not wearing that home, are you?"

He looks down and runs a hand over his chest. "Yeah, why?"

I point to his crotch. "I can see the outline of your peen, which means everyone else can too."

"Who else is going to see it when I'm in the truck?"

"What if we have to stop for gas, or a bathroom break?"

"We're like an hour drive from Chicago, and I filled up before I picked you up from the airport. I haven't driven anywhere since, so I won't need gas. And I can hold it for an hour, and I'm assuming you can too. Unless you're planning to drink a liter of water before we hit the road."

"It'll be distracting."

He arches a brow.

I throw my hands in the air. "I don't want to leave this bubble!" I drop my head so he can't see how close I am to the edge.

His socked feet appear in my vision, along with the crotch of his gray sweatpants, and the prominent bulge looks even more obvious this close up. I don't know whether to laugh or cry or both.

"Hey." He wraps his arms around me. "I'm yours whenever you want me."

"It would be smarter for both of us if we stopped seeing each other." The words feel like a serrated blade to my heart.

"Is that what you want?"

"No. But you having to sneak around and hide what's going on isn't what I want either."

"We can take it one day at a time, Clover. It doesn't have to be all or nothing. It can be whatever we want it to be, for as long as we want."

I melt into his embrace. In this moment, it feels like there's somehow both a million miles and no years separating us.

RETURNING to school and the start of the semester brings a new set of complications. When we can coordinate our schedules, Maverick resorts to sneaking over to my place after dark and leaving before the sun rises. But I find myself running into him on campus constantly, which creates anxiety I'm not used to.

At the beginning of the third week of the spring semester, I'm on the way to the gym, which I've been avoiding since the sauna incident. The need to release some of this nervous energy wins out, though. And so does the desire to swim, despite the chlorinated water.

Just as I reach the door to the building, it flies open, and I'm face-to-face with Maverick. His hair is wet, the ends curling around a beanie, and he has a gym bag slung over his shoulder.

"Hey, Cl—Professor Sweet." He glances over his shoulder, maybe checking to see who's around. When he's sure it's the two of us, his gaze moves over me on a slow sweep.

"Hi." I fight to keep my voice from coming out pitchy and barely win, but I lose the battle not to fidget and tuck my hair behind my ear. Then I try to make it less obvious by adjusting my glasses. I feel like I have a scarlet letter tattooed on my forehead, as though everyone can see through me.

"You know I can come over in a few hours, and we can work out together." One corner of his mouth tips up in a smirk, but he steps aside, making room for me to pass.

I'm about to make a comment about this being my warmup, but another student comes jogging through the foyer, heading straight for us.

"Hey, Mav. Wait up. Can you give me a ride home?"

He has hair so dark it's nearly black and eyes so green they appear luminescent. I recognize him from pictures on Maverick's phone as his best friend, Kody. His piercing gaze lands on me for a second and slides past, like he sees me, but not really.

"Have a good swim, Professor," Maverick says.

"You too. I mean, have a good evening." I rush off, not looking back, and push through the door to the women's changing room. I head straight for the individual stalls, lock myself inside, and sink down on the bench, fighting with myself to stay calm. *No one heard him. No one knows.*

Once I stop shaking, I spend an hour and a half in the pool, swimming laps, warring with myself and questioning what I'm doing and whether this is fair to Maverick. He's said he's okay with the secrecy, but I worry about how long that's going to last, and how long it reasonably should.

I take a long shower after my swim. After rinsing the chemicals out of my hair, I tuck it up in a beanie and huddle into my winter coat as I rush across the athletic facility's parking lot. It's dark already, and fat snowflakes swirl around in the air, the promise of a storm coming. I parked under one of the lights, so it's easy to find my car in the half-empty lot. It isn't until I'm behind the wheel that I notice something tucked under my wiper blade.

I glance around the lot. A few students are walking down the sidewalk, heads bowed against the biting winter wind and snow flurries. I open my door and quickly nab it, expecting it to be a flyer or something. I drop back into my seat and hit the lock button on the door, then tap the interior light. It's not a flyer, though. It's an origami crane made from the cellophane wrapper on a soda bottle. The number eight hundred seventy-three is written in silver marker on the wing.

It's like he knows where my head goes before I do.

TWO DAYS LATER, I work late, marking essays in my office. When I finally leave the building, I step out into a blizzard-level storm. The snow has been nearly constant over the past week, and we must have gotten more than eight inches this afternoon.

Plows are out, trying to keep the roads clear, but the snow is falling fast, the black asphalt disappearing under a fresh blanket of white as soon as they pass. The sun has long since set. I can't see more than a few feet in front of me and trying to locate my car in the parking lot proves to be a feat.

I end up hitting my panic button, setting off the car alarm so I can find it among the snow-covered cars. I'd be embarrassed about how loud it is, but there's zero chance I'd be able to find my Prius otherwise. When I finally reach it, I deflate. The entire driver's side is covered in a drift of snow that's waist high. Add to that more than eight inches of snow blanketing the rest of my car, and I have no idea how I'm going to clean it off, let alone drive it out of here.

A vehicle comes down the aisle, moving slowly, headlights illuminating me and the road ahead. As it gets closer, I realize it's a black truck. It slows and comes to a stop beside me, and the passenger window whirs down.

Maverick is alone behind the wheel. "You on your way home?"

"Eventually. When I'm done digging my car out." I thumb over my shoulder.

"Might be better to do that in the morning. I have practice at six thirty. I can come a little early with a shovel. It'll be a lot easier to manage when the snow has stopped. Hop in, and I'll drive you home."

I glance around the parking lot, which is close to empty. Anyone left on the sidewalks is rushing with their head tucked down, desperate to get out of the storm.

"No one is paying attention to us, Clover. Let me drive you home."

I know I'm being paranoid, but I'm struggling to find the balance. "Okay."

I climb up into the cab as Maverick rolls the window back up. It's warm inside, and I breathe in the scent of his deodorant mixed with cologne and a faint hint of cinnamon and cloves.

There's an empty travel mug sitting in the center console, and it's clear Bengal Spice has become Maverick's new favorite tea as well.

I buckle my seat belt, remembering the last time I was in his truck. The drive home from Pearl Bay felt like a punishment, like I was losing something important. Despite Maverick offering to give me space upon our return, I hadn't been inclined to take it. But with our schedules being what they are this semester, some of that space has been forced on us. Hockey takes up a lot of his time, so with the need for secrecy, we've only seen each other a few times since we returned. It was so much easier at the cabin . . .

Maverick shifts into gear and heads for the parking lot exit, driving cautiously. I slouch in my seat, feeling conspicuous despite the fact that the snow is falling so fast and heavy that he can't see more than a few feet in front of him, so there's no way anyone can see inside.

"You doing okay? Kind of feels like you've been in avoidance mode since I ran into you in the athletic facility the other day." There's no accusation in his tone, just concern. He takes his foot off the gas and touches the brake. The back end starts to fishtail, so he eases off until it evens out. Then he rolls to a stop in front of a sign that's nearly completely covered with snow, except for a hint of red on the top left corner.

"I'm okay." I don't know how true that statement really is.

"Hold on." He puts the truck in park and opens the door. He rushes around the hood, uses his forearm to clear off the stop sign, then returns to the driver's seat and buckles himself back in. "Talk to me, Clover. What's going on? It doesn't do either of us any good if you're holding stuff in."

I swallow the lump in my throat. "This is harder than I thought it was going to be."

He glances over before he focuses on the road again. "Which part?"

"I barely ran into you on campus last semester, but I see you all the time there now. It's just . . . conflicting."

"Because I'm your dirty little secret?" he asks.

"You're not a dirty secret, Maverick."

He brakes when the light ahead turns yellow. When the truck is stopped, he extends his arm along the back of the seat, fingertips skimming the side of my neck. Despite the cold outside, his hand is warm. "I'm sorry. I didn't mean that to come out the way it did, and that was a shitty thing to say. I used to see *you* all the time on campus outside of class last semester, but back then, you were trying *not* to see me. I know this is hard for you—harder than it is for me because of the position you're in. I also know why it has to be this way, and I accept that. But if it's too much for you, tell me, and I'll back off."

He turns down Hackett Street. It hasn't been plowed yet, at least not recently, so the snow is several inches deep, and since it's windy, there are drifts along our side that are deeper closer to the sidewalk. He stops in front of my house and puts the truck in park.

"That's not what I want at all," I tell him. "It's more that every time I see you, I'm reminded of how easy it was when we were at the cabin and we didn't have to worry about anything but us."

"I'll understand if the risk is too great for you."

"That's not what I mean. It feels unfair to you. When it's you and me, I can forget about the rest of the world. But outside of our bubble . . ." I take in his beautiful face and consider what the next few months will be like if we keep seeing each other. How much harder it will be to let him go when the end of the semester comes. It'll be messy and painful, but I'm not ready to walk away now. "What's going to happen when you're in another state and I move to Pearl Bay?"

"We'll figure it out then, I guess? I want to be with you, even if we're confined to me sneaking over after dark and leaving before dawn. I'd rather have something than nothing. Even if it's limited to the next few months, I'll take it." His eyes meet mine, imploring. "I'll be more careful when I run into you on campus. No one will know but us."

Right now, my heart is clearly in the driver's seat. "Do you want to come inside?"

A relieved smile breaks across his face. "Of course I do. Let me drop my truck off at home. I'll walk back over and deal with your driveway before I deal with you."

My stomach flutters at the unspoken promise of what's to come. "I'll leave the sliding door unlocked."

I reach for the door handle, but his warm hand curves around my neck. "Hold on a second."

I turn back to him, and his mouth covers mine. I sink into the kiss, letting myself get lost in him for a minute before I pull away. "To be continued."

He nods. "I'll be back as soon as I can."

29

The Sweetest Secret

MAVERICK

I rarely sleep in my own bed in the weeks that follow. Most nights I wait until darkness falls and make the short trek to Clover's house. It's not hard to evade my siblings, or Kody and BJ, since we're all focused on studies and extracurriculars.

I've gotten good at staying in the shadows when I reach her driveway, and until the weather warmed, we always kept the walkway clear so I didn't leave footprints in the snow on the off chance her ex—who is less present lately but still holding Clover hostage with paperwork—should do a drive-by. The threat of an order of protection seems to have been enough for him to back off, but not enough to persuade him to sign the fucking paperwork and set her free.

We've made the trip to her cabin in Pearl Bay a couple of times. Other times, we'll stay the night at a hotel in Richmond or Elgin and sometimes even Rockford, so we can get dressed up and go for nice dinners. When I'm wearing a suit and tie, polished dress shoes and clean-shaven, and Clover wears her hair down and leaves her glasses at home, the age difference doesn't seem quite so glaring.

On nights like those, everything feels much more real. And it's hard to return to Chicago and go back to hiding.

A couple weeks before the end of the semester, the hockey team is heading into playoffs. We're currently in second place. The next game is home advantage, but it's against the team in first place, and we've struggled to beat them this season. It doesn't help that this is also Russo's team, the guy who constantly needles me when we're on the ice.

I have an early skate tomorrow morning, but it doesn't stop me from going over to Clover's once the sun has gone down. The days have started to get longer again, which means it's been impossible to avoid dinners at home. It's not a bad thing, though, because my presence in the house keeps my family from asking too many questions. It isn't until everyone else disappears for the evening that I do too, and I'm always home first thing in the morning, before anyone else is up.

Besides, Lavender is busy with the play she's making costumes for, and Kody is busy studying and spending time with my sister. BJ is finally putting some time in with his courses, so even he's been scarce lately, and River spends most of his nights at Josiah's.

Tonight, I escape the house without running into anyone in the kitchen. I walk the three blocks to Clover's and slip inside the back door. I take off my shoes and carry them to the mat at the front door, so I don't leave dirty shoe prints on the floor.

Clover's already in the kitchen, making her famous pasta Bolognese. The blinds are always closed in there now, giving us the privacy we need.

"Hey, can you grab me the parmesan? It's on the second shelf, right-hand side," Clover asks, her back to me, an apron tied around her waist, hair pulled up in a ponytail.

"Yeah, for sure. Do you need anything else?" I find it exactly where she said it would be and come to where she's standing in front of the stove, setting it on the counter next to her.

"That's it for now. Thanks."

I wrap an arm around her waist, kissing up the side of her neck. "How was your day?"

"It was okay."

"Just okay?" The tightness in her voice sets me on edge. "Did something happen?"

"Just Gabriel making things difficult."

"Did he stop by here or something?"

"No. I think he enjoys making this divorce cost more than it needs to." She sets the wooden spoon on the counter and turns around, sliding her hands up my chest and hooking them behind my neck. "But I don't want to talk about that. It puts me in a mood." She tugs, and I drop my head so she can reach my lips. After a few minutes, she pulls back. "How hungry are you? Can you wait on dinner for a bit?"

"Sure, why?"

"I want you to take me to bed, make me feel good."

"I can do that." I reach behind her and turn the burner off, then grab her ass and hoist her up. She wraps her legs around my waist, and I carry her down the hall to the bedroom.

We spend the rest of the night not talking about Gabriel and whatever happened. We eat a late dinner, and I study for my exams—my grades are a lot better this semester, thanks to all the time I spend with Clover—while she grades papers.

We might spend a lot of our time together naked, but we spend just as much time talking. We make meals, hang out, watch TV, read, play Scrabble, and I teach Clover how to make origami cranes. I've made so many this year that I've filled an entire tote bin. It's the first time I've ever felt like I'm in a real relationship. And the closer we get to the end of the semester, the more I struggle with what's likely the inevitable end. I don't know how I'd deal with being halfway across the country and in a relationship. And she's still fighting her way out of a bad marriage. I don't want to put that kind of pressure on her.

Clover is sitting between my legs, the most recent issue of *Psychology Today* open to an article on the psychology of deep-fake. I'm only half paying attention, my mind wandering to tomorrow's game.

"Mav?" She pats my cheek. "You still with me?"

"Huh?"

"Are you done with this page?"

"Oh. Yeah."

She gives me a doubtful look. "What's up? What's going on in your head?"

"We have a big game tomorrow night, exams are coming up —just a lot on my mind." I take her hand in mine and kiss each knuckle.

"What are you worried most about?"

"In the immediate future? Losing the game. After that? Exam stress, which I'm not as worried about because I have this professor girlfriend who keeps me on the straight and narrow, and I've been way more diligent about my studies this semester."

She smiles up at me. "You have proven to be very studious. It's impressive. But is there anything besides the game and exams? Is this related to the nightmares you've been having lately?"

Over the past few weeks, I've been waking up from dreams that leave me with cold sweats and the shakes. I'm locked in a small room that smells like gasoline, and all I have with me is a dead cell phone. I can hear someone calling for help, but I can't find a way out of the room. I also have one where I'm trying to skate, but I can't get my feet to move on the ice, and I end up missing all the important shots. Then I end up on camera for an interview and everyone keeps telling me how I let my team down.

"I'm just thinking about contract talks, and convocation," I tell her. "Not necessarily in that order."

Clover shifts so she can look at my face. "Are you worried about not getting called up?" Over the past couple of months, I've taught Clover a lot about hockey—what the stats mean, how Nashville has my rights, that Vancouver picked up Kody, but there are other teams who have eyes on him.

"I don't know. The closer I get to contract talks, the worse the anxiety gets."

"The anxiety about what, exactly?"

"A lot of things. This thing between us ending, having to pick up and move across the country, starting a career with guys I've never played with before. Or worse, they could release my rights and I could end up in Europe if they don't see me as NHL ready. What if I'm not good enough? What if I can't keep up with my teammates?"

"Well, logically speaking, you wouldn't get called up if you weren't good enough."

"Sometimes I think the only reason I got drafted when I did was because of my last name. I'm never going to be as good as my dad was."

"You've said that before. Why do you feel that way?"

"I have to work my ass off and run extra drills, work out harder, watch more videos, and practice a ton more to be even a fraction as good as he is. It doesn't help that my best friend is basically a hockey savant. Kody works hard, but he's a natural on the ice. He skates circles around me. And I'm not jealous of how good he is. He lives and breathes the sport, and he loves it. It's more that he's so certain of his future, and I'm not."

"But you're at practice and on the ice every day," she says gently.

"Yeah, but if someone told me I couldn't play hockey again? I'd be sad, but I wouldn't be devastated the way Kody and a lot of my teammates would. Honestly, the reason I'm worried about contract talks not going well isn't because of me; it's because I don't want to disappoint my dad. I've trained my entire life for this, and if I don't make it . . . I don't want to see that disappointment on his face. But the possibility of having to spend the next half decade or more being compared to him?" I twirl a lock of her hair around my finger and watch it unfurl, trying to find the words. "I don't know . . . Half of me almost hopes I won't get called up, even if I do have to face his disappointment. In some ways, that would be better than never being able to live up to his legacy."

"Does he know that you feel like this?"

I shake my head. "Of course not."

"Do you think it's something you should talk to him about? I can't imagine he would want you to feel this kind of pressure."

"It's not his fault I feel this way."

"But keeping it to yourself isn't helping you either. I'm going to ask you a question, and I want you to think about it before you answer. I want you to be honest with yourself and with me."

"I'm always honest with you."

"You are, but this is a tough question, and you're going to want to knee-jerk respond. Which is why I need you to take a minute to sort out your thoughts before you answer."

"Okay." I lace my fingers with hers. This is what I need, a

real conversation with someone whose input I value, and whose focus isn't on the glamour of an NHL career.

"How much of an impact does our current relationship have on you not wanting to sign a contract?"

I sigh. And I force myself to wait a beat before I open my mouth. "I've thought about this a lot, and I've tried to logic out my feelings, but I can't. I don't know what's going to happen with us, but I do know that I've been a better version of myself in a lot of ways this semester." I meet her eyes. "Even if you weren't part of my life, I would still feel the way I do about my future as a hockey player."

"And if you weren't a hockey player, what would you want to do? Work in sports rehab?"

"I don't know. My whole life has been focused on this one goal, and the closer I get to it, the less appealing it looks. I don't want to spend the next decade floundering in a career I don't love." I wrap my arms around her. "And I don't want to walk away from you. Can you have a midlife crisis at twenty-one?"

"There's a lot happening in your life, and I'm an added layer of complication."

"You're the best thing that's happened to me, not a complication." I press a soft kiss to her lips. "I know it's a big ask, but would you come to my game tomorrow? It would be good to have you there."

She settles her hand on my cheek, expression pensive. For a moment I think she's going to say no, but a small smile forms on her perfect lips. "I can be there. I want to be there for you."

Everything Was Good
Until It Wasn't

MAVERICK

Kody elbows me in the arm. "Isn't your professor from last semester sitting over there?" He tips his chin toward the seats across from our bench.

The arena is packed tonight, since we're playing one of our biggest rivals for the top spot in the league. I need to keep my head in the game and not let Russo get under my skin. I was stressed out about the game last night and had restless sleep, which Clover experienced right along with me.

So far, we're winning, but our opposition is keeping us on our toes. I've managed an assist and haven't missed any stupid shots. But I'd love a goal, because it's been a few games since I've had one. Plus, with Clover being here, there's real incentive to do well.

I glance in the direction Kody pointed and shrug. "Might be. Why?"

"She keeps looking at you."

"She's probably keeping an eye on the action." I nod toward the ice.

"I don't know, man. Every time I look over there, her eyes are over here."

"Maybe because you're staring at her? Or maybe she recognizes me because I was in her class and I was a giant asshole for ninety percent of the semester." In my peripheral vision, two girls stop in front of Clover. Probably students of hers.

I can feel Kody looking at me and then back at her.

This time I'm the one who elbows him in the arm. "Would you stop looking over there? You're about as inconspicuous as a fully dressed person in a nudist colony."

His brow furrows, like he's trying to make sense of what I said, but the buzzer goes off, so we get back on the ice. Instead of stressing about messing up plays or being the one who scored the goal instead of an assist, I just play the game. Kody gets control of the puck right away, so I get into position, making sure the path is clear to the net. When I get close to the end zone, I switch directions and edge my way between defense for the opposition and the goalie.

Kody must realize what I'm doing, because he sets it up, passing me the puck, giving me the opportunity to circle behind the net and take a shot. Defense knocks it away as it kisses the goal line, but Kody is right there to steal it and tap it in.

He skates over to me, gives me a rough hug, and tells me that was one of my best plays this season. The back pats and praise keep coming from my teammates. It should make me feel good, but for whatever reason, it has the opposite effect. Instead of feeling awesome about the goal I set up, it creates a pit in my stomach—the one that's been growing all year and getting bigger the closer we get to the end of the season.

We win the game by three goals. It's the best we've ever played against Russo and his pals, and for sure they're going home sore. In the last period, they ended up with two penalties for chippy playing, and Russo kept on with the digs, but for once, I didn't react. In part because I didn't want to end up in the penalty box while Clover was watching.

I get what my dad has been saying about settling down and finding someone who balances me out. He's always talked about how he became a better player when he found my mom. She made him want to do better, be better—play with integrity and not testosterone. And I see what he means now.

I glance across the rink to where Clover's gathering her things, looking more like a student than a woman who works at the university with her pom-pom beanie and school-colors scarf.

She reminds me of a Hogwarts student with the stripes and glasses, which she seems to love to wear these days just to get a rise out of me. And they've grown on me over the past several months. I used to think they overwhelmed her face, but now I like the way those thick, dark frames make the ring of blue in her eyes pop.

It isn't until we're gathering our stuff from the bench that I spot my parents in the stands behind us, sitting up near the back of center ice. There are a couple of guys in suits right behind them, scouts keeping an eye on their investments, since Kody and I aren't the only guys on the team to have been drafted. It's probably good that I was too distracted by Clover to notice them until now.

My parents wave, and my dad gives me a thumbs-up.

"Looks like you're going out for a celebratory dinner with your 'rents," Kody says as he shucks off his gloves and grabs his water bottle.

"Seems like it."

"Nice work out there, guys." Quinn claps us both on the shoulders as he passes, heading for the shower.

"Thanks, man," we say in unison.

I don't message Clover like I want to, not with Kody sitting beside me, taking off his equipment in his organized, methodical way, folding everything neatly, even though it's all going to end up getting washed.

My plan had been to shower, get dressed, drop my truck off at home, and meet Clover at her place, but my parents being here throws a wrench in things.

Kody and I shower, dress, and hang our equipment. Quinn falls into step with us as we head to the foyer, where my parents are waiting.

"I feel like you get bigger every time I see you," Mom says to Quinn, pulling him in for a hug.

"Maybe you're starting to shrink." He pats her gently on the back.

"It's entirely possible. How's the master's thesis going? Poppy says you're applying for your PhD."

"It's good. A lot of work, but worth it. And yeah, that's the plan."

My dad commends him on his dedication, then gives Kody the usual greeting, telling him he had a great game and making a comment about how he hopes Kody's treating his baby girl right. It's predictable and hilarious, because Kody never fails to get flustered and turn bright red.

My mom rolls her eyes. "Give Kody a break, Alex. You've known him since he was in diapers. You don't need to give him the 'treat my daughter like I'm watching your every move' speech whenever we see him. It's awkward for everyone. Especially since there are images of you and me playing dueling tongues all over social media from when we were their age."

Dad gives Mom a look. "That's not the point."

"Then what is the point? We all know you're Dad of the Year. You don't need any more accolades, and Kody doesn't need to have an anxiety attack every time he sees you. Besides, they're moving in together next month. I think it's time to let go of the whole she's-my-baby-girl-forever ideal."

Quinn and I stand off to the side, watching this all go down. I'm just happy that the focus isn't on me. I missed it when my parents and Kody's came for a visit after my sister announced she was taking a summer internship at an off-Broadway theater to design costumes. And that Kody was coming with her. Apparently, it was a real come-to-Jesus talk, where Lavender told our parents she was tired of living in a bubble. It also happened on the same day River brought his boyfriend home, unaware the 'rents were there, and finally came out to them. This semester has been eventful, that's for sure.

Anyway, I'm a little disappointed that Lavender isn't here tonight to endure the embarrassment along with Kody. But she's neck-deep in making costumes for the next school performance. Having her here would probably just prolong this, though, and as fun as it is to watch Kody squirm, I'm antsy to get the inevitable dinner with the parents over with so I can do the celebrating I want to, which is the naked kind. With Clover.

My dad invites Kody and Quinn out to dinner with us, but they both cite homework. Kody probably wants to take another shower because he hates the locker room ones and Quinn is likely being honest. But my parents don't hassle them about it. Quinn and Kody head to the parking lot on the north side of the arena.

"I noticed the scouts, were they checking up on us?" I ask as we make our way through the lobby and head for the doors.

Dad nods and claps me on the shoulder. "You had a great game tonight, and they noticed."

"That's good." It's a relief that I played well.

The parking lot is mostly empty at this point, with only a few small groups of people left heading for their cars. The sun is close to the horizon, and the sky a murky gray, clouds heavy and threatening rain. I scan the lot, assuming Clover is long gone. I'll have to let her know I'm going to be a lot later than I planned.

I notice a couple standing near the back of the lot. At first, I don't think anything of it, until I recognize the woman as Clover. She's easy to spot with her green jacket. The problem is the man—it's freaking Gabriel. *What the hell is he up to?*

I don't weigh the consequences of my actions as I drop my backpack on the sidewalk. "I gotta handle this."

"Handle what?" my mom asks.

I leave my parents standing there and jog in Clover's direction. "Hey!" I shout.

Gabriel's head swings around, and so does Clover's. Her eyes flare when she sees me walking toward them. She gives me a quick headshake, but it's too late. Gabriel's expression turns stormy. At least they're in the corner of the lot, and it's mostly empty at this point. The bad part is that my parents are following me.

It's too late to turn around and walk away—not that I want to—but I stop about fifteen feet from where they're standing. "Everything okay, Professor?"

"It's fine. Thank you," she calls. If she weren't wearing a jacket, she'd definitely be holding the edges of her cardigan together.

I can tell she's anything but fine. And the fact that her ex is here, after staying away for weeks, is a huge red flag.

Gabriel's lip curls, eyes shifting between the two of us. "What the hell are you thinking, Clover?" He turns to me. "You need to stay away from my wife."

When he takes a step toward me, Clover grabs for his

sleeve, but he shakes her off. "I don't know what you think you're doing, but it needs to stop. Now."

"What's going on?" my dad asks.

I raise my hands, as if I have no idea what he's talking about, as if he's lost his mind. "I'm just checking in since you seem pretty hostile."

"I'm not an idiot. I know what you're doing. She's still married to me." He points at himself. "And you need to back off."

Clover's fingers are at her lips, and thankfully the hood of her jacket is pulled up, shielding her face and her identity. "Gabriel, this is inappropriate, and you have no idea what you're talking about," she says. "He's a student." Her voice wavers.

"Well, that's the fucking problem, isn't it?" he spits.

"You should go." I look at her for a moment before returning my gaze to him. "I've got this."

He huffs a humorless laugh and shakes his head. "You've got this? What's inappropriate is you thinking you have a right to tell *my* wife what to do."

"What the hell is going on, son?" My dad steps up beside me and rests a protective hand on my shoulder as Gabriel approaches.

I wish I'd thought this through better, but I'm not sure what other options I had. I'm not worried about myself, or about my parents finding out. In fact, it would be a hell of a lot easier if I could stop pretending I'm still on a dating hiatus. It would be even better if I didn't have to keep sneaking around like a criminal—leaving Clover's place before the sun comes up and waiting until it goes down before I can steal my way back into her house and her bed.

But we're almost at the end of the semester. Just a couple more weeks and exams will be over, and she'll no longer be an employee of the university, and I'll no longer be a student. Not long after that, I should be signing a contract.

"Isn't that the question we'd both like an answer to?" Gabriel smiles, but it's stiff and unfriendly, not like the previous time I met him. Then, he was cocky and dismissive, charming almost. His angry glare swings to my dad and then to my mom, who's standing a step behind us.

I glance between Clover and her car, a silent request for her to get the hell out of here already.

Her expression tells me she doesn't want to, but she ducks into the driver's seat of her car.

My dad puts out a protective hand as Gabriel takes another step closer. "You should wait in the car, Vi."

My mom isn't always the most logical person on the face of the earth, and she also raised four kids, so she isn't one to back down. "Like hell I'm waiting in the car when a forty-year-old man is coming at my son."

"Your son is sleeping with *my* wife." Gabriel's voice is eerily calm.

"She's only your wife because you won't give her a divorce." I realize, belatedly, that the smarter move would've been to keep my mouth shut. But it's clear, at least to me, that he's been keeping tabs on Clover. Watching her somehow. Otherwise, what the hell would he be doing stalking her on campus?

"Clover and I have been trying to work it out, and you're getting in the way," he says through gritted teeth.

I cross my arms. I honestly have nothing to lose at this point. "Correct me if I'm wrong, but aren't you supposed to be going through her lawyer if you want to talk to Clover? I'm not sure that constitutes an attempt at working it out. And if you mean I've been getting in the way by being someone she can rely on and talk to about the fact that you've been refusing to sign the papers for more than half a year, then yeah, I guess I am."

Clover pulls out of her spot and heads for the exit. Gabriel is too focused on me to notice. He moves closer, getting up in my personal space. "Do you really think you're what she wants? She's only fucking you to piss me off."

"Well, clearly, it's working. Feel free to take a swing at me so I have a reason to knock your ass out."

"Step down, Maverick." My dad pushes between us, shaking his head. "You need to back off. If you so much as lay a finger on my son, I'll have you so wrapped up in legal red tape, it'll make your head spin and your bank account cry."

Gabriel runs his tongue over his teeth and takes an exaggerated step back, holding his hands up in surrender, gaze moving over my dad's shoulder to where I'm standing. "Leave my wife alone. She's a bleeding heart. It's one of her personality flaws. I did some digging. I know about you and your family." His gaze shifts to my mom. "Your golden boy is just a pawn in a game." He turns to walk away but pauses and spins to face us. "In case you weren't aware, you should know that my wife is your son's professor."

He grins when my mom gasps, like he's proud of the bomb he dropped. He tucks his hands in his pockets and starts whistling as he crosses the parking lot, disappearing around the side of the arena. I'm sure he parked his car in another lot on purpose. This feels orchestrated, like he's been waiting to pull this shit.

My dad puts a hand on my shoulder. "Come on. You need to get in the truck."

31

The Verbal Diarrhea Match

MAVERICK

Tonight, more than any other night, I wish I hadn't driven in with Kody and Quinn, because then I'd have an escape route that isn't sitting in my dad's truck, fielding twenty questions. I try to climb into the back seat, but my mom elbows me out of the way.

"Oh, hell no. You're sitting up front with the human time bomb." She gives me a look and holds out her hand. I give her mine, and she hoists herself into the back seat, shimmying over until she's in the middle of the bench while I climb into the front passenger seat.

"Are you trying to sleep your way to a degree?" she asks.

"No, Mom. And most of my professors are old dudes. There's no way I would sleep with any of them."

"Are you an escort, then? Is that what's going on? Are you pimping yourself out like . . . like . . . one of those pool boys?"

"What?"

"Kids do it all the time in college. They get a sugar daddy, or mommy, who pays for all their things in college! Tuition, clothes, boob jobs, which obviously you don't need because you don't have boobs—but that's not the point! We have literally millions of dollars. You do not need to sell your body for money!"

"How do you know that's what girls do in college?" Dad asks.

I give my dad a look. "Leave it to you to get all territorial about Mom thirty years after the fact. You didn't even know Mom back then. So what if she had a sugar daddy?" If I can defend my mom, I might get her to calm down.

She makes a gagging sound. "I never had a sugar daddy in college! As if I wanted to sleep with guys with saggy balls before I had the saggy boobs to match! But I had friends who did it."

"Friends, huh?" Dad arches a brow and glances at her in the rearview mirror.

"Focus, Alex! We're talking about our son and what happened in that parking lot." She points at me.

"I'm not an escort, Mom. I don't have time to fake-date people."

"She's a professor! How old is she?"

"She's not even thirty. It's not a big deal."

"What does that mean? She's twenty-nine? Professors aren't that young."

"She is."

She slaps the center console. "You are twenty-one years old, Maverick Alexander Waters. You are supposed to be dating nineteen-year-old girls!" My mom's voice is shrill. Her head is right beside mine, and she's basically shouting in my ear.

"According to what freaking handbook?" I shift in my seat

so I'm looking right at her. "I don't know if you're aware, but I've *never* dated a girl my own age, or younger. In high school, I dated girls who were at least the year above me, until I became a senior, and then I didn't have a lot of options. Having a dick that's like a third freaking arm scares the fuck out of high school girls, FYI."

"He has a point, Vi," Dad mutters.

"Why are you showing your dick to high school girls? That's illegal!"

The shrillness isn't abating.

I hold up a hand. "Calm down. I'm not showing my dick to high school girls. I'm just saying, when I was in high school, there was no way I was going to lose my virginity with someone who had zero dick experience. Like I wanted to scar some poor sophomore for life with this thing." I point to my crotch.

I wish I could shut the fuck up about this, because it isn't a conversation I want to have with my parents, but my mouth keeps moving, spouting nonsense. *Thanks, Mom.*

"You were having sex at fifteen?" My mother looks horrified.

"I was almost sixteen. And I'm a dude. I was basically a walking hormone from the time I got my first boner until . . . well, I still am. The point is, college girls are not my jam. They're work and drama, and I don't have time for that shit."

"Your sister is a college girl, and she's not drama," Mom says pointedly.

"Really? Because if I'm remembering correctly, there was a viral picture of Lav on social media last semester wearing a white thong bikini in our backyard, and right before it was taken, she was flirting with the biggest dirtbag on the school hockey team. It's a wonder she didn't get an STI from standing next to him, he's so dirty."

My mom looks scandalized. "Why was Lavender talking to

him? And why didn't you or your brother or your cousins, who I know for a fact are always at your place, do something about it?"

"Since when does Lavender have thong bikinis?" Dad interjects. "And why are you inviting dirtbags to your house when your sister is around? You're the one who insisted she live with you in the first place!"

I close my eyes a moment. I probably should have left the dirtbag part out. "A few guys from the team were over, and the dirtbag invited himself. We were all keeping an eye on Lavender." I turn back to Mom. "And we didn't do anything because she was trying to piss Kody off, and it worked since he was the one who turned into a caveman and carried her inside. Now everything is fucking sunshine and rainbows with those two, so you're welcome for that."

Mom purses her lips.

I cross my arms. "I'm not apologizing for swearing. I'm a grown-ass man."

"Grown-ass men don't sleep with other men's wives!" she shouts.

"Yes, they do! All the damn time."

"Just because someone else is doing it doesn't mean you should too," she fires back.

I suppress an eye roll. "She handed him divorce papers in August, and they'd already been separated for a year. He's refusing to sign. They're only still married because he's a delusional jackass."

Mom pinches the bridge of her nose. "Do you have mommy issues? Did I screw you up that badly?"

"No, Mom, I don't have mommy issues. And you didn't screw me up."

"I just can't believe you're sleeping with your professor."

So far, my dad hasn't said much. I don't know if that's good or bad. "*Was.* Past tense. We hooked up in the summer—"

"You hooked up with her in the summer? How in the world did that even happen? You were twenty years old!"

I wish my mom would stop yelling. It's giving me a headache. I'm also worried she's going to stress herself out to the point where she either has a panic attack or breaks out in hives.

"It was a hookup, Mom. I didn't know she was going to be my professor until she started teaching my class."

"But, but . . ." She flails her hands around. "Are you telling me you didn't even know each other and you slept together? How did she not know you were a college student?"

"Well, Mom, hookups are usually about chemistry and not conversation, so the fact that I was a college student didn't come up. And neither did the fact that she was a professor. I'd also like to point out that you and Dad were supposed to be a freaking one-night stand, except Dad is tenacious as fuck, apparently."

"What?" Dad frowns. "That's not true. Your mother had an early flight to catch. And she left her glasses behind, which is the universal sign for *I want a repeat.*"

"I actually couldn't find my glasses, and I was trying to get out of there before you woke up," Mom says. "Maverick, stop trying to divert the conversation. Isn't it against the law or the rules or whatever to sleep with your professor?"

"It's not against the law to have sex, even with your professor. And we didn't start sleeping together again until I wasn't her student anymore."

"Well, that's reassuring." Her voice drips sarcasm. "I don't understand what the two of you could possibly have in common."

"We both read *Psychology Today*. We like walks on the beach, piña coladas, and getting caught—"

"What if she's just using you for—for sex!"

"Seriously, Mom? You think this would be the first time I've been used for sex? Half the girls who come to my games are just looking to hook up with a hockey player because they want the notoriety that comes with sleeping with someone who may or may not be headed for the NHL. And I'm the son of this guy." I thumb over at my dad. "He did all those freaking condom endorsements, and I look exactly like him when he was my age. Girls hope if I look like him, I'm packing like him too. At least until reality hits. Then sometimes they cry, or scream, or run away."

Okay, maybe I'm exaggerating about the tears, but I'm trying to make a point here, and I have had a couple of potential partners back out.

"You did ask if I had some kind of disorder," Dad says to Mom.

This conversation is so fucking weird. We pull into the driveway. My sister's car is there, but River's isn't. I'm guessing he's at Josiah's for the night.

"Look, I'm a student for two more weeks, and her contract with the university ends this semester because she's a visiting professor."

"And then what? Are you going to openly date her?" Mom sounds aghast at the prospect.

"I don't know. Maybe? Maybe not. She's the one who has something to lose, not me. So it really depends on what she wants."

I hate the turn this conversation has taken. I don't want to think about what happens after contract talks. Nashville is far—farther than I'd like. And who knows if they'll decide I need time on the farm team first. And Clover's moving to Pearl Bay once the lease is up on the house in Chicago. If I was sticking around here, that would be fantastic, but I have no idea where I'll be next year.

"Would you feel differently if it was six months from now and I was an NHL player, and she wasn't associated with the college?" I ask.

Mom sighs. "But it's not different. It's right now. We're worried about you. Is this why you were so . . . morose over the Christmas holidays? Did you leave early so you could be with her?"

I don't see the point in lying. "Yeah, that's exactly why I left early." I reach for the door handle. I'm relieved the dinner plan went out the window after Gabriel showed up. My mom losing her shit on me in the truck is one thing, in a public restaurant is another. "I gotta put in some hours on the books tonight since exams start next week."

"Son." My dad puts his hand on my arm to stop me from getting out of the truck.

I sigh. "What?"

"I don't know if this relationship is good for you or not. I do know that I love you. What do you know about this ex of hers, other than he's been making it hard on her by not signing the divorce papers? And how does he know about your relationship?"

"I gotta assume he's been keeping tabs on her, or me, or both of us." I run my fingers through my hair, really wishing like hell I could call Clover and find out what's going on. "We've been careful because of her position."

"Because she knows she shouldn't be sleeping with her twenty-one-year-old student," Mom grumbles.

"Uncle Darren is almost a decade older than Aunt Charlene, and no one seems to think he's too old for her."

"It's not the same."

"Why? Because the roles are reversed? Because she's the older one? You're perpetuating a stereotype. I get that you think I'm young, but how many twenty-one-year-olds have the kind of responsibilities I do? I'm a full-time student. I play varsity hockey seven days a week. I teach self-defense classes two days a week at the gym. I've been a summer hockey coach for kids since I was fifteen. I run a house, and I make sure my brother and sister are dealing with life okay. I think I'm beyond dating college girls whose biggest worry is how many views their fucking video got on TikTok. I'm not the first twenty-one-year-old in the history of the world who's dated an older woman."

"Who's married to a lunatic!"

"Vi, I know you're upset, but can we focus on the more important detail here, which is the fact that this woman's husband sought her out in a very public place and then came after our son?" He turns back to me. "I'm worried about your safety."

"And I'm worried about Clover's."

"Clover?" Mom parrots.

"Yeah. Her name is Clover."

"Is that a nickname?"

"You named me Maverick."

"Vi, please." My dad holds up his hand, and Mom flops back in her seat with a huff.

"What else has happened with this guy? Do you need me to call in a favor with the Chicago PD?"

There are good and bad sides to having a dad who was basically famous, not just for his illustrious hockey career, but also his brief stint in sportscasting and his time as a coach for the NHL, not to mention the condom ads, among other endorsements. The bad side is that because I look like my dad, people also expect me to be exactly like him. The good side is that there are a lot of guys on the force who have sons who play hockey. So my dad can call in favors when he needs them.

"Honestly? I don't know," I tell him. "At the beginning, he was sending her gift baskets and stuff. That was back in late October or early November, but it's escalated since then."

Mom's head appears between us. "I thought you said you weren't sleeping with her when you were her student."

"I wasn't. It wasn't like that at first. I wrote this paper . . . and I wanted to talk to her about it."

"A paper about what?" Dad asks.

"Does it matter?"

"Based on the way your leg is going a million miles a minute, I'd say yes, it does," Mom points out.

"It was about childhood memories. I wrote about the carnival." I keep my eyes on the dash and avoid looking at either of my parents. "Anyway, that's not the point. We started talking."

"About what happened to Lavender?" Dad asks.

I nod. "Yeah, but you're missing the point. Clover was very clear about the lines. We had a history and chemistry, and she was my professor, so at first, I mostly kept my distance." I don't feel the need to go into the details of the sauna incident, or the drunk assholes who scared the crap out of her, or the self-defense lessons. "One day I was running by, and her ex was in the driveway. He seemed nice enough at the time, I guess. But when I think back on it, it was clear that Clover was uncomfortable with him being there. They weren't married long before things went south. He was controlling, and he's a manipulator, and from what I've seen, that hasn't changed. He's making it impossible for her to move on with her life."

"Are you sure she's being honest with you? She could be playing both of you."

I shake my head. "She's not."

"How can you know for sure?"

"Because I sleep beside her almost every night." I rub the space between my eyes. "Look, this is the realest thing I've ever had. And you saw my midterm grades this term. They were solid, and my finals are going to be just as good because she's a positive influence on me, not a bad one. I don't know what's going to happen when I graduate, but I do know that I care about her. A lot. She's important to me. Just please try not to judge her before you even give her a chance, okay?"

"Okay, son." My dad drums his fingers on the center console. "I feel like it might be a good idea to take this to the police, though."

"What are we going to tell them? That my girlfriend's ex approached me in a parking lot and told me to stop sleeping with his wife? He didn't throw a punch, and he didn't threaten me. The only thing he did was allude to having done some research, which wouldn't be all that difficult because I have a famous parent." Although he is supposed to be going through her lawyer to speak to her, so that might be something. "I don't want to draw more attention to Clover than I need to. It's bad enough that it was in a public place." I look over my shoulder and give my mom a look. "I can feel your judgment. You need to find some chill, Mom."

"I just don't know how to handle this," she admits.

"You have a gay son. I'm pretty sure you can handle me dating an older woman."

"River being gay wasn't a surprise to anyone, least of all me. You being involved with your professor . . . Maybe it also shouldn't be a surprise, but it is." She sighs.

I nod. "I need to check in with Clover and see how she's doing. I don't want her to be on her own tonight." Might as well keep on with the honesty—and prevent my parents from inviting themselves inside to continue this discussion.

"I'll call you tomorrow, okay? So you can update me," Dad

says. "And if there are concerns about this husband of hers, please tell us so we can help."

I nod once and let him pull me in for an awkward hug before I get out. My mom slides along the back seat and meets me at the side of the truck.

Her lips are pursed, and her brow is furrowed. She looks . . . tired and worried. She settles her palm against my cheek. "I feel like I'm missing a lot of pieces of this story. I'm worried about you for a lot of reasons."

"I've got it handled, Mom."

She stares at me. "I'm concerned that you're giving me lip service to shut me up, and that I've been missing a lot of signs." She steps in and wraps her arms around my waist. "I love you. Please be safe. And use condoms."

I laugh.

She leans back and gives me a look. "I'm serious. I can handle a lot of things, but you getting your professor pregnant before you graduate isn't one of them."

"We're safe, Mom. Don't worry."

"It's my job to worry. Especially about you."

I help her into the passenger seat and stand in the driveway, waving as they back out. I wait until their taillights disappear down the street before I pull my phone out and send Clover a message. My gut tells me not to go to her until I get the all clear. I don't want to make an already-shitty situation worse.

32

The Crossroads

CLOVER

My heart rate calms slightly once I'm out of the athletic facility's parking lot, though I don't feel great about leaving Maverick behind—and with his family, no less. I'm on edge as I turn onto Hackett Street, looking for Gabriel's black BMW. He'd been quiet all semester, ever since the holidays—too quiet. Going through our lawyers, playing by the rules I set . . . That isn't like him. He's always liked setting the parameters of our relationship.

The street is empty of cars, though. I'm nervous as I pull in, terrified that Gabriel is going to be waiting for me. But there's no one lurking in the shadows, at least not that I can see.

As soon as I walk in the door, I call Sophia, and she comes down right away. I fill her in on what happened after the hockey game and how it seems Gabriel has been watching me somehow, even if he hasn't come around.

"This is not good," I conclude, wringing my hands. "I have no idea how many people witnessed that. What the hell was Gabriel thinking?" I clasp my hands, resisting the urge to bite my nails.

Sophia shakes her head. "I don't know, but now might be a good time to consider that order of protection. Gabriel was quiet for a while, but he's really been escalating since you filed for divorce."

I think back to the beginning of the end of our marriage, when his control started to slip, and his behavior became erratic. "I thought him showing up at my parents' over the holidays was bad, but this is something else. What if he reports me to the school? What will I do?"

"Take a breath, Clover." She reaches over and squeezes my hand. "You were very careful. You followed all the rules, and based on the official protocol, you didn't do anything wrong."

"Logically yes, but you and I both know that my colleagues —*our* colleagues—won't see it that way. The double standard in this profession is ridiculous. No one even bats an eyelash when one of the men professors ends up marrying the PhD candidate he mentored. This won't be viewed the same way. I might not want to be a professor in the long-term, but it could still have a very negative impact on my future career."

"You're assuming the worst is going to happen. Do you really think Gabriel would report you to the school? And wouldn't he need tangible proof?"

"It was stupid to go to Maverick's game. What the hell was I thinking?"

"He asked you to come support him, so you did. Lots of faculty attend school sporting events. I doubt you were the only one there tonight."

"That might be true, but how many of those faculty members are sleeping with one of the players?" I run a hand down my face. "That was such a bad call, Sophia. I should've known better."

She sighs. "You can't go backwards, though, so we need to make a plan for how you're going to deal with this. Regular classes are almost finished, and then we're into exams. What's the worst that can happen? I'm asking sincerely—in your mind, what's the worst-case scenario? What are you most afraid of?"

I stop and consider that. "It's so complicated."

"Okay. Unpack that for me. Tell me what makes it complicated. Are you truly concerned about what our peers will think?"

"I don't want people to think I'm taking advantage of one of my former students, or that I would abuse my power like that." I press my fingers to my temple, the truth of it finally settling in. "Oh my God, Soph. What if I'm exactly like Gabriel?"

Her eyes widen. "Why would you think that? Where's the connection? How do you make the leap from going to see your boyfriend play hockey to being a manipulating control freak who intentionally removed all your support systems and now refuses to sign divorce papers?"

One of the best things about Sophia is her ability to make me vocalize my thought process. It's why she's so good at what she does.

"I pursued my student, just like Gabriel pursued me." My chest tightens at the thought. "Am I repeating history?"

"Let's back up for a second. As soon as Maverick became your student, you did exactly what you should have to protect yourself and him. You passed his assignments over to your TA to avoid a conflict of interest. And you didn't pursue Maverick; he pursued you."

"But I kept letting him into my life." I close my eyes a moment. "Okay, okay. Think about how this looks from the outside, though. My ex-husband shows up at a school sporting event to what? Confront me publicly? Did he come into the arena? How long was he watching me?"

At the end of the game, I'd been stopped by a few students who wanted to chat. My plan had *not* been to stick around so long that the team came out.

I hadn't noticed Gabriel until I was at my car, and he stepped out of the shadows. He seemed ready to snap, not in control the way he usually presents. He told me he knew what was going on, and then Maverick had come outside with his parents, and Gabriel had homed in on him, instead.

I finger the tiny origami charm at my throat. "Has he been following me this entire time? Or is this another one of his tactics to gaslight me?"

"This is why I think it might be time to consider the order of protection. He knows he's supposed to go through the lawyers."

"But then I'll have to admit I'm involved with a student. Is he purposely backing me into a corner so I have to out myself? Or is this some convoluted way to try to get me to stop seeing Maverick?" I can't get any of these answers if I don't talk to Gabriel, but I also don't want to give him the satisfaction of caving, which again, is what he wants.

Sophia echoes my thoughts. "Based on what I know about him, I don't think you're too far off base. This was clearly a ploy to get a reaction out of you. I don't like that this seems to be his new strategy."

"I'll talk to my lawyer in the morning and find out the procedure for an order of protection." It's not an answer, but it's something. "This is such a mess, Soph. I can't even begin to consider how difficult this is going to be for Maverick or what his parents must think. How could I ever face them after this?"

That's a pointless question since I don't even know where Maverick and I stand. Whatever we are is supposed to end when he signs a contract.

Sophia shifts to look at me carefully. "The bigger question is, do you *want* to face them?"

"I don't know." But even as I say it, my heart tells me it's not the truth.

"You don't know because of what happened with Gabriel, or you don't know because you haven't thought that far into the future?"

"Why do you always ask the hard questions?"

"Because I'm your best friend and I'm a therapist. It's what we do."

"I feel like an idiot."

"Why?"

"Because I allowed myself to fall for someone I can't logically have a future with."

"Because his career path is going to take him to another state."

"That's one reason," I mutter.

"Here's what I think. You've set up a whole bunch of barricades to make this relationship more difficult than it needs to be. I understand keeping it quiet until you're no longer part of the faculty for all the reasons we've talked about. No one wants to be the fodder for that kind of gossip, so I get it. But if you shed the other fears, particularly the age gap between you, and just look at the relationship you've formed with him, would you want to try to make it work, distance or no distance? Do you think he's worth the risks and the challenges?"

I voice the truth I've been trying to suppress for months now. "I feel like I've met my soul mate."

"So that's a yes." She reaches over and squeezes my hand.

"Find out if he's in the same place you are, and if he is, decide where this is going to go."

I nod. I know she's right.

It feels a lot like my stomach is going to turn itself inside out as the minutes tick by while I wait to hear from Maverick. It takes more than half an hour before that happens, and all I can do is run through worst-case scenarios with Sophia.

Five minutes after he messages asking if it's okay for him to come over, there's a knock on my patio door. As soon as he steps over the threshold and closes the door behind him, my face is in his hands, and his lips are on mine.

It's just a soft press, but even as brief as it is, it provides comfort. He pulls back, his eyes searching. "Are you okay?"

I cover his hands with mine. "I'm fine."

"Such a liar." He dips down to kiss me again.

Sophia clears her throat, and he pulls back, dropping his hands this time.

"Hey, bestie." Maverick lifts a hand in a slightly awkward wave.

"Hi, Maverick." She mirrors the wave and points to the ceiling. "I'm going upstairs, so you two can talk. Text if you need anything."

"Maybe don't sleep with your earplugs in tonight," I suggest.

"I was thinking the same thing. I'll text when I'm locked in." She slips her feet back into her shoes and leaves through the sliding glass door. Less than a minute later, I get a text, and I send one back in response while Maverick makes sure all the doors and windows are locked and the house alarm is set.

We go to the kitchen together, and he pulls out two mugs while I fill the kettle.

"I'm sorry about tonight. I saw him and reacted and didn't think about the mess I might be making for you," he says softly.

I set the kettle to boil and turn to him, resting my hip against the counter. "Don't apologize. I know you did it because you were worried. It was probably good that you interrupted."

"What was he even doing on campus? I'm really starting to wonder if you need an order of protection. My dad has friends on the force, I'm sure he can get it pushed through."

"You're not the first person to suggest that tonight. And he's tired of going through the lawyers." I shrug. "It's hard to manipulate me when he can't get to me." I pinch the bridge of my nose. "I'll talk to my lawyer in the morning, but I'd really like to be done at the school before I resort to an order of protection."

He nods. "Because of the potential backlash, which I understand, but it also concerns me. I'm worried he knows you're not likely to go to the police *because* I'm a student."

"I know. We're so close, Maverick. The year is almost over. I just don't want the gossip."

He nods and taps his lips. "I get it. No matter what, you get tarred with the professor-who-slept-with-her-student brush, whereas I get to be the undergrad who got into bed with his hot professor. It frustrates the hell out of me that if our roles were reversed, it would be the student everyone tried to blame."

"Society is full of double standards, and I don't know that they're ever going to disappear."

"I shouldn't have asked you to come to the game." He drops his head, shaking it slowly. "That was stupid on my part, and I put you in an impossible position."

I take a step closer and put my hand on his chest. "I wanted to be there to support you."

"It put you at risk, and that's not what I *want*." He covers my hand with his and brings it to his lips, kissing the tips of my fingers.

"It was a calculated risk. Gabriel showing up was unexpected. How are things with your parents?"

He smiles wryly. "My mom asked if I was a paid escort."

"I'm sorry, what?"

"Her head goes to weird places." He rolls his eyes. "They had questions, and I told them the truth, that we were seeing each other, that I wasn't your student anymore when we got involved, and that you're in the middle of a divorce and your ex is a problem because he's refusing to let you go."

"Were they upset about your involvement with me?"

"They don't know you. My dad's most worried about Gabriel and whether he's unstable. He wanted to file a report, but I told them I wouldn't put you in that situation." He pokes at his bottom lip with his tongue. "Mostly I was worried you were going to call it quits on us because it's becoming too risky for you . . ." He swallows. "I would understand that, even if it's the opposite of what I want."

"It's not what I want either," I say softly.

"Okay." He blows out a breath. "Good. That's good." His eyes dart around before landing on me again. He strokes my cheek, and his voice is soft and slightly pained when he whispers. "I don't want to lose you. I don't want to lose this."

"I feel the same way." My heart feels like it's going to beat out of my chest as I prepare to be completely honest.

"I need to tell you something," we say at the same time.

He grins, and so do I. "You can go first." I squeeze his hand.

"I was about to say, *ladies* first." He gives me a chagrined smile, then nods like he's psyching himself up. "I know things are kind of up in the air as to where I'm going to be after contract talks, and that you have plans of your own, but the way I feel about you . . ." He stops, shakes his head, and clears his throat. "This is—this doesn't feel temporary. Not for me, anyway."

I take a step closer, until our toes touch. "It doesn't feel temporary to me either."

"No?" Hope and fear swim behind his eyes.

I shake my head. "Not temporary at all."

"You feel permanent. Like you're inside my heart and my soul, and I want to keep that. This is the most grounded I've ever felt in my life." He raises a hand, as if he's expecting me to interrupt. "I know that's twenty-five-ish percent shorter than yours, but that doesn't negate this feeling. I'm in love with you. And I know the odds don't seem stacked in our favor, but I still want this. You. Us. I don't want to put an end date on you and me."

"I don't want that either." I smile softly up at him. "And as much as I tried to fight against it, my heart took the reins. I love you too."

His eyes flare, as if my response is unexpected. "Yeah?"

I nod.

"So once the semester is over, no more hiding?"

"No more hiding."

"I can take you on dates whenever and wherever? Call you my girlfriend in public? Hold your hand?" He gives me a lopsided, dimpled grin.

I mirror his smile. "We can do all of those things."

"I can embarrass you with public displays of affection?" He bites my knuckle and tugs me forward, wrapping his arm around my waist.

"I don't know about these embarrassing PDAs."

"What about innocent kisses?" His lips skim the column of my throat. He nips at the edge of my jaw.

"What's happening behind the fly of your pants doesn't feel very innocent, Maverick."

"We have privacy, though, and parts below the waist are highly aware of that. Plus, this feels like a defining moment in our relationship, and all of me is appropriately excited about you being my girlfriend outside this bubble." He smooths his thumb across my bottom lip, backing up so I can see his face. "I know it's still going to be complicated, but I'll do everything I can to be worth that for you."

I smile. "You already are."

33

The Fears We Can't Control

CLOVER

A few days later, I wake up at three in the morning to the sound of Maverick's deep groan. There's nothing sensual about it, though. It's followed by a panicked cry and thrashing.

I flick on the bedside lamp. His hair is damp with sweat, and there's a furrow in his brow.

I give him a solid shake. "Maverick, wake up. Hey, hey. Wake up for me."

He sucks in a breath, and his eyes pop open. Then he bolts upright in bed, his breaths coming fast and shallow.

I put a hand on his damp cheek. "Hey, look at me. It was a dream. Everybody's safe."

His gaze flits around the room. "Fuck. I'm sorry." His voice is gritty and low. He covers my hand with his and drags the other one down his face. The sheets are twisted around his legs, and two of the pillows are on the floor. "This is getting ridiculous."

"Was it the dream about the shed or about hockey?" I rub slow circles on his back, hoping to soothe him and bring him back from whatever edge he's been on in his mind.

He shakes his head a couple of times and blinks rapidly, as if he's trying to get rid of whatever threads of the dream are still clinging to him. "This time it was the closet. It's like all my childhood memories are merging and fusing with the present. I keep making mistakes on the ice, missing stupid shots, or I'm frozen, or when I get a penalty, it's not the box anymore. It's the fucking shed, or a closet, and when I open the door, it's you in there, and there's all this blood." He rubs his eyes. "But when I try to get you out, you disappear. And they lock me inside, and there's all this screaming, but I can't figure out where it's coming from. So I keep calling for help and pounding on the door until my hands fucking shatter."

"Oh, Mav, that's awful." I drag my fingernails down the back of his neck. The closet is new, and not something I know anything about. "Can you tell me about the closet? Where is that coming from?"

He taps restlessly on his thigh. "A couple of years after Lavender went missing, she got locked in one of our closets during a game of hide-and-seek. She was probably in there for, like, I don't know, twenty minutes? Kody was the one who found her, and when we found them . . ." He shakes his head, gaze lifting to mine. "There was all this blood."

"From what? What happened?"

His gaze shifts to the side, suddenly distant, as if he's back in the past with the memory. "At first, I thought maybe they were dead. There was blood all over Lavender's face and her hands and Kody's neck. She'd been so terrified, she bit right through her bottom lip, bad enough that she needed stitches, and she'd done that thing with her nails. She got a lot worse after that for a couple of years. It probably triggered the memory of the carnival for her. I know it did for me. And the rest of my family. My dad lost it. He totally freaked out." He rubs at his bottom lip. "And the worst part is that she ended up locked in there because of me."

I want to ask more questions about his dad, but I need to keep the focus on him for now. "What do you mean, because of you?"

"I was the seeker. I was supposed to find her. She always hid in the same three places, though. So I assumed she was in one of those spots, and I didn't go looking for her the way I should have." He scrubs at his eyes with his palms. "Every time I think I've let one shitty memory go, another one pops up."

There's so much old trauma he's holding on to, and it seems that now that the door to his past is open, more of those tough memories keep surfacing. I wish I could convince him to talk to someone, but I worry he'll shut down on me like the last time I mentioned it.

"What can I do to help?"

"I need finals to be over. Once finals are over, it'll be better. Then it's just contract talks. It'll be better then."

He wraps his arm around my waist and pulls me into his lap. I rearrange myself so I'm straddling his thighs.

He glances at the clock on the nightstand. "I'm so sorry this keeps happening. I should probably sleep at my place until it stops. Or maybe the spare room. I don't want you to be alone at night."

I take his face in my hands. "Hey, look at me."

His gaze moves away from the clock, his exhaustion and guilt obvious. "It's no good if neither of us are sleeping through the night."

I caress the edge of his jaw. "I can handle a few broken nights of sleep."

"This has been nearly constant for the past week. I have an exam in six hours, and you have to proctor one." His fingers drift up my arms, then down my back.

"We'll both survive the day with coffee, and then one more exam for you and it's done."

All I can do is reassure him for now, but the truth is, this lack of sleep stems from a lot more than his nightmares. It's everything. Since the incident with Gabriel, Maverick has been hyperattentive, worried about my safety to the point that he's double- and triple-checking the locks and the alarm before bed.

Even on the nights when he has a late shift at the gym, or practice, he still comes to stay the night. Before this, he stayed often, but there were always a couple of nights of the week where he'd sleep in his own bed. Now it doesn't matter what time it is; he comes here.

He wraps his arms around me, dropping his head and pressing his face against my neck. He breathes me in. "I'm sorry," he murmurs, whether to me or an invisible force that's shredding his mind with painful memories he can't exorcise, I can't be sure.

"It's okay. Tell me what you need. How can I help?"

"It's late. I should let you sleep." His hand settles on my hip, thumb slipping under my thin shirt, skimming bare skin.

"I can sleep later. Do you need a distraction from whatever is in your head?"

His brows pull together, his expression uncertain even as his eyes darken with lust. "Are you sure you're down for that? It's stupid o'clock in the morning, and I know it's not exactly a sedative for you like it is for me."

"I wouldn't offer if I wasn't sure." I lean in and press my

lips to his, sucking the bottom one, letting it slide between my teeth.

"I love you so much," Maverick says on a low groan.

"I love you too." I pull back, grab the hem of my sleep shirt and lift it over my head, dropping it on the bed beside us, leaving me naked.

He cups my breasts in his palms, thumbs brushing over my nipples before he takes one into his mouth, gentle at first, then applying more suction.

I push the covers down and free his erection from the sheets. His teeth sink into my breast when I wrap my fingers around his cock.

He exhales heavily, thickening and lengthening with each stroke. Over the months we've been together, I've grown accustomed to his size. I don't think there will ever be a point that I don't need at least a little preparation before we have sex, but we can manage a semi-quickie on occasion.

Tonight, though, I feel his need to lose himself in me, and I want the same. I don't care if I'm exhausted tomorrow. The closer we get to the end of the semester, the closer we get to contract talks and all the uncertainties that brings with it—which is another layer to his nightmares, I'm sure.

"I want you in my mouth." I shimmy back on his thighs and nudge his legs apart so I can settle between them. I leave wet kisses on the shaft, working my way up to the head and running my tongue over the slit before I take him in my mouth.

"Fuck, Clover. Why are you so good to me?" His fingers drift down my cheek, skimming the place where my lips and his cock meet.

I pop off and kiss the tip. "Because you're my favorite person in the world, and I love you." I wrap my lips around the head again.

Maverick gathers my hair in his hand to keep it from getting stuck to my lips. He folds his other arm behind his head, propping himself up so he has a better view.

I take my time, alternating teasing strokes of tongue with gentle suction. And I take as much of him as I can until the head hits the back of my throat and my eyes threaten to water—which, incidentally, is the point at which Maverick always stops me.

"It's your turn." He cups my face in his hands and eases me off. "And I need a minute or ten." He sits up and kisses me. It's sloppy and wet, full of pent-up desire. He moves me to lie on top of the comforter, head at the foot of the bed, and settles his massive body between my thighs, hiking one over his shoulder and pushing the other out to the side.

He drops his head and licks up my center. I pull in a gasping breath and grip his hair in preparation. But he doesn't lick me again. Instead, he moves to the inside of my thigh, kissing me softly before he sucks on the skin.

"I can't ever get enough of you." He nibbles his way back up the inside of my thigh. "I want you all the time."

"It's the same for me," I assure him. I don't want to think about what it's going to be like when he's in another state. Not now.

When he reaches my center, he lifts his eyes and drags a single finger from my clit to my entrance, easing it inside as he flicks my clit with his tongue. Every muscle below my waist clenches, and my eyes roll up. He pumps a few times, curls his finger, and adds a second one. Then he presses his tongue against my opening, where his fingers curl inside, and licks up my slit. He continues to tease me in the best way, in no hurry to give me the orgasm that hovers just out of reach. My body aches with the need for release, but he keeps me at the edge, the most delicious torment.

"I don't want to come until you're inside me," I groan, legs shaking with the effort it takes to hold back.

He flutters his fingers and flicks my clit again. "Is that you telling me you're close and asking me to be inside you?"

"Yes, and please."

He gives me one last, sweet lick, and when he withdraws his fingers, I groan at the loss. He prowls up my body, dropping kisses along the way until his mouth meets mine. I lick inside, tasting myself on him, and we both make a low, needy sound as his cock glides over my clit.

I wrap my legs around his waist to keep him from breaking the contact. Maverick pushes up on one arm, eyes falling closed, and his erection slides low, nudging at my entrance. His throat bobs, and his fingers skim my cheek. "Let me get a condom."

"Or we could go without this time."

It's half question, half suggestion. In all the months we've been together, we've always used protection—even though he's seen my birth control pills sitting on the night-stand. I take them at the same time every night, just before bed.

"If it makes you more comfortable, you can pull out instead of coming inside me," I offer when he doesn't answer right away.

"I, uh . . ." He closes his eyes and licks his lips when I shift again.

I run my fingers through his hair. "You can say no, Maverick."

His eyes open, and his cock twitches between us. "I haven't ever gone without a condom."

"Okay. I don't want to do anything that's going to make you uncomfortable."

"It's not that it's going to make me uncomfortable. It's just not something I've done before, so I'm not sure how it's going to affect my performance."

I smile at his expression, a mixture of chagrin, anticipation, and desire. "That's okay. I'm at the edge anyway, so you won't need to worry about me." My fingers trail from the nape of his neck, down between his shoulder blades, and lower. "I'd like the closeness, if you would too."

"Yeah, I'd like that." He nods once.

I curve my palm over his ass and press down as I tilt my hips up and the head slips inside. Maverick blinks once, twice, and we exhale the same shuddery breath.

"I want more of you," I whisper, brushing my lips over his.

His eyes never leave mine as he sinks into me. His brows pull together in a furrow, and he murmurs, "Oh, fuck."

I curve one hand around the back of his neck. "Is that a good, *oh fuck?*"

He clamps his teeth together before grinding out, "This is . . . not the same."

"No, it's not. It's better, isn't it?"

"You're so soft." He pulls his hips back. "And so warm." He pushes in again.

"I can feel all of you."

His hands move along my shoulder blades, fingers curling to reach my collarbones, anchoring me so I don't slide into the footboard or off the bed as he continues to move over me.

It doesn't take much to send me freefalling into bliss.

His jaw clenches. "This is too intense. I don't think I can hold back much longer."

"So don't." I watch the goose bumps rise along his shoulders and make their way up his neck and down his arms. It happens every time he comes.

"I don't want to pull out."

"Then don't do that either."

He runs a hand down my side and unhooks one of my legs from around his waist. He pulls it higher and slides his forearm underneath, the inside of his elbow resting against the crook in my knee, allowing him to go deeper. Every thrust hits that spot inside, taking me higher right along with him.

I can't take my eyes off him, his expression almost feral as he moves over me.

Another orgasm slams through me as Maverick pushes inside one last time, his entire body taut, muscles quaking with his own orgasm.

He collapses on top of me for a few seconds, the weight of his entire body pressing me into the mattress. I revel in the closeness as he pants against the side of my neck, then slowly kisses his way back to my mouth as he pushes up on one arm.

His mouth covers mine, and we kiss lazily for long minutes, bodies still connected, sweaty and sated.

Eventually he pulls back, and I can see already the sedative effect sex has on him. His smile is slow and easy, movements languid. "Gotta admit, it's going to be hard to go back to condoms after that."

I push his hair back from his forehead, watching the thick, dark curl spring back into place. "We don't have to. It's really whatever you're comfortable with. It's a different kind of connection."

He nods once. "It's deeper, literally and figuratively." He rolls his eyes at himself. "Leave it to me to ruin epic sex with stupid jokes." His expression turns serious. "I've never felt this connected to anyone before. It feels like you live not only in my heart, but in my soul as well."

We kiss again, unhurried, just like before. I want to stay like this, wrapped in the comfort of each other. But as the heat settles and the sweat dries on our skin, he finally pulls out. I excuse myself to the bathroom to clean up, and by the time I come back to bed, Maverick's blinks have slowed considerably.

I tuck myself into his side, and he wraps his arm around me, pulling me close. He turns his head and kisses my temple. "Thank you."

"For what?"

"For knowing what I need when I need it."

"That's what partners do." I kiss his chest and listen as his breathing regulates, along with his heart rate. I match my breaths to his, but my mind takes longer to settle. Just like Maverick, I have no idea what contract talks are going to bring our way.

34

One Step Closer
to the Unknown

MAVERICK

I step out of my bedroom, which I haven't slept in much lately, and nearly collide with Kody. Right behind him is Lavender.

"I'll see you when you get home," she says. "Hey, Mav, it's nice to see your face. I'd ask where you've been for the past two weeks, but I don't have time to wait for you to concoct a lie. Good luck on your last exam today." She kisses Kody on the cheek and rushes down the hall.

"Slow down, babe. I'd like you to be in one piece when we leave for New York!" he calls after her.

She flips him the bird but grabs the railing as she rushes down the steps. From the *oof*, I'm guessing she missed one.

"Why is she rushing? She gonna be late or something?" I ask.

"Nah." He rubs the back of his neck. "She wants to get to

campus with lots of time to spare in case some random, unforeseen thing happens that could possibly make her late. Also, she anxiety pees like three times before every final, so she hangs out near the bathroom for about fifteen minutes because she doesn't want to have to go in the middle of the test."

"Huh. That's . . . weird."

He shrugs. "Seems to run in your family. You ready for your final exam? You really haven't been around much lately."

I follow him down the stairs to the kitchen. The front door slams shut, indicating that Lavender is gone, and it's just the two of us.

"I saw you yesterday at hockey practice," I tell him. The season is over, but it doesn't mean we don't make the most of ice time when it's available. There were some rumblings about what happened in the parking lot after the game when Gabriel showed up, but I dispelled the rumors, saying some drunk dude was getting out of hand. No one pushed it or questioned it, so I let it be.

"I mean outside of hockey." Kody grabs a box of cereal from the cupboard and the jug of milk from the fridge, setting them both on the table. "For the past couple of weeks, every time I knock on your bedroom door, no one answers. I was kinda hoping we'd get to hang out a bit more since Lavender and I are basically jumping on a plane right after convocation." He opens another cabinet and retrieves two bowls, passing me one.

I grab two spoons, and we take a seat across from each other. "I'm sorry, man. It hasn't been intentional. I've been juggling a lot with classes, the gym, and hockey. Why don't we hang out after our exams today?"

I grab the box of Harvest Crunch, and Kody goes for Life. Clover has to work all day, and she's clearing out her office—not that she's accumulated all that much since she's only been here a year. Since that last showdown with Gabriel, I've been off the grid, and Kody and I haven't had much time together outside of hockey. He's leaving for the summer tomorrow, and then who the hell knows how often we'll see each other after that. Unless one of us has our rights traded so we end up on the same team—I still like to fantasize about that sometimes, even though the odds are slim.

His eyes flare, like he's shocked I would suggest we hang out. "Yeah. That would be great. Wanna grab lunch at the campus bar? I should be wrapped up by eleven thirty. What time is your last exam?"

"Starts at nine thirty, so I should be done around the same time."

"All right, cool." Kody shovels in a mouthful of cereal.

"Cool," I echo, and do the same. We both nod a bunch of times while chewing. "Why does this feel like we're awkwardly making a date again?"

"Uh, I don't know, but it does." I can see he's working up the nerve to say something. "I feel like there's this divide I don't know how to cross with you, and it keeps getting wider."

I sigh, realizing we need to have this conversation and it probably should have happened long before now. "I'm not mad at you for dating Lavender. I knew it was going to happen. All of us have known it was coming."

"But there's *something*, Mav. If it's not me and Lav, what is it?"

I lace my fingers behind my head. "It's not you, man, it's me."

"This sounds like the beginning of a breakup speech." Kody's shoulders hunch forward, like I've physically harmed him.

I guess if that's what he believes, I have. I need to fix that. "I'm not breaking up with you, asshole." I smile but clear my throat. "When you and Lav finally got together, like we all knew you should be, I was relieved because you'd spent so much time beating yourself up over what happened."

"And you didn't?" Kody challenges.

I poke at my cereal. "I did. Sometimes I still do. But the point is, I knew when Lavender came here this year that you two were probably going to end up together. What I didn't plan for was how hard it was going to be. You and I had three years of hockey and hanging out, and it felt like when we were kids—then it was gone. I knew it was coming, but I didn't realize how lost I would end up feeling."

Kody leans back in his chair, brow furrowed. "Lost how?"

"You've always known exactly where you were headed. You played hockey before you could walk. You knew it was going to be your thing."

"You've been the same way."

I shake my head. "It's different for me. I play because it keeps me connected to the people I care about, like my dad and you. And it took the onus off River. Your whole life is mapped out for you and has been since you were a kid, and I'm not in the same place as you. That's not your fault, but watching you and Lav this year, seeing you so sure of your future, it made me realize how unsure I am of my own."

"You'll get called up this year. There's no way you won't."

"Maybe. Yeah. But what I'm saying is, I've probably been a shit best friend this year. And I'm really fucking sorry because it's not about you or my sister, it's just me, trying to figure shit out."

"You haven't been a shit best friend. You're the reason Lavender and I are together at all," he says with a conviction I envy.

"You're together because you're supposed to be. I just gave you a nudge in the right direction."

"Gotta admit, when you said I should move in here, I

wasn't sure how well that was going to go." Kody pokes at his cereal with his spoon.

"It wasn't my subtlest move, but it was probably my best one." I chuckle and change the subject, feeling like I've finally cleared the air with him the way I should have months ago, but didn't know how. "You excited about the summer in New York?"

"For the most part, yeah," he says. "I mean, it's kinda bittersweet, you know? I feels like this year has flown by, and as excited as I am for everything that's coming, I'm going to miss this." He gives me a sad half smile.

"We had the last four years together. And you're gonna marry my sister one day, so you'll be my brother-in-law, and we'll definitely see each other on holidays at the very least."

"Yeah. That's true." He nods as he mulls that over.

It's all coming together for him. And here I am, still hiding my relationship with Clover, unsure of what the next month will look like, let alone the years that follow. I'd like to tell him about Clover, but I don't want to put him in a position where he has to keep it from Lavender. It's better to wait until convocation is over.

His jaw works for a second. "You never know, though. Maybe we will end up playing for the same team. How cool would that be?"

"Really fucking cool." I dig into my cereal, trying to figure out why the idea of having to be on the ice, with or against him, makes me want to crawl out of my skin.

I FINISH my exam with twenty minutes to spare and go over the questions I had the most trouble with one last time before I hand it in. Now all that's left is convocation. Kody and I go out for lunch, which turns into beers, which turns into us getting so wasted we need Lavender to pick up our stupid, drunk asses because the Uber driver said no.

I pass out in my bed for several hours and wake up feeling like a bag of shit. I shower, hoping the beer that's still seeping out of my pores is diluted enough by the gallon of water I drink that Clover won't smell it on me.

My ability to cover up the beer stench fails, but she seems to think it's funny, and very appropriate college almost-graduate behavior. We spend the rest of the night playing dirty strip Scrabble, and I sweat out the rest of the beer I drank this afternoon when we end up naked on her living room floor, acting out all the dirty words we made. It got a little kinky, since I played the word *shocker*, and I found out it wasn't something she'd experienced before.

The next morning, I get up early, wake Clover with oral, get inside her, make a mess of her sheets, and then pull her into the shower with me where we have more sex before we get dressed and make breakfast.

"My parents are going to be there this afternoon," I tell her as I beat several eggs in a mixing bowl, adding shredded cheddar and some chili flakes.

"I figured they would be." Clover fries onions and hash browns in a pan, stirring them continually. "It's kind of a big deal to graduate."

"It's a lot bigger of a deal to get your PhD, but I think they're just relieved I finished with a degree." I add the eggs to another frying pan. "My sister and Kody are leaving this afternoon for New York, basically right after convocation is over. We have enough time for a quick lunch, and then they go to the airport."

"How do you feel about that?" she asks.

I poke at the edges of the egg with the spatula. "I'm happy for them. He'll be my brother-in-law one day, so he'll always be part of my life, one way or another."

"Change is hard."

"But necessary."

She hums her agreement. "Do you want to come back here after? We can celebrate together? I'll pick up a bottle of champagne."

"That sounds better than perfect. I can make us a dinner reservation somewhere if you like? Unless you'd rather order in?"

She runs her hands over my chest and fidgets nervously with my collar. "Maybe we could stay in? Save dinner out for another night? Unless you want to celebrate with your friends?"

"The only person I want to celebrate with is you." I kiss her on the cheek and reach around her for the spatula.

"Okay." She smiles, but it seems a little sad.

WHEN I GET HOME, the front foyer is crowded with Lavender and Kody's suitcases. Their flight to New York leaves this afternoon, and now that the day is here, I feel like I haven't had enough time with either of them. I've been so wrapped up in my own relationship. I guess that's normal, but I still don't love that this may be the last time the three of us are in the same city for what could be a lot of years.

It makes me nostalgic for my youth. I can almost see Clover rolling her eyes and biting back a comment if she could see inside my head. I drop my backpack on the bench and kick off my running shoes, tucking them into a corner so they're not in the middle of the floor, and head for the kitchen.

"What're you smiling about? And where the hell have you been? You can't wear jogging pants to your convocation. Mom will lecture you for hours, and we'll all have to listen to it." I look up to find River leaning against the counter with a bowl of cereal in one hand and a spoon in the other. He's wearing black dress pants, a white button-down, and a rainbow tie, his customary scowl decorating his face.

"Nice tie."

The furrow in his brow deepens as he looks down. "Josiah gave it to me."

"Yeah, he did." I grin.

River smirks. "I have matching boxers too."

"What about condoms? You got those to match as well?"

"Not yet. But I'm sure they're coming. Seriously, though, where the hell have you been?" He sets the empty bowl in the sink.

"Just tying up some loose ends. I'll be down in fifteen. I need to put on a suit, and I'm good to go. You catching a ride in with Mom and Dad?"

"Nah. I'm gonna drive over with Lav, spend a little time with her before she gets on the plane." He tucks his hand in his pocket, and his lips pull to the side.

"She's gonna be fine. She'll have Kody there with her, and she'll be back at the end of August."

"Yeah." He tugs at his bottom lip with his teeth. "I don't know if she'll be back, though."

"It's just a summer internship."

"I feel like she's spreading her wings, and when she flies, she's going to soar," River adds.

"How you feeling about that?"

"Okay, I think. Kody loves the fuck out of her, and she's got bigger balls than all of us. If anyone deserves this, it's her." He smiles, and even though it looks a little sad, it's genuine.

River has always worn his heart on his sleeve. If he felt something, we knew about it. But he hid the most important part of himself, who he really is. And I realize maybe I wasn't here for him as much as I should have been this year. Or maybe we've all just found our own ways of dealing.

I clap him on the shoulder. "You know, it seems a lot like you and Lavender are in the same place at the same time. It's fitting."

"I never thought about it like that, but yeah, I can see it." He nods slowly. "I don't think I realized until recently how much you sacrificed for us."

I give him a questioning look. "I don't know what you mean."

"This was your senior year. You could have lived with your hockey buddies, probably should have, but you put me and Lav first. So I hope that whatever's going on with you, it's because you're putting yourself first for once."

I stare at my younger brother. "Are you high?"

He rolls his eyes. "No. I'm not dumb enough to do that when we're going to see Mom and Dad. I'm just saying, you're a good brother."

"Oh. Well, thanks."

He pulls me in for a hug I don't expect, then pushes me toward the stairs, telling me I need to shower off my stank.

River's words stick with me as I get ready for convocation—and not the ones about the stank. I'm ready for this chapter of my life to be over.

35

Awkward Conversations

CLOVER

I feel ill, like I might toss my cookies at any moment. I'm trying to stay engaged in conversation with my colleagues, but it's a challenge when my boyfriend and his parents are less than a hundred feet away and currently celebrating the fact that their son has graduated college.

Professor Longley—a man in his mid-forties, who has on more than one occasion this semester asked if I'd like to have coffee, and I've always been busy—is droning on and on about the different kinds of coffee beans and how the ones they use at some café downtown are the best. Mary Connor, one of the sociology professors, is hanging on his every word. I wish he would get a clue and ask *her* out, since it's clear she's into him.

It makes me question what the hell I'm doing and how this thing with Maverick can ever work. But I remind myself that I have one more week in my contract, and then I'm finished. Then we're just two people in a relationship.

I excuse myself to the bathroom. My mouth is dry, my palms are sweaty, and I'm ridiculously jittery, as though I've consumed a gallon of coffee and followed it up by chugging a bottle of maple syrup.

I use the ladies' room, gather my senses, and exit, prepared to excuse myself to my office. I need to get out of here so I don't start second-guessing myself and what I'm doing more than I already am. The hardest part has been watching Maverick and his parents talk to his professors from this semester, knowing that they're discussing how bright he is, probably asking if he's interested in pursuing a master's, despite being aware of his NHL future. I can't approach them, speak with them, tell them how amazing I think their son is, because of our relationship.

He can do anything he wants. Be anything he wants. The world is at his fingertips. And instead of hanging out at bars on the weekends or talking to girls his own age, he's playing Scrabble with me in the evening, reading *Psychology Today*, and having sex all over my house.

"What am I doing?" I chastise myself. I step out into the hall and almost run into another woman.

"I'm so sorry." I stumble back, and my mouth goes even drier. Because I'm standing face-to-face with Maverick's mother.

She's a tiny woman, slight and curvy with long, wavy auburn hair. I realize I've seen her daughter on campus, Maverick's younger sister, because she looks almost exactly like her.

"I was wondering if I could have a word." Her expression is pinched, uncertain.

Saying no is not an option. Not if I want an actual relationship with Maverick, and even though I'm questioning myself today, my heart already knows what it wants.

"Of course." I glance down the hallway. There are conference rooms to the right. "We can go in here; there's more privacy." I use my faculty card to unlock the door and turn on the lights, ushering her inside before I follow and close the door.

She clutches her purse in her hands. It's ornate, decorated with beads, and looks like a math textbook. Her gaze moves over me. "You don't look old enough to be a professor. If you came to a liquor store and I was working the cash, I would definitely card you. Even if you were buying a fifty-dollar bottle of wine."

"Fifty-dollar bottles of wine are a little above my current paygrade." *Oh my God.* Did I just lip off to my boyfriend's mother?

She shakes her head. "I would never work the cash register at a liquor store. It would be super depressing to see the same guy come in every day and buy Colt 45. Mouthwash would be a better option than that shit. It tastes like lighter fluid that's been marinating in a toilet."

"I will take your word for it." I wait, because obviously she didn't pull me in here to talk about malt liquor.

"What exactly are your intentions with my son?"

"Can you be more specific?"

She blows out a breath. "Are you reliving your twenties because you missed out on them the first time around? That ex-husband of yours seems like a bit of a bomb waiting to go off, and you had to have been young when you met him. Early twenties, maybe? So you took a pass on all the fun stuff because you settled down with a douchecanoe, and then you saw my son and thought he would be a good way to get your rocks off for a while? Or maybe he's a ticket to a life of leisure?"

"Wow. Okay. Um, my ex-husband is the worst choice I've ever made."

"That's saying something, since you're sleeping with one of your students."

I have to give it to her, she's a straight shooter and a protective momma bear, which isn't a surprise given the way Maverick talks about her. Her children are a top priority. I need to put myself in her shoes.

"I realize we don't know each other, and maybe you have concerns—"

"Concerns? You're sleeping with a twenty-one-year-old who happens to be my *son*." She crosses her arms. "What could you possibly have in common, other than the fact that he's in his sexual prime and you're approaching yours?"

Blaming the man who likes to hold the blame would be a terrible betrayal to him and what we mean to each other. I wait again, unsure if she's done or if she's planning to rip into me some more. She has a right. It tells me what I need to know. That he's important to her. That she cares. Just like I do.

"Well? Are you into hockey? Or just hockey players? Or is it limited to my son?"

The sarcasm is strong with this one. "Do you actually want an answer, or do you just want to attack me?" I ask.

"He's my baby, and you're taking advantage of him!" Her eyes are on fire. "He has a bright future, and you are not going to get in the way of that."

"I don't want to get in the way of his future. I know he's on track to be called up by an NHL team. Whether we'll be able to manage a long-distance relationship remains to be seen, but I would never try to persuade him not to go down that path, if that's what he wants."

"*If?* He's been training his entire life for this. He's lived and breathed hockey since he could walk. This is what he's worked for, and I'll be damned if I'm going to let some woman with relationship issues drag my son down and ruin his future."

If she could breathe fire, I'm sure she would. I can appreciate her conviction and her love for her son.

"I realize how this must look from where you're standing, and I don't think there's anything I can say that's going to make you see it differently. I don't know if Maverick told you this, but he intervened when I was almost attacked by a group of men."

"What? When?"

"It was the end of October. I was putting out my garbage, and a group of drunk men started heckling me. They surrounded me, and Maverick stopped whatever was or wasn't going to happen. And then he made sure I was okay and suggested I take the self-defense class he teaches."

Her brows pull together. "That sounds like him, but it doesn't explain how you ended up in a relationship."

"I'm getting to that. I want you to know it didn't start with any sinister intentions."

"He told me you hooked up in the summer."

My eyebrows rise. "Wow. He's really open with you, isn't he?" I feel my face heat with embarrassment. Interesting that he'll divulge that kind of information but talking about what happened to his sister is such a closed subject.

"He has verbal diarrhea. It's hereditary. I'm sure if he could have kept that part to himself, he would have. As a mother of a daughter, I have to say, you are incredibly lucky that you hooked up with my son, and not some asshole."

"It was . . . impulsive, and out of character, and not something I would typically do. I don't know how to explain it, but I felt safe with him, despite not knowing him as well as I should have."

"He wouldn't hurt a fly—unless he's on the ice, anyway."

I nod. "He's more likely to catch it so he can set it free outside. Anyway, I went to the self-defense class. Only once, but he was insistent, and I thought it was a good idea. He told me he started teaching them because of what happened to his sister."

She takes a step back, and her fingers go to her bottom lip. She rubs the center of it, like Maverick does every time he talks about his sister. That scar. The one that came after the trauma, when she was locked in the closet during the game of hide-and-seek. "I don't understand how all of this connects."

"I got to know him as a person." I look up at the ceiling. "He is very charismatic and also hard to say no to."

"It's the dimples. They're a curse. His dad has them. Man can convince a desert dweller to buy a space heater like—" She snaps her fingers.

"The dimples are hard to resist," I agree.

"This still doesn't tell me what your intentions are. He's young. A lot happens in your twenties, as I'm sure you're aware. And his career is just starting, where yours is already established. How will that work? Are you planning to follow him wherever he signs?"

I shake my head. "I'll be staying here." *Or at least close to here.*

"And how will that work? Being the wife of an NHL player isn't easy. There are a lot of sacrifices. Your career comes second." It sounds like both a warning and a challenge.

"I don't know what the future holds for him and me, but I'll support whatever path he wants to take, whether it's to pursue a career in the NHL or something else. And I realize it won't be easy, but I don't want to give up on us before we've even had a chance to try to make it work."

"He's been training for this his entire life. He needs to stay focused on his goals."

"Is this a polite way of telling me I should step back?" I arch a brow.

"I don't want Maverick to get sidetracked by a fling and throw his entire future away. And some of the things he's said recently concern me, and they very conveniently coincide with his relationship with you."

"I don't want to get in the middle of you and your family, but I also won't minimize my relationship with Maverick. He's far too important to me, and I understand if this is difficult for you, but at least try to see it from his perspective." I hold up a hand before she has a chance to interrupt. "Maverick is incredibly selfless. He puts everyone else's needs ahead of his own. Particularly when it involves the people he loves, and that includes but isn't limited to his family, his friends, and his teammates. This year hasn't been easy for him." I want his mother to understand that there's more to this than just my relationship with her son, and that blaming it on me is convenient.

"Because of contract talks?" It's a question, not a statement.

"Among other things. He carries the weight of the world on his shoulders, and the path he's on is a challenging one. He has some big shoes to fill. Look, I won't betray Maverick's confidence, but know he's grappling with a lot. Our life circumstances and what we've both been going through brought us together in ways neither of us expected. I didn't intend to fall in love with him, no more than he intended to fall in love with me. But it happened. You don't have to like our relationship, but it seems a lot like you've already condemned it."

"His life is just starting."

"I know. And I won't get in the way of that. Whatever he wants, I will support and encourage, because that's what partners do. I know this is unconventional, but I would have walked away long before now if I didn't think our relationship was worth the challenges. He's under a lot of pressure. Feel however you want to feel about me but stand beside him. He's already fighting enough demons. He needs your love right now more than anything."

I turn and walk out of the room, hoping I haven't done more damage than good.

36

Rough Road Ahead

MAVERICK

I lose track of Clover sometime after the convocation, but it's not as though I'm going to make idle chitchat with her in front of her colleagues and my peers.

Since Lavender and Kody are leaving for New York this afternoon, we're under a bit of a time constraint, but his parents and my parents have still managed to put together a combined graduation and going-away party. They rented out an entire restaurant and invited all their hockey friends and our cousins and friends.

Of course, my dad and his buddies are all about discussing the coming contract talks, and this year's draft class and how they think things are going to go. Our school team ended up in first place overall, which is great, but my stats this year are slightly lower than they were last year. Kody, on the other hand, has had his best year yet.

My dad keeps reassuring me, telling me it wasn't until he was on the farm team that he really found his groove. I nod and agree, even though I'm worried I've already peaked. That the only reason I was drafted in the first place is because of my last name. And there are loads of players who make the pros, but never get a chance to play, and I don't know how I'll feel if I'm one of those.

At three, Kody and Lavender have to leave to catch their flight. There's a flurry of hugs and goodbyes, and because Mom is always emotional when it comes to Lavender, she starts crying.

Kody pulls me in for a hug, which isn't something he would usually do, so it takes me off guard. "Thanks for everything this year."

"You know I always have your back."

He steps back and nods, blowing out a breath. "I'll see you in a few weeks. We'll get some bro time when I'm back in Chicago in a few weeks, okay?"

He's coming back the weekend of the draft because it's what we always do. "For sure. Take care of my sister, okay?"

He gives me a wry smile. "Eh, it's more her taking care of me than the other way around these days, but I promise I'll keep her safe."

"I know you will. You always have, even when it was hard on you."

Lavender squeezes her way between us and wraps her arms around me. She's wearing a dress she most definitely made and is the same color as her name. She's so short, her face is in my armpit. "I'm gonna miss you, even though you were basically a ghost this semester." She lets me go and tips her head up so she can meet my eyes. I think she's a little drunk. I'm guessing she had Kody sneak her champagne on the sly, or my mom gave it to her. Either option is possible. "I hope whoever she is, I get to meet her one day."

I roll my eyes. "How are you fishing when you're about to get on a plane?"

"That was not a no, which is as good as a yes." She pats my cheek. "I love you. Thank you—for everything. I know it hasn't always been easy to be my brother."

"Don't." I shake my head. "Do not get emotional on me." I pull her in for another hug and bend down until I'm close enough to her ear that I can whisper. "I'm always on your side, Lavender. Always. You taught me what strength is. I'm so fucking proud of you."

I don't know why I'm suddenly all choked up, but I'm grateful when my mom pushes her way between us again and basically sobs all over Lavender. My dad gives Kody one last be-responsible lecture, which is pointless since they're driving them to the airport, along with Kody's parents, and they'll have at least forty minutes for be-safe lectures on the way.

Mom threads her arm through mine on the way out to our cars. "When are you coming to Lake Geneva for a visit?"

I guide us around a sewer grate, because my mom could trip over a toothpick. "I'm basically full-time at the gym now until training camp starts. I can check the schedule and see about an overnight, but I'm not coming up to visit if all you're gonna do is lecture me on my life choices." Nashville is out of the play-offs, which buys me some time, and it's the same for Kody.

She makes a face. "I'm worried about you."

"I graduated with a degree. I'm on track with hockey. What are you worried about?"

She stops walking, which forces me to stop as well. She glances around, checking to see if anyone is listening, but they're all busy hugging and chatting. "You're still seeing that woman." It's a statement.

"Why does it matter?"

She pokes at her cheek with her tongue. "I don't want you to make life-altering decisions influenced by someone you've never formally introduced to us."

"Is that you asking to meet her?"

"Has she managed to get the divorce papers signed yet? What about the husband? Have you seen him around?"

A week and a half ago, I started to suspect that he may have switched cars from the black BMW to a blue Kia. I can't prove that it's him because the windows are tinted and always rolled up, but I've taken down the license plate and I've seen it a few times. Unfortunately, there are two other blue Kias in the neighborhood, also with tinted windows, belonging to students. Now I see blue Kias everywhere, and I'm forever checking the license plates. So is Clover. But I'm not telling Mom that.

"I don't think anything I say right now is going to make you happy, and you need to focus your energy on Lavender and getting her on a plane to New York. Your issues with my life choices are still going to be here after you've dropped her off."

"Don't think I won't corner you when I get the chance."

"I know you will." I kiss her on top of the head. "I love you, and I know you love me back, and that's why you're being over-bearing. I'm an adult. I can make adult decisions. You're emotional because your baby girl is about to spread her wings and fly. This conversation can wait until another day when your feelings aren't on fire."

She huffs, likely aware that I'm right. "I love you too. All of my gray hairs came from you." I know she's joking, and she doesn't mean it the way I've taken it, but the sting is still there.

"I know." I smile, but it feels stiff. "I'm sorry for that. I'm trying my best to atone for my mistakes, but I don't always get it right."

"Vi, honey, we need to get going so the kids have lots of time to get checked in," Dad calls.

She frowns. "What did you just say?"

"I'm sorry about the gray hairs. Come on, everyone's waiting on you." I guide her over to the Bowman's massive SUV and help her into the passenger side. My dad and Rook are up front, the moms are in the middle and Kody and Lavender are in the back. I step back as Kody's dad pulls out of the spot. Lavender waves, grinning like she's won the lottery, and Kody looks somewhere between excited and like he wants to vomit. I keep waving as they pull away, but I don't love the concerned expression my mom continues to wear.

I thought Clover and I had gotten over our biggest hurdles, but maybe I'm wrong.

Twenty minutes later, I make a left down my street and notice the blue Kia parked halfway down the block. My brother's car isn't in the driveway, but Lavender's is, and that's where it will stay until she comes back at the end of summer.

River has a job at a sporting goods store, and he's planning to stay in the city since Josiah has a job here too. It seems like our house is destined to be empty a good part of the summer, seeing as I plan to spend my nights in Clover's bed, at least until her lease is up at the end of July.

I drive past my house and slow as I approach the blue Kia on the other side of the road. I grab my phone, roll down my window, and hit the brakes, snapping a picture and making sure I have the license plate and the house number in the background before I keep going.

For the very first time since this thing with Clover started, I don't circle the block and leave my truck at my place. Instead, I pull into her driveway. And I don't walk around back to the sliding glass door. I walk up the front steps and knock.

It swings open a moment later. She's no longer wearing the

dress and cardigan ensemble she had on earlier. Instead, she's in a pair of black skinny jeans and one of my old school T-shirts, from freshman year, before I packed on another forty pounds of muscle. I was going to donate it to the Salvation Army when I cleaned out my closet a month ago, but Clover saw the bag in the back seat of the truck and snagged it for herself.

"Hello, graduate." She's holding two champagne flutes in her hands and a bottle of bubbly.

"Hello, girlfriend." I step inside, take her face between my hands, and dip to brush my lips over hers. "I'm not planning to need a glass, but it's cute that you thought we might be civilized enough to use them tonight."

ONCE SCHOOL HAS OFFICIALLY CONCLUDED for both of us, there's a tangible shift in my relationship with Clover. While we still don't frequent restaurants inside the college catchment area, we've stopped driving way outside the city. Sometimes I'll leave my truck at my place, but if I have an early shift at the gym, I park in her driveway.

And every time I see that blue Kia, I take a picture. Even as June grows hotter, the windows remain rolled up so I can't see inside, but at this point, I'm positive it's Gabriel. He stays away from Clover, as per the order of protection that was filed shortly after her contract with the university ended, but I worry that he's on the edge of too close.

She and I have fallen into a routine of domestic comfort. Her lease is up at the end of July and Clover plans to move to her cabin in Pearl Bay. She's secured a position at the local library on the outskirts of Lake Geneva.

Our relationship feels more solid and stable than ever, but with the new draft class and contract talks hanging over my head, the nightmares have been ramping up, right along with my anxiety levels.

My dad has taken to calling every other day to check in. I should want to practice. I should want to know what my agent is saying, whether they think I'm NHL ready, or if I'll be sent to an AHL affiliate. But the more I talk about it, the more stressed I get.

"Are you okay, son? Why don't you come visit for a couple of days and we can follow the draft together, get ready for the contract deadlines, hear what your agent has to say? I'll book us some ice time. We can shoot the puck around."

"I can't. I'm working all week." I am working, but I have Friday and Saturday off because everyone knows this weekend is all about hockey.

"But you have the weekend off, right? I thought we planned this out."

Clover sets a cup of tea beside me and mouths, "*You should go.*"

I grab her hand, pulling her close enough that I can kiss her knuckles before I release her again. I found out she ran into my mother in the bathroom at convocation. It took her forty-eight hours to tell me, and only because my mom called asking if I was okay, and did I need to talk, and a bunch of other stuff about loving me unconditionally.

Also, Clover has a terrible poker face, at least with me. I only know what she's told me about their conversation, and she gets a little flustered when I ask about it, so I'm on the fence as to how truthful she's being. I don't think she's lying; I just don't know if she's omitting in a bid to protect me, or my mother, or both. It seems a lot like something she would do.

"I can come up Friday morning."

Clover gives me a look.

"I'll leave right after work on Thursday," I amend. "I finish at five, so I should be able to get there by seven or so."

"We'll have a late dinner." I can almost hear his relief, like he's walking on eggshells with me. Which sucks. "We can shoot the puck in the yard if you want, or go to the arena. Whatever works for you."

"That sounds good, Dad."

"I'll call you later this week, just to check in, okay?"

"Sure."

We end the call. I toss my phone on the coffee table, and I hold my hand out to Clover, who's still standing beside the arm of my chair. As soon as she lets me take her hand, I pull her into my lap and wrap my arms around her. "I should be excited about this." I mutter into her neck, breathing in that clove and cinnamon scent mixed with citrus.

"But you're not," she finishes.

"No. Not even a little."

"Do you want to talk about why?"

"I don't know if I can deal with the disappointment if I don't get offered a spot at training camp."

"You can't deal with your own disappointment or someone else's?" She shifts so her back is against the armrest, and she's curled up like a cat in my lap.

This isn't the first time we've had this conversation, and regardless of how many times I go over the same points, she still walks through them with me, every single time.

"Both? I should be living and breathing hockey. I should want to be on the ice every day."

"Says who?"

"Says everyone who's ever had the dream of becoming a professional player."

"You're living in extremes, though. Every life decision isn't all or nothing, and I feel like that's where you're currently situated. There doesn't seem to be any balance. You don't have to be like Kody, who from the sound of it can *only* live in extremes. Look at his relationship with your sister. It's always been all or nothing. He couldn't do it any other way, so that's how he lives his life. It doesn't have to be how you live yours."

"What if I make it and tank my career? I'm caught up in this shitty spiral, and I don't know how to get out of it."

"Okay. I have a question for you, and it's probably not one you're going to want to answer truthfully, but it's valid all the same."

I nod, waiting for her to go on.

"Is it less about you not being as good and more about you not *wanting* to be as good?"

"My stats answer that question." I was mid-range at best this season, and half of what's carrying me is my name. Or at least that's how it feels.

"But do they answer it because it's accurate or because you're consciously or subconsciously making sure they're not the stats you need to get where you've planned to go your entire life?"

"Honestly?" I rub my temple. "I have no idea anymore."

She sighs and smiles sadly. "I can't make this decision for you, Maverick. Only you know in your heart what's right. But I will tell you that you can't base your decision on our relationship, or on what you think your parents expect from you. This is your life, your future, your career. You need to decide what's best for *you*."

"I know." I take her hand in mine and lace our fingers together. "I feel like I've been on this path for so long, and now that I'm almost at the end, I'm questioning everything. And then there's you and me. This whole time I've been focused on the optics and how much easier it will be for us to be a couple when I'm playing professional hockey and I'm not just a college kid."

She props her elbow on the arm of the chair and settles her cheek on her knuckles. "You've never been just a college kid, Maverick. And my issues with the age gap between us are mine, not yours. And the optics of us shouldn't be a reason for you to sign or not sign a contract."

"I know you're right. I'm also trying to be realistic, because some NHL careers are short, and having a backup plan is essential."

"I agree on the backup plan, and your degree gives you the foundation you need for that. I think you need to see what you're offered and take it from there. Talk it through with your dad. Be honest with him. Tell him how you're feeling, and make your decision not based on what you're afraid of, but on what's going to make you happy."

"I really love you. You know that, right?" I tell her.

"I do. And I love you back." She runs her fingers through my hair. "And whatever you decide, I will stand beside you, and we'll figure out how we move forward from there, okay?"

"Okay." Even though everything else in my life seems uncertain, this thing between me and Clover doesn't.

"What else do you need from me right now?"

"Nothing." I take her face in my hands and kiss her softly. "Well, maybe one thing."

She smiles against my lips. "Take me to bed then."

ON THURSDAY EVENING, I toss my hockey equipment and an overnight bag into the back of my truck. Before I leave,

Clover and I have slow, needy sex. Well, I'm needy, and she's accommodating.

"I'm going to head up to Pearl Bay on Saturday, probably in the evening," she says as I put my shoes on. "That way I can be close, if you want to see me."

"Okay. Why don't I meet you at your cabin on Saturday night? Unless you want to come to my parents' place? Or we could do brunch on Sunday?"

"That's up to you. Maybe we play it by ear? I'll head to the cabin, and you can message and let me know what you'd prefer. I'm ready to meet them, and the rest of the people who are important to you. We can't be an us if we're just a you and me."

I kiss her again, but she stops before I can turn it into more. It's already six. I'm going to be late getting to Lake Geneva as it is.

When I pull into the driveway, my dad greets me at the door and grabs me in a hug. I wish I felt half as excited as he looks. He helps me with my bags, and I follow him to the kitchen. "You hungry? I've got pizza in the oven and beers in the fridge."

"Carb-and-cheese-a-thon since Mom's in New York, huh?"

Mom took the Butterson twins and River and Josiah along for the trip. They planned to surprise Lavender, so she isn't alone while Kody is here for contract talks. He's already here, but I won't see him until tomorrow.

"You know it. We can eat and then shoot the puck around?" He hands me a beer. "You're almost there, Mav. The world is at your fingertips."

I smile, but it feels a lot like all the things I want are slipping through them, or just out of reach.

37

Choices and Confessions

MAVERICK

I'm skating over the ice, but it's dark, and shadows move under my feet. I can't keep my eye on the puck, and I can't move fast enough. Everyone is skating circles around me. And there's a sound—a scream, lots of screams.

The lights in the arena are too bright, too much. So I look back down at the ice, trying to find my focus again. That's when I see the figures moving below the surface. Their fists pound against the ice under my feet, their screams muffled by the barrier.

I try to tell the other players, but I can't speak, and now the ice under me is turning red, obscuring faces that are all too familiar—my sister, my mother, Clover. I drop to my knees and slam my fists into the solid surface, scrambling to find a way to get there before the shadows envelop them.

There's a hand on my shoulder. Someone is trying to pull

me back, but I struggle to stay where I am. Everything goes blurry, and the voice gets louder and louder in my head.

"Mav, Maverick! Son, wake up."

I shoot up in bed, disoriented, unnerved. I'm covered in sweat, my sheets are twisted around my legs, the comforter thrown off, and my bedside lamp lies on its side, casting eerie shadows over the walls. I look down at my hands, expecting to see blood and bone, but they're fine.

"Fuck." I'm breathing heavy, feeling light-headed and like I'm going to vomit. I struggle to free myself from my sheets and stumble to the bathroom. I don't even have a chance to close the door before I'm retching into the toilet. I heave until all that's left is bile. A glass of water appears in my peripheral vision, and I take it. I swish and spit a few times before I take a tentative sip.

My dad flushes the toilet for me, and I drop to the floor in front of the bowl, glad I'm not a disgusting pig who leaves the bathroom a wreck. I drop my head between my knees, trying to find some calm. I don't close my eyes, though. I don't want those images back.

His hand comes to rest on my shoulder. "Take a few deep breaths."

I do as he says, tracing the pattern in the tile floor with my eyes, trying to shake the dream, and wishing Clover were here, but at the same time glad she didn't witness this.

She'd tell me I need to talk to someone.

She'd be right too.

"You all right?" Dad asks after a minute—or longer. I'm not sure.

"Yeah, just a bad dream," I mumble.

"Sounded like a lot more than a bad dream." He clears his throat. "Talk to me. What's going on? I feel like I'm on the outside, and I'm not used to that when it comes to you."

I raise my head and hate the expression on his face, the concern, but more prevalent is the hurt. I realize this isn't fair to either of us. I've spent my life nodding in agreement, following the path that's been set out for me, because it felt like the easier thing to do.

"I don't know if I want this."

"Want what?" he says.

I shift so my back is to the wall. He sits on the edge of the tub, hands clasped, elbows resting on his knees.

I take a deep breath and say the words I've been choking on for a while now. "I don't know if I want to play professional hockey."

"You've got contract talk jitters. Those are completely normal."

I shake my head. "No, Dad, I don't think that's it."

"You've been playing your whole life," he says gently. "This is what you've worked so hard for."

"I don't know that I should have been a first-round pick. I'm not as good a player as you."

"Nashville saw your potential. Give yourself some time at training camp to get comfortable. You'll get your feet under you. The skill is there. And you have the discipline."

He's not wrong about the discipline. I have that. But the skill set? That's been a struggle. I see it every day when I'm on the ice with my team, Kody especially. So, I go with blatant honesty, because I feel like I have nothing left to lose—except years of my life doing something I'm not sure will make me happy.

"Even if I have the discipline and skill, I don't know that I can spend my entire career on the ice trying to live up to your legacy, Dad."

His expression softens, and I see it, how hard this is for him too. "I don't expect that from you. Your career is yours. I'm not asking you to follow in my footsteps like that."

"I don't want to disappoint you." I stare down at my hands, wishing I had something to do with them other than inspect my hangnail.

"Son, look at me." He waits until I drag my eyes away from the floor. "You could never disappoint me. What's going on in your head? Does this have to do with the woman you're seeing?"

"No, it doesn't have to do with Clover." I shake my head. "Actually, yes, it does, but not in the way you think." I drop my hand and meet his imploring gaze. "She's not trying to sway me one way or the other. If anything, me playing professional hockey would be better for us. Then at least I'd look legit." I sigh. "She's been a great sounding board. We've talked it all through. She knows you not as Alex Waters the hockey legend, but as my dad. She's not subjected to the chatter of me following the same path." I run my hands over my thighs. "I've been having a lot of nightmares—tonight was probably the worst yet—and they've been ramping up the closer we get to training camp. I can already see what this is going to look like. My stats aren't like Kody's. I know you've been keeping it positive, but I don't know if I'm NHL ready, or if I'm ever going to be. If I didn't have a dad who was a hockey legend, that might be okay, but the reality is, you've had an incredible career, and no matter what, I'm always going to feel like I'm in your shadow—not because you've done anything to make it that way, but that's just the way it is. It's different with Kody. He's a natural. He's better than his dad, and that's saying something. Because Rook was and still is an amazing player." I hold up my hand to stop Dad from interrupting. "And maybe I could be as good as you. Maybe I could even be better, but I don't think I *want* to be."

I run a hand through my damp hair and shake my head. "You know, I've spent so much time avoiding relationships because I was terrified to ever feel the way you do about Mom. And I sure as hell never wanted to feel about someone the way Kody feels about Lavender. That guy stewed in his own misery for more than half a decade because he was afraid he would screw her up." I blow out a breath. "And I really had no intention of falling in love with anyone, let alone my fucking professor, but I just see the world differently. I think I always have. And I see that for all the good this career has done for you and our family, there's another side to it. Some people can handle it all, and maybe I could, but I don't want to."

My dad is silent for a long while before he finally asks, "If not a career in hockey, what do you want?"

I pull a square of toilet paper free, start folding it, and give voice to the thoughts that have been rolling around in my head for a while now. "Just a normal life. I don't deal well with the excess. I think . . . I just want to be a regular guy. I like my job at the gym, and they've been asking me if I want to move into management. I can see maybe wanting to open my own self-defense studio down the line. I can see myself going back to school and getting a degree in sports psychology, because it fits what I love. And I'd love to work with you, teaching kids how to play hockey—get 'em ready for the kind of future you always wanted for me." I set the crane on the edge of the tub and lift my gaze, afraid I'm going to see his disappointment and crack.

Dad rubs his bottom lip. It's a habit everyone in our family has, I realize. His expression doesn't hold the emotion I worried it would. Instead, he looks sad. "I only wanted that future for you because I thought it was something *you* wanted. I don't want you to feel like you *have* to follow this path. But I want to make sure, if you're going to say no, that you're doing it for the right reasons."

"Clover and I have talked about this a lot lately. She's been good for me on a lot of levels, even if you probably think the opposite. For a while, it felt like the only way my relationship with her would feel balanced was after I made the NHL. It's a lot less scandalous for a professor to be dating a professional hockey player than a student. But at the same time, that would make it even more complicated, and it would put our relationship under a microscope. That's another thing I don't want. Not just for us, or her, but for me in general."

"But is that the right reason to turn down an offer?" My dad shakes his head. "And I'm not telling you what you should or shouldn't do. I'm just asking questions, so I understand where you're coming from."

"I don't want to say there's no offer out there I would entertain, but playing professionally isn't where my heart is. When I look at my future, I don't see me on the ice for a decade and then coaching pro, or sportscasting, or any of those things. Maybe I'm a little bit more like Aunt Lily? I know she didn't go to the Olympics because of financial constraints, but she didn't let that define her. She's an amazing teacher, and I think I could be good at that. I'd rather help other people get there. I know myself, and I know how hard that life is on a family. I don't want to be one of those guys with a semi-decent career who's also been divorced three times because all of my relationships suffer."

"You've thought this through, haven't you?"

"This year has been eye-opening for me in a lot of ways. And I've loved playing for the college team. But it's not so much because of the sport as it is because it connects me to you and to Kody. Even if by some fluke I got traded and we did wind up together, it's unlikely we'd play on the same line. He's on another level."

"I keep wanting to say things like, *you can get there too*, but I don't think that's what you want to hear."

I've only ever seen my dad look this helpless once before, and it shreds me in ways I don't expect. But backtracking isn't going to change how I feel about this.

"I might be able to get there," I agree. "But I won't have a life, and I won't be happy trying to make it happen."

Dad is silent for a few very long, very terrifying seconds. "I'm sorry you didn't feel like you could tell me this sooner."

I shake my head. "I don't think I realized it until recently. I feel like I've let you down a lot, and I didn't want to do that again, especially with this."

"You've never let me down."

I drop my head, fighting with the words, but needing to get them out all the same. I need to make peace not just with myself, but with him as well. I see it all now, the way it links together, how the past keeps coming up because I haven't ever dealt with it the way I need to. "I feel like I did—not so much with hockey, but with Lavender."

He moves from the edge of the tub and drops down, crouching in front of me. "Look at me, Maverick."

I lift my gaze and find him on the edge of emotion. I feel his anguish like fresh wounds.

"Are you talking about the carnival?"

"That's one instance, yeah." I swallow bile, uncertain if there's anything left to purge apart from words and what remains of the guilt I'm trying to let go of.

"And the time she got locked in the closet?" His voice is soft and unsteady.

I nod once, not trusting my voice.

He closes his eyes. "Fuck."

When they open, they're swimming. I don't think I've ever seen my dad cry. I've seen him get angry, lose his shit, but the only time I've seen him this kind of emotional is when he talked about the accident that nearly ended his career. And the night Lavender went missing. "Are you referring to what happened in my office after? When I lost it?"

"Yeah."

"I'm so sorry, son. I'm so fucking sorry." His voice breaks, and he turns his head, like he's trying to keep it together. "I didn't realize you were still holding onto that after all these years. Not like this. Your mom and I made a mistake—one we can't ever take back. You didn't do anything wrong. You were just a kid. You weren't responsible for any of it, and you weren't responsible for what happened when Lavender got locked in the closet either. There were adults in the house who were supposed to be paying attention. And I knew that lock was prone to jamming. I'd meant to fix it the week before, but I forgot. Your mom had dresses in there, and she'd been going through the closet that afternoon and forgot to close the door and lock it." He pauses, taking a breath. "I know I lost it on you that night, and I shouldn't have. I couldn't get my emotions under control, and it wasn't fair."

"I told you it was my fault. It made sense that you'd be upset with me," I tell him, not wanting to shift that burden off my shoulders and onto his. I'd been the seeker. I should have found Lavender sooner. And he'd gone off in a way that had terrified me. But I felt like I'd deserved it, because for the second time, my selfishness was the reason something bad had happened to her. Rook had eventually come in and told me to go upstairs.

I perceived it as anger back then, but when I think about it now, through an adult lens, I realize he was terrified, that it triggered the memory of when we'd lost Lavender.

He shakes his head. "You were kids. It was an accident. I should never have made you feel like it was yours to own. It wasn't your fault. If I'd known you were still dealing with this . . ." He looks away, choking on emotion. "I don't know how I didn't see it." He pulls me into a bone-crushing hug—awkward since we're both still on the floor. "You have always been your sister's protector and her biggest advocate. Always. You put everyone ahead of yourself." He pulls back, eyes red-rimmed. "I'm sorry I failed you."

"You didn't fail me, Dad."

"But I did, because I didn't see how much this was weighing you down, how *my* actions are responsible for making you feel this way all these years." He rubs at the corner of his eye, expression despondent. "How can I ease the burden, son?"

"You just did." I feel like that kid all over again, but instead of the weight of guilt dragging me down, it's been lifted from my shoulders—a lot like a different weight was lifted after Lavender and I had that heart-to-heart.

For years I've carried around that blame, wore it like a punishment, believing everyone felt the same way. Now to be absolved again, to see it through a different lens, brings with it a peace I've never experienced before. It's almost a terrifying feeling, and one I don't know how to handle.

My dad hugs me again, and I break, really and truly in a way I don't expect. I didn't know how much I needed to hear those words until he spoke them. I needed the absolution so I can finally move on from this.

Eventually he sits back and reaches over, yanking several feet of toilet paper free. He tears off a handful of squares and passes them to me. He uses the rest to blow his nose. I do the same.

"I feel like I have a lot of years of making up to do when it comes to you," he says.

"You don't." I shake my head. "I loved the time I had with you more than I loved playing hockey. It was worth it, though.

Taught me solid work ethic." I toss my wad of TP into the toilet. "But, uh, if you're really serious, I wouldn't say no to you dealing with Mom if I don't end up accepting a training camp offer."

He laughs and runs a hand through his hair. "I can handle your mom on this one."

My alarm goes off, signaling that it's six, the time I usually get up for work. There's not much point in going back to bed. I wouldn't be able to sleep.

"You think you can handle coffee?" Dad asks.

"Yeah." I pick myself up off the floor and hold out a hand, helping my dad up.

He grimaces and limps a couple of steps before he finds his footing, another reason I'm not entirely sold on a professional hockey career. I see the toll it's taken on my dad's body, and what that might mean down the road.

I pull on a shirt and shorts and follow him downstairs. We make a pot of coffee, and I throw some whole grain bread in the toaster. And instead of talking about this year's draft and who we think is going first round, we pull out the Scrabble board, and my dad lets me kick his ass.

Once the day gets started, Kody and I message back and forth all morning. He's meeting with his agent and while Vancouver drafted him, there are trade talks and apparently Philly is pushing for him. He lived in Philly for years, and it's the closest to Chicago he can get.

Kody comes over later in the evening, and we head down to the beach, beers in hand. Our dads hang back, probably trying to give us space.

I leave my flip-flops on the beach and dip my toes in the water. It's hot, being the end of June, but the water is still cold.

"You all right?" he asks.

I nod and drop down in the sand, close enough so the water

comes up to my toes, but not so close that my shorts get wet. "Even if I get an offer for training camp, I'm not sure I'm going to go."

"What do you mean *if?* You'll get an offer. There's no way you won't."

I appreciate his conviction, even though I'm not so sure it's accurate. "Have you called Lavender and told her yet?"

He shakes his head. "We decided we'd wait until I was back in New York before I say anything. I'm ninety-nine percent sure I'll be going to Philly, but my agent is negotiating, so we'll see. And Lavender and I want to be together when I give her the news. She threatened to break up with me if I didn't accept an offer."

I frown. "Why the fuck wouldn't you accept?"

He answers my question with a question. "Why are you on the fence about training camp?"

"I haven't been offered yet. The only thing you love more than hockey is my sister." I pause. "Ah, that's it, isn't it? You're worried about being away from her."

He pulls something out of his pocket and flips it between his fingers. "I just got her back. I don't want to risk losing her."

"You won't lose her. You might have a hard time with the distance, but you'll manage."

"Yeah. I know. But Philly's looking a hell of a lot more alluring than Vancouver."

"You gotta do what's going to make you happy."

"It's about more than my career now." He settles his forearms on his knees. "Talk to me about why you're on the fence? What's going on?"

"I don't think I want it, not the way I should. And taking a spot from someone who's driven to play just because I think it's what I'm *supposed* to do doesn't seem like a good idea."

"What's really going on, Mav? I know I've been wrapped up in my own stuff, but this is about more than just hockey." I catch a glimpse of the tiny purple fabric heart between his fingers and know it has to be something Lavender gave him—a talisman of sorts, I'm sure. Something to calm him while he's away from her.

"You remember when I told you I hooked up with someone before the end of summer? I was late for skate practice and Coach made everyone do suicides?"

His brow furrows. "Oh yeah, that was brutal. Half the guys vomited."

"I felt bad about that." I was one of the people who vomited. Lack of sleep, food, and too much exertion is not a winning combination. "My hookup ended up being one of my professors in the fall semester."

He fumbles the heart but manages to recover it before it hits the ground. "Wait, what? You slept with your professor?"

"Yeah, and to make a long story short, now, uh, we're kind of dating."

He purses his lips. "Is that the woman who was at the game a while back? Close to the end of the season? You two kept looking at each other."

"For someone who's usually oblivious to that kind of shit, you sure picked up on that fast."

"Well, shit. That explains a lot." He keeps flipping the heart between his fingers. "I knew something was going on. I hadn't seen you with anyone in months. And even when your truck was in the driveway, you were hardly ever home. I guess now I know where you were always disappearing to. I can't believe you kept that under wraps all this time."

"I didn't want to put you in an awkward position before the school year was over, and I couldn't put Clover's career in jeopardy. And then you and Lav moved to New York."

"I get it. We were students; she was a professor. The fewer people who knew the better."

"I wanted to tell you."

He clinks his bottle against mine. "You don't have to explain. Or feel bad, Mav. You always put everyone else before yourself." His smile is a little sad. "I'm sorry you couldn't talk to me about it."

"It was the circumstances, and it wasn't your fault. Hopefully you'll get to meet her before you head to training camp."

"That'd be good. I'd like that." He leans back on his hands, looking at the sky. "How old is she, anyway?"

"Thirty."

"Wow. That's settling-down age."

"Says the guy who's been waiting to settle down with my sister since you could say her name."

"Touché," he says dryly. "You really do live up to your name."

"How do you mean?"

"You've never been one to conform. You make your own rules. And you never take the path of least resistance."

"Nothing good ever comes easy."

"Isn't that the truth?"

He clinks his beer against mine again, and we both tip our bottles back.

I know the road ahead is going to be bumpy, but I'm ready for the ride.

NASHVILLE OFFERS me a spot at training camp. I don't have to accept right away, but based on the way my palms start to sweat and I nearly have a panic attack, I already know I don't want to accept.

I don't think I want it enough—not judging from the invisible weight that seems to lift when I make a list of pros and cons and it leans heavily on the con side.

I'm not disappointed by the offer, or jealous of Kody's choices. I'm happy for my best friend and relieved for me. And that tells me everything I need to know. But I ask my dad if we can sit on my decision. I don't want Kody's dad to try to convince me to change my mind. And I don't want to steal Kody's thunder.

I call Clover, and she and I plan to meet up at her cabin in Pearl Bay later in the evening. Today has been intense, and while it's been good to have the support of my dad and my best friend, I want to run it all by Clover and tell her everything that's happened over the past forty-eight hours. I feel like my entire life has changed course, and this new path is the one I really want.

At six fifty-two, I get a message from Clover that she's heading for Pearl Bay soon, and she'll let me know when she arrives. But when I still haven't heard from her by eight, I start to get antsy, especially when my text messages go unanswered. She turns her alerts off when she gets in the car to avoid distractions, but maybe she forgot to turn them back on. It's happened before. When I call, it goes to voicemail.

"Maybe her cell died, and she doesn't have a charger?" Kody suggests.

"She's usually prepared for things like that." Although if her charger isn't in her car, it could explain the issue. "I'm gonna drive over there and see what's going on."

"I should probably head back to my parents' since I have to be on a plane balls early." Kody is meeting with the general manager of Philly tomorrow morning and then flying back to New York in the evening.

"We could follow you, to make sure everything is cool?" BJ pushes out of the Adirondack chair. He drove over from Pearl Lake with Kody this afternoon so the three of us could hang out before Kody leaves again for New York.

"Yeah, sure. I think that'd be good." I don't like the gnawing feeling in my gut that has nothing to do with my decision not to take Nashville's offer.

The drive to Pearl Bay only takes twenty minutes, but the sun is going down, casting murky shadows over the road.

"You all right, man?" Kody asks from his spot in the passenger seat. BJ is following in his Jeep.

"I don't know. I don't like that she's not responding."

"Maybe she stopped to pick up groceries or something?"

"Maybe. That's possible." She hasn't been to the cabin in a few weeks, so it's entirely possible that she made a pit stop to stock up on essential items.

The uneasy feeling in my gut settles when I pull down the driveway and her car comes into view. "Thank fuck."

It looks like she's just arrived. The trunk of her car is open, her overnight bag still inside. I grab it and head for the front porch. But my blood runs cold at the shrill scream that comes from the other side of the partly open door.

38

The Edge of Awful

CLOVER

I set the grocery bags on the porch and slide the key into the lock, letting myself into the cabin. I'm not sure what to expect in the next twenty-four hours, whether Maverick will be going to Nashville, or somewhere else, or if he'll decide to pursue another career. But whatever his decision, I'm on his side.

I pick up the bags, leaving the door open because my overnight bag is still in the trunk. I want to get the groceries unpacked first and the champagne in the fridge. I pull my phone out and bring up Maverick's contact, ready to fire off a message to let him know I'm here and he can come by whenever he's ready.

I pick up the bottle of champagne in my other hand and turn to the fridge, but I startle at the sound of the door hitting the wall. I spin around, thinking maybe we're in for a storm.

There were some dark clouds on the drive in, and sometimes the wind acts like a funnel in the bay, depending on the direction it's coming from.

But it's not wind.

It's Gabriel.

Message half-composed, I fumble my phone, and it drops to the floor. "What the hell are you doing here?"

"I'd ask you the same question, but I already know the answer, so that would be pointless." He steps inside the cabin, looking around the space. His gaze lands on the kitchen table, where two paper cranes sit in the empty fruit bowl. One from the first night we met, the other from our New Year's celebration.

"How much longer is this going to continue? What you're doing is embarrassing for both of us," he says as he crosses the room.

I take a step back, the floorboards squeaking under my feet. "You're violating the order of protection. You need to leave."

He ignores me. "I'm done with the bullshit. I've been more than patient, more than understanding about this whole thing. But you're taking this way too fucking far, and it needs to stop."

"You've been understanding? About what?" I don't like the wild look in his eyes, or the way he doesn't seem to be tracking quite the way he should. I glance down. My phone is only a few feet away, almost within reach, but I don't want to take my eyes off him, and I don't like that he's between me and the front door. There's a sliding door in my bedroom, but that's on the other side of the cabin.

"You and this *kid* you're fucking." He spits the words, like they taste sour in his mouth.

"That's none of your business, is it?"

He takes another step closer, and my only option is to back up, moving me farther from the front door, but marginally closer to the bedroom. I'll still have to cross the living room to get there, though.

He sneers, and his voice is mostly a growl. "Have you forgotten? You're still *my* wife."

I keep my hold on the bottle of champagne. If nothing else, it'll make a good, albeit expensive, weapon. "Not willingly! It's been two years since we separated." And at this moment, I realize today is the anniversary of the day I packed a bag and left him.

"I'm not giving you a divorce, Clover. You don't get to run away from me anymore."

"You can't hold me hostage forever." I glance at the clock on the stove. It's already after eight. It only takes an hour or so to get here, and I told Maverick I would message when I arrived. He'll worry if he doesn't hear from me soon.

"Oh, I can, and I absolutely will." His lips curl into a sneer as he reaches the island, and he slams his fist on the counter. "You are *my* fucking *wife*!"

The hairs on the back of my neck rise. "Why won't you just let me go, Gabriel?"

"Because you are mine, and you don't get to decide when you're done with me. I've waited two years for you to come to your senses."

I've never seen him unhinged like this. "I've already moved on." I motion between us, bottle of champagne still fisted in my other hand. "We are over."

"No." He shakes his head. "We're not over until I say we're over. I'm done being patient. I should've burned this goddamn place to the ground when I realized what you were doing."

"What?"

"I know you've been sneaking out here for months with that little shit. Playing house. Whatever plan you think you have, it's going to be awfully hard to execute if this place is a pile of ash."

My phone lights up on the floor, and I glance down as Maverick's name flashes across the screen. I should have messaged him as soon as I pulled into the driveway. I always forget to take it off the do-not-disturb setting when I'm done in the car.

The momentary distraction is all it takes. Gabriel darts around the counter, and I raise the champagne bottle. His face is a mask of fury, and he grabs my wrist on the downswing. I lose my grip and the bottle flies out of my hand, smashing on the kitchen floor. Shards of glass skitter across the tile and ping off the cabinets.

At first, I panic, and all those self-defense moves I learned with Maverick fly out the window. Gabriel grabs me by the hair, fingers anchoring near my scalp, and spins me around. When my cheek hits the counter, stars burst in my vision with the pain.

Real fear settles under my skin as Gabriel's legs bracket mine, feet pressed against my heels, knees on either side of mine, pinning me against the lower cabinets on the island. I'm bent over the edge, chest pressed flat against the granite counter. He grabs my arm with his other hand, fingers digging into the skin as he forces it to the counter, holding me down.

The front door is open a few inches, and I spot the gas can sitting just inside the cabin on the shoe mat.

"What are you doing?" I struggle to keep my voice even.

"Helping you make better decisions." His fingers slide along the back of my scalp, nails digging in, keeping me pinned to the counter.

Pain shoots across the side of my face. "You're hurting me," I grit out.

"I know. How does it feel to be the one with no control,

Clover?" I try to shrink away as his lips brush my ear. "Sometimes tough love is the only way to get through to someone like you."

The teapot on the counter is just beyond my reach. If I were a few inches closer, I could grab it. There's a pencil next to it. It's one of Maverick's mechanical ones. We used it to record our scores when we played Scrabble the last time we were here.

My phone buzzes on the floor again. This time with a call.

"Someone wants your attention. I think he's had enough of it, don't you?"

More of Gabriel's weight presses into my right side, like he's looking over his shoulder. I take the opportunity and try to grab the pencil. I skim the end with my fingertips, but it's just out of my reach.

"What do you think you're doing?" Gabriel's rage is a roar and a red shroud that blankets me.

He yanks my head back, and in that moment, I realize if I don't do something *now*, this may end very badly for me. And I can't let that happen. I won't let this man take anything else away from me. Calm washes over me as I reach behind, grabbing hold of Gabriel's hair. At the same time, I pull his head forward and snap mine back, head-butting him. The muscles in my neck strain with the movement, but it has the desired effect. Gabriel's hold on my hair loosens, and he rears back, giving me enough room to maneuver.

I elbow him in the side and try to get out from under him, but he manages to grab my arm. I drop my shoulder and jam it into his diaphragm, and on the way up I twist my way out of his grasp. I try to sprint for the door, but he manages to grab me by the hair again, and I go down, landing in the middle of the champagne and shards of glass. My face hits the floor, and my teeth cut into my lip.

I taste copper as sharp pain radiates up my arm, but at least I'm not the only one lying in a pool of champagne and glass. I slam an elbow into Gabriel's neck. He splutters, choking on a curse, and it gives me enough time to get to my feet and out from behind the counter.

I run for the door, the floor slippery under my feet. I grab the gas can, adrenaline the only thing keeping me going. Gabriel is right on my heels, so I do what I must to stop him. I swing the can around, slamming it into his knee.

The horrible crunching sound is accompanied by Gabriel's roar of pain. He lands on the floor and clutches his leg.

Just then I hear my name being called from outside.

Maverick.

39

Down the Hole

MAVERICK

When I push open the door, it bumps into something, and I quickly realize that something is a someone, and that someone is Clover. Less than ten feet away from her is Gabriel, lying on his side on the floor, clutching his knee. A gas can—the metal kind, not the plastic ones you'd use to fill a riding lawn mower—sits on the floor next to her.

It doesn't take long for me to process the scene. But the thing that sends me into full-blown panic is the blood. Clover's lip is bleeding, and the sleeve of her pale green cardigan is tinted dark red.

"The fuck?" I drop to my knees, angling my body so I can still see Gabriel, but my focus is on Clover. "What do I do? What can I do?"

Her eyes—wide with mirroring panic—lock on mine. "I'm okay. Outside. Let's get outside." She grabs my shoulders.

"You're bleeding."

"I'm fine," she assures me. "Grab the gas can."

I help her to her feet and do as she asks, ushering her outside. The sun has nearly set, so I flick on the porch lights, illuminating the space where BJ and Kody are standing.

"What the hell is going on? Are you okay?" Kody's gaze darts from Clover to me to Gabriel, who is still on the floor, but working to pick himself up.

I point a finger at him. "Stay the fuck down unless you want a whole pile of broken bones."

I turn my attention back to Clover. She's shaking, adrenaline probably coursing through her veins. When she crashes, it's going to be rough. She has a bruise on her cheek that's quickly turning dark purple, and there's a thin trail of blood making its way down her chin. I don't have anything to wipe it away with, and the sight of it takes me back to the night Lavender got locked in the closet. I try to push those memories down, though, and stay in the present, where I'm needed.

I take her face between my palms. "Sweetheart, can you tell me what happened?"

"He must have followed me here. He said he was going to torch the place. He came at me, and I dropped a bottle of champagne and fell in the glass. It's all surface wounds. We need to call the police."

"I already called 911. They're on the way." BJ holds up his phone. "Ambulance included."

"You should sit down," I tell her.

She nods, and I guide her to one of the chairs. When she's sitting, I use the hem of my shirt to wipe the blood from her chin and inspect the wound. It doesn't look serious enough to need stitches.

At the sound of a grunt, I turn to find Gabriel gripping the doorjamb, trying to stay upright.

I move around BJ and Kody, who have formed a barricade between us and him. I grab him by his shirt and slam him against the wood siding. And in that moment, I understand exactly what murderous rage feels like—how a person can be so blind with hatred that they could take a life. "I'll fucking end you, you son of a bitch." I slam my fist into his face, once, twice, a third time. Blood gushes from his nose, and his lip splits.

The memories I've been fighting come to the surface.

Lavender's torn dress.

Her bleeding palms.

Her haunted eyes.

My father's rage.

The way the SUV smelled like gas after that night, and my dad traded it in a week later and got a new one for my mom.

"Mav, that's enough. You're gonna do damage you can't come back from," BJ says calmly. "The cops are coming; they'll handle it. You gotta let him go."

Kody's arm comes around me, and BJ pries my hands free from Gabriel's shirt.

As soon as I let Gabriel go, he sinks to the deck, head lolling back, knocked out cold. I glance down at my hands, knuckles split and bloody, not just with mine but his too.

Kody grips my shoulder. "Look at me, Mav. Look at me."

I meet his gaze and see a haunted expression I'm familiar with echoed back at me. "She's safe now, and she needs you. Take a breath. Be what she needs."

I nod once and wipe my hands on the back of my jeans to hide the worst of the damage. Clover reaches out a hand and I take it, dropping to my knees in front of her.

"I'm sorry I wasn't here. I should have met you here."

She takes my face in her hands. "It's okay. I'm okay because of you. It's a few surface wounds. Nothing a few Band-Aids and a little TLC can't fix."

"Let me see." I kiss her fingertips before I gently turn them over, inspecting her arms. The right sleeve is patchy with seeping blood along her forearm. "Is this the only place you landed in the glass?"

She nods. "I tried to roll the other way, but I couldn't avoid all of it."

"Does it hurt?" I rub my thumb over the center of her palm, memories bubbling up of when Lavender used to come to my room and ask me to help with her hands.

"Not much. I think the adrenaline is still at work, though."

The sound of sirens in the distance brings another barrage of memories, but I shove them down and lock them in the box, needing to stay present with Clover.

"Do you want me to have a look at them? Do you have a first aid kit here?"

She strokes my cheek. "The ambulance will be here soon. We can wait for them."

Kody appears in my peripheral vision, holding two bottles of water. He sets them on the arm of the chair and holds out a blanket. "I grabbed this. The temperature is dropping, and the shock might be starting to wear off." He puts his hand on my shoulder. "You should sit."

I shift out of the crouch and let my knees settle on the deck, still keeping a barrier between Gabriel and Clover. He groans from the other side of the porch, starting to come around. Blood seeps out of his nose and runs down his chin. If Kody and BJ hadn't been here, I don't know if I would have stopped.

Emergency services shows up, bringing with them the police, an ambulance, and fire truck. The fire truck doesn't stay, but the ambulance and police do. Pearl Bay is a tiny community, with only a few police officers assigned to the area, but

Pearl Lake is slightly larger, and Lake Geneva has a much more substantial force. Our families are well known around here, and the officer assigned to the call has a son who plays hockey. My dad coaches him. It's times like this when the blessing of having a famous parent weighs out over the negatives.

Gabriel violated the terms of his order of protection and physically attacked Clover, so he's taken away in cuffs and will likely spend the night in the local jail after he's been checked over for injuries. He seems to be struggling to put weight on his left leg. He's not entirely coherent as they put him in the back of the cruiser, still ranting about how he should have burned the place to the ground months ago.

Clover gives her statement, and I give mine, and then she's loaded into the back of the ambulance and taken to the Pearl Bay Emergency Clinic so a doctor can look at her injuries. I go along with them, leaving Kody and BJ to give their statements with promises to check in later.

While Clover is getting X-rays on her cheek, I call my dad and fill him in. He tells me he'll be at the clinic as quickly as he can.

I'm allowed back in the treatment room with Clover after the X-rays. There are no fractures or broken bones. But I hold her hand as they remove several pieces of glass from her forearm and use Steri-Strips on the shallower wounds, stitching up the worst of them. In the end, she has more than twenty stitches in her forearm, but otherwise she's okay—physically, at least. The doctor gives her a prescription for painkillers, and she has a follow-up appointment in a few days.

My dad is sitting in one of the too-small-for-his-frame chairs when we step out of the exam room. He pushes out of his seat. His hair is a mess, like his hand has been in it a bunch. "Are you two okay?" His gaze shifts from me to Clover and back.

"It's all surface wounds." I repeat the words Clover keeps

giving me, as if they're somehow going to dampen the fears that continue to claw their way up from the box of memories I don't want anymore.

He looks at Clover. "Kody and BJ told me what happened. If it's all right, it'd make me feel a lot better if the two of you came home with me."

"That would be great." She squeezes my hand.

The twenty-five-minute ride from the clinic to my parents' place in Lake Geneva is quiet. I sit in the back with Clover. The adrenaline has likely long worn off, but I can feel the nervous energy seeping out of her.

I press my lips to her temple. "It's okay. My dad is on our side, and my mom is in New York with my sister." I know she's the one Clover is most worried about, and the last thing she needs is more stress after what happened tonight. My phone is blowing up with messages in my group chat with Kody and BJ. I fire one off to let them know we're fine and we're going back to my parents' place. I wish Kody luck tomorrow and thank them both for having my back.

We pull into the driveway, and I help Clover out of the truck. The stiffness and aches are starting to set in, based on the tentative way she moves. Once we're inside, I offer to make her a cup of tea.

Clover gives me a tremulous smile. "That would be good, I think."

"Do you want to sit in the living room while I make it, or do you want to stay in the kitchen with me?"

"I'd like to stay with you, if that's okay."

"Yeah. Of course." I guide her to one of the bar stools at the kitchen island and help her up, then grab a thin blanket from the living room and drape it over her shoulders. Her cardigan went into the trash at the clinic. Most of her right forearm is covered in gauze and bandages.

My dad goes to the cupboard and retrieves two mugs. He squeezes my shoulder. "Sit down, son. I've got this."

I don't argue. I don't feel particularly steady on my feet—more like I'm going through the motions, trying to keep my head in the present. I take the seat to the left of Clover and thread my fingers with hers.

Dad sets the kettle to boil and pulls out the box of Bengal Spice tea. It's become a staple at my parents' place since I introduced them to it during the holidays. He drops a bag in both cups.

"Are either of you hungry?" he asks. "Sometimes trauma does that. Makes us hungry. Or not. I'll put out one of the board things your mom loves to make with all the crackers and stuff on it, yeah?"

I don't stop him. I know he's doing his best to be helpful. He starts pulling out boxes of crackers and cookies. He finds two blocks of random cheese in the fridge, breaks up a couple of chocolate bars, fills a bowl with nuts and another with pretzels, and sets it on the counter in front of us.

Clover picks up a cracker and nibbles on it.

"The police said they're going to stop by in the morning again to get any additional details they need from the two of you about what happened. Gabriel has been officially charged with violating the order of protection you filed." My dad raps on the counter. "If you need any help with legal advice, I can give you my lawyer's number."

Clover nods. "I have a divorce lawyer I've been working with."

My dad bites the inside of his cheek. "No offense, Clover, but since you're still fighting to get that divorce you so clearly want, it might be time to switch things up. Not saying you need to decide that right now after the night you've had, but, uh, I have someone on retainer who could probably help expedite things for you."

"Maybe we could talk about that later, Dad?" I suggest.

"Yeah. Of course. Sorry." He shakes his head. "I just . . . I know how important you are to Maverick, and I want to keep you both safe."

A buzz sounds, and Dad pulls his phone from his back pocket. "That's your mom."

"You haven't told her about this, have you?" I ask, suddenly on high alert.

He gives me a look. "Not a chance in hell. The only thing your mother knows is that you've been offered a spot at training camp and we're in discussions. She's got enough to deal with keeping your sister calm while Kody's here. The less she knows right now, the better. Kody and BJ know not to say anything, and I've already talked to Rook and Lainey and your aunt and uncle, so they'll keep an eye on those boys. The police aren't offering information to local outlets for twenty-four hours. The important part is that everyone is safe. I'm just going to take this." He clears his throat and brings the phone to his ear. "How's my beautiful wife? You and the kids having a good time?"

He squeezes my shoulder and heads down the hall toward his office.

I turn and press a kiss to Clover's temple. "How you hanging in there?"

"Nashville called you up."

I can't read her tone or her expression. "Yeah. But I'm not making any decisions about that right now. And we can talk about it later, okay? You and your well-being are the top priority."

She nods slowly, and I have to wonder how much of this she's really processing.

I tuck her hair behind her ear. "You okay, sweetheart?"

She leans into my touch, seeking comfort maybe. "This all feels so surreal. I don't want to think about what could have happened, but it's hard not to let your mind go there."

"We need to get a proper security system set up at your place before you move in there for good," I tell her.

"That's a good idea." She takes another sip of her tea. "Is it okay if I lie down? I'm exhausted in a way I can't describe."

"Of course." I take her upstairs to my bedroom, help her into one of my T-shirts, and lie down beside her.

"Thank you," she murmurs, snuggling into my side.

"For what?"

"For coming into my life. For teaching me that I'm stronger than I think. For saving me."

"I didn't save you. You saved yourself."

"Because you taught me how."

I kiss her softly and stroke her hair until she falls asleep.

When I'm sure she's out, I head back downstairs to check on my dad. He's a lot like me in that he'll go into fix-the-problem mode right away, but it doesn't mean the gravity of this isn't going to hit him eventually.

I find him sitting in the living room, flipping one of the many paper cranes I've made over the past two days between his fingers. A glass of scotch sits on the table beside him. My dad isn't a big drinker. Mostly he reserves scotch for holidays and parties. Sometimes he'll kick back and have a beer with dinner, and of course there's the dock days of summer, but the good scotch is usually reserved for special occasions.

"How is she doing?" he asks.

I take the chair across from him. "She's asleep. She was exhausted."

He nods and rubs his bottom lip. "That cabin, is it going to be Clover's primary residence? Or is it her vacation spot?"

"Her lease runs out on her place in Chicago at the end of July, so her plan is to move into the cabin. But, uh, obviously there have been some issues since the ex keeps fighting her on the place."

He pokes at his cheek with his tongue. "If it's okay with you, I'm going to make a call in the morning and get a security system installed. It's pretty isolated, and there's a lot of tree coverage between her and her neighbors. I think there's going to be some building happening there soon, but the added protection would be good. And maybe a dog wouldn't be the worst thing in the world." He sets the crane on the coffee table. "I take it if she's going to be living there, you'll be spending a lot of time there too."

"Yeah, probably. I don't really want her to be on her own out there, not with her ex threatening to light the place on fire." I scrub a hand over my face, trying to get the scene I witnessed out of my head.

"Why don't the two of you stay here for a bit? Take the pool house so you have some privacy."

"You think Mom's going to be cool with that?" I don't like the idea of Clover in that cabin all by herself any more than my dad does.

"Despite your mom's feelings about who you're dating, what she wants most is for her kids to be happy. I see the way you and Clover are together." He looks up at me. "Give Mom a chance to see that too. She'll come around."

40

The Hand in the Dark

CLOVER

The police show up first thing the next morning. Maverick's father brings me an assortment of his wife's clothing to choose from. She's much shorter and bustier than me, but I find a pair of leggings and a loose, flowy tank top and cardigan that fit fine. Based on the interactions I've had with Violet, it would be safe to say she would not be excited to see me wearing her clothes.

Maverick's eyes are red-rimmed, and he looks as exhausted as I feel. I slept okay, but I woke up every time I tried to roll onto my right side, and I had to get up in the middle of the night to take a painkiller. At the time, I thought I'd woken him up, but I'm wondering now if he was awake already.

"Do you want privacy for this part?" Maverick asks when they start to ask questions about my relationship with Gabriel.

I shake my head, needing the emotional support more than anything else. "Can you stay?"

"Of course, sweetheart." He presses his lips to my temple and frees another tissue from the box. But he doesn't pass it over, instead he gently dabs under my eyes and wraps his arm around my shoulder.

I start at the beginning, when I met Gabriel at a conference, how it had been a whirlwind romance, that we'd only been dating a handful of months when he proposed, that the engagement was equally short, and that once I was his wife, the expectations had started to change.

The dynamics shifted slowly at first. It started with moving us away from my family and friends, so he was the sole source of support. Then he began belittling my job, telling me my PhD didn't matter, that he would take care of me. Then the gaslighting. At one point, I'd felt like I was losing my mind.

"What does this look like moving forward?" Maverick asks.

"We can hold him for forty-eight hours, but after that, his bail is set at five hundred thousand."

"Will he be able to come up with that kind of money?" Maverick asks.

"I don't know. Maybe?" I feel like I'm being choked by fear. Not just for myself, but for Maverick and his family.

Maverick brushes tears away. "Hey, it's okay. We'll keep you safe, sweetheart."

The police assure us he'll be monitored closely, and we're given direct numbers so we can call with any other information. Then they escort us to the cabin so we can pick up the things I need.

I grab a few extra changes of clothes and my toiletries from the bathroom. I avoid looking at the kitchen area, not wanting to see the broken glass still on the floor or the blood that's dried overnight. The mat at the entryway is black, so it hides what the pale tile can't.

I hope this place hasn't been ruined for me after this settles. I worry that the memories Maverick and I have created will be overshadowed, and this place I considered a haven will be tainted.

Once I have my things, the police follow us out and promise to keep us updated. I guess one of the great things about Maverick having a father who's a hockey legend and genuinely nice guy is that people will bend over backwards to help him.

Maverick's father has been more than accommodating. And I have to wonder if it's mostly attributed to the fact that he's seen this kind of trauma before.

"You sure you're all right to drive, Mav? I can get one of your uncles to come back here with me and grab the truck."

"Nah, I'm okay. Just . . ." He gives his head a shake. "Thinking about how differently yesterday could have gone. I'm real glad it didn't." Maverick wraps one arm around my shoulder, giving it a gentle squeeze.

I push up on my toes so I can press my lips to the edge of his jaw. "You taught me how to handle this kind of situation. Why don't we go back to your parents'? You look like you could use a nap."

"Let's get back and get you settled in," he agrees.

The morning has taken more out of me than I anticipated. Maverick and his dad offer to make us lunch when we get back to their house, but all I want to do is sleep. We head out to the pool house and climb into bed, Maverick wrapped protectively around me.

I wake up in the same position I fell asleep in, Maverick's hand twitching against my side. He makes a plaintive sound. I lie there for a minute, listening to his uneven breathing, worried he's caught in yet another bad dream. I shift so I can see his face. His brows are pulled together, and he makes another low, despondent sound.

I sit up, hoping he's going to fall back into peaceful sleep. He's been struggling for weeks now, and what happened last night isn't going to make it any better. I'd hoped things would settle after contract talks, but I fear that won't be the case. I know he's been offered a spot at training camp now, but I don't know what he's thinking.

I consider that a moment. What will I do if he's moving to Nashville? Can I stay in that cabin on my own? Do I want to? My brain automatically rejects the possibility. Would following him mean potentially falling into the same pattern I had with Gabriel—leaving my support system behind and relying on only him? Would it be fair to either of us?

Everything feels too fresh for me to be able to think this through rationally. I don't even know if he plans to accept it. Anyway, this situation with Gabriel needs resolution before I can start planning my future.

Maverick's lip twitches, along with his fingers. I put my hand on his cheek. "Shh, you're okay."

He sucks in a ragged breath, and his eyes flip open. They zing around the room, frantic and unnerved.

I drop my hand, and he catches it in his. "Shit. I fell asleep. How long have I been out?"

"I'm not sure. Were you dreaming?" I ask.

"Yeah." He blows out a breath. "How long have you been awake?"

"Just a couple minutes."

"Did I wake you? Are you feeling okay?"

"Just stiff and sore, which is to be expected. How are you?" I shift and tuck my legs under me, leaning into his side.

"I'm okay. Fine. Worried about you and all this shit with Gabriel. I knew he was a problem. I just didn't realize he was this dangerous." He massages his temple. "If I'd met you at the cabin, it wouldn't have happened."

"You can't take the blame for this, Maverick." I settle a palm on his chest, feeling the heavy beat of his heart. "Talk to me. Tell me what's happening in your head."

"I don't know. It just . . . It could have been so much worse." He picks up my hand and brings it to his lips. "I want to keep you safe."

"You have, and you taught me how to take care of myself. That's even better, don't you think?"

He nods. "I might be a lot to handle for the next little while, so I'm going to apologize in advance. If I'm driving you up the wall, let me know, and I'll try my best to tone it down."

"I think we'll probably be two peas in a pod." I lean down and kiss his lips, then rest my uninjured forearm on his broad chest. "Tell me how the weekend went. You were offered a spot at training camp?" He's on the fence about what he wants, so I can imagine that getting the offer is both good and bad.

"Nashville offered, but I haven't agreed to go yet."

"Because you're undecided?"

He reaches up and traces the contours of my face. "I keep going back and forth, trying to figure out what I really want. For a good while, I wanted the contract not because of the career, but because it would make the optics for you and me better."

I nod. "I could turn that around and say that because of who you are, the stigma would most definitely affect you, because you'd own it." I curl the rogue wave swooping over his forehead around my finger and let it go.

"Mmm . . . Yeah, which is what I realized and why I had to do a mental reset and take into consideration not just how it impacted optics, but how it would impact the rest of my life. I started thinking about what it would look like if I don't accept the offer. Am I going to regret walking away?"

"And what did you decide?" My heart is in my throat, because I can see the changes that have slowly been taking place over the past few months—how instead of putting everyone he loves before himself, Mav is finally also taking his own needs into consideration.

"I don't think I'll regret it if I don't accept. I had a talk with my dad, and I laid it all out for him. When I put the money I could be making aside—and I know that's not an easy thing for people to do—but when I take out the paycheck and look critically at what I'm being offered . . . Maybe I could rise, do well in the league. But I'm always going to be compared to my dad, and he's had a legendary career. He's blown records out of the water as both a player and a coach. I don't want to live in a shadow. And if I take the offer, that's what I'm signing on for." He laces his fingers with mine. "I want to build my own legacy. When I look five years into the future, I don't see me playing for the NHL. I see me working with my dad, getting kids ready for their own shot. I see myself running a self-defense program. I see a normal life."

"Then that's what you should have." I lean down and press my lips to his.

He runs his fingers through my hair and parts his lips, inviting me in. I sink into the kiss and the connection, wanting to get lost in him. In us.

His hand eases down my side but stops at my hip.

"Are you okay with this? It doesn't have to lead to anything," he murmurs.

I nod. "I want you. I need the closeness."

"Can I take care of you, then? Make you feel good?" His lips move along the edge of my jaw.

I suck his bottom lip between mine. "I would love that, but I would love it more if we could take care of each other."

He pulls back, eyes roving over my face. "I'll just get you ready, then?"

We undress each other carefully, and his face falls when he sees the bruises that have formed over the past twenty-four hours. He kisses every single one before he settles between my thighs and brings me to orgasm with his mouth. I get lost in feeling good. In his attentiveness. In his love.

When I'm sated and boneless, he sits up and settles me in his lap. "Is this still okay? I want you to have full control."

"This is perfect." I brace my hands on his shoulders and lift as he positions himself at my entrance.

My eyes flutter closed as I take him inside on a needy sigh. When my ass rests on his thighs, I open my eyes and meet his gaze, which is laced with concern.

I link my fingers behind his neck. "How did you become exactly the person I need?"

He skims my cheek with his knuckle. "I don't know, but I'll love you for as long as you want me."

Our mouths connect, and we make slow, gentle love, finding a fragment of peace within our connection, keeping the chaos of the world at bay, if only for a little while.

An hour later, his phone buzzes on his nightstand with a message. DAD appears on the screen, and Maverick picks up the phone and checks it.

"My mom is home, and dinner is in half an hour, if we're interested." He quirks a brow. "It's okay if you're not in the mood to deal with family dinner. This whole thing is a lot, and my mom . . . She's intense on a good day."

As much as I'd like to avoid the awkwardness of it all, if Maverick and I are going to try to make this work, I need to win over his mother. And with an ex-husband who isn't technically an ex yet, and who also threatened to burn my cabin down yesterday, I'm climbing a serious uphill battle.

I must mull it over too long because Maverick adds, "I'll tell them you're still sleeping."

I shake my head. "You don't need to do that. I want to come." I can't hide from the reality I've created for myself. And I don't want to do that to Maverick.

We get dressed, and I check my reflection in the mirror. There's nothing I can do to hide the bruise on my cheek. Maverick laces his fingers with mine, and we leave the cocoon of the pool house. It's built into the side of a hill to the left of the main house. The view from the backyard is stunning, and there's a covered outdoor dining area, where his parents are currently setting up for dinner.

His mother's gaze lifts as soon as we cross the patio and goes directly to our clasped hands. For a moment, she's guarded, and then her eyes shift and settle on my face. The silverware she's holding clatters to the table. "Oh my God."

She rushes out to meet us. Her hands flutter around in the air and then she takes my free one in hers.

"Mom, careful, please," Maverick chastises.

She looks down at my bandaged arm and releases my hand. "Oh, God. You poor thing. Are you okay? You should sit down." She shoots a look over her shoulder at Alex, who's wearing a grimace. "You didn't tell me it was like this."

He grips the back of his chair. "I didn't really have much of an opportunity to explain, did I?"

She turns back, envelops me in a gentle hug, and whispers, "I'm so sorry this happened to you."

Something in her tone and her unexpected affection tips the emotional scale, and much to my horror, a quiet sob works its way up my throat. I realize then that I've been in a state of shock. I haven't even called Sophia to tell her what happened, or my parents. I've been in a tiny bubble, wading through my own disbelief and fears, trying to understand how all of this happened. *And* worrying about how my boyfriend's mother is going to feel about my presence in her home. We might not need her permission to date, but Mav is so close to his family, and I want their acceptance on top of everything else.

"You must have been so brave." She gives me a soft squeeze before she releases me. When she steps back, her eyes go wide in horror. "Oh, God. Did I hurt you?"

I shake my head. "No. I'm fine. Just emotional. It's been an intense twenty-four hours."

"Of course, it has. And now you're staying with your potential future in-laws while the nightmare you've been through gets sorted out, and our first and second introductions probably weren't the best representation of either of us. I'd have the moops, for sure."

"Mom."

She looks at Maverick, whose expression reflects horror.

"What?"

"Can you be less . . ." His hands flail as he searches for the right word.

"No, honey. I can't be less. It's both part of my charm and the reason all of my children need therapy." She gives him what looks to be a semi-apologetic smile. "I'm sorry. I hope you'll still visit me in the retirement home when I'm old and making penises out of clay during craft time."

I choke on a laugh. Maverick wasn't lying about his mother, or exaggerating. Not even a little bit.

"My lack of filter only gets worse with age. By the time I'm in my sixties, I have a feeling the only child who will willingly be seen in public with me is my daughter." Violet pats my shoulder. "Come on, let's sit down. Can I get you a glass of wine? Maybe a bottle with a straw?" She takes me by the elbow and guides me to the table. "Maverick, there's a bottle of white in the fridge and a red on the counter. Bring them both out, please."

Dinner is not what I expected. At all. I don't get the third degree from his mother. No one pushes me to talk about Gabriel. In fact, the only time it's brought up is when Alex mentions that the security company he uses is going to install cameras and invisible fences along the perimeter of my property, and that he'd like to cover the cost.

And when Violet eventually mentions Nashville and asks what Maverick's thoughts are on the offer, she listens to what he has to say and doesn't push him one way or the other. Instead, she tells him to weigh the pros and cons before he makes a final decision.

After we finish, Alex and Maverick clear the dishes and put away the leftovers, leaving me and his mother alone for a few minutes.

"Thank you for being so hospitable," I tell her. "I know this can't be easy for you—not with your daughter in New York and Maverick making big decisions about his future, and here I am turning everything upside down."

She hums a quiet laugh and picks up one of the napkins Maverick turned into a crane. "I don't think you're the one turning everything upside down, Clover. Alex filled me in on what happened yesterday, and while the circumstances are certainly less than ideal, you are not the reason your ex-husband did what he did." She blows out a breath. "That must have been terrifying for you."

"I'm still processing, if I'm going to be quite honest."

"That seems reasonable, all things considered." She smiles sadly and rubs her bottom lip with her fingertips. Her nails are painted lavender, with little white hearts decorating them. "I've had some time to think about what you said at Maverick's convocation. It's hard not to be protective of your children, even when they're adults. He'll always be my little boy, even though he weighs twice what I do and has more than a foot on me. And it's hard, as a mother, to realize that you've failed your child. It's the last thing I ever wanted to do." She reaches for another napkin and dabs at her eyes.

"You didn't fail him, Violet."

"I did, though. I should have seen it—what he was doing, how he wasn't dealing with things. He's always been very much his name, and yet totally the opposite. He's had to balance so many different roles. He's such a good man. And it breaks my heart that he's been carrying around so much guilt over some-thing that wasn't his fault, and that he's felt compelled to step into shoes he never wanted to fill."

"Maverick is very good at showing people what they want to see," I tell her. "And until recently, he's always put himself last. It's his nature to protect and to care for people. That's who he is, and you and Alex have done a great job of giving him a stable and loving family he can rely on. Trust the job you've done. He's never made any decision without fully weighing the consequences."

Her expression softens. "You really are in love with him, aren't you?"

"As complicated as it is, I am."

"You know, I shouldn't be surprised that he ended up falling in love with his professor. He was forever flirting with Robbie's girlfriends when he first started bringing them around. And the last time he went out with a girl his own age was when he took a girl in his class to the eighth-grade dance." She sets the crane on the table. "It's taken me some time to get my head around the two of you as a couple, but I can see that you really care about him, and that he is head-over-ass in love with you. He seems . . . settled in a way I've never seen him before, like he's sure of himself." She smiles at me. "Whatever he decides moving forward, personally and professionally, Alex and I will support him."

41

All the Ways to Break

MAVERICK

I've gone through bouts of insomnia before, but it's never been like this. Every time I close my eyes, images of Clover in the cabin and Lavender when they found her at the carnival flash through my mind. And when I fall asleep, the nightmares are brain-melting. So it's been nearly forty-eight hours since I slept, apart from that nap I took with Clover.

She's just fallen asleep, and my phone is buzzing on the nightstand. It's Lavender. I shouldn't be surprised.

I can't see Kody being able to keep what happened from her, and I honestly wouldn't want him to. What happened yesterday was some crazy shit, and today he met with the coach from Philly and then flew back to New York. His head must be spinning. I know mine sure as hell is.

I roll out of bed and pad across the floor, answering the call with a whispered, "Hold on a sec." I unlock the sliding door and step out into the warm summer air.

"Okay. Hey. What's up?"

"Okay. Hey. What's up?" she repeats.

"I'm taking it Kody is home."

"Yes, Kodiak is home." She's silent for a moment before she asks, "Are you okay? And I don't mean are you okay with the current state of the world. I mean, Kodiak told me what happened, so I know you have a girlfriend, which I called, by the way, but gotta be honest, the professor angle was a bit of a shocker. Also, the fact that her name is Clover is fitting. But when I'm asking if you're okay, I mean mentally and emotionally, how are you handling what happened?"

"I'm okay?"

"I'm hanging up and calling you back on video chat." The screen goes blank and then lights up again a second later.

I answer the call and drop down into one of the Adirondack chairs. Lavender's face appears in the small screen. She's sitting on a couch, cheek propped on her fist. "You look exhausted," she says. "Are you even sleeping?"

"Right now, no."

She purses her lips. "I mean in general. You have bags under your eyes. Big ones."

I adjust the brim of my hat. "The whole training camp deal was stressful, and then this shit with Clover's ex happened, so my sleep hasn't been the most restful. But things should get better now, so you don't need to worry about me."

"That sounds like an awful lot of placating and bullshit."

"Where's Kody?"

"He's passed out from his stress-purge pillow talk. My vagina is his truth serum. The poor guy. I don't know how he managed to keep all that bottled up until after we had thank-God-he's-not-going-far-away nookie."

I cringe. "That's way more information than I needed."

"I know. I do it on purpose. But seriously, he filled me in on everything. I feel bad because I was over here making jokes to Mom about you and your four-week relationships, mostly as a way to get dirt on whatever's going on with you, and all this shit was going down. I'm really worried about you, Mav, and not because you're dating your professor, or because you're on the fence about training camp."

"What are you worried about, then?"

"What happened to your girlfriend yesterday seems a lot like an echo of what happened to me, and I don't know that you've ever really dealt with the fallout of that. I want to tell you something important. And I need you to listen to what I'm saying and know that it comes from a place of love and concern. I know you have the tendency to take blame and hold on to it like it's yours—kind of like Gollum and his precious. Please don't do that with this. You couldn't have known her ex was going to end up being a full-blown psychopath."

"I actually don't think you're far off the mark there. He really just . . . lost his mind. And you're right, it felt exactly like an echo of that day. Keep an eye on Kody, maybe?"

"Maybe stop trying to take care of everyone and focus on yourself, okay?"

I laugh and nod. "I'm working on that too. And as far as holding on to the blame, I'm learning how to let it go. I kept looking for forgiveness, and in some ways, I needed to hear it from the people I love. But now I realize the only way to get past any of this is if I give *myself* the forgiveness I need." And as I say it, I know it's true, and this is one step closer to that goal.

She gives me a soft smile. "I don't know if you still need to hear it from me, but I forgive you for being a frustrated eight-year-old boy. It's okay that you were jealous. It's okay that you ran ahead. I forgave you before I realized you even wanted forgiveness. You're an awesome brother. You always have been."

"And you're an awesome sister."

"You have no one else to compare me to, which is good." She sighs. "Now let's get back to the important stuff. How is your girlfriend? Is she okay?"

"Physically, it's all surface wounds, and she seems to be dealing okay. I think it scared the hell out of her like it did me, but, uh, it looks like she'll be able to press charges. Doesn't make it any less traumatic for her."

She nods pensively. "Or you. Can you stay with Mom and Dad for a while?"

"Yeah. They've been awesome about the whole thing. Really supportive. I think it's gonna take some time for Clover to get comfortable with the idea of being in her cabin again. It's pretty secluded. But Dad's going to have a security system installed."

"Sounds like a dad thing to do and a good idea. How's Mom handling the fact that you're dating your professor?"

"She didn't love it at first, for obvious reasons, but she seems to be coming around now."

"That's good. She's had a lot thrown at her this weekend, so I'm sure coming home to find out that your girlfriend's ex threatened to burn her cabin down was the icing on the cake."

"What do you mean she's had a lot thrown at her? What's going on with you?"

"The production company offered me a full-time residency. I'm going to transfer to a college program here."

"Holy shit, you're going to live in New York?"

"Seems that way. And with Kodiak in Philly, we'll be able to make the distance thing manageable. He said Nashville offered you training camp but you're not all that inclined to take it."

"I don't think I want to live in Dad's shadow for the rest of my life."

She nods, her smile knowing. "He casts a big one. Sometimes you have to forge a new path so you can find your own light."

BY THE MIDDLE OF JULY, I still haven't made a decision about training camp. I have until mid-August to either accept or pass, and I'm taking that time to think the decision through.

In the meantime, I help Clover pack up her things in Chicago and move what she needs back to my parents' pool house in Lake Geneva. We're still waiting on Gabriel's trial, but her lawyer is confident he'll do jail time. It doesn't make me happy, but there is some relief in knowing he's on house arrest and can't be in the same state as Clover anymore. And the charges against him made it a lot easier to get the divorce papers signed, so Clover is legally free of him as well.

Clover has convinced me to start talking to a professional. It didn't take much work on her part to get me to see the validity of it. Lavender was right. What happened with Gabriel unearthed more of the shit from my childhood, and if I don't deal with it now, it's going to make my life impossible.

I can't be attached to Clover at the hip, and anyway, I need to find a way to manage the fear and worry without smothering her. It isn't logical or possible or healthy to be with her twenty-four hours a day. So I get myself a therapist and talk through all the crap my family has been through, sorting through damage so I can be a better version of myself.

I transfer to the Pump It Up location in Lake Geneva, agreeing to also stay on at the Chicago gym for a while to train self-defense instructors once a week, since they want to keep the program running, and it's one of the things I feel passionate about.

For a couple weeks, Clover and I stay at my parents' place, but at the end of July, we do move into her cabin on Pearl Bay. Clover starts her position at the local library, and I start working part-time with my dad at his hockey training program.

MY ALARM GOES off at five fifteen in the morning. I hit the snooze button and wrap my arm around Clover. I nuzzle into her hair, breathing in her cloves and citrus shampoo. She makes a little noise but doesn't stir otherwise.

Practice skate starts early, and I have to be on the ice at seven thirty. Still, I lie here, body curved around Clover's, until my alarm goes off again. Then I reluctantly roll away from her warmth and carefully climb out of bed.

Although Clover's day doesn't start until nine, she often gets up at the same time I do so we can have coffee and breakfast together. But yesterday, the verdict for Gabriel's trial was finally read. In the end, he was given five years. It was an emotional day for her, and we stayed up later than we should have. I'm glad that chapter is finally over. It means she can move on with her life.

And I feel like I'm ready to move forward with mine.

42

From Here

MAVERICK

Six months later

I step down out of the moving truck and take in the neighborhood. It's a nice area on the outskirts of Lake Geneva. A couple walking a dog passes us on the sidewalk, looking curiously from us to the neatly manicured brownstone with the blue BMW parked in the driveway. The license plate reads *Dr. Dave.*

I flip the keys around my finger, then tuck them into my pocket. "You guys ready to do this?"

"Is it bad that I kinda hope he gives us a hard time?" River cracks his knuckles and laces his hands behind his head.

Our cousin Logan gives him the side-eye and taps his badge. "That's what I'm here for."

"And also why we're here." My dad motions between himself and Rook.

River shrugs. "I'm just saying, that time you had to taser the guy was pretty unforgettable."

"Especially when he peed himself." BJ grins.

I give them both a stern look. "Our job is to get her in and out as quickly as possible with the least amount of trauma. She's already been through enough. Seeing her ex get tasered and pee his pants, while vindicating, is the opposite of what we're trying to accomplish here."

River and BJ have the decency to look chagrined. "We know. Sorry."

We all turn toward the house. The curtains in the living room fall back into place. I walk across the lawn to the car parked behind the truck, rounding the driver's side.

The window rolls down, and my beautiful girlfriend's face appears. I rest my arm on the frame and duck down. "How's it going in here?"

"We're ready whenever you are," Clover says. "Right, Soph?"

Sophia nods and gives me the thumbs-up.

"Great." I look to the woman sitting in the back seat, hands clasped in her lap. "Mindy, you can stay in here until we've got the situation handled in the house. Does that sound good?"

Mindy gives me a faint nod. "What if he won't let me get my things?"

"We have a court order, so that won't be a problem. We're going to do our best to ensure you don't have to see or speak to him, okay?"

She blows out a nervous breath. "Okay. Thank you."

"Just give us a few minutes to get him out of the house, and then we'll get you in." I give Clover a quick peck on the cheek and meet Logan on the front porch.

BJ and River are busy unloading cardboard boxes from the moving truck, and my dad and Rook are standing off to the side, ready to intervene if necessary.

Over the past six months, Clover and I have done a lot of talking, and we came up with an idea—one that's probably going to turn into a full-time gig eventually.

When she started working at the library in Pearl Lake, she discovered they'd created a reading program for kids of the women who live in the shelter on the outskirts of Lake Geneva. These women are escaping abusive relationships and living in temporary accommodations, with most of their belongings still in their homes, which they're unable to access without facing their abuser.

So we put our heads together and came up with a volunteer program in which former and current athletes escort the women to court or to help retrieve their belongings from their residence. I proposed it to my dad to see if he would be interested in helping me get it off the ground. He was all for it, and my aunt Sunny, who oversees several not-for-profit ventures, came on board as well.

It started as a community initiative, but it's quickly picking up steam.

I knock and wait for the ex-dickbag to open the door. It's nine on Saturday morning. He's aware we're coming, but it doesn't mean he's going to be easy about it.

A man in his early forties, wearing dress pants and a button-down, stands in the open doorway. Abusers come in all forms. They can be everything from drugged-out lowlifes to doctors. This guy happens to be a surgeon and a well-respected member of his community. He also has a habit of getting drunk when he's not on call and knocking his wife around.

"Where's my wife?"

I ignore the question and give him my best patient smile.

"Hello, Dr. Doran. We have a court order that indicates you need to allow your wife to enter the premises so she can collect her things."

"I'd like to speak to her. Is she in that car?" He points to Clover's black car. It's not the one she drives every day, just the one we take when we make visits to asshole exes.

He tries to push his way between us, but Logan holds his arm out, barring his way. "I can escort you to your vehicle so you can leave while Mindy collects her things."

"I'm not leaving. If she wants her things, she has to talk to me."

"Actually, according to the court order, which was hand delivered to you, you must leave the premises while your wife is here." I clasp my hands behind my back and roll up on the balls of my feet, smiling serenely. My heart is beating a million miles a minute. Adrenaline is a beast and my best friend in these situations. "Failure to do so will result in an arrest. Now I'm sure you have a reputation you're trying to uphold in this neighborhood, which we're clearly doing an awesome job of ruining by being here in the first place. Unfortunately, your inability to work *with* us instead of against us is the reason you're in this situation in the first place. If you would prefer Officer Butterson to cuff you and escort you to his police car, that's absolutely an option."

"I'm going to sue your ass."

"You can go ahead and try, but we have the court order, so you're not going to get very far. You have caused someone you're supposed to care for and love an incredible amount of pain. Your wife's arm is in a cast because you can't control your temper. Do you think, Dave, just this one time, you could behave like a human being with a shred of decency instead of an untamed animal?"

His jaw works, and his fists clench.

"You throw a punch, and you're in the back of the cruiser, and no one here is going to be kind about how we get you in there. Just something to think about," Logan offers calmly.

Dave's lip twitches. "I'll get my keys."

We wait at the door while he aggressively gets what he needs.

"Eyes on the ground. Do not look at that car," Logan warns.

"I'm not a fucking criminal."

"Don't kid yourself. You abuse women. You're pretty low on the human-decency meter." Logan escorts him to his vehicle and positions himself so Dave can't see past him. "We'll text you when we're done here."

We wait until the car disappears down the street and then check the house before we deem it safe.

Two hours later, we have all of Mindy's belongings in the truck. We drive to her new apartment, bring all the boxes and furniture in, and set up what we can before we leave her and the friend who met her here to finish.

"That went pretty well," I say to Clover as I walk her back to the car.

"It did. She was really nervous that he wasn't going to leave, or that he was going to make it difficult."

"Having a group of guys who look like they would happily use him as a punching bag is pretty good incentive. And having a cop tag along doesn't hurt either." I open the driver's side door.

"Mmm . . . . This is true." She smooths her hands over my chest and laces her fingers behind my neck. "Can you head home now, or do you have other things to take care of first?"

"I'm running a practice with my dad at four thirty."

Two weeks after Gabriel went to jail, I officially rejected the offer from Nashville. I knew it wasn't what I wanted for my life, that there was another path I needed to take—one that still included hockey, but didn't require the same amount of travel, the fame, or the stress.

"You mind a spectator?"

"Of course not."

"I'll pick up coffees?"

"That'd be great." I tuck my finger under her chin and drop a chaste kiss on her lips. "You were amazing today, as usual, by the way."

"So were you. You're very sexy when you're standing up for women's rights." She bites her bottom lip.

"You're very sexy, period." I smirk when she blushes.

"Mav, practice is in half an hour. We gotta get going," my dad calls.

"Coming," I yell before I return my attention to Clover. "Tonight. You and me. Strip Scrabble."

She grins and blushes further. "My favorite. I can't wait."

"That makes two of us." I drop another kiss on her lips and hold the door while she gets behind the wheel. Then I close it for her and start toward my dad's truck.

She rolls down the window. "Hey."

I turn and quirk a brow.

"I love you."

"And I love you. Every minute of every day until forever ends." I wink and turn back around, a smile on my face, my heart full.

I know I made the right choice when I turned down Nashville's offer. This is exactly where I'm supposed to be: surrounded by the people I love most and helping people who need a hand up out of the dark and back into the light, so they can learn how to shine again.

Birthday Gift

Maverick's 25th birthday

Strong arms wrap around my waist from behind, and warm lips sweep along my neck. I let my eyes flutter closed and angle my head, giving him access to more skin, should he want it.

And he does.

He nips his way up to my earlobe, and his fingertips find the hem of my shirt and glide under the fabric, drifting up my stomach to cup a breast.

"What are you doing?"

"Kissing you." He slides a hand into my bra and grazes a nipple. "Touching one of my many favorite parts of you." His other hand finds the button on my jeans.

"Your family and mine are going to be here in less than an hour."

"I guess I better be quick then, huh?"

"I still have to prepare the appetizer platter."

"Our moms and my sister will help you with that. It's my birthday. I want one of your orgasms as a gift." I don't stop him when he flicks the button open and slides his hand down the front of my pants, cupping me over my panties.

"We had sex three hours ago."

"It feels like days, not hours. Whose idea was it to invite our families over anyway? Why aren't we going out for dinner?"

"Because we decided it would be nice to host them here. Remember?" My parents flew in from Florida yesterday. They're staying with Maverick's parents. Over the past few years, huge family celebrations have become a regular thing.

"We must have had this conversation after sex when my brain wasn't really functioning." He pushes my panties to the side, fingertips gliding over my clit.

"Are we really going to do this right here? What if someone shows up early?" I arch, my butt pressing against his erection.

"Hmm . . . Good point." His lips leave my neck, and the hand down my pants disappears, as does the one in my bra. He dips down and picks me up, carrying me fireman-style across the room.

Herman, our two-year-old German Shepherd, jumps up and starts to follow us to the bedroom, but Maverick closes the door on him. He barks once and whines. When we come out, we'll find him lying beside the bedroom door, all dejected and sad.

Maverick drops me on the bed and straddles my hips, his bottom lip caught between his teeth. I reach to take my glasses off, but he shakes his head. "Leave them on, Professor Sweet."

I roll my eyes. "I was a professor for all of a year."

"You'll always be my favorite teacher. Every day I learn something new from you." He pulls my shirt over my head and rids me of my jeans. He pauses, taking in my bra and panties. "This is new. Is this one of my birthday presents?"

"You like?" The bra is pale green lace, the panties the same. I flip over on my stomach.

"Oh fuck, yes. I love it when you get all naughty and pull out the thongs." He grabs my ass and bites each cheek. "This is, like, my ultimate fantasy, right here." He pulls his shirt over his head and drops it on the floor. His jeans and boxers follow.

He straddles my thighs and then stretches out on top of me. I turn my head, and his lips connect with my cheek as his erection settles against my lower back. "I want to do dirty things to you."

"You better do them fast unless you want to spend the rest of the evening wishing you'd planned this out better."

He chuckles and folds back on his knees, tucking a finger under the waistband and tugging gently. "So fucking sexy."

I look over my shoulder as he slides his thick cock under the string and along the divide.

"I don't care what birthday it is; you're not getting in there with that thing," I tell him on a low moan.

He chuckles. "Oh, I know. But I can tease you, can't I?"

I answer with a hum, then moan softly when he stops. I try to push my butt up. He presses a knee between my legs, and I part for him. His fingers find my most sensitive skin as he kisses a path up my back. When I'm on the edge of an orgasm, he covers my body with his again and enters me from behind.

It's become one of my favorite positions. He's so deep, and with every thrust, he strokes my G-spot. He takes my chin in his palm and turns my head gently until our lips meet. He keeps rolling his hips, a slow and steady climb all the way to the peak.

After I come, he pulls out and flips me over. He tugs my panties down my thighs and stretches out over me again. His hands curl around my shoulders. "I love you so much," he murmurs against my lips.

"And I love you." I wrap my hand around the back of his neck. "You gonna come for me now, Mr. Waters?"

One side of his mouth quirks up in a salacious grin, and his thrusts grow harder, pushing deeper, moving faster. After a moment, he comes on a low groan and collapses on top of me. "Can we play strip Scrabble after everyone leaves?" he mumbles into my neck.

"Absolutely. Now can I get dressed so I'm not scrambling when your family arrives?"

"Definitely. I'll even help. That's how much of a team player I am."

I change into another new bra and panty set while Maverick stands there, still naked, biting his knuckle. "You're gonna be the best dessert in the world. I'm actually considering skipping dessert entirely so I can cover you in chocolate syrup and lick it off your body."

I pull my jeans on. "I made a cake. From scratch."

"Right. You'll be dessert round two." He jabs his legs into his boxers.

He's just pulled his shirt over his head when Herman starts barking.

"Oh my God. People are here. I need to make sure my hair doesn't scream *freshly fucked*." I grab my brush and yank it through, smoothing out knots at the crown. My cheeks are flushed, but there's nothing I can do about that.

It could be from running around the kitchen as easily as it could be from sex.

The first people to arrive are Lavender, Kody, and River. Lavender and Kody flew in from New York this morning, and they're staying at his parents' place. It worked out well because he has a game tomorrow night in Chicago, and we're all going to see him play.

Lavender pulls me in for a hug. "FYI, my mom is going to bring up a trip to New York for a girls' weekend. She's already got the whole itinerary planned, and she's convinced your mom it's a great idea. Sorry in advance, but I promise we'll have fun, even if it will also be mildly embarrassing."

Kody lifts his hand in a wave. He's an interesting guy. Mostly quiet and pretty serious, but he lightens up a lot when he's around Maverick, and it's very, very clear that he's painfully in love with Lavender. The sun rises and sets on her.

Our little cabin slowly fills with family. All the parents arrive next, and his cousin BJ. His brother Robbie couldn't make it because he's still out in British Columbia managing a crop harvest, but he visited this summer, and this morning he and Maverick had a video chat. He also sent a giant bag of edibles that arrived last week. I put those in the freezer.

Over the past three years, Maverick and I have grown, both individually and as a couple. He took classes part-time and completed a master's in business administration. I'm still working at the library, but only part-time now, because last year we opened Lavender House, a not-for-profit women's shelter designed to give women in abusive relationships and their children a safe place to get back on their feet.

We've hired an entire team of counselors, including Sophia, and part of the program includes self-defense classes. In addition, we've managed to grow the volunteer program of both professional and non-professional athletes who escort these women to court dates and help them retrieve their personal effects from their homes while we transition them into new housing.

None of it would have been possible without the help of Mav's parents. And part of our staff includes Queenie Kingston. Her husband, Ryan, was the team's goalie when Maverick's dad was the coach in Seattle. They've been friends with his parents for a long time, and their family moved out this way a couple of years ago. She developed an art therapy program for children coming out of abusive homes, and I run their literacy program.

Every day I get to see Maverick shine his light on people who are struggling to find their way out of the dark. He's a beautiful soul, and I'm lucky to have fallen in love with him.

We eat dinner, laugh, joke, and talk about our plans for the Chrismukkah celebration at Lavender House. We've been able to secure donations from local businesses, so all the kids will have presents, as well as their mothers, and we have a huge dinner planned with a movie night for the kids. Violet is a tremendous support, as are all the other women in their hockey family.

Being part of Maverick's world and his family has opened my eyes to exactly how supportive they all are of each other. And I love that my parents have been folded right in. My brother and his girlfriend couldn't make it this time, but they came and spent a week with us this summer, and they're coming out this way again for Thanksgiving. And I see now, in a way that I couldn't before, exactly why hockey has been such an important part of Mav's life and why choosing a different path was such a challenge for him.

Maverick opens his gifts after dinner. It's almost a surprise when his mother doesn't give him something embarrassing. Instead, she gives him the Onyx Scrabble edition, which he gets irrationally excited about. She seems pleased, and she doesn't need to know that his excitement is more about the fact that we play by a very different set of rules.

"You have to come outside to see your gift from me," I tell him.

"Did you buy me a star?"

I shake my head. "You'll never guess. Come on." We all put on our shoes and head out to the small garage. Over the past few months, I've been working on a project with some help from his family.

"Did you get me a riding lawn mower?"

"We already have one."

"A tractor? We have two acres. We should definitely have a tractor."

"No. It's not a tractor." I hit the button, and the door whirrs as it opens. I thread my arm through his and watch as his expression turns from questioning to surprise. "It's a home office. I know how important it is for you to have space carved out for working, and the cabin isn't really set up for it, so on the days you're not in the office or on the ice, you'll have this."

"Holy crap, Clover. How the hell did you manage to do this without me knowing?"

"Careful planning and a lot of help." I look over my shoulder, smiling at his family and mine, who seem just as excited as me for this unveiling.

He takes a few steps forward, pulling me along with him. "Holy shit, is that . . . are those my cranes?" He reaches up and touches one. They're hanging from the ceiling in a spiral design. They're every color of the rainbow, and some of them sport inappropriate and hilarious designs, which I found out from Violet was old wrapping paper from Christmas and other holidays over the years. She always held on to them.

In the very center of the spiral is the first crane he ever gave me. The one he left on my nightstand. It wasn't until we moved in together that I realized there was a note inside that read:

Clover,
I wanted to leave my number, but I don't think I could handle the disappointment if you didn't call. 1000 cranes equal a single wish.
Mine is that the universe brings you back to me.
Only 999 to go.
~x Maverick

I put it in a special box and kept it safe, until now.

"Your mom brought a few boxes over from the house, and we spent a couple of days putting them up. There are a thousand. Exactly enough for a wish."

He takes my face between his hands. "You are everything I never knew I needed." He presses his lips to mine and wraps me in a hug I feel all the way to my soul. "Thank you for this," he adds. "I can't tell you how much it means that I have all of you backing me ." His voice cracks at the end, and he releases me to hug the rest of his family, all of whom helped make this happen, not just for him, but for us.

"I have something for you." Maverick reaches into the pocket of his hoodie.

"For me? It's your birthday. The presents are supposed to be for you."

"It is for me." He takes one of my hands in his and drops to his knee.

"Maverick?" I glance over at our families, who are all standing there like they knew this was going to happen. His mother smiles and then gives me her cringey face. It looks like she's going to cry—but happy tears. I turn my attention back to him.

"Thank you for being my light in the dark, for opening my eyes and for taking a chance on us. For saving me from myself. The only thing I want for this birthday, and every single one yet to come, is to know I get to celebrate with you. You're already my partner in every way that matters. Marry me, Clover. You have my heart, I want you to have my soul too."

He flips open the box, and inside is a beautiful diamond ring—three stones arranged in what could be a clover.

My eyes well, and my lip trembles.

He nods toward his family and winks at me. "No pressure or anything."

I laugh. "Of course I'll marry you. I'm yours, until the end of forever and whatever comes after."

Our families clap and whistle.

He puts the ring on my finger and stands to kiss me. And of course, because he's Maverick, he slips me the tongue. Just a quick stroke and then he pulls back. "I'm really glad you said yes. Otherwise this would've gotten real awkward."

We're enveloped in a huge hug, one that speaks of unconditional love. I know that however unconventional our beginning, Maverick and I are supported and celebrated by the people who matter most to both of us.

I might have been the hand that pulled him up from the darkness, but Maverick is the light. And I get to watch him shine every day.

OTHER TITLES BY HELENA HUNTING

Lies, Hearts & Truths Series

Little Lies

Bitter Sweet Heart

All In Series

A Lie for a Lie

A Favor for a Favor

A Secret for a Secret

A Kiss for a Kiss

Pucked Series

Pucked (Pucked #1)

Pucked Up (Pucked #2)

Pucked Over (Pucked #3)

Forever Pucked (Pucked #4)

Pucked Under (Pucked #5)

Pucked Off (Pucked #6)

Pucked Love (Pucked #7)

AREA 51: Deleted Scenes & Outtakes

Get Inked

Pucks & Penalties

Standalone Novels

The Librarian Principle

Felony Ever After

Before You Ghost (with Debra Anastasia)

FOREVER ROMANCE STANDALONES

The Good Luck Charm

Meet Cute

Kiss my Cupcake

ABOUT THE AUTHOR H. HUNTING

NYT and *USA Today* bestselling author, Helena Hunting, lives on the outskirts of Toronto with her incredibly tolerant family and two moderately intolerant cats. She writes contemporary romance and romantic comedies, and when she wants to dive into her angsty side, she writes new adult romance under H. Hunting.

Scan this code to stay connected with Helena

ORIGAMI CRANE INSTRUCTIONS

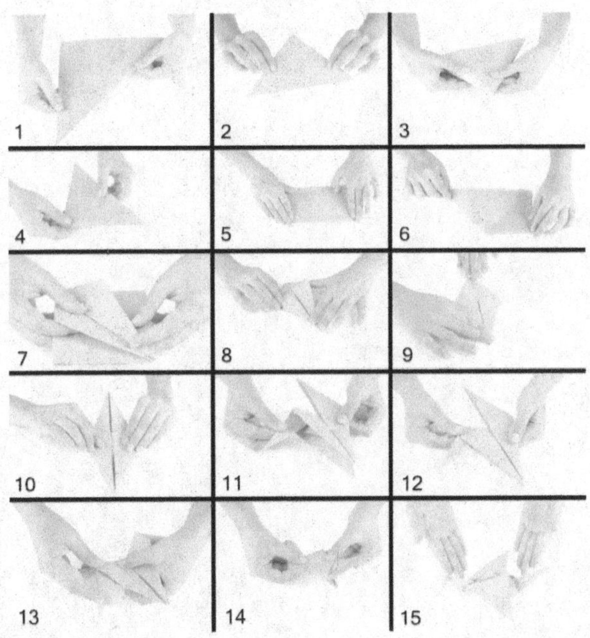